D0915986

JACKAL

JACKAL

A NOVEL

ERIN E. ADAMS

BANTAM BOOKS | NEW YORK

Jackal is a work of fiction. Names, characters, places, and incidents either are the products of the author's imagination or are used fictitiously. Any resemblance to actual persons, living or dead, events, or locales is entirely coincidental.

Published in the United States by Bantam Books, an imprint of Random House, a division of Penguin Random House LLC, New York.

BANTAM BOOKS is a registered trademark and the B colophon is a trademark of Penguin Random House LLC.

Hardback ISBN 978-0-593-49930-6
Ebook ISBN 978-0-593-49931-3

Printed in the United States of America on acid-free paper

randomhousebooks.com

2 4 6 8 9 7 5 3 1

First Edition

Title-page and part-title images: edb_16 / stock.adobe.com (forest)
Chapter-opening images: MysticLink / stock.adobe.com (heart); setory / stock.adobe.com (feather); Sete / stock.adobe.com (scales)

For my first cheerleaders and biggest supporters.
I love you, Mom and Dad.

JACKAL

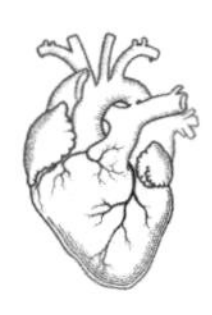

ALICE

June 1985

Tanisha Walker loved the stars. She didn't memorize the paths of the cosmos or their patterns. She just loved the look of them. The fact that she could see them so clearly was the only part she liked about moving to a town as small as Johnstown. Her husband told her their daughter would be safe. After all, the only place safer than the suburbs was the middle of nowhere. They'd moved because he'd gotten a job at the steel mill. With the finite resource running low, he was brought in to help put the place to rest. A full transition would take years, but the town knew men like him coming meant the beginning of the end. The industry had dried up.

Upon arriving, Tanisha didn't trust the place. If pressed, she couldn't say why. The best answer she could give was: It felt too safe. Tanisha had grown up in the city and was numb to loud noises and erratic personalities; her calm demeanor belied her understanding that danger always lurked right around the corner. But they had moved to a town without corners. Danger didn't need a place to hide, it preferred to fester. First it would smile and bring you German chocolate cake. Then it would wait out in the open on your front porch until it felt good and ready.

Tanisha's daughter, Alice, was named for the writer of a book Tanisha had read in high school. The book was banned. Tanisha read it anyway because she liked the cover. Alice was Tanisha's only child.

Born a full two months early, at thirty-two weeks, she was three pounds, four ounces, and fit in the palm of her father's hand.

I think Alice came early because she couldn't wait to see the world.

However, her premature arrival meant they'd kept her in the hospital for those two months while her lungs grew to their full capacity. There the nurses talked to her on their lunch breaks, the residents checked on her between rotations, and every night at 11:00, her parents came to bathe her and rock her to sleep. They were both dead tired but elated to spend time with their daughter.

From the beginning, Alice was loved.

She was always loved.

She will always be loved.

Small-town living agreed with Alice. She loved to explore the forest and play "Let's Get Lost." Her favorite meal was sauerkraut and sausage. She had no tolerance for anything remotely spicy. And she had never met a potato she didn't like. Like her mother, she loved the night sky. But unlike her mother, she was not dazzled by the stars. She loved how the darkness between them went on forever. If she stared long enough, she felt like she could fall up into the vast blackness above.

Alice wasn't a picky child, but she did have a favorite jacket. No matter the weather, she'd wear it. Tanisha hated it. Unable to say no to his daughter, her husband got it for Alice anyway. It had unfinished denim edges and its fluffy white shearling reminded Tanisha of the rich white girls who had stuck gum in her hair on her train rides to school in the city. Even so, Tanisha would have lived as that jacket, wrapped around her daughter, for the rest of her life.

When she turned ten, Alice finally felt the differences between herself and her peers. Ever the optimist, Tanisha let her daughter live in blissful ignorance for as long as she could. Of course Alice was aware of the color of her skin, but she hadn't yet mastered what it meant. At first, the differences were slight and revolved around her hair. To get it done, she went to a lady's house, not a salon. She got braids *before* she went on vacation. And in swim class, she had to wrap her hair in a tight swim cap or else her mother would "kill" her. She forgot the cap once and cried. She told her instructor about her mother's stance on getting her hair wet, and her mom had to have a meeting with a lady from the state that day. Alice wasn't allowed to say "Mom would kill me" ever again, unless she really, really meant it. Alice was beginning to understand how she was different. She just didn't have all the words yet.

Early summer is fickle. On Friday, June 21, 1985, the temperature dipped just enough to be chilly. Still, Alice begged to go exploring outside with her friends, a request Tanisha almost always denied if there wasn't an adult. Mostly because of the stories about the woods. Always some nonsense about shadows. Tanisha hadn't lived in Johnstown long enough to have mastered the adage "if you think you saw something . . . no, you didn't," but she was wise enough to glean the truth behind the lore. Shadows hid danger. Danger for Black girls was different. It didn't obey the boundaries of stories. For them, it was always real.

But so much time in this small town had made Tanisha easy. She didn't always lock her doors anymore. She had stopped interlacing her keys between her fingers when she walked alone at night. After a few years, her guard had finally come down. For the first time, she agreed and offered Alice her favorite jacket.

"Mom," Alice whined, "I don't need it. It's fine."

"If you get sick, you'll be upset," Tanisha warned. "And don't forget to wear your bandana if you happen to 'find' yourself in the woods." Tanisha looked down at her daughter knowingly. "I put it in the pocket. Please, Munchkin."

Alice looked at the jacket and the bandana and for the first time she understood that these two totems were more than Day-Glo and denim, they were her mother's care. Alice took the jacket and did her best to conceal her smile as she ran out the front door and off to play.

With her jacket around her waist, Alice and her friends streaked past houses and haphazard gardens until they reached the last house on the block before the woods began. The dirt driveway extended past the garage and dissolved into an array of Eastern hemlock trees. At the end of the driveway, there was a boy she'd never seen before.

One of Alice's friends whispered, "He said he found a deer skull last night! There're still brains inside."

Another rolled their eyes to the back of their head and let out a zombie groan, "Braaaainnns . . ."

Without a second thought, all her friends took off toward the tree line. Alice faltered. This new boy looked odd. Too young to be out there alone or very small for his age. He looked angry. For the first time, she felt a hint of her mother's worry. She fished around in her jacket for the bandana. In the afternoon sun, its orange hue made her eyes ache. She would look like a total loser and she knew it. Alice shoved it back into her pocket and then remembered the swimming cap incident. She had never seen her mother cry until that lady from the state talked to her. Alice didn't like seeing her mother cry. Her mother asked her to wear the bandana like a necklace, but Alice had a better idea. She flipped the stiff fabric up and wrapped it around her head, like a crown.

"Alice," someone called. The voice was soft, she couldn't be sure who it was, but it was coming from the trees. She took a step toward the woods. A chill passed through her. Her mom was right. It wasn't as warm as she thought. Freshly crowned, Alice put on her favorite jacket, turned up its fluffy collar, and ran into the woods after her friends.

The streetlights came on.

Night fell.

Her friends made their way home.

Alice didn't.

Before Tanisha could call them, the police knocked on her door. They sent a female officer because the department thought this needed a woman's touch. In reality, none of the men on the force was up for the task. When Tanisha answered, the officer spoke with a heavy sense of duty.

"Ma'am, do you recognize this?" she asked. The officer held up a plastic bag.

Tanisha shook her head. "No. Wait." She leaned in to get a closer look. The officer tried to pull the bag back, but it was too late. Tanisha could smell it. The plastic couldn't contain the sharp metallic tang of blood. The evidence bag slid over the fabric—whatever it was, was soaked. The bag moved in the officer's hand and a shearling collar shifted into view. Tanisha reached out and grabbed it to get a closer look. The cold slickness of the bag did not match the warmth that the liquid inside once contained. While the officer stepped back, she could not stop the realization building in Tanisha. Though the denim jacket was stained with blood and mud, the collar shone through.

Tanisha's life stopped. Time continued, but she was forever divided: There would always be before this moment and after it. With each passing second, the pain of the present robbed the past of its luster. Tanisha, like any mother would, tried to do the impossible. She saw time marching forward, and she wanted to turn it back. But like the heavy bag in her hands, time slid out of her grip. The weight of the jacket brought her to her knees.

Tanisha had wanted Alice to be seen so she wouldn't become a hunter's prey. She'd had that title long before she reached my eyes.

You can't stop a mother from seeing the good in her child, even in their most abject state. After hours of questions and paperwork. After her husband broke down and put himself back together. After they walked down the long hallway to the morgue. When they showed her Alice, all Tanisha saw was her daughter's serene face. She didn't look at the hole in her chest. She didn't ask about the innocence taken. She didn't seek out Alice's missing organ, her heart. Instead, Tanisha chose to see what little serenity Alice had left.

Walker Tragedy Ruled an Accident

March 13, 1986

JOHNSTOWN, PA—Alice Walker's tragic death has been ruled accidental after months of investigation. The medical examiner's office released this statement: "After a thorough investigation, we have concluded that Walker got lost and succumbed to the elements. Injuries previously considered to be foul play have been deemed animal activity. We take this time to remind parents to ensure their children's safety when hiking and playing in the woods. Children should be under adult supervision at all times. Our thoughts and prayers are with the Walker family tonight. We hope this answer offers them some solace." Walker's parents could not be reached for comment.

THE HEART

ONE

June 17, 2017

Welcome to Johnstown: Home of the World's Steepest Vehicular Inclined Plane.

All of that, every single word, is emblazoned on a massive billboard visible about a mile outside of town. Because of the angle of the train's approach, the Inclined Plane is the first and only landmark I see. It means I've reached my final destination. The journey here has been rife with spotty cell service, dotted with tiny towns and abandoned industries consumed by thick forests. Yes. After fourteen years away, I, Liz Rocher, am returning to Johnstown, Pennsylvania. The rust belt.

Home.

I take another gulp of my train wine. The cheap varietal burns my palate. *Varietal. Palate. Who do you think you are?* There it is. Judgment. One of the many things I ran from when I left.

The train slows. I catch a glimpse of my reflection in the window. With my thick natural hair and dark skin, my Appalachian origins are unexpected. I buzzed all my hair off a little over three months ago. It's finally settled into its new length. Returning home with no hair means no protection. That's why this trek required a trip to Harlem to get a decent wig. Her name is Valerie. On the box, she looked like a pop star. On me, she looks like a PTA mom. Between the wig and my rumpled business casual, I look like a mockery of what I've become: a "city girl."

You'll never be rid of that backwoods, small-town stink. There it is again. My therapist, a tall white woman who gives me names for my feelings, would call that voice my anxiety. The tightness in my chest is my imposter syndrome. The occasional inability to catch my breath is a perfectionist tendency. Neat little notes in her records. My next sip of wine becomes a full gulp, finishing off the split.

"This stop is Johnstown, Pennsylvania."

I gather my things. My phone lights up with a notification from the office. Sales never sleeps. I've taken the weekend off, but I have work to do. I always have work to do. If I don't, I ask for more. The first time I did, my then-boss laughed and asked, "Trouble at home?" Implying that I didn't have ambition, I had misplaced avoidance. I smiled back at him with all my teeth. In two years, I had his job and an engagement ring on my finger. I don't have the ring anymore, but the work is a constant. Sometimes I wonder how he knew. I try to open the document but it refuses to load. A single bar of service flickers in and out. *Great.* I cling to my technology, like the rind of this place won't get on me if I'm shiny enough.

Moving into the aisle, I have to peel my dress pants off the backs of my thighs. I chose slacks over sweats because I feel powerful in a suit. In control. Every sweaty wrinkle threatens to break that illusion.

The train comes to a stop. What should have been an eight-hour journey became ten because of delays, and my body is sore and stiff. I turn my head to stretch my neck. A ligament pulls tight all the way down the center of my back, pinching right behind my heart. My eyes land on a red sign at the top of the open train door.

Exit.

My suitcase is above my head. One good pull and I can roll off this train. Or I could stay? Ride on to Pittsburgh. Take a flight back to New York.

My phone rings.

Melissa Parker.

How does she always know exactly when to call? I answer it.

"You're here!" she says.

I glance across the car, half expecting her to pop out from one of the empty seats. "How do you— I've been delayed for— Are you tracking my trip?"

"*Someone* won't stop asking when you're going to get here." Mel is more than enough reason to come home. Her daughter, my goddaughter, Caroline, is another.

I lift my bag into the aisle, but I don't leave the train just yet. A few passengers slide by me.

"Last call for Johnstown!"

I look back at my seat. *Seats.* Plural. I paid for both of them back in January when Mel called me and said, "I'm getting married." No hello. No how are you. No delighted scream. No girlish cheering. Mel started the call with a statement. She ended it with a date. That's how I knew she was serious. I bought tickets. The details would come later. She'd made a New Year's resolution to live in the "present." After more than ten years of living with her boyfriend, Garrett Washington, Melissa Parker was going to take his last name. Then, I had been all too eager to attend because I was finally who I imagined myself to be: Successful. Great job. Great fiancé. I'd become a New Yorker who had plans to move to Connecticut in three years.

"How does it feel to be home?" Mel asks.

"My home is dead." The phone is warm on my ear by the time this unprompted observation spills out of me.

"Liz," she replies. "Stop being so damn dramatic. It's one weekend."

"Fine."

Let it be known, I buried this place. When I look at a map of the United States, my eyes drift over all 309 miles of a state that isn't quite the heartland or the coast. As I stand in this Appalachian intercostal of America, I find myself in a liminal expanse. A cruel riddle.

"Can I get a weekend for my wedding?"

I see the conductor waving at me. This is it. *Last chance, Liz.*

I knew Melissa Parker was a good person when she shielded me from spitballs in the cafeteria in middle school. I'd stumbled into some quintessential '90s bullying. My sin? Being the only Black kid who wasn't "Black." One of three in my entire school, I was the one who didn't fit in. I didn't sound like them or listen to rap or have any rhythm. To my white classmates, these were compulsory to the definition, leaving me at the mercy of this shameful smattering of stereotypes. Cue the spitballs. The other Black kids were no help. I don't blame them; they were swimming for their own social lives and I was tainted water. Branded an Oreo, through and through. Whiteness influenced my speech, mannerisms, and pop-culture preferences. Mel and I hadn't said more than a few words to each other before then, but when she saw my matching lunch of a soft pretzel and fries, she knew we were meant to be. That's what she says. We both know it was because she herself was a white girl who didn't fit in. She wasn't rich, her blond wasn't from a box, and she wasn't interested in power over kindness.

"You get exactly forty-eight hours," I say before yelling to the conductor, "Wait!" A quick hoist of my bag, a sprint down the aisle, and I'm off the train. It lets out directly onto the tracks. "My God, this place is remote," I say to Mel.

"That's just the station."

The train pulls away. The landscape mounts. The flat coast is a distant memory now. Eastern hemlock trees crowd in, bringing darkness with their density despite the dwindling daylight. I'm in the wild. *Breathe*. I name the things around me:

Phone.

Gravel.

Trees.

"Garrett just sent me a picture of the view at the venue. It's stunning," Mel says. I can hear the tinny sound of her mixing something in her kitchen. Baking. Probably her cake. Mel got the *idea* to get married in January. She only seriously started *planning* two months ago. This ceremony is the definition of haphazard, last-minute, and thrown together with a hope and a prayer.

"Glad you finally decided on a place the day before the ceremony," I tease. "Where is it?"

"We're using Nick's place?" The upward inflection is there to make sure I'm okay. I'm not the biggest fan of her brother, Nick.

"Like, his house?"

"His land," she clarifies. "It's . . . picturesque?"

Saliva pushes past the wine on my tongue. I don't reply. I'm not gonna say it until she does.

"It's . . . the woods. We're in the woods, okay?" This double insistence tells me all I need to know. "Elizabeth Rocher. Please tell me you're gonna be cool."

"Wh—what do you mean?" I almost fool myself with the validity of that question.

"I don't know—we were going to grab the ballroom at the Holiday Inn, but they're closed for the weekend because a pipe burst. We were gonna do it in the yard, but Nick offered. It's beautiful, Liz. Just beautiful—"

"I understand, but I—"

"Please don't tell me you're gonna run?" Her voice gets tight with emotion.

I choke back my laugh. *Too late.*

"I didn't mean that," Mel backtracks.

"Yes, you did." Mel is the only reason I survived Johnstown. I know what this wedding means to her. "You are so lucky—" I start.

"Thank you!"

"So lucky," I repeat as I walk toward the station.

Because everything here is on a hill, the station itself is a ways from the tracks, down two flights of suspiciously steep steps. I stop at the top.

Before I confess something to Mel that she already knows, I look over my shoulder, checking that I'm alone. "It's, umm . . . it's just me. Okay?"

"I know." Mel brightens her voice, instantly adjusting to the pain in mine. "I don't want that asshole here. I want you." After a beat she adds,

"I need you here. Believe me." As much as she can read me, I can read her. Something's wrong.

"What's up—"

Snap!

A loud sound cuts through the air. It's something distinctly natural, like the breaking of a massive branch or a tree. I whirl around, nearly dropping my phone.

"Liz, you still there?"

I scan the train tracks. In the corridor between mountains, I see forest on either side. The sound doesn't return. It must have been a branch on the tracks. Or my imagination. It wouldn't be the first time my mind has birthed something out of fear. Or boredom.

"Yeah. I'm—I'm here, Mel."

"All right. I'll see you tomorrow."

I hang up. We don't need to say hello and we've never said goodbye. This conversation is an extension of the one started in middle school when we'd tie up the internet connection talking about boys and the depth of our feelings. No matter what, we can pick back up without ever missing a beat.

I descend the steps to the station. There is a kiosk at one end and bathrooms at the other. Straight ahead of me is a set of doors leading to the street. A few passengers go through them to meet their rides. The conductor climbs the stairs behind me and locks the exit to the tracks. Now there's only one way out. A bottleneck.

Sweat pools in the kitchen of my hair. I push my nails under the back of my wig and dig through my short, thick curls. My fingers find the hollow where my skull joins my spine. I massage it. The bruise that was once there is gone, but the tightness and tenderness remain. Instead of giving me any release, my muscles tense and wetness trickles down the back of my neck. I give my scalp one last good scratch and fix my wig.

I sit on the metal bench near the door of the station and call a cab. If I could stand being in an enclosed space with my mother for more than five minutes, I would have had her pick me up. Another reason I've spent so many years away. I need protection from every aspect of "home."

I'm here for Mel's wedding and to answer a question:

If I can't trust myself, then who?

One thing any breakup does is make you doubt every part of yourself. A bad breakup? A nasty one? The first few weeks I mismatched my shoes. The second month I skipped meals because I couldn't tell when I was hungry. After almost fumbling a major account, I had to do something. I was planning to cancel on Mel. But Mel, this wedding, and this town are the only certainties I have left in my life. The last person I trusted was Mel. The last right choice I made, beyond any doubt, was leaving this town. I'm here to confirm that. This weekend is going to be uncomfortable. Awkward. Painful. And it should be. I can't wait. Because once I remember how to trust myself, I will start to mend.

Waiting for the car, using the pad of my thumb, I search the underside of my left wrist. There, I find a thick, shiny melanin relic of my childhood trauma in the woods. The scar blanches under the pressure of my fingers. It was roughly made and badly healed. I search it for the uncomfortable spot where the nerves go awry. Depending on the day, it's either too sensitive or strikingly numb. I prefer numb.

I look out. On the wall across from me is a massive topographic map of Johnstown. Another bottleneck. Built in the bottom of a valley, layers of mountains jut out at the edges and everything spirals open from the Conemaugh River at its center. When I first saw this map in fourth grade, I said, *Whose idea was it to build a town in a ditch?* I can already hear my therapist wanting me to unpack that statement. What has this town ever done to me?

It's a wonder it didn't flood immediately. It did eventually. Three times. When we visited the Flood Museum in elementary school—because it was a disaster, of course there's a museum—I don't remember who, but someone (not me) asked: *Where are all the Black people?* My teacher, Mrs. Kohler, replied, *Look at the pictures, sweetie. They weren't here yet.* Like every small-town citizen in America, my teacher believed

Black people were an alien anomaly in white suburban perfection. She never questioned where the photographer focused their lens or the history of this town. I should have. I didn't stay long enough to start.

The sun dips in the sky, sending the first traces of orange rays through the station window. For a sunset, it's bright and rich. I can't help but trail my fingers in the amber of it. If there's one thing you don't get in the city, it's this: unblemished nature. I push the door to the street open and step outside.

The light but distinct smell of stagnant water hits my nose. Water and something else. Something rotten. The scent isn't coming from the river. It's seeping off the buildings and into the air. No matter how long ago the floodwaters receded, in some places, the smell of river water and decay never left.

This station must be older than I thought. I turn back and look up at the walls. There, at least fourteen feet above my head, sits a plain brass bar. Some buildings have the muddy lines, others have these ominous indicators. Either way, they mark where the waters reached in 1889, 1936, and 1977. The 1889 tragedy is the only one known by name. It was so devastating people here simply call it "the flood." Water got up to sixty feet in some places, more than four times the height of the bar above me. Thinking of water that deep reminds me I don't know how to swim. Kind of, but not really. I know how to not-drown, does that count?

I don't need my grade school history unit to know that this town was once a true industrial center. I can tell by the brick buildings. They're sturdy even in their decay. The business of removing things from the earth didn't work out in the long run. Still, this town persisted. New, flimsy-looking developments are piecemealed between abandoned properties. While the new buildings are bright white with modernity, the weight of this place won't be lost so easily. Just like the people here, it will take much more to wash it away.

Where the town stops, the mountains and the woods begin. Wild, enveloping, and vast, the forest is thick enough to inspire campfire stories of monsters and mayhem. I'd forgotten how much wild there is.

Trees surround the town and carry on into the distance as far as I can see. Looking out, my heart beats uncomfortably in my chest.

Something makes the small of my back prickle. Attention. Someone's watching me. I turn around and see that the station is empty. I look over to the parking lot. Immediately, I find a pair of eyes burrowing into me. I push back with my stare. People in this town smile and nod and say hello. I don't. I meet the gaze with an unspoken challenge. *What the fuck are you looking at?* That usually works. Not this time.

The eyes staring at me belong to a woman. Nondescript in her Blackness and her clothing. Jeans. Short salt-and-pepper hair. A worn gray T-shirt. No jacket. No bags. She's in the middle of the parking lot, perched on the base of a streetlamp, with seemingly no destination in mind. She isn't even turned toward the town. Her body faces the trees, but she's looking at me. Strangely comfortable, like I've had the audacity to wander into her living room. Her eyes are bright and hollow at the same time. Like a drowning person, her stare can't help but pull me in. This woman needs something and I am *not* about to give it to her. As I turn away, I see her stand and start making a beeline toward me.

"Ma'am?" Her voice is loud and harsh. She picks up her pace and holds a flyer out in front of her. What was once white and crisp is now folded and yellowed. Someone clearly threw this one away and she fished it out of the trash.

I turn away. "No, thank you."

"Just a minute of your time. I need your help—" She launches into some pitch. I try to tune her out, but her eyes draw me in. I don't listen to her words, but she has my focus now. I'm judging her before I realize it. I make a catalogue of her appearance: Her clothes are dirty, she is unkempt, there's dirt under her uneven nails, her shoes are worn. It felt like I walked into her living room, because I did. She lives outside this station. The shame that wells up in me is unavoidable. I know I'm supposed to think kindly about homelessness. I know what I should say and what I should do. Smile. Listen. But all I want to do is scream at this woman to get away from me. It's not her fault. It's this place. This is what it can do to a person. A city can do the same, but in a city I won't be mistaken for this woman. I've been mistaken for nannies, retail employees, any Black woman other than myself. Here, the make of my bag, the quality of my clothes, the timbre of my voice, the style of my hair, none of that matters. My skin speaks first, and it is too close to this woman's for comfort.

"No, thank you," I say in a huff to end our one-sided conversation.

She cuts her eyes at me. "Well, aren't you bitter?"

Looks like I'm not the only one judging. "Excuse me?"

"Nothing good comes from being hateful and hollow."

"I don't—I'm not . . ." I start, but stop myself. Do I hate this woman? I don't want to, but I can't deny the feeling.

She steps closer to me, and I stay still. "But if you're angry?" She raises an eyebrow. "That's useful." She offers the flyer again.

I frown back at her. "I'm not angry." The paper flutters between us. It's something homemade and sad. I grab it.

A car horn honks. It's my cab. *Thank God.*

"Coming!" I wave. I fold the flyer in my hand and scan for a trash can. Of course, there aren't any. I shove it into the narrow back pocket of my pants. My suitcase rumbles over the pavement as I race toward the car. Before I get in, I glance back at the woman and see her hunched figure retreating across the parking lot. Like before, her focus is on the trees, not the town.

I get in the car. The driver loads my bag in the back. He pulls away and we head up into the hills. My hands fidget, looking for a task. I check my phone. No service. No access to work. No access to me. I look out my window and breathe and name:

Purse.

Phone.

Wrist.

Tree.

Tree.

Tree.

TWO

I stand in the doorway to my childhood home. Before I ring the bell, I smile the way my mother likes, with my top teeth only. She'll think that I've maintained her investment in my braces and still wear my retainer. I don't. My bottom teeth are far from the crowded mess they once were, but they aren't perfect. That's the problem.

Knock knock.

My mother opens the door. I brace for questions, tears, delight. Without saying a word, my mother reaches out and grabs the wig off my head.

"Why did you cut all of your hair off? You look like a boy."

Here we go. "I needed a change," I say as I drag my bag up the front steps and into the mudroom. My mother frowns as I strain to lift my suitcase, but she doesn't make a move to help. I wouldn't let her anyway.

"Why is your bag so heavy?"

"It's a wedding. I had to bring . . . stuff." My bridesmaid's dress, sweats for the day of, and an outfit for the train ride home. Supplies. I meant it. Forty-eight hours. No more, no less.

I roll my bag into the kitchen and attempt to sit on one of the stools before she can comment about the size of my hips, but she stops me.

"Do not sit yet. Let me get a good look at you." Like any well-educated Haitian, my mother pronounces every letter of her English. She paid dearly to learn those words, and she's going to make sure you hear all of them.

She looks at me.

She saw me six months ago. Christmas. Right before things got bad. She has seen me since I've left town, just not in this house.

She frowns.

My mother, Marie, is a perfectionist. This made her an excellent doctor but a hard person to live with. Everyone in front of her is a patient who needs to be fixed. If I didn't fit the textbook definition of success, I was a failure: An A-minus was no better than an F, a size four was a slippery slope toward morbid obesity, and single after thirty meant I was doomed to die alone. I will say this: Being over thirty and being away for so long, I'm starting to figure her out. I know she holds me to these standards because someone did the same for her. Society and the root of my last name, my father.

My mother found a Black man with a French last name, Rocher. Only he had no real connection to the country or its colonies. He held her to impossible standards because, as a Black female physician, the woman was a walking miracle. She subverted expectations and defied inherent bias just by existing. Constantly moving the finish line, he used her need for perfection to guarantee she'd never attain it. My father told me to be independent, smart, and self-sufficient because he loved me. But when it came to the woman he married, the *idea* of her earning more than him grated away at his core until he left. Step by step, he faded into the background of our lives. In the end, he resented my mother. Nothing kills a relationship faster than that. I know that now.

After their divorce, as soon as my mother could, she bought the biggest house she could find and filled it with the nicest things money could buy. Within reasonable taste, of course. Everything in her house has a specific purpose and place. In my childhood, through trial and error, I memorized each one. My mother stayed thin. She didn't date again. She tells the truth no matter how much it hurts. For her, pain is part of the healing process.

After a long beat, my mother renders her verdict. "You gained weight." Single. Check. Fat. Check. My mother hasn't seen me since before the breakup. Yes, when I do remember to eat, I've been coping with wine and take-out. No, I don't need a definitive reminder.

"I got a promotion," I offer.

My mother shrugs.

"Thanks."

"You have a new dress for this wedding? What if you got the wrong size, *eh*?"

"Thank you," I repeat, expressionless. This is new. This is therapy. I've never told my mother about going to therapy to help with the breakup. She's not ready to hear I've learned that prayers alone aren't enough. I used to deconstruct everything my mother said, but my therapist suggested I try the opposite. As expected, my mother doubles down on her judgments.

"It is the truth," she insists. I wonder how often the truth and my mother's observations are conflated. "Did you gain weight before or after he left you?"

I never did inherit her Haitian bluntness. I don't answer.

"What?" My mother has already answered for me in her head. And without saying a word, I've managed to start a fight. "Men care about these things. Even if they refuse to admit it. Beauty is not without effort. And being fat is bad for your health." The bait she's laying is too tempting. "The way people eat in this country is the problem."

I can't let that comment slide. "How do you know how everyone eats all the time?"

"That is not what I'm saying."

"How is that not—?"

"You are not *everyone*, Elizabeth." She faces me to drive her point home. "You do not need to be like everyone else. Remember that."

I do my best to keep a lid on all the things I want to say. *Why don't you ask what* he *did wrong? Would you ask me to work it out if you knew what he was like when we were alone?* But the truth, more than any sort of self-control or temperance, cools me. I'm *her* daughter. Much is expected of me, my friends, my life, every second I'm here, because my life was never mine. Instead, it's a summation of her sacrifices. What do I have to show for them? A one-bedroom apartment in Manhattan that I can barely afford and a degree from an out-of-state school I'm still paying for.

Looking at the house, my mother has decorated like she was expecting company. Not me. She's put out two bouquets of fresh flowers to welcome a fiancé. Me standing here, alone, is confirmation that her daughter is a spinster.

I get up to grab my suitcase. She blocks the way.

"Yes?" I ask.

She separates my hands and pulls me to her. My mother is at the age where I've started to notice it. Her medium-brown skin has picked up lines of living that stay in her face after she makes her expressions. Grays streak her straight shoulder-length hair no matter how often she dyes it. She has more freckles along her collarbone, which now juts out from her slender frame, not just because of her weight, but her age. She smells the same, like warm spices and bitter shea butter. I hold her and she feels like a bird in my arms. As I struggle not to crush her, her hug offers me the opposite of comfort.

"*Cherie*, did you try—"

"I did," I say as firmly as I can. With her, I must always walk a careful balance between ending a conversation and sounding disrespectful. This means I smooth out the rough edges of things for my mother.

"Misunderstandings happen. Relationships are hard."

I press my bottom lip into my mouth, between my teeth, and focus on the dry split skin there. I taste metallic flesh and papery tissue. I think of the truth. My throat aches as it forms on my tongue. No. Not ready.

"It's over." All this pressure is because she loves me. Her love is overwhelming. If she learned that I've come home with a broken heart, she would pry my chest open with her bare hands to fix me.

After one last squeeze, she lets me go.

I glance around at my childhood home. It's exactly as I remember. Clean. It looks more like a magazine spread than a place where anyone lives. My mother is predictable. Any bit of class is polished and cared for within an inch of its life.

I reach for my bag and something drifts into the corner of my eye. On the far side of the front door, in the mudroom, I see a solid but frantic shadow. I take a step toward it. On a wide white card is a little creature. The fur is long and wild. It begs the title of "rat," but it's too small. Jerking forward on the glue trap, the mouse reaches for a dark corner and the small hole it probably came from. It cries as it moves. It's not screaming because of me or the light, it's screaming because of what it's done trying to free itself. More pink flesh than blood, the chewed sinew and bone of its leg sits exposed in the glue. Like a half-mounted insect, the poor thing struggles to gnaw itself free of its dead limb. I see a white tendon snap free. It tries to rip the skin by running. The trap trails after the creature like a sad flag.

I scream.

My mother rushes to my side. "*Eh-eh!* Just a small one. They keep getting in." I hear her retreat to get a broom and a bag to dispose of it. My wrist aches. The wound there was deep enough to see the tendon. My mother swoops in with the bag. Muted little cries come and go as she smacks the bag with the broom. Three hard whacks. Red splatters. The mouse is dead. I watch her as she heads outside to throw it away. She's in matching gray unwrinkled sweatpants and fur-lined slippers. None of that can change the fact that she lives in a pristine home with a pest problem.

When she returns, she jumps right back into her assessment.

"Your hair looks dry. I have *lwil maskriti*. It will help." And she is off to grab the thick, spicy brown oil. She shouts over her shoulder as she races back into the house. "The spare keys are—"

"I remember!" The house is huge compared to my apartment in New York.

My hands shake as I open the drawer for the spare keys. Death is still a moment for me. In America, the cycle of life is hidden. Broken. Beef ends up on our plates without reminding us of the process. My mother was raised on an island where meat meant cutting the throat of the chicken yourself. I reach into the drawer and feel cool metal hidden behind hard plastic. I pull the drawer farther out and see little baggies of unpopped popcorn. It's strange, but I don't say anything. If they are there, it's because my mother wants them to be. I take the spare keys.

My mother returns with the oil. It is just as thick and musky as I remember. She dumps a sizable amount in her palms before I can stop her.

"Wait! I don't have *that* much hair."

"*Le sech.*" She hurls Creole at me before I can process it. In the seconds it takes me to translate the word "dry," her hands are on my scalp and massaging in the smoky oil.

Her strong fingers carry me back to elementary school and firm braids in my hair in the mornings. Her steady hand pulling my strands through the brush to join in her palm. Girlhood rushes back to me. Perfectly parted plaits. Summer braids. A flash of long box braids and the jammy smell of hair gel creeps in the sides of my memory. I snap away from her.

"Elizabeth, what's wrong?"

"Nothing. You pulled my hair." I press my hands to my short Afro and bring them to my nose. Just the spicy oil. No sweet gel.

"You have no hair to pull." Her sharp tongue is harder to avoid in person than it is on the phone. I wish it could shock the memory away.

I scramble for a topic shift. "Have you put out the patio furniture yet?" I move over toward the sliding back door and start to unlock it. "I need some air." It doesn't budge.

"Wait!" She pulls a bar out of the track. Finally, the door opens.

"When did you get that?"

"Just"—she hesitates—"extra security."

I duck outside and, thankfully, she doesn't follow me. I breathe in deep with closed eyes. When I open them, the dark remains. I feel a strangeness I haven't felt in years. An untethered fear latches in me. Instead of listening to anything roiling around inside, I look up. I search the night sky for stars. Ursa Major. The Great Bear. The Big Dipper. I trace the dark vastness between the dots to the handle of the Little Dipper and there it is. Polaris. The center of the sky. The North Star blazes like the beacon it is. I know where I am again. Johnstown. Pennsylvania. June. Near midnight. The day before Mel's wedding.

My phone chimes. Despite the history, an impersonal row of numbers titles the thread:

212-555-1564: Hey.

The period is shitty and unnecessary. It's meant to irk me. It's working. I reply. I'm home. After a breath, I add, Asshole.

Send.

I flip the phone over. *You just told him where you are, stupid.* I grab my wrist and search my scar. I press away my panic. This time, everything hurts. I press anyway.

My phone buzzes.

Message failed to send.

No bars. The isolation of this place just saved me from myself. For now. I delete the reply, ensuring it never goes through.

Breathe.

I can still smell my memory of the hair gel. My mind is locked on it, searching for it in the night air. Another breath clears my lungs. My stomach churns. Finally, I listen to what my body has been trying to tell me. I'm home.

Home.

Coming back here was a huge mistake.

THREE

June 18, 2017

A man and his shadow live in the trees.
When they walk in time, both are pleased.
If one calls your name, or the other tempts you off the path,
You must ignore both, or face their wrath.

The same way I'm hesitant around large bodies of water and the police, I'm nervous around the woods. Not that I can't trust these things, they just need to be proven worthy. Look at that rhyme. It's two couplets of "Stay Out of the Woods." The first time I heard it was junior year of high school. Mel recited it as she guided us out of the trees. Said her dad taught it to her. She tried to make it sound like fairies or something twee. She was attempting to comfort me and tell me I was going to be okay. She clutched my hand and assured me that I wasn't going to bleed to death from the gash in my arm.

Now I'm standing outside her wedding venue. There is no mistaking it. Mel has dragged me back to the woods. I have to resist the urge to whirl around in circles, checking the spaces between the branches. Instead, I focus on the bits of civilization in front of me. In the middle of a clearing, there's a barn—not one of those built for photographs and parties, a real barn. Thank God Nick has put some work into making it wedding-ready. Fresh coat of paint. There are outlets, a dance floor, and if I peer in, I can see a small kitchen and a bar. A few feet away from the barn are bathrooms, a welcome amenity. Two matching buildings on the side are dressing areas. Beyond all this, the field drops off to reveal a stunning view. Interlocking symmetrical hills. Densely packed greenery. It stretches out in front of me. I search for the end of it. There is none. Not a hint of a brick building or a paved road. My mouth goes dry. I try to swallow, but my throat clutches against itself in vain.

I turn away.

Walking toward the dressing rooms, I search for water when someone catches my eye. "Garrett?" I ask, because the Black man I spot in the corner of the venue is smoking. The love of Mel's life, Garrett, does not smoke. He coughs to disperse the cloud around him. Too late. I've caught him.

"Liz!" Garrett smiles too big and greets me too enthusiastically. "How the hell are you?" Garrett Washington is fundamentally kind. I can tell. Some men, you can sense the danger lurking behind their eyes. Like with Nick. Men don't have to be kind the way women do.

"I think I should be asking you that. How's . . . well . . . everything?"

"Got everyone here in one piece." He glances toward the dressing rooms. "Plan to stay that way if Mel and Mrs. Parker don't tear each other's heads off."

"That bad?"

He gives a low whistle. "We thought they'd get it together for the wedding, try to make the day easy." He leans in to share the secret. "It seems she thinks she can turn Mel into a runaway bride."

"Jesus Christ." I can't help but feel bad. For Mel's parents, it was okay to be friends with "The Blacks," just don't bring one home. It didn't help that Mel was three months pregnant when she had.

Garrett manages a dry laugh. "Mrs. Parker loves my daughter. Always there if we need a sitter, picks her up from school, just *loves* her, right? Me?" Garrett points to himself and takes in what he's about to say. "I'm the problem."

I shake my head in solidarity. "That sucks. I'm sorry." Someone needs to apologize for what they've been through. Might as well be me.

"You didn't do anything." Garrett puts out the cigarette. "Won't have to put up with it much longer anyways."

"Yeah, marriage has a way of shutting people up."

"Exactly. I got to pick the location for the baptism. She gets the wedding." I'm forever grateful they had Caroline's baptism at a church in Philadelphia. It was closer for Garrett's extended family and I didn't have to travel all the way back here, till now. A wave of groomsmen descends on us and Garrett is pulled in another direction. I head for the dressing rooms.

There, I see that while there's been a gesture at uniformity with the peach bridesmaid dresses, each is slightly different because we all got them on our own.

With finished hardwood floors and mirrored walls, the dressing room exceeds my expectations. I find a corner and am instantly reminded of gym class, where I perfected the art of changing clothes while remaining fully dressed. For the first time since arriving, I unzip my garment bag. My dress is peach tulle, midlength, and strapless. It was the only thing Bloomingdale's had in stock that fit Mel's parameters. Already sweaty, I get undressed as painlessly as possible and throw on my peach explosion. I try to shimmy it over my hips, but the dress stops at my upper thighs. I look at the tag—it's my usual size. My mother's right, I have gained weight. I pull it over my head. The slim hidden zipper slips out of my fingers. I pinch it hard and twist my shoulder down.

"Liz Rocher!" a woman shrieks inches away from my face. Instantly, she pulls me in for a hug. Gripped in her arms, I search the mirrored walls for clues. No luck. When she finally lets me go, she steps back and I get a good look at her. Her black hair and blue eyes make her pale skin even whiter; despite a full face of makeup, she looks washed-out. I'm quiet for so long she catches me thinking. "Lauren Bristol. I have a mind for faces. Don't worry, it freaks people out."

"Not freaked out at all," I lie. My shoulder strains and I finally pull up my zipper. I do my best to hold my face. The Lauren Bristol I remember was not this friendly. We weren't friends in school and we haven't spoken since. While she hadn't gone out of her way to make school absolute hell for me, she hadn't helped. She'd been too busy trading gossip for social clout. She was that girl who was only in student government to get institutional levels of dirt.

I can feel Lauren giving me a once-over as I smooth out my dress, stretching it over my hips. I expect as much. This is what this weekend is going to be. Lauren, along with anyone else I meet, is going to be checking to see how I've changed: Do I have any visible tattoos? What kind of clothes am I wearing now? All of it fodder for small-town gossip later.

"Aren't your eyes bright," she says.

"Th—thank you?" Not sure about that comment.

"Where's your plus-one? I can't wait to meet him." How does she know I had a plus-one? She's been following the guest book, she had to be.

"Uh." I got this. I have rehearsed this answer in my bathroom mirror for the past four months. "No. Not anymore." *Crap*. The practiced answer gave Lauren more information than she asked for.

"'Anymore'? What happened, hon?"

Shame burns in my face before I can stop it. "Um. Well. I. Um—" Each breath threatens to betray me. Tears wait beyond the hitch in my throat I'm desperately trying to control. I remember what my therapist says: *Name things. Ground yourself.*

False eyelashes.

Lipstick.

Peach nail polish bottle.

Blow-dryer.

Heels.

"I should stretch these shoes, or else they'll give me blisters." I rush away from the conversation to the other side of the room.

There is no privacy, so I literally turn in to a corner. I'm coming apart. Tears race out of my eyes. I press my hands to my face like I might physically put myself back together. It's not just the breakup or my mother or the woods or being home again. It's all of it and everything else. I clutch my shoes. I'm here to change all that. To conquer this. To prove to myself who I am: Someone who can come home. A good friend. Someone who can go to my best friend's wedding. And have a good time. I can laugh. I am good.

"Liz!"

I turn at my name and see Mel. She's in a white robe and slippers. Her thick blond locks are now in a curled mom-length bob. Her cherubic features never age. Mel is pretty in that way that can't be named. Examine her for her secret, there isn't one, which should make you hate her. But hating Mel is hard. She's too damn nice. My dress crunches as a teenage hunch forms in my back. My red face matches hers. We've each found the other in tears.

Melissa reaches out and holds me so tight it makes my shoulders hurt. She pulls me over to the bridal dressing area and definitively pulls the curtain shut.

"You okay?" I ask.

A hardness washes over Mel's face. "It's a mess. All of it is just a . . . nightmare."

"Where's your mom?" I ask.

"I'm *this* close to asking her to leave," Mel says in a rushed whisper. "I know my parents aren't the biggest fans of Garrett, but I thought he'd won them over. *We'd* won them over."

"What happened?"

Mel's face shows her fatigue. She unzips a garment bag to reveal her dress. It's beautiful, intricate lace. Off the shoulder. Open-backed. With a long sheer train.

"That's *stunning*."

"This was my third-choice dress. Only one I could get in time. Mom was like, 'It's a sign.'"

"Seriously? It's perfect."

Mel removes her robe and shimmies into the gown. "And when the first venue canceled on us, Dad was like, 'Well, I guess that's it.' Like, *that* could stop a wedding? Thank God for Nick. All this is his next . . . investment." Even though Mel grumbles, she can't hide her awe. "He's been building it up for weddings anyway. Wasn't supposed to be open till next summer. He worked overnight to get things ready for us." Mel leans in for a whisper. "It's a trap, right? I mean, of all people, he'd be the one to pull something." She laughs.

Try as I might, I can't.

"So, you got your speech ready?" Mel asks.

I almost throw up. "You said nothing about a speech—I don't have one—I barely got the dress—"

"I'm kidding!" She chuckles. "Kidding. Trying to get you to snap out of whatever is going on with you."

"Oh." I attempt another laugh, but it falls out of me like a cough.

Mel finally speaks to my discomfort. "Don't tell me that's why you're— You still have that thing about the woods?"

"I don't have a *thing*. I have a real, justifiable fear."

"There's electricity and working toilets. This is not some kegger in the trees." She turns around. "Help, please?"

I button a column of tight little loops cinching in at her lower back. "I know."

"You can still make a speech. But only if you want—if it will get you to calm down."

"No. Thank you. I'm terrible at them. I never know what to—" I stop midsentence and shriek when I see something dart across the tiny dressing room and out under the curtain. It looked like a mouse. Or a bug. "Did you see—"

"No, you didn't." Mel digs into one of her many bags. I try to perch on a chair, but she grabs the edge of my dress before I can shrink away. "Elizabeth Rocher, don't you flake on me." She produces a small flask from a bag, prompts me to tip my head back, and fills my mouth with a shot of vodka. Then she takes one herself.

"You're here."

"So are mice. Or bugs. Both."

"There's an open bar. Even if everything goes horribly wrong, we can still have one hell of a party."

I breathe in Melissa's confidence. "Right. You're right. We're gonna have a total *rager*!" I haven't used that word in years. It feels good to whip it back out again.

Melissa laughs loudly. "I expect nothing less!"

Maybe it's the vodka, or finally seeing Mel, but I relax. She's right, today is going to be exactly what both of us need. She's going to get married, and I'm finally going to have some much-needed fun.

A sweet-looking nine-year-old brown girl peers into Melissa's dressing room. "Auntie Liz!" Her enormous curly hair blooms from her head.

"Caroline!" Mrs. Parker, Mel's mother, says as she races in after the girl. "Now, you—"

Mrs. Parker stops still when she enters. Both Mel and I stare at her expectantly. She presses her fingers to the edges of her eyes, blotting back tears. She's seeing Mel in her dress for the first time.

"Oh, Melissa" comes out of Mrs. Parker as a whisper.

Mel deals with Caroline first. "I told you Auntie Liz would make it." Melissa turns to me. "Caroline has been asking for you since I told her you were—" Caroline doesn't wait for her mother to finish, she races to me and hugs me. The white ruffles of her dress flutter with the speed of her impact. It's the best hug I've received since coming home.

"Care-bear, when did you get so tall?" I ask. When I saw her around this time last summer, she came up to right above my elbow and now she's up to my shoulder. I gave Garrett and Mel a date night and took Caroline to see some bright, loud show on Broadway. I got her a light-up headband thing from the gift shop. We got sushi. She fell asleep against me on the subway ride home.

Mrs. Parker answers my rhetorical question. "She's gonna be tall, like her father. I keep telling Mel to get her on the basketball team."

"MeMaw, I don't like sports," Caroline mumbles with a slight edge.

Maybe her teenage years are closer than I thought. Caroline carries a sketch pad and sullenly clutches crayons. I can tell they embarrass her. I got her fancy ones for her birthday last month. White wrapping. Vivid colors. Satisfying waxy feel. I feel silly. She's clearly grown out of them.

Caroline looks at Mel in her dress. "What happened to the sequins?"

"You got all the sparkles, remember?" She has. Caroline's dress is a white shimmery explosion of ruffles. Melissa looks back at me. "Oh my goodness."

"What?" I ask.

"That looks exactly like your prom dress."

I look down. Melissa's right; it isn't just the town that's reminding me of high school. Add a little more volume to the skirt, sprinkle some shine on the bodice, and it would be a carbon copy. High school prom is why I avoid dances and clubs and holiday parties. Prom was the first social event I attended where it was no longer acceptable to show up alone. I had this shattering realization during the first slow dance of the night. Watching everyone paired and happy, I wept in public in a way I never had before. When Melissa noticed my puffy eyes, she ditched her date and spent the evening with me instead. We danced, laughed, and snuck cups of spiked punch for the rest of the night.

"Mom! Can you do a zigzag part?" Caroline asks.

Mel doesn't respond. She can't avoid her mother anymore. Sensing the weight of a needed conversation, I seize the opportunity.

"I can do zigzags, Care-bear," I say.

Mel flashes me a quick look of thanks. She straightens her back and faces her mother. I grab Caroline's hand and close the curtain behind me.

I lead her out to where my things are and settle her on the floor between my knees. Her hair needs water, leave-in conditioner, and curl cream. I grab a bottle of water, wet my hand, and sprinkle till her hair is damp. I massage the leave-in thoroughly till it reaches her scalp. Then I grab a rat-tail comb and a paddle brush. I part and gather her hair on one side. Caroline relaxes in my grip.

"Auntie Liz." Caroline's high voice carries in the busy room. "When you were on the train from New York, did you tell them to go faster—" I thought Lauren was nosy; Caroline wants to know every single detail of my life since I last saw her. Unlike Lauren, she hasn't mentioned my ex once. She's too concerned about what I've eaten every day since we had sushi. I catch her up as best as I can while I do her hair. After a brief pause she asks, "Am I behaving today?"

"So far? Yeah, you are. Why?"

Caroline grins. "Because if I'm good, Mom said she'll think about getting me a dog." The girl vibrates with excitement.

"Well, keep it up. Your mom had—" I pause. *Did Mel ever have a dog?* While we were childhood friends, I forget that there were years before when we weren't. Before I can follow up, Caroline is already on to her next topic.

"Do you like my dress?"

"Yes."

Caroline slouches and I guide her upright. *That was the wrong answer.* Already the girl is seeking external validation. She picked the dress. She liked the dress. But she wants to know that I like it too.

"It's really pretty. Like a princess."

Caroline beams from the inside.

I see movement from Mel's dressing area. After a shuffle, Mrs. Parker pulls back the curtain and leaves her daughter to finish getting ready. I watch her, looking for a clue as to how it went. Mrs. Parker's face is an enigma. She scans the floor of the room, checking the corners and crevices for something. Examining the craftsmanship of the wall, she catches my eyes in the mirror. I bury myself back in Caroline's hair.

Mrs. Parker comes over to us. "You're so good at that." She hovers. Her voice is tinged with the slightest bit of jealousy.

I keep making twists. "Practice." I take the time to roll the ends with a little extra cream so that they pop back with a curl. When I'm done, I swoop the girl's edges into little waves. Caroline watches me in the mirror. I wonder when's the last time someone did her hair like this. She reaches up to touch it, but I brush her hand away. I search in my bag for a scarf and tie it around the girl's head.

"Okay," I level with not-so-little Caroline. "I did zigzags. Now promise me something, okay?"

"What?"

"Do not take this scarf off and do not touch your hair." My voice is heavy with well-earned wisdom.

"What about your hair, Auntie Liz?" she asks.

I look back in the mirror. My wig is catching hell in this humidity. The plastic strands curl up in unorthodox shapes around the sweat on my temples. Leave it to a child to call me out. I look at everyone else getting ready. They are almost done, blotting away shine or adding one last spritz of hairspray. I look at the products in front of me, the ones I've just used to do Caroline's hair. Water, leave-in, and curl cream. I didn't bring anything for the synthetic strands on my head.

"Caroline!" It's Mrs. Parker. She's getting everyone set. I know she'll be calling my name next if I don't hurry.

"Go ahead." I nudge Caroline. She doesn't move. The girl looks at me like she wants to ask a question she's been told not to. "What is it, Care-bear?"

"Are you sad because your hair looks funny?" She's right. I am sad because my hair looks funny. Lace-front or not, the straight strands would never grow out of my scalp.

The room is empty. I reach up and pull the wig off. I brace for Caroline's questions, maybe even a few well-timed teases. Instead, she reaches out with both hands and touches either side of my head with such care. Like she's checking to make sure it's real. Then she takes her left hand and touches the back of her head, where, though her curls are looser, her hair is tight like mine.

"I like it. You look like"—she considers this—"a superhero."

"Caroline!" Mrs. Parker ducks her head back in. "Come on, honey. You need to line up."

That's my cue too. I admit, I already feel better without the confines of the wig. I rub a bit of product into my hair to get my curls to pop. I start my makeup, keeping it simple; cover the perpetual bags under my eyes and some blush. I'll sweat most of it off anyway, as the temperature is already at 80 degrees and rising. The lines around my mouth are deeper than I remember. And there's a hollowing to my cheeks. My baby fat is gone. I look like someone's mother. Then again, I could be.

This is the shortest my hair has ever been. Instantly, I think of when it was at its longest. I went all the way to Pittsburgh to get waist-length microbraids, once and only once, for vacation. It took two days to put them in. The kids here acted like I was . . . something. It was the first time someone other than my mother called me beautiful.

"You're . . . beautiful," Mel said when she saw me in school the next day. The way she uttered it was like she was relieved that I'd finally realized it myself. It was a fact to her. A fact that had never occurred to me. I kept those braids in until they matted and my mom had to cut them out. It would be a long time before someone called me beautiful again. That's why I straightened my hair all through high school. And after. Months ago, when I cut it all off, I saw my natural hair for the first time in years. I was sick of length and the perm–new growth cycle. I wanted off the wheel. Also, my ex liked my hair straight. He'd grip me by it so he could give me sloppy kisses. Thick. Heavy. Full of saliva and tongue. I start to feel nauseous all over again. A chill runs up my spine.

"Lizzy?" Mrs. Parker catches me mid-shiver. "Oh no."

"What?"

"No, no." She gathers me up by my arm, looking down near my feet. "If you saw something, I don't want to know. Nick rushed this place through, I wouldn't be surprised if there are . . . vermin." She carefully scans the floor.

"Nope. Just a chill."

She continues to peer over the construction as she leads me out. "You know what they say. If you think you saw something out here . . . no, you didn't."

FOUR

Here's how to survive a wedding after a breakup. You'll need: A dress you look amazing in. Good shoes. Wine. I have: A polyester peach poof. Stunning but painful shoes. And an open bar (I just have to get through the ceremony). Also I have an intangible promotion. Will it be enough?

I'm happy for Mel. She did it. I didn't. I went through the stages of a proper relationship, but I always knew it was off. When love feels like a series of checked-off boxes, something is wrong. Relationships aren't meant to be itemized. Now that it's over, I'm working on getting back what I lost: My pride. My joy. My peace. Reviewing the list in my head, I wonder if I ever had any of them.

Mel and Garrett came together like a story. They were from different sides of the tracks, or in this case, altitudes. Every level of Johnstown has a different demographic. Like most Black people, Garrett grew up in the valley. Mel and I grew up high in the hills. Spread evenly throughout, the forest is the only thing every area has in common.

After living in the same town for their entire lives, Mel and Garrett met for the first time in college. They started dating almost immediately. Senior year they advanced to meeting the parents. When Garrett brought Melissa to Thanksgiving dinner, his mother cornered Melissa in the bathroom to demand her intentions. Melissa blinked and told her the truth. Next Thanksgiving it was Mel's turn. Melissa's pregnancy had just started to show when she brought Garrett home. Her father physically chased him out of the house. Garrett calmly declared his truth from his exile in the front yard. Over the years, their love stayed the talk of the town.

Now, on their wedding day, Mel and Garrett's love is so true that it has done the impossible: rendered them unremarkable.

They are in love. Simple. Fact.

The wedding party stands in the negative spaces between the dark branches in the scenery. Rows of white chairs arrange the attendees in two perfect squares. Guests fan themselves and shield their eyes from the piercing summer sun. Lauren, Claire—Mel's friend from college—and I teeter in our heels in the grass. Throughout the ceremony, there are only a few shifts in the audience. That's it. I can sense the relief in Mel. She and Garrett kiss. The applause comes instantly.

The air cools as the sun sets. The reception starts. Summer blossoms fill the centerpieces on the tables and everything is cloaked in a glow from the soft, battery-powered votive candles. The lights cast strange shadows in the woods surrounding us, but there is light and that comforts me.

I gear up for the entrance of the bridal party. My last obligation. We all wait for our cue outside the barn. Claire puts her long red hair up into a bun to get it off her shoulders. Lauren futilely fans herself with her hands. Unable to sink our heels into the grass, we all hobble on the balls of our sore feet. The groomsmen rehearse a dance step they plan to march in with, balancing from one side to the other and somehow ending up on beat with the music. Claire notices.

"I'm not letting those boys show us up"—she smiles—"and neither is Liz."

"Oh! I don't dance," I say. That's not enough of an answer for Claire. Before I know it, my hobbling has become a step-touch with a snap, twirl, and pose. It's much simpler than the guys', but we can do our routine cleanly and in sync.

Our cue comes.

"Here we go!" Claire grabs my hand and pulls me into formation. Nerves and adrenaline take the details away from me, but the feelings stay. My face aches from laughing. And smiling. I'm having a silly dance battle at my best friend's wedding in a barn in the middle of nowhere—and I'm having fun.

After we pose for pictures, we head for our seats. I'm the first one to arrive at my table, nestled in one of the corners. As the others come, I realize that I'm at the singles table. The seats comprise Garrett's two single cousins, myself, and Claire—all the unpaired wedding guests. While the others make conversation, I nurse my water and peel my feet out of my shoes. I spread my toes out on the cool concrete and it feels like heaven. Claire gradually unlatches from her phone and attaches herself to Garrett's cousin Tré. Seeing them flirt fills me with a dose of envy. There's no hint of failure in either of them. It's like the world has deemed them beautiful, and because of this they have no need to question anything about themselves.

Once the bridal party is seated, Melissa and Garrett make an entrance to a song everyone except me seems to recognize. It's catchy. I can't help but hum along to the predictable tune. The couple takes their seats at the place of honor and the toasts start. Thankfully, because of the rush, my duty as part of the wedding party is over. I just had to show up and put on a dress. The Parkers are all smiles and laughs and telling stories about triumph over uncertainty. This is acceptance.

The band starts to play and I bob my head along to the music. I can't remember the last time I've had a good time like this. I feel myself shaking off a fog. A few guests make their way to the dance floor. I take this opportunity to head to the bar.

Before I get there, I stumble because I can feel someone watching me. Small-town watching is so different from city watching. In the city it's a quick glance, the person being watched might look back. Here people will stare, utterly unaware of themselves. I turn around to find that I've drawn the eyes of the man who saved the day. Mel's brother.

"Hey, Nick." I make myself smile wide. "Beautiful ceremony." He's at the edge of the doorway between outside and the barn.

"It's official. Mel's not a Parker anymore. She's a Washington now."

The name sounds rank in his mouth. I know Nick despises more than Garrett's last name. The first time I went over to Melissa's house to hang out, Nick tried to put rubber cement in my hair. A few visits later he tried to burn me with a lighter. When I screamed, he told me, *Niggers aren't supposed to feel pain*. Wouldn't be the last time a white boy told me what did or didn't hurt. He got grounded for that. I notice a faded American flag tattoo on his hand. His reddish-blond hair is buzzed short. Though he isn't much older than me, his face has a rough quality to it.

I flash him another full smile, begging him to wipe it off my face. "You did a great job with the venue." That's an honest compliment.

"Least I could do." It's like pulling teeth to get him to be excited. This is easily one of the nicest parties this town has ever seen and he should know. He threw it. Yet, he looks absolutely miserable.

"How have things been?" I ask.

"You still working in sales?" He drives the conversation.

I correct him. "Wholesale and imports. Just got promoted to manager of Northeastern Regional."

"Son of a bitch." Nick nods. "You left town and just—" He makes an explosion noise. "I might be coming into a promotion myself soon." He literally puffs up his chest; I have to bite my tongue to keep from laughing. "I've *been* qualified for detective. Just waiting for the right time." The last Mel said, he was a rookie. A beat cop scrambling to get ahead. Thinking about it now, that was back when Caroline was a toddler.

My small talk falls away for an honest question. "Then why build all this?"

Nick gives me a beleaguered smile. "Titles and money aren't the same thing."

Amen to that.

"Auntie Liz!"

I whirl around at the sound of Caroline's voice. "What's up, Carebear?"

She shows me a battery-powered candle. "It's a game!"

"O-kay?"

Caroline launches into a dizzying explanation that boils down to: "We're throwing lights into the woods outside the barn!" She points to two of her cousins. Their hands are filled with bunches of battery-powered votives.

"I'll tell the kids to put them back," I say to Nick.

"Let 'em play," he says. "You good to keep an eye on her?"

"Yeah." Whatever the game is, it seems like much more fun than forced small talk.

In the sticky summer humidity, Caroline's hair blossoms as she sweats. She has a powerful arm. When she throws, she does so with her entire body. Every limb organizes to accomplish the task at hand. Her little cousin Petey's throws barely break the tree line. Tyler can get the candles to whiz pretty far, but Caroline's throws sink deep into the woods every time. It takes two rounds for one of the boys to beat her.

"It's your turn, Auntie Liz." Caroline hands me a candle.

I face the forest.

Here I am after all this time. I wait for the panic to come. For my heart to race. Nothing. Even in the dark, with long shadows dancing between branches, when I look out at the woods, they look like what they are: trees.

I throw the votive. It spins off my fingertips and lands lamely a few feet in front of me. Caroline laughs. I take up the candle again. When I throw it, it curves through the branches; when it hits the ground, it rolls. After many rotations, Caroline's is still farther than mine.

"I got 'em," Tyler says, preparing to collect the votives.

"I gotta go!" Petey whines, stopping his brother in his tracks.

"Then go," Caroline says.

"No, I gotta," Petey's voice sinks to a whisper, "do number two."

Caroline lets out another high-pitched laugh.

Tyler looks at his little brother. "There are bathrooms inside, Petey."

"Mom said not to go alone if I'm not at home."

"Yeah, but this is . . . different." Tyler is clearly making this up. "You can go alone here."

Petey thinks, picks up one foot after the other, pinches his knees together, and waddles his way to the bathroom. Tyler runs into the woods.

The lights flicker like little fireflies in the tree line. They float, one by one, as Tyler gathers them. Seeing Caroline in her dress, I can't help but be reminded of school. I hope it's better for her than it was for me.

"How's school going, Care-bear?"

"Fine." Caroline hides her response behind her hand as she wipes her sweat off her face. I know that tell all too well.

"What's up? Kids being assholes?"

Caroline grins at my swear. I forget that I shouldn't do that around her. I'm her godmother, mentor, and role model. But since she doesn't flinch, I think she understands that bad words exist and that sometimes they need to be used.

"My best friend, Vicky, couldn't come. Her parents wouldn't let her." Caroline frowns. "Said only dumb people are out tonight."

"Her parents sound dumb." And overprotective. "Any dumb kids at school?"

"Vicky and I . . . they don't tease us or anything like that. It's just . . . I don't know." Caroline's gaze drifts off.

I get it. Vicky is Black. She and Caroline are probably the "onlys" in school. I'm glad they're friends. I know that wasn't the case for me. Johnstown isn't as much white as it is segregated. Not officially. Just in historical ways, like by postal code.

"You two are different." Which, at the age Caroline is heading into, means potential devastation. "I know people can make that seem like a terrible thing. It's not. They're just afraid of what they don't know."

"I want to be like everyone else."

If the phrase wasn't coming out of a nine-year-old, I would have mocked her for sounding clichéd. She's so earnest.

"Well, you aren't." A pained smile crosses my lips before I can stop it. "That's not a bad thing." I'm repeating a version of the hard truth from my mother. Caroline leans into me and I wrap an arm around her. Instead of pushing her in one direction or the other, I stay present in this uncomfortable moment. I hope I'm not the only person in Caroline's life to do so.

"Oh!" She hops up and rushes to the edge of the barn. She comes back with her sketchbook and crayons. "I didn't show you my drawing." She opens the book and shows me her depiction of the ceremony. The level of detail she got out of the crayons tells me that she clearly sketched through dinner.

"It's good." An honest compliment. "Too good. Did you eat a bite of your food?"

She avoids my question and sits on the ground. I join her. She looks up at the stars. "I gotta get the stars right." She grabs a yellow crayon and maps them out.

"It's almost the first day of summer. Make sure you get the Summer Triangle. Three of the brightest stars in the sky. I find them using their constellations." I try to spare her the Latin and point out the shapes in the sky. "In the winter there's Orion and, um . . ." I search for the name. "Canis Major?"

"What do they look like?" Caroline asks. I sketch them out. I miss this. There are no stars in the city. Not like this. If there is anything I miss about home, it's the stars. They feel more like home to me than anywhere else. Looking up, I remember memorizing the patterns and constellations and stories as a kid.

Tyler emerges from the trees and dumps the candles on the ground in front of us. Caroline is quick to pick up the game again. I need another diversion.

"I'm getting something to drink. You two want anything?" I ask. Tyler shakes his head no.

"A Shirley Temple?" Caroline seals the request with a smile. She has already reached her quota for the night, but now that I know she's running on sugar, I'm getting her another one.

"You got it. Stay here, where I can see you."

When I step back into the barn, I'm distracted by a roar in the corner. I look and see Nick laughing loudly with a group of men across the way. They all carry that telltale stiffness to them: They're police officers. Or military. From the look of it, at least half the department must be here. Most of the people I know from town are here.

It looks like everyone stayed connected; all of their stories woven together and added to the fabric that is Johnstown. In this room full of "friends" I am alone. The fact that I'm dressed up makes it just unbearable enough for me. As if I needed any more reasons, I make a beeline for the bar.

FIVE

The bar isn't too busy, but I don't see the bartender. I see Lauren. She is content to wait. I have no other choice but to stand next to her. Dancing isn't my thing. Or it is, but only when I'm alone in the safety of my apartment. The people on the dance floor are jumping. That isn't my thing, at all. There isn't any style or grace on those boards, just pure movement and joy. Some people find a strange rhythm in their abandon. I do not.

"I haven't been to a party like this in years—remember Bonfire Nights?" Lauren smiles. Her voice warms with the memory.

"I didn't go to bonfires, I just went to the . . . um, the last one, you know?" Tragedy settles in me like a stone. Lauren doesn't notice.

"They were amazing! Why not—" She catches herself. "Oh." A respectful heaviness enters her voice. The dead must be respected. I try to shift the conversation, but Lauren insists. "I'd almost forgotten about that . . ." She lowers her voice, now self-conscious about her previous delight. "Wh—what was her name again?"

"Keisha Woodson." Every letter is burned in my brain. I'll never forget Keisha's face.

"You two must have been really close, right?"

"No more than you and I."

"But you two . . ." Lauren starts and purposely doesn't finish.

"What?" I see her trying to work around the logic in her head. In Lauren's mind, Keisha and I were as thick as thieves because of the color of our skin and its difference from her own. I don't feel like explaining how not all Black people know one another, especially not in this horrible context. It's clear that Lauren is used to thinking of Black people as a monolith, because when confronted with the spectrum, she can't see it.

I end the conversation. "What happened was— "

"Terrible," Lauren finishes for me. "Wait." She's unable to control her need to gossip. "Did you hear about how they found her?"

I can't help but give Lauren a look. "How could you forget?" That shuts her up for a moment.

Keisha was found by a hiker in the woods a week after Bonfire Night, with her insides strewn across the forest floor. A gash from under her chin to the bottom of her sternum ripped her chest cavity open. Like an animal. Once all the parts of her were gathered, they found that her heart was missing. Taken. There was evidence of other things done to her too. Sexual trauma. But I never knew if that was kids embellishing an already awful truth. After a long investigation, all this was ruled out. "A *very* bad fall compounded by animal activity" was what I heard. I never delved. I didn't want to think about what animals would do to a body left out in the open for long.

"Having a good time, Rocher?" It's Mr. Parker, Mel's father. Never thought he would come to my rescue.

"Yes. Congratulations." I smile and stay on guard. Nick learned his racism from somewhere. I've long suspected Mr. Parker. Always hiding behind a smile, he knew how to mask it.

"Glad to hear it." He grins. The expression doesn't reach his eyes. His teeth are a telltale smoker's yellow. "Haven't seen you back here in years—this place exciting enough for you?"

"No." I tell the truth.

Parker laughs long and hard at that. He did always appreciate a dry sense of humor.

I scan for the bartender.

"Where's your plus-one?" he asks. "Mel told me she had you down for two."

"Ah. That. We broke up." I'm too sober for this conversation.

"That's right. That's right." I can tell by the way his face flushes that he knows he's just put his foot in his mouth. Mel told him about my breakup, but he got distracted by something. He's nervous. He recovers and leans against the bar. "You'll find someone else. There are plenty of men in that city." He makes the city sound like *The Dating Game*. It is, if the game is a sick carnival booth of "Guess Who's a Narcissist." (The secret is: everyone.)

The bartender returns. Parker turns to me.

"What're you having, Rocher?"

Before I can answer, the bartender cuts in.

"Liz? Liz Rocher?"

I am so sick of being recognized. I never know who I'm going to get. When I finally look at the bartender's face I know exactly who it is.

Chris Hartmann.

He was the first boy to make me feel heady. In my thirties, he still can. Suddenly teenaged again, my voice crawls under my sternum and refuses to come out.

"Chris?" I mouth, questioning reality for a moment.

"Hey." He looks at me like he's seeing a ghost.

The last time I spoke to Chris was fifteen years ago, at the party in the woods Keisha Woodson disappeared from. It was dark. Chris and I looked at the stars. I'm not a junior at a graduating-senior party anymore. He's not the twenty-one-year-old buying beer for high school kids. When he smiles, he gets crow's feet. The lines in his forehead stay there despite the sweat on his brow. His eyes are still that striking green. His thick golden curls proved untamable, so he has sheared his hair short, like mine.

Mr. Parker orders for his wife, giving me time to gather my thoughts. Which is good because, dear lord, my teenage crush is exhausting. A quick reply is beyond my grasp. In college, I looked Chris up on the internet, but he didn't have any social media accounts. Or at least, none in his given name. I haven't looked again since. By the time Parker leaves the bar, I've coaxed my heart back down from where it had climbed into my throat. I finally notice that Chris is in all-black attire.

"Um . . . so, are you the barkeep for this evening?" Feeling grounded, I start to go through my bag of tricks, eager to show off the wit I've acquired since high school.

"God, I hope so, or else I think I might have crashed the wrong funeral," he replies in mock horror. I give him a laugh even though it's a bad joke.

Lauren laughs louder than me.

"What can I get you?" He asks me the order like it might save him.

"Red."

The bottle he starts to pour from empties. He struggles to open a new one. I notice how focused he is. His shoulder is rolled forward. He's trying to escape Lauren's attentions. Back when I cared about things like who Chris Hartmann was dating, Mel told me he and Lauren were a thing when she was in college. Judging by Lauren's ring finger, I'd say she is married. Looking at his bare hands, I assume Chris is not.

Lauren is at my side before I know it. She rests a hand on my wrist.

"How's today going? Not too much for you?" She doesn't care how I am, she's just trying to get Chris's attention. "Weddings *alone* are always so hard. Right?"

"I'm having fun."

"When I saw that you"—she barely drops her voice—"took off your wig, I got worried. So happy this is a breakup haircut and not cancer." She gives a quick glance to Chris; he's still working. "Men have no loyalty."

Chris hands me my wine.

"Oh, I know, Lauren." I cheers her, thank Chris, and leave the bar. There's only one drink in my hands and I came for two. I've forgotten Caroline's Shirley Temple. I'll try again when the bar is less treacherous.

I take in the room. Standing there in my dress, I feel my old high school hope mounting. I breathe and remind myself that Chris probably has a girlfriend. Maybe even a kid. Or there's something else, something horribly wrong with him. There is no way a man like him is still single. Then I realize I have no idea what kind of man he has become.

SIX

Outside the barn, night and a pile of votives greet me. Their battery-powered embers pool orange light. I pick one up and look for my playmate.

"Caroline?" I spot a group of teens just outside the barn. They're sneaking shots. I can tell by the faces they make after they drink. Caroline isn't among them. They probably wouldn't have taken her in. I look for Tyler and Petey. A quick glance inside the barn shows me they both have returned to their mother. Little Petey is asleep in her lap.

"Caroline?" I yell.

I walk the perimeter of the barn. Even though it's dark, she should be easy to spot in her sparkly white dress. A careful lap around and I'm back to the candles. I go to the tree line. The cool dark of the forest spreads out in front of me. I call her name again.

"Caroline?"

I look at the edge of the woods and will Caroline to emerge. I've checked inside. I've walked the perimeter of the reception. This is the last place.

No. Look again.

Back to the barn. I confirm, yes, Petey and Tyler are with their mother. I look through the crowd of cops. Nick is nowhere to be seen. At the bar, someone else has taken Chris's position. Lauren is much less interested in them. No Caroline weaving between the barstools. Mrs. Parker and the aunties are gossiping at a table. Garrett's family is uncomfortably seated, because of course they are. The disconnect between Garrett and his family glares back at me. His family is laughing and smiling, but there is a tightness. A guard. For two families recently joined, they couldn't be more separated. I search the brown faces for Caroline's. She's not there. Garrett and Mel are on the dance floor. She holds the end of her dress in one hand and her husband in the other.

I turn back to the woods, a new tension building in my chest. Then, I see something. A flicker in the trees. I peer out and sure enough, there's a candle.

"Care-bear?" I call softly.

When I get no reply, I'm able to focus only on the obvious answer: Caroline is with the candle in the woods. I blink. Again. Again. Like I can make her appear.

"Caroline!" I'm loud. I hear my voice echo in the branches.

No response.

I look at the candle one more time. Caroline wouldn't run out there. She would want to keep her dress clean. She didn't even get any food on it at dinner because she spent most of the time drawing. She's hungry! I head back into the reception. If she wanted food, she'd go to someone who'd always sneak her some sweets.

"Mrs. Parker?" I don't even try to be graceful in my disruption. "Have you seen Caroline?"

"Yes," she says.

"Good." I sigh.

"She was out there throwing those little lights." She gestures out to the side of the barn.

I nod. I drink some of my wine. I nod again. She smiles and goes back to her conversation.

Another lap around the room.

I check the bathrooms. I check in with Petey and Tyler's mother. I check in with Garrett's parents. I check in with strangers I haven't spoken to all night. No one has seen Caroline. Everyone I talk to, I make sure I laugh and smile and hold up my quickly disappearing glass of wine. Everything is fine.

I look again.

And again.

And again.

I'm back, standing where I started: facing the candle in the trees.

I have to check for her. The faster I do it, the faster I'll confirm that she's somewhere in the barn. Instantly sober, I am stilled by adrenaline. My breath slows and I shift my weight. Here it is. My test. There's nothing in the trees. Nothing in the woods. I take a step into the darkness and toward the votive.

As I leave the light of the barn, strange shadows shimmer between the branches. The reception is loud enough to scare off any animals. I think about getting Nick or Chris—no. I can do this. I can face this.

I take a step in. Mud wraps around my feet and takes my shoes with it. *Shit.* I grab the muddy heels and keep moving. Dirty and determined, I press forward.

"Caroline!" Farther from the party, the noise fades. The quiet of the woods takes over. This is the quiet I remember. The quiet I dread.

I race toward the light. The candle flickers in a bush. Nothing else. I look for any other signs. Only shadows greet me. Suddenly my skin prickles. I'm being watched. Whipping around, I see nothing but black.

Wait.

In the trees, there's something. I struggle to glean the image. I open my eyes wider, willing my pupils to expand, taking in all the light they can. The moment my eyes perceive what's in front of me, my mind refuses to make sense of it. The mess of shadows shifts into the shape of a dog. No, this is too big to be a dog. A hound. My breath catches in my chest. A deep tremor roots in me and vibrates my entire frame. My mind is making shapes with the dark. It's trying to assign a form to nothing. That's it. That's all. There is nothing in the woods. I blink to reset the image. My eyes refocus and the shadows melt. A mess of misleading branches and brush are all that lay in front of me. No dog. Nothing.

I faced the darkness. I stood in the quiet. Neither has produced Caroline. There must be somewhere at the reception I haven't tried. I turn around. A flicker of white stops me. There, in the underbrush, I see unmistakable shimmery fabric. I grab it. The strip is covered in sparkly shredded ruffles, heavy with mud and something else. It's slippery. I have to clutch the fabric to keep it from sliding out of my hands. I bring the ruffle to my nose.

Nausea overtakes me. My mind scrambles for the name of the smell, my body knows it instantly.

Blood.

I focus on my hands. Through the snatches of light, the mud slides off my skin. The blood stays. *Keisha died out here. Alone. Afraid. In pain. This place ripped her body apart.* I remember kids talking about how animals go for the "soft parts" first. Scavengers ate her eyes. Then her face and neck. With her sternum broken in half by a fall, I wonder how long the animals out here waited to dig out her heart. Focusing is all I can do to keep from screaming. I search for something else. Anything else. Another hint of Caroline in the trees. I drag myself onward through the mud and search around the flickering votive. Nothing. I turn my gaze deeper into the woods. Only blackness lies ahead. I shift my weight again to take a step forward. Fear makes me question the mechanics of walking. *Go after her.* I curl my toes under me like they can drag my body forward. *Coward!* When I have no rebuttal in my body or my mind, I earn that title. I can't bring myself to go any farther. I retrace my steps back toward the reception. I pause when I reach the pile of candles, hoping she's returned, waiting for me to play again.

Nothing.

In the space between the trees and the barn, no one stops me. I race through all the places she could be again in my head. I looked. I *really* looked. A strange whine follows me. My muddy feet slip on the concrete. The sound wavers. It's coming from me. The edges of my peach dress are covered in mud. My face is warm and wet with tears. Overwhelmed, I gather myself between breaths and move forward, searching the faces on the floor. When I reach Melissa and Garrett in the center, I stop.

"Liz?" Mel looks so happy.

"I can't—I can't—I can't." I pull away when Melissa reaches for me. She's going to hate me. I've ruined this day. "She was right there. Right there. I can't find her."

"Who?" Mel asks.

"Caroline."

Mel flinches, but she holds her face.

"I'm sorry—I'm so sorry," I mumble. Before she can ask him, Garrett breaks away and calls for his daughter. Someone turns the lights on.

"It's fine. Everything's fine," Mel whispers. "Calm down."

"We were near the trees—and—and—"

"The wedding is in the woods, Liz, we're all near the trees." Melissa grips my shoulders. "She's here. We'll find her. She's okay."

I meet Mel's eyes and the words refuse to come. This is it. The nightmare. I show Mel the bloody piece of Caroline's dress.

A new grounding possesses Melissa; it is something I've never seen in her before.

"Caroline?" she says. Someone tells the band to stop. "Caroline?" The other guests fall silent. The only sounds are Melissa's and Garrett's measured voices. "Caroline?" Melissa yells, Garrett echoes. "Caroline!" Every child shudders, they all know what that drop in her voice means. Caroline is in trouble. The other mothers round up their children. Garrett's cries don't carry like his wife's. After a few minutes, all I can hear is Mel screaming her daughter's name into the night.

"Caroline!"

Silence.

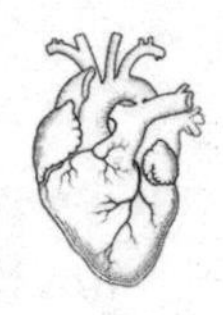

KEISHA

June 2002

Keisha was used to the rich kids. They were fun. Because she didn't belong to them, it was easy to manipulate parts of her personality to fit in. Like the best kind of game, this one was constantly changing and adapting. She had long realized the cultural currency of Blackness. Black was cool. It gave her a set of unique pieces and perceptions to play. Keisha found it funny that what she learned at home helped her get ahead at school. On the other hand, it was taking longer to apply what she learned at school to home. Between the two, her future was bright.

Her mother worked hard to maintain that luminous fate. She was why Keisha was going to school up the hill in the first place. Her mother had seen too many people get stuck. "Stuck is more than a location," she said. "It's a state of mind." Keisha didn't understand what her mother meant until Keisha met the other Black girl in school, Liz Rocher. The girl embodied the word. Stuck finding friends. Stuck focusing on grades. Stuck obsessing over these white boys. Unlike Liz, Keisha didn't question her interest in these white boys. She didn't flush when she thought of them. One of them had told her he was in love with her. She didn't know if she loved him back. Not that her desires weren't as deep as Liz's, but she didn't funnel everything into one of these young men like they were her saviors. She already knew what they were. Boys.

When Keisha arrived at the bonfire, she did a welcome tour affirming her place inside this ecosystem.

"I love your braids!" Lauren Bristol yelled. "How long did they take?"

"Eight hours," Keisha said.

"Ohmigod, I could never sit that long." Seasick from her beer, she looked at Keisha and counted her long plaits. Keisha simply kept moving.

As the night went on, Keisha found herself in one corner of the party. The boys around her drank beer and broke the bottles. She kept up with the conversation, entertaining and one-upping where she could. Then Melissa Parker entered the circle.

"Where's your shadow, Parker?" Bobby Hoffer asked. Everyone knew who he meant. The little Black girl who followed Mel around. Liz Rocher.

"She's not my . . . my . . ." Mel stumbled over the word *shadow,* unsure if it was a slur. "She's over there, looking at the stars." They all turned. There was Liz, across the field, looking up. The kids laughed. Mel didn't see what was funny about it. Liz loved the stars. "You guys should go talk to her. She knows tons of cool stories about them," Mel added. No one moved to take Mel up on the offer.

Keisha didn't dislike Liz. In all honesty, Keisha wanted to take Liz under her wing, but the girl required too much work. Liz didn't even know how to be *this* version of Black. How could she ever learn to manipulate it with fluency? Keisha braced herself—the need to take care of Liz finally moved her to act.

Keisha walked over to her. "Liz?"

Liz beamed back, earnest as ever.

Keisha frowned. "You finally snuck out for one of these. Stop being a goody-good and have some fun." Keisha said the word "good" like an insult. To her, it was.

"I am having fun."

Keisha knew that was a lie. The beer in Liz's hands was full.

"Liz." She sighed. "Mel's not your friend. Look." She pointed. "She left you. At a party. With drinking and stuff. You'uns should stick together."

"Mel's my friend. She can go where she wants."

"Mm-hmm." Keisha narrowed her eyes at Liz. Liz was too trusting.

Keisha would have been successful in life if she hadn't fallen victim to one of its worst lies. It wasn't her fault; it was ingrained in her by her parents and they learned it from theirs. She believed that there was only space for one successful Black person. That meant one popular Black girl, one pretty Black girl, and one Black girl at this party. Liz could be the smart one; Keisha was going to be the one who rode her connections to the top because she was better at playing the game.

Soon the kids coupled up and broke off into the trees. Someone pulled out a joint and a pint of Malibu. The teens courted in that awkward way teenagers do. It is a shame this unusual courtship usually stays with people for the rest of their lives. With behaviors that strong and careless, I wonder how anyone ever meets their mates.

The leftover girls huddled around the rum and cooled their feet in the river. Melissa's laugh carried in the night. The girl was always so loud.

Keisha sought out her "boyfriend" and wondered if she could use the title with him yet. This was something couples agreed upon—were they that? He told her to meet him deep in the trees. Just below the bonfire field was a maze of old hiking trails, newly made paths, and animal migration patterns. The locals called it The Rounds, and it was almost impossible to navigate in the dark. Keisha's boyfriend knew a way through them. He was older. Cooler. Keisha didn't question his need to keep their relationship a secret. The people in this town could talk.

Oh, to be a teenage girl.

Excited and scared all at once, Keisha didn't notice eyes watching her until well after she was lost. When she glimpsed movements following hers, she froze. She looked in the branches behind her, trying to decide if it was friend or foe. A strange, large, dark shadow moved in and out of her sight line. All her life she'd heard the stories like this.

"Hello?" she asked.

"You aren't Liz," it replied.

Unsure if it was a question or a statement, Keisha told the truth. "No?" The shadows moved and she gasped. She'd done it. She saw something strange in the woods and she did the worst thing. She looked. Keisha drew breath to scream. The shadow simply raised a limb to signal her to be quiet.

"Help!"

Her refusal forced the shadow to emerge from its hiding place and take the shape of a man. He wrapped a gloved hand over her mouth and led her farther off the trail. That's when the shouts from the party started.

"Cops! Police! Five-Oh! Run, run, run!" someone yelled.

The party devolved into chaos. They all ran. Keisha was marched deeper into The Rounds. No kids dared to flee there. Once they were far enough away, the man removed his hand from over her mouth.

"You a cop?" she whispered to the dark figure.

Silence.

"It's just a party. Okay?" she pleaded. "They have them all the time." Ever resourceful, as she spoke, she searched for a way out. She looked to her left and right. The trees were too dense. She looked ahead, and she saw more unknown paths. She looked up. She couldn't see the stars through the branches. Ahead, she saw a massive downed tree trunk. It looked rotten and hollow. Maybe if she could roll inside, she could distract him enough to get away. She counted the steps it took to get to the tree. After twenty, she fell to her chest and pressed herself into the dirt to roll.

"Keisha?"

There. In the hollowed-out tree was Liz. This is when the unknotting in Keisha began. If she had really been the only Black girl, if Liz hadn't come, she wouldn't have had this moment, then she wouldn't have been out there with someone who was just as afraid as she was.

Fear moves in people differently.

When Liz's and Keisha's fears aligned, Keisha stepped out of her pattern. If there was room for only one Black girl, one of them wouldn't survive. Keisha wanted to live.

I watched Keisha.

She reached out for Liz's hand before she was pulled away.

Keisha taught me that a heart can change.

Hers changed me.

Keisha Woodson

CLASS OF 2003

[KEISHA'S YEARBOOK PHOTO: A rainbow laser backdrop. Keisha is sixteen years old. Black. Smiling with her top teeth. Long box braids. A crisp white shirt. Clear lip gloss. Pink stud earrings.]

In Loving Memory.

SEVEN

"What did you get up to, party girl?" The clerk's familiarity makes me take a step back. I look up and brace myself for another reunion. Behind the desk sits an older Black woman. Her short gray hair looks soft. Her smile seems kind. I dim my focus to the space between us as I search for my answer. The haze of the night is still heavy on me.

The wedding dissolved into a search party. Tables were overturned. Harsh light invaded. The police not already at the wedding were called. Then the fire department. Both arrived at alarming speed. It's a small town, after all. Then, while the party guests flocked to the flashing lights, the two departments argued for what felt like an agonizing amount of time. There was some sort of math that had to be done around the missing child. Hundreds of scenarios were whispered between men in uniforms before they decided to have the cops search the woods.

Something in my brain clicks. I'm in a police station. My focus goes back to the clerk.

"They, um . . . need my fingerprints," I mumble and shift my gaze to my feet. To my surprise, I'm still in my bridesmaid's dress, but someone has given me flip-flops. They are at least two sizes too big and bright green.

"A VIP party girl, huh?" The clerk gives me a smile. She wants a smile out of me. Not tonight. "You can take a seat, honey. Doug will be out to get you in a second." She hands me a form to fill out. I shuffle back to what I have decided is my chair and sit. Once I do, the rest of the night unfolds itself to me again in a rush.

There were lots of lights. Questions. The bloody edge of Caroline's dress was bagged. My hands were wiped. Seeing the blood disappear was comforting, but it also felt wrong. Like they were taking away something important. Outside, the officers were cool, calm, and collected, but the same feeling simmered inside all of them. Something was off. While children got lost, they didn't disappear like this. That was why Melissa, Garrett, and I had all been asked to go to the station. Well, it wasn't so much a request as it was an implication. If we had nothing to hide, we could come in for questions. The weight of each new memory sinks my shoulders.

That's when I realize I'm wrapped in something. A jacket. It's heavy and denim. I run my finger along the raw edge. This is Chris's. He gave it to me. I can't remember if he drove me to the station. I can't remember how I got here at all. I bring the collar of the jacket to my nose and inhale.

"Liz . . . R-Roach—?" a voice asks, giving up on the French midway through my last name. I bolt to my feet.

"It's Ro-shay," I correct reflexively.

The voice belongs to a lanky white man with brown hair. He's in a blue polo, not a uniform, and holds a clipboard. While he isn't dressed in the institutional green that covers the walls, something about him blends into the background.

"But there's an 'r' in it." His eyes peer over his glasses at my name again. Maybe it's a poor attempt at a joke? I'm too tired to laugh. All I can do is shuffle over to him.

At the end of a long hall, through a series of unmarked doors and past rows of filing cabinets, I arrive at a desk. This is not this man's desk, I can tell by how he orbits around it, only dipping in where he's allowed. And by the fact that he's not the one sitting at it. Instead, there is a man heavy with muscle despite his years. He moves economically and in a way that makes me realize how much energy I'm wasting by slouching. I don't straighten up. He rubs his eyes and adjusts his tie. His crumpled suit reveals that he was there. He was at the wedding. I find a nameplate on the desk: *Sydney Oswald.*

"Doug?" Oswald doesn't look up to address the man who led me here. Doug twitters around him like a gnat. Somehow both invisible and annoyingly present. This is a strange symbiotic relationship. Or a work relationship.

Doug holds an electronic pad in front of my face.

"Yes?" I ask. He's going to have to explain that before I touch it.

Oswald points to my hands. "Left, then right."

They want my fingerprints. I don't move, but I'm curious. "No ink?"

"It's all digital now." Doug gives me a forced smile, trying to make things easy. It's nice that someone is responding to the tension in the room.

I cross my arms over my chest. "You're supposed to tell me why." My thoughts build as I voice them. "You're also supposed to tell me where my prints are going, and if I'm being considered in the investigation—"

Oswald cuts me off. "We need your prints so I can rule them out when we process the scene—"

"I thought this was a search. Why are you calling it a 'scene'?"

That makes him take his eyes off his paperwork and look at me. "You don't want to cooperate?" He doesn't need to raise an eyebrow in accusation, it's clear by the tone in his voice.

"Of course I do. I just want to know what I'm cooperating in."

He sets down his paperwork. With his attention comes a familiar hostility. My cooperation isn't just expected, it is required.

"We're searching for the girl," Doug cuts in. "We need to make sure we cover all our bases, just in case. Now, your fingerprints are going into the computer. If you don't want to give them to us now, that's fine. But—"

"You were holding evidence." Oswald glares at me. "We'll be getting your prints one way or another."

"What my colleague here means is, if we find anything out in the woods, we'll be tracking you down to get them anyway." Doug extends the pad to me again. He smiles. Punctuated by a gray line across the front of his teeth, even that kind gesture looks sad. What a perfect good-cop/bad-cop duo. Like a put-upon service worker, Doug makes me want to cooperate just to relieve him. Like a poor manager, Oswald makes me want to dig my heels in at every step. Neither of these men are officers. Nothing about Doug is threatening. He's childlike. Everything he says has a genuine directness to it. He's probably gotten his ass kicked more than a few times because of this. Hence the smiles. Someone must have told him those helped. Meanwhile, Oswald doesn't need to lift a finger to terrify me.

I extend my left hand to Doug. Carefully, he rolls my digits on the pad one at a time. Oswald inserts his presence between us, watching Doug's work. Three prints are closely observed like this until Doug says, "I got it." I recognize the lift in his voice. Somewhere underneath his pleasant front, Doug hates being micromanaged.

"I called you back in on your first day of vacation, I want to make sure you have your head in the game," Oswald replies, unmoving.

"I am sharp as a tack," Doug says. "I swear."

Satisfied, Oswald retrieves something from the back of the room. He doesn't turn on the light. He's comfortable moving in the dark. Beyond him, the space expands, but it's too dim to tell how far it goes. My eyes strain to make out shapes in the black. When I'm reminded of the last time I sought shapes in the darkness—of the woods—I focus back on the men in front of me. I don't need to find any more horror this evening.

"Can I have your right hand, please?" Doug scans my face like he knows me. I look back with a mirrored curiosity. I fold my right hand under my arm.

"Have they found Caroline yet?"

"No," Doug replies.

"Do they think I . . . took her? Or . . ." I don't finish a sentence that could implicate myself in something I'm not guilty of.

"Is there something you want to tell us?" Oswald's voice rumbles from the darkness.

"Is there anything I should know?" I'm already regretting volunteering my prints.

"You found a piece of Caroline's dress." Oswald makes no effort to hide his frustration. "Her blood was on your hands. The more you cooperate, the better you look."

He is right; it doesn't look good for me. But I have nothing to hide. I offer my other hand to Doug. Before he takes it, the men share a glance. Doug rolls my fingers. There's a lot more tension in his arm this time. I want my hand back. Oswald makes a production of collecting the documents he was working on.

"Nowak, you good to finish up these prints?"

Doug nods. I watch Oswald as he grabs more forms. Papers.

"Blood type?" Doug asks.

"A positive," I say. Doug takes notes. He puts a swab in my face.

"What the hell is that?"

"There's blood at the scene," Doug explains. "If any of your DNA is there too, we want to rule it out."

I open my mouth.

He swabs. "You're about thirty, right?"

Once the rough cotton is out of my gums, I look back at him and catch him clocking every telltale sign of age on my face. "I'm thirty-two."

"Thirty-two and"—he refers to my ring finger—"still not married?" There's that genuine directness again.

"Yeah, I'm one of those awful women who has the audacity to wait for a decent man."

"Well, there must be someone."

"Oh, Doug." I sigh. "I'd love to live in your world." I am not recounting my dating life to this stranger. "Am I free to go?"

"I'm sorry. My mouth gets ahead of my mind sometimes."

"A word of advice. Don't ask a bridesmaid why she isn't married."

"That explains the dress!" He is genuinely delighted. I've solved the riddle of my appearance for him. I can't tell if I should be offended or concerned.

"Can I go?"

"Yeah—no," he stumbles, putting the pad away, and races over to the computer. "Just, wh—where are you from?"

"Here. Born and raised." My patience is starting to wear. "You know, there are Black people in Johnstown too, Doug."

"Oh, I know that. Johnstown is fourteen percent African American."

Oswald makes sure I don't have a smart response. "Nowak, don't talk her ear off, get her prints and pack it up. We need to prep for the debrief." He walks out of the room.

"What was that about?" I need Doug to know that I'm not a fool. Or at least I don't think I am.

"I, umm. I study town history. Historical population trends. Migrant communities. Who lives here and why. That kinda stuff."

I'm honestly surprised. "Ever heard the term 'brain drain'?"

"Human capital flight," Doug replies.

"Exactly." I rub my eyes. "Do you know where they took Melissa and Garrett?"

Doug nods. "If they're with the detectives, they're back the way you came. The receptionist can point you to the waiting room."

Before I leave I ask, "You going back on vacation?"

"Not anymore. This is all hands on deck." He starts to lead me out the door.

I don't move. "Give me your card."

"I'm not a detective. If you have any information—"

"You took my fingerprints and my DNA. I get a card."

That makes Doug stumble. "Uh—I'm not the medical examiner. I just run tests—"

"And if something goes wrong with my tests or prints, I don't want you to hide behind that guy." I try to match the intensity of his stare, but I can't. Ever since he called me back, he has been watching me. I hold my hand out.

He grabs a card from Oswald's desk. "Honestly, this is who you want to follow up with. I'm staying as far away from this as possible."

"I thought everyone was working on it?"

"I, um . . . cases involving kids are tough for me. Anything with kids can be." For a moment Doug gets a melancholy look, rife with vulnerability. He recovers. I wasn't supposed to see that.

"Sorry to hear that." I mean it, but keep my hand out.

Doug grabs a pen. He writes his number on the back of Oswald's card. He hands it to me and I tuck it into my phone case.

EIGHT

After being released by reception multiple times and after they assure me they will tell Mel to call me, I leave the precinct. I send a few follow-up texts, just in case, but I don't get a reply. I'm not expecting one. I have no other choice but to go home.

When my mom arrives at the station, her hair is done, but she is still in her pajamas, robe, and slippers. Marie had decided long ago she would never leave the house in her headscarf. Today is no exception. According to her, it's "ghetto." I think a woman in a headscarf isn't to be messed with. A Black woman with her head wrapped clearly didn't plan on leaving the house, but there she is. Best get out of her way.

In the car, I lean against the passenger-side door. The early morning air smells sharp and clean. The sun rises. We drive home in silence. The motion of the car threatens to rock me to sleep as we make our way back up the mountain. By the time we arrive home, the sun is up.

"Mom, I—"

"Shh-shh." She helps me out of the car.

In the warmth of the kitchen, she holds my hands under her nose and grimaces. "Your skin is going to crack from what they washed it with." Too tired to fight her, I let my mother guide me to sit on a stool.

"Do you want hot chocolate?" she asks. My appetite is soured by the idea of sweetness now. It's somewhere between too early and too late.

"No, thank you." My stomach gurgles.

"You look cold."

"It's already seventy-five degrees outside."

"But inside?" she asks. "It will help."

Before I can reply, she retrieves a ball of raw cocoa. She boils some evaporated milk on the stove and grates the cocoa into it. She stirs in all the spices. Cinnamon. Anise. And a pinch of something I've never asked about. Whatever it is, it warms you right down to your core. She strains the mixture into two mugs and we sit in the kitchen. The overhead fan whirls and I blow on my hot chocolate to cool it down.

"How are you, *cherie*?" she asks.

I sip the cocoa. The steam from the mug makes me sweat. With the first swallow, the cocoa warms me. With the second, the world feels soft. She was right. I was cold inside.

"Tired," I confess.

"I know," she says between sips. Then, "On my first rotation in the ER here, I lost a child."

My mother never talks about her patients. Even in retirement.

"They . . . died?"

"I—I do not know," my mother confesses. She takes a breath to steady herself. "This child, he comes in all by himself. Will not speak to anyone. Sick as I have ever seen." She takes another sip and so do I. "Fever. Chills. Productive cough. The attending is asking him his medical history and all that. The boy could not be more than eight or nine. He does not know any of that. I ask to sit with him alone. I take his temperature. I take notes. Slowly, when he sees that I want to help, to listen, he starts to tell me his symptoms. I go to tell the social worker the diagnosis—a respiratory infection. When I came back, he was gone. Missing." My mother finishes her cocoa. "I thought I told one of the nurses to watch him—or the attending would come back. I still think about that boy and wonder if he got the help he needed. The way he watched me . . . if he survived, he will do something healing. I know it." My perfect mother admitted to making a mistake. A big one. Looks like I'm not the only one who has changed during our time apart. I finish my cocoa. I don't have to reach for her, my mom knows I need a hug. Because she's not forcing it on me, the embrace gives me some comfort.

"I want them to find Caroline," I say.

"They will." Though she hasn't done it in years, my mother gets me ready for bed.

Up in my room, she unzips my dress, wraps my hair, and gets me into clean pajamas. She wipes away my blurred makeup, puts Vaseline on my dry hands, and runs her fingers over my cracked cuticles. Instead of interrogating me about them, she puts my hands together with hers and prays.

"*Bondye, mèsi pou pwoteje pitit mwen an.*" The rhythm of the words washes over me with familiarity. They bring me ease even though I have long forgotten what they mean. "*Mèsi paske ou kenbe li an sekirite.*" She puts me in my bed. "*Mèsi pou retounen pitit mwen an.*" She kisses me on the forehead. When she pulls away I notice tears in the corners of her eyes. I want to reach out to comfort her, but by the time the impulse comes, my mother has tucked me in.

I used to speak Creole with her at home. When I went to school, my classmates were far less understanding of my "broken" French. In the first grade, right when I'd mastered being at school, it was cold, so I asked someone to turn up the *chalè* and the entire class laughed. They called me "valet" all day. I stopped speaking Creole at school from then on. Then I stopped speaking it at home. Then in my dreams. For years I corrected myself in my mind, commanding myself to speak English. The funny thing is, after that, I spent five years learning French. I was always careful to only speak French at school and never to bring it home. I didn't correct my French in my dreams. I don't remember most of my dreams from early childhood. They were too boring.

Daylight streaks my room. I reach out to close the blinds behind my bed. Straining a hand through the intricate cast-iron headboard, I search for the dowel. I grasp it and I twist it till the blinds shut. As I do, I see a car sitting in front of my house. It's positioned purposefully, right past the end of my driveway. I crack the blinds open again to get a better look at it but, in the time it took me to have the thought, the car starts to pull away. Quickly. Decisively. As if the driver saw the movement from my window. I search my memory for the car, to see if it's a neighbor's, but nothing comes to me. I crane my neck to get more details, but the vehicle is long gone.

NINE

Caroline's First Day Missing

"I don't know!" Melissa shouts at the female officer. It is too early for shouting. It is also too early to ask a mother how much her child knows about outdoor survival. Outside what was once Melissa's wedding venue, the police and the fire department have set up camp. A handful of officers work in teams to sweep the woods. Firefighters lean against their truck, waiting to be rallied. The tension between the two factions is palpable but familiar. While the officer continues to question Melissa about Caroline, I clutch Mel's hand, subtly telling her to back off. Mel, unaccustomed to this side of the police, misses my signals entirely.

"Why the hell would— She's not a Boy Scout or anything. I already told you, the last time I saw her, she was in her dress from the wedding."

"Could she have taken any food with her?" The officer holds a professional facade and braces herself for Melissa's rage. The patience she is extending to Mel wouldn't be extended to me. Never mind. Fuck subtlety. Give 'em hell, Mel.

"I told you. I don't know!" Melissa's voice carries in the field and draws a few stares, but the authorities continue to busy themselves. "Where are the dogs? Don't you all have dogs for this?"

"You don't want us to call in the dogs. Trust me," the officer says a little too casually.

"Don't tell me what I do or do not want. I want you to do everything to get my child back. Now!" Melissa gets in the officer's face. "I want dogs and helicopters and sweeps and radar and whatever the fuck else you have. I want it all and I want it now!" Angry tears stream down worn paths in Melissa's makeup, a strange facsimile of the night before. Her hair is piled in a hurried bun. Her jeans are muddy and torn. "If you won't do anything, let me go back out there." She tries to push past the officer, the officer does her best to get Mel back to the barn. I help her. Mel's been called off the searches because of her clear exhaustion. If she passes out like this in the trees, they'll have another emergency on their hands.

"You could use some water," I offer. "Maybe a coffee, right? Let's get coffee and then you can go back out there, okay?" I get her away from the officer.

Melissa looks dead tired. ". . . A quick minute."

In the barn, I'm greeted by a deconstructed moment in time. The remains of Mel's wedding reception sag and sour. Tables are stacked in one corner, there's a pile of tablecloths in the center of the barn floor, and the wilted roses that line the stage smell sharp. It's all rotten. In the gravity of the events of the evening prior, none of the guests took the floral arrangements home. Mel grips a walkie-talkie in her hands. It occasionally crackles with messages, updates. I take it and turn down the hum of radio chatter. We've all quickly realized how unreliable cellphones are this far into the mountains.

We retrieve our coffees and Mel walks back out to the edge of the barn. She stands and scans the trees, willing Caroline to stumble out of them. She can't take a break. Every sip, no matter how scalding, is counted. The moment she finishes, she is getting back out there. I know she hasn't eaten yet. And I can tell by the grimace she makes, that first sip of coffee is turning her stomach.

We're far enough out into the forest for the police to discourage volunteers who aren't experienced with the terrain. It's too easy to get lost out here. I top off Melissa's coffee with a creamer packet. I hold my coffee with both of my hands, warming myself with the cup. This high up, this early in the morning, the temperature fluctuates. Out here, early summer means cold mornings and hot afternoons. Melissa keeps taking full gulps. This is fuel.

She points to the police in the field. "Look at their uniforms. What are they, rookies?"

"I think they're detectives." I'm reminded of Nick's aspiration. These officers look like they have their shit more together than he does.

"They're young." Melissa swallows another painful gulp. "Look at that one over there. She questioned me last night. She kept asking me if I was sure someone was watching Caroline. She must not have kids." Melissa pauses. She's remembered that I don't have kids. I clear a space for us in the wilting floral arrangements and sit Mel down on the stage. She downs the rest of her coffee in fury. I keep sipping. Unoccupied, Melissa sinks into herself. Her head falls into her hands and then rests between her legs. I reach over and massage her back.

"When you were watching her, did she say anything about the woods?"

I swallow hard. I was the last person to see Caroline. Guilt makes my stomach hurt.

"No."

"Did you see anything out there?" Melissa asks like it's been running around in her mind all night. "When you went in looking for her, did you see *anything*?"

My mind conjures the shadowy figure I saw in the trees. I know it was a trick of the light. Not helpful right now. I brush it aside.

"No. Nothing."

Mel settles with a finality that says she isn't moving anytime soon.

"Looks like your mom could use a coffee," I say. "Want me to check on her?"

Melissa nods. I get up and head toward the coffee station.

Mrs. Parker has busied herself by tidying up after the officers. By the time I reach her, her hands are full of empty cups.

"No manners," she mutters to herself, as she dumps the cups in the trash.

"Let me get a new pot started," I offer. Mrs. Parker gives me a tight smile.

"Thank you." She wraps a jacket around her shoulders. "I'm gonna be sick to my stomach later. I never have more than one cup a day." Her candor surprises me, but I go with it.

"How many is that?"

"Coffee number three. It's not even good." She takes a deep breath. "Nice of you to stay out here with her."

"Of course."

"It's the least you could do." She smiles at me to hide the jab.

"I . . . I didn't—"

"Children are slippery. If you aren't used to them, you'd be surprised by the trouble they get into. That's all."

I offer Mrs. Parker a truce. "Caroline is a smart girl."

"She is." Mrs. Parker sips more coffee. She spots another empty cup and rolls her eyes. Without finishing the conversation, she goes after it. I follow her out to the field and spot the rest of Mel's family.

Mr. Parker, Garrett, and Nick talk with a clump of officers in the field. It looks like the officers are on a break, their bodies relaxed. Except for Nick, of course. The man always looks like he's on edge. At the ready. The officers laugh while Mr. Parker tells a story. Garrett stands by their sides at respectful attention, but not relaxation.

Mr. Parker's laugh carries in the air. "Now, I've seen people catch tires and cans and stuff on cartoons, you know?" he says. "I never thought I'd catch one of them in real life!"

"Not my fault. The river is a dump." Nick shrugs sharply, trying to lift some humor out of his body. "I still got that tire in my trunk, just in case! You know?" The father and son laugh loudly. Their jollity echoes in the officers. I see Garrett standing slightly apart. He rubs his face to stay awake.

"Caffeine?" I offer. Garrett's smile tells me that he's grateful, but his eyes are red, hollow, and impossibly sad.

"Please."

"Don't worry, I got your wife to take a rest."

Garrett smiles back reflexively, happy to have a wife, but his happiness fades as the events of the last night seep back into him.

"Rocher!" Mr. Parker yells. I attempt to smile and accept his side hug. "This one here is a real champ." The officers turn to me and I wilt. I don't like their attention in any capacity, even if it's positive.

"Just doing what anyone would do," I say.

"Came all the way in from NYC to hike in the woods. Never expected that, did you?" he says with a wide smile.

I can't stop my scowl. "It's not a hike. At all."

Mr. Parker lets me go, aware he's hit a nerve. Unwilling to witness the awkwardness, the officers disperse. Mr. Parker turns toward the woods. Instead, it's Nick who's going to deal with me.

"He knows that, Rocher, just trying to keep their spirits up. Keep 'em motivated."

"It's their job."

Garrett, also uncomfortable, leans away from the conversation.

I gesture at the search. "Where's the FBI?"

"Feds are looped in." Nick rubs his hand over his mouth. "First forty-eight hours are the most important."

"No," I correct. "*Where* are they?"

"They have been—" Nick catches himself. "If Caroline isn't found in the first twenty-four, the next twenty-four are gonna determine everything. Don't tell me how to do my job and I won't tell you how to do yours, saleslady." He spits that title at me. "I'm making sure those boys put in the work. They're going to find the girl you were supposed to be watching."

"I looked away for a second."

"That's all it takes."

"Half the department was at the wedding."

"Off duty. And now," he challenges me, "I'm gonna find her."

I think of everything I've been through since coming home. Who was that woman at the station the moment I walked into town? She had the flyers.

"Y'all can't even keep the train station clear from grifters. How are you gonna handle something like this?" I watch as Nick puzzles over what I mean. "There's a homeless woman harassing people at the—"

"That's Denise. She's . . . harmless— I'll call it in." Nick looks back at me. "See if we can spare the manpower." He doesn't have coffee. Doesn't need it. Out of everyone here, he's the only one who doesn't seem fatigued by the night. Just the opposite, the man is wired.

TEN

By the time night falls, tire tracks from the emergency vehicles carve up the field. I do my best to avoid the resulting mud puddles and deep holes, but before I know it, my shoes are hopelessly wet and covered in earth. The cops and the fire department stick to their respective corners. Once the police have claimed full jurisdiction, officers start setting up huge floodlights. I haven't been able to join a sweep yet. Still tense from the last time I was in the woods, I've been staying at the base offering support. I scan the faces for a familiar one. When every visage is a stranger's, I take refuge in the barn.

Swerving out of the way of a stray moth, I head for the dance floor. I turn and my eyes land on Chris. He's loading up wine bottles and kegs, grabbing inventory from the wedding. He moves quickly, like he doesn't want to be here longer than necessary. He makes a tally on a small piece of paper. The only familiar face I see—I wave and make my way over to him.

"Got any whiskey back there?" I ask, somewhat honestly. I could use a drink.

"Bourbon?" He holds up a half-finished bottle and I see that he has on gloves. Dead fruit flies speckle the liquor.

I frown. "My favorite."

He laughs and adds the bottle to the tally he's building. I peer behind the bar. Overturned bottles float and mix in the wells. Judging by the smell and the fruit flies, they've been sitting like this—in the heat—since the wedding.

"I knew it would be bad, but . . ." He sighs. Chris pops a speed pour out and adds another bottle to the growing stack on the bar. Slowly, a sticky-sweet stink fills the air. He notices the disgust on my face.

"Sorry. I'm used to it." He works in silence and we both track the scene in the barn. As much as he's here to count bottles, he's also watching the investigation.

I turn in time to see two more cops cross behind me. When I look back, Chris has made another tally: cops and bottles.

Before I can bring it up, he asks me, "You staying in town?"

"Yeah, to help."

Chris nods while he chucks more bottles. "What are you doing tomorrow night?"

"This," I say without a second thought.

"Wanna grab a drink or something sometime? Catch up? I own the Hearth now, so drinks are on me."

I freeze. I scan his face for a smirk, a smile, a lift in his speckled eyebrows. Nothing. He's serious. His breath does a tight cycle in his throat, not reaching his chest. He's nervous.

"I'm—I'm here." I'm too stunned to say much more than that.

"Great. Umm." His words release the tension and he's back to the task at hand. "I'll text you." He smiles. With his teeth. He has good teeth. I reach for his paper tally. When I write my number down, I glance at it. His totals make no sense.

A whistle sounds.

I turn and see officers spill out of the trees. Mr. Parker, Garrett, and Nick emerge. I spot Mel as she comes out from a different section of the woods from the men. She looks frazzled. Mrs. Parker is nowhere to be seen. But, based on the last time I was here, she's probably making sure the search doesn't wreck the place. I keep forgetting this is Nick's land. I give Chris a quick wave goodbye and bound over to Mel.

"You out there alone?" I ask.

"I have a radio."

"Mel, it's dark. That's not safe."

"Caroline isn't safe until she's home." She turns down the chatter and latches the device back on to her hip. Then she works her boots through the grass, wiping the mud from the treads. It comes off in long streaks.

Neon ribbons flutter in the trees and draw both our gazes to the taped-off section of the woods: the spot where I found the piece of Caroline's dress.

"Have they asked you to walk them through what you saw?" She leans away from me, like she doesn't want anyone to notice we're talking.

"No." I admit, I too think that's strange.

Her rage simmers away her sadness. "Of course. They don't—" She drops her voice. "They don't know what they're doing." Mel starts to move back toward the forest. I don't follow her. She looks back at me. "C'mon."

I stall. "Where?"

"If they won't walk you through, I will."

Anxiety roils in my belly. "They questioned me. Took prints, DNA, and—"

"Liz." Mel doesn't try to modulate the command in her voice. "Let's go."

I take a step forward. The ground slips under my feet. Slick mud takes my heel. My vision in the trees flashes back to me. Dark. Shadows. Teeth. Mel catches me by the elbow.

She hefts me up and leans her face toward mine. "Just a few steps in. That's all I need."

We approach the trees.

"What was that rhyme about poison ivy?" I point to the suspicious-looking greenery on the forest floor. "Was it three leaves or five?"

"Leaves of three, leave it be. Berries of white, best take flight." Mel stands about a foot beyond the tree line, waiting.

I take a step in. Moss, leaves, and earth cradle my feet. Unlike the mud, it supports me with a spongy strength. I take another step and I note how much the forest floor feels like flesh. Cold flesh.

"Liz?"

Another step.

Another.

I'm past the first row of trees now. The bustle of the site dampens. The temperature dips. I shiver. It's always cooler in the trees. I wrap myself deeper in the shell of my old ski jacket, the only extra layer I have at my mother's house. The zipper still has a mangled lift sticker attached to it. I run my fingers over the worn paper. The thin wire feels like a bone underneath. I look out at the forest in the night. Its vastness threatens to swallow me whole. I focus on the task at hand.

Another step.

Moving along my path from last night, I make my way farther in. "The candle was in that bush, right behind you." I look back at the field. Even in the dark, the way to the wedding is obvious. Mel shines a light on the yellow tape just beyond, marking off where I found the piece of Caroline's dress.

"It's like . . ." Her flashlight flits from the bush to the neon tape and back to the field beyond. "They don't care." She looks at me. The bags under her eyes are more apparent in the dim light. Before I can answer, she continues, "Where are the dogs? The human chains? The sweeps? They don't fucking care." Mel takes a moment. "It's 'cause she's a little Black girl, right?"

"Mel?" She didn't want me out here only to walk the scene—she needs to speak freely.

"The cops don't care and there are no reporters, or whatever, because she's Black, right?"

I'm at a loss. "We're looking, Mel."

"My . . . um. My family wouldn't talk to me when I was pregnant?" A question is the only way that statement can come out of her. "It was around Thanksgiving. Right after college. When you had that crazy roommate. I didn't tell *anyone*. I couldn't . . ."

I let her confession settle in the space between us. "What happened?"

"I moved in with Garrett 'cause my parents kicked me out. Didn't speak to Dad for a year. After Caroline was born, Mom and Nick visited us. Dad didn't. He said I wasn't his daughter anymore."

"What changed?"

"Garrett saw how miserable I was. He called my dad, asked if they could talk. To see if they could find an understanding. He invited Garrett out hunting with him. Just the two of them."

"No."

"He went," Melissa says.

I frown. "What?"

"I know it— I know! He didn't tell me till after." The memory comforts Melissa. "They went out, had some beers, and shot a deer. The next day, Dad came over and met Caroline. He and Garrett have been good ever since."

"Who knew the cure to racism was hunting?" My sarcasm is lost in this moment, but it's all I have to keep myself from shaking some sense into Mel. As a kid, Melissa shielded herself from racism the way most white people did. She held on to a well-rehearsed lesson from after-school specials in the 1990s: *I don't see color.* Mel would say that instead, she saw *me*. Teenage Liz loved that. From what Caroline said last night, Mel is still avoiding the truth: Being blind to color only makes you blind.

"My dad's not a racist, he's just old-fashioned," Melissa insists.

"Those two things aren't mutually exclusive and it's not just your dad, Mel."

"Nick?"

"For starters."

"Nick is an asshole, and Dad was scared." Her voice mounts, getting defensive. "They didn't know any Black people."

"What about me?"

"Of course, you. They know you, but you're not . . ." Melissa shifts, unsure of the thought. "Dad needed to meet Garrett on even ground."

"In the woods, with a gun?" I push.

"No. On his own terms." Mel watches the officers through the trees. "I just— I mean— You ever needed someone to tell you what they think?"

Yeah. I did. I asked Mel that question two years ago. Our conversation was punctuated with the taste of vodka sauce from the nice Italian place around the corner from my apartment. I ordered the finest red I could find on the menu to wash away my feelings. Mel was there, all laughs after she met my ex. I had asked her the same thing.

"What do you think?"

"Liz." She fiddled with the base of her full wineglass. "He's an asshole."

"He was so nice to you!"

Mel shook her head. "You're different around him. Dim. Dull. Dumb. Not . . . you."

"I don't know what you're talking about." I did.

"Liz?" Mel looked at me with pity. "Look at me. Is he who you want?"

I couldn't meet her eyes. She was right. I shoved the feeling down.

"Liz?" Mel taps my shoulder and I'm back. In the woods. "Tell me, what do you think?"

I focus on the current emergency. "Caroline is lost, but they're gonna find her any second and she's gonna have a story to tell about the whole thing." Again, I ignore my fears.

Mel looks at me. She squints. She knows what I'm doing.

"But something is off, right?" She looks at me, desperate.

I've only ever lied by omission to Mel. Evidently, it's the same way she's lied to me. I think she didn't tell me what occurred between Garrett and her parents to protect herself. If she didn't repeat it, it didn't really happen.

"Mel . . ." I consider my words carefully.

Impatient, she checks her phone. Bright light illuminates her face and the time: 9:30 P.M. It's been twenty-four hours since Caroline went missing. I twist my wrist in the dark and my scar pulls tight.

"Everything is going to be fine. I know it." This lie is to protect her. I can't tell Mel what I think. I think this reminds me of the time another Black girl wasn't found after she'd been missing for twenty-four hours. The girl who disappeared from a party in the woods. Keisha Woodson. Bonfire Night. That was fifteen years ago. Keisha was found dead, her body mutilated, a week later. I don't wish that for Caroline. It's cruel to draw a parallel between the two. Especially when it's just a feeling. No proof.

Be it denial or belief, Mel silently accepts my assessment.

The trees around us swell with a soft breeze. Their leaves blow, making a wide sound. After a few moments, I can make out my own stilted breathing. Mel goes still in the dark. Her breath is soft. My ears throb from the effort of my heart. We are two opposites in the wood. Like Garrett and Mr. Parker. Listening to the way Mel told it, I had wondered what Garrett had gained that day. Now I ask myself, *What did he lose?*

ELEVEN

"And?" my mother asks the moment I walk in.

"They haven't found her yet." I take off my shoes and notice, for the first time, there's mud in the mudroom. My mother has a pair of sneakers drying upside down.

"What happened?"

"I was in the garden." She waves her hand, conjuring the memory for herself. "I like to work in the sunset, the heat is less, and today, one of the neighbors, she comes up to me. She tries to offer me a cutting from her rhododendron. Blue flowers." My mother scrunches her nose. "*Non*. Once they take root, you will never be rid of them. And this is not the time of year for cuttings. They will not take."

"Mom? The neighbor?"

"Yes! This one, she is not a close neighbor. She is from a few streets over. She likes to visit with Mrs. Cleary across the road. This woman is a 'gossip woman' and the stories from this part of town are more suited to her taste. Well, she wants to talk about the missing girl, the search, all of that." My mother leans on the kitchen counter and sips her evening coffee.

"What did you tell her?" I ask.

"The truth: I do not know. These people are bored, *cherie*. Do not give them something to talk about."

I laugh. "You make it sound easy."

"It is," she insists. "When you are here, remember, there are eyes everywhere. You help your friend and that is it."

I call her bluff. "What if—I don't know—doing something 'crazy' is helping her?"

"No, no. This is different. You do not want your name in these people's mouths."

"People talk no matter what. And not just here." This isn't about the town anymore, this is about me. "I'm . . . I'm . . ." Everything I've kept a lid on, busied away, and left in New York lurches up to the surface.

My mother seizes the break in my thoughts. "Was there no way to work things out with him, or were you being stubborn?" She's trying to make me admit I'm the reason the relationship fell apart. "Did you care for him? Though they seldom ask, men need to be cared for."

"Like Dad?"

"Your father and I were different," she insists.

"How?"

"I do not like to revisit such things, Elizabeth. I am talking about you, not me."

"Yeah, well, I don't wanna revisit things either."

I think of all she doesn't know about my relationship, how I nearly lost myself. I want to tell her, but I don't know what I will do if she still blames me.

"Elizabeth?"

I cross my arms. I'm not answering her questions and I'm not backing down.

My mother waves the air again to banish the argument. I let her. I don't have the energy to fight. She comes in for one of her strange hugs. Her embrace locks around me like a shackle. I'm not the daughter she wants. I'm not thin enough. I don't live close enough. Unmarried. The moment I feel her arms start to part, I make my way out of them.

"I'm gonna check out the garden," I mumble. Before she can stop me, I head outside.

Using my phone as a flashlight, I go to the front of the house. I wasn't lying. I am truly interested in these flowers. Gardening has been one of my mother's only consistent hobbies. When she worked, she never could keep it up. She refused to hire someone to do it. *This is my land. My piece of earth. I will make it mine.* And she did. Her garden is a chance to engage with a bit of her from a distance. Space has helped us before. Now that I'm home, I'll take any separation I can get.

It's quiet outside. Another difference from the city. I search for a siren or a loud conversation out a car window. I find my thoughts instead. Mel and I have the same gut feeling: Something isn't right. But there's nothing the police can do about a feeling. They're taking the best course of action with the evidence they have.

I get to the front of my mother's house. The motion detector turns the floodlights on. Before I can find the garden, I see a car sitting at the end of my driveway. The same car as last night. Lights off. Idling. Blue. Four doors. Before I can glean any other details, it pulls away with a definitive screech, leaving no doubt in my mind.

Someone is watching me. Watching the house.

I chase after the car, determined to get more information. Racing past the end of the driveway, I can make out part of the license plate. I recognize the PA colors but can get only the first letter and the last three digits: Q and then 588. The car turns at the end of the street and speeds off into the dark.

"Q-five-eight-eight," I whisper. I take a moment to catch my breath, only to realize I'm breathing normally. I look back at my house. I covered a good distance at a full sprint and I'm not winded. Maybe I'm not as out of shape as I thought? That puts a spring in my step as I speed-walk back to the house.

Thanks to my newfound cardio endurance, I keep my cool demeanor when I come back inside.

"What did you think?" my mother asks.

"Lovely," I lie. I didn't even look at the flowers. I make my way up to my room. I recite the plate number.

Q-588.

The light striped wallpaper of my room mocks me. I'll always be a little girl here. Looking around the room, everything is still the way it was when I went to college. That's because this isn't so much my room as it is my mother's. I was never allowed to decorate it. No posters. No fun colors. Just white and pink. I guess my mother saved me from any unfortunate boy band posters. It means that my apartment in New York is colorful. Bright. Teal accent wall with a red couch. Statement on statement. Bold and bold. Tacky for the sake of tacky. I've had time to develop my style, but owning things my mother would consider "in poor taste" is my minor act of daily rebellion. I have my limits, though. I still have white ceilings.

Q-588.

I look at my face in the full-length mirror. Bothered, I zero in on my eyes. They look normal. Not bright or tired. Okay, maybe a little tired. I yawn. My hair catches my eye. It looks longer. I reach up and stretch a curl with my fingertips. I can't remember how long it was before.

Q-588. Q-588. Q-588. Q-588.

I need paper. I search.

Mirror.

Phone.

Flyer.

Denise's flyer. My mother must have found it and left it for me. I grab a pen, open it to write the plate number down.

Keisha Woodson stares back at me.

It's her high school yearbook photo. We had the same background, those rainbow lasers. Her box braids are fresh. Her smile is genuine. Her eyes are bright.

Beneath her picture is: *Justice for Keisha Woodson.*

I tremble, but I don't look away. I'm not leaving Johnstown until I bring home the girl I lost.

THE FEATHER

MORGAN

June 1994

Morgan learned she was beautiful at the age of twelve. Her mother, Latoya, had always called her "cute." Her father, Reggie, crowned her "princess." It was church that taught her she was beautiful. Through glances during sermons, pointed looks from women in enormous hats, and lingering gazes from deacons, Morgan figured out her beauty. It was a problem. Girls were pretty. Women were beautiful.

A luxury of girlhood is being able to play on other people's anxieties without consequence. If you make a girl cry, you must be sorry. If a girl offers you an imaginary phone, you answer it. If a girl reaches for your hand, you take it. In womanhood, all those exchanges become contingent on her ability to pay a price. Sometimes this toll is exacted with no regard for the willingness of the woman.

Morgan's girlhood, like many Black girls', was so brief she almost missed it. One moment she was a child and the next her mother was concerned about the length of her dresses and the color of her shirts. Morgan had seen enough girls grow up. She thought she knew what to expect. She was lucky to be beautiful. It was what you prayed for. She thought that was because beauty made your life easier.

Her mother, Latoya, corrected her. "It isn't ease, it's attention. Wherever you go, you are remembered."

Morgan still felt like a girl. Sometimes being a woman made her sad. Other times, it made her reckless.

"Look at them," Morgan said, referring to her older teenage co-workers. "Never want to help close up." Even though it was late, it was still bright. Summer was here. After a long day of selling ice cream, Taylor, the co-worker closest to her age, could only nod in agreement. Morgan worked at the job the way only a fourteen-year-old could. She outpaced employees years older than her. She had her first taste of agency, and she loved it. Someone other than her parents gave her money and she could do whatever she wanted with it.

Breaking down a table that should have been a two-person job by herself, Morgan tracked the sun. They were behind. She looked over at her other co-workers and saw the reason. They were watching cars pass on the road. Checking. Waiting. Giggling.

"They're looking for boys." Taylor frowned.

Morgan folded her arms. "Stupid." The teens weren't much older than she was. From the way they spoke, how they practiced accentuating the curves of their bodies, who they smiled at and why: They were conjuring power.

"Hurry up!" the manager yelled. They shot the man a look. He backed off. "Please?" he added. The teens laughed. It was clear Morgan and Taylor were going to be the only ones to accomplish anything.

Morgan continued to stack the tables and chairs.

"Here they come," Taylor said. She slouched, keeping her head down.

Morgan looked.

Boys, older boys, approached slowly in a car. The other girls were suddenly busy, engaging in the most diligent effort of ignoring them. Morgan couldn't believe her eyes. After all that, they were going to pretend like these boys didn't exist.

"Hey!" the boys yelled. The teens played coy.

"Hello!" Morgan waved at the boys. She smiled brazenly. The boys waved back to her in awe.

When they drove off, Morgan didn't look over her shoulder. She knew she was remembered.

Her walk home was only a few blocks. The streetlights, though spread out, lit the way. That was the only reason she was allowed to be out after dark. Her mother told her to stay in the light. Not that bad things wouldn't happen there, but anyone who would do something in the light would do much worse in the dark.

"Hey!" This man's voice wasn't like the boys'. The boys spoke to her with a wide-eyed sense of awe. Mutual excitement. "Hey, baby, where are you going?"

Morgan knew better than to look at him. She walked faster.

"You too good for me?"

Morgan did not know how to answer that question yet. No matter what the world deemed her, she was still a girl.

"I just want to talk." He wanted her to be afraid. She knew that. When someone is afraid, they are easier to manipulate. Morgan set her face in stone, stayed in the light, and kept going. Glancing over her shoulder, she saw him and noted his appearance. He was short for a man but taller than her.

"Bitch." How quickly she went from baby to bitch.

One more turn to home. She stopped. If she went that way, he'd know where she slept. She didn't know what to do. Morgan remembered what her father had taught her about bullies. Confront them. Don't let them see you hunch your back. Show them you will fight. Morgan lashed out with the only weapon she had. She turned to face the man and smiled with all of her teeth.

"You have a pretty smile," he said.

Her smile stayed. She crossed her arms over her chest but tilted her head. Her eyes burned with anger. Full of contradictions. She wanted to shove the man away, but she needed him to think it was his idea.

"You hear me?" he asked.

She grinned wider. Her lips cracked at the strain. Her cheeks ached. She showed her gums. She made the most horrifying image she knew, it was one she saw on a decaying box of pancake mix in the bottom cabinet in the kitchen. The red-lipped mammy on the box haunted her dreams with its image of forced jollity. She widened her eyes, to show the whites.

"What's wrong with you?"

She let out a wild laugh. And without realizing it, she did exactly what her mother would have told her to do in the situation. Act crazy. People will try to mess with you if you look small, but not if you look crazy.

After taking in her strange behavior one last time, the man left.

Morgan's expression relaxed. She felt a flutter in her neck. She pressed there and felt her heart pounding. Home was a block away.

Morgan could have become a woman who asked for things her mother would never have dared to. She could have shattered glass ceilings. She could have demanded the world give her what she was worth. Beauty aside, she wasn't easily forgotten.

At the edge of her vision, she saw a shadow. She knew the childhood rhyme about the dangers of looking at shadows. That was in the woods. This was home. But in a town like this, the trees were always close. That fact was made very clear to her as she plotted her way back to her house. All the way at the end of the street, nestled in trees that bore gold leaves in the fall, her home was at the edge of the woods.

A new voice called out to her, "Morgan. There you are." The shadow moved between her and her destination. She turned away. Don't answer if your name is called, don't go off the path.

Real violence doesn't give you the chance to scream. It cuts through you before you feel the blade. Then comes pain. Then fear.

Snap!

A hand twisted around her wrist and yanked her down, taking her off balance. At first Morgan thought the man handled her without care, but when he twisted her arm, grating it hard in her shoulder socket, she knew he felt the opposite. He wanted to hurt her. He wanted to scare her. He wanted to destroy something in her. She was unsure of what.

The violence of the abduction was swift. One moment she was there, the next she was gone. In the seconds before she was dragged into the trees, she still wasn't afraid. She'd reached past that feeling to find something more useful.

Hope.

She prayed—not that nothing bad would happen. She clung to the hope she'd see daylight again. She'd have a chance to laugh with her friends again. She'd see her family. Whispers of these desires escaped her lips. With each one that did, his grip on her grew tighter. When her shoulder gave in a painful *pop,* she cried out. He looked back at her. He witnessed her pain with curiosity. Like it had never occurred to him she could feel the sensation at all.

Beyond this disconnect, Morgan saw him. Sadness morphed into apathetic hate: He made his misery hers. That was when Morgan felt true fear. She didn't need to be an adult to know that sad men are the most dangerous.

Though I know Morgan's heart well, they never found her body. Morgan, who was always remembered, slowly was forgotten. Her heart taught me the monstrosity in beauty. It showed me how people are often pulled to what hurts them the most. Desire and destruction. With her heart, I learned to wield both.

FIRST BAPTIST NEW YEAR NEWSLETTER

January 15, 2017

NEW HELP IN LOCATING MORGAN DANIELS

May the New Year usher in a season of blessings upon you. Thank you all for your years of support and care in locating our daughter, Morgan Daniels. She was last seen on the evening of June 21, 1994. She disappeared between the hours of 7 P.M. and 11 P.M. She was 14 years old, 5'3", and about 105–115 lbs.

In this new year, we are pleased to share this age progression to help find her:

[AGE PROGRESSION PHOTO: Morgan with glasses. Bright eyes. Full cheeks. Cupid's bow lip. Delicate jawline. Smooth, clear forehead. Short hair. A girlish light pink shirt.]

She would be 36 years old today.

ONE

For the first time in a long time, I dream:

I'm outside.

Running.

It's a sticky summer morning. The rising sun warms me, while a slow breeze keeps me cool. I run past the houses on the street I grew up on. The Lombardis' three-story stone house looms at the top of the hill on my right. The organized field stones cast strange, heavy shadows on the ground as I run past. I reach the next street. The Bernardis' place is coming up. They locked their pool behind tall, sinister gates.

I keep running.

Finally, I reach the end of the neighborhood and I'm ready to loop back around. The small outlet at the end of the cul-de-sac leads into the woods beyond.

I stop.

I catch my breath.

I look back the way I came and plan my route home.

Suddenly, I feel like I'm being

watched.

I turn.

And turn.

And turn.

I see no one.

TWO

Caroline's Second Day Missing

I read the flyer with Keisha Woodson's face on it at least a dozen times before I go to bed. The girl I can't get out of my head was handed to me moments after I got into town. Below her face is a call for justice. The only reason to demand justice for an accident is if it wasn't one. I wonder if Denise is her mother. I call the number and it tells me the mailbox is full. But I don't have much time to focus on Keisha because someone has been watching my mother's house. And Mel's family has much more tension than I ever knew. In all this, there's something beyond my grasp. A piece that, once I hold it, will snap everything into focus.

After I wake from my dream, I can't go back to sleep. Up before dawn, I start getting ready. I need to head back to the train station to find Denise. Keeping an eye on my phone for an update, I head downtown with the rising sun.

Sitting outside the station, I don't see a hint of Denise. Nothing in the parking lot. Nothing near the station itself. I check the time: 6:00 A.M. I need to get back to Mel at the site.

I text her. I'm on my way.

I start my mother's car. Before I can pull away, my phone buzzes.

Trapped. Mel replies.

I fight the urge to call her back. She could be in a situation where a ringing phone could make it worse.

Where are you? I type with one hand and use the other to steer. The moment I send the message, I split my focus between the road and the screen, checking for Mel's reply. I get to an intersection and pull over. With all the one-way streets, a turn in the wrong direction means I'll have to go a long distance to get back on track.

My phone buzzes.

Home.

Mel's curt reply makes my heart race. If she's home, they must have found Caroline. If she's okay, Mel'd tell me. If she's not . . . I break the suburban speed limit driving to her house.

When I get there, I have to park all the way at the end of the street. Every bit of space is taken. I grab a spot and turn off the car. Before I get out, I glance around, trying to get a clue of what I'm walking into. If Caroline has been found, there'd be police to take her statement or an ambulance to make sure she's okay—if she's been found alive. I get out of the car and break into a jog. Moving past the cars clogging up the street, I see they all are congregated around Mel's. I run.

A navy-blue car stops me.

It's like the one I saw outside my mother's. I check the license plate. No match. As I get closer to Mel's I scan the plates of other cars. It was dark, so navy blue could have easily been black or even green. None of the plates are a match.

When I arrive in front of Mel's house, I'm dizzy. I'm forced to stop and catch my breath, not out of exhaustion but anxiety.

Breathe.

I need help. I can't be here for Mel and keep up with the investigation all on my own. I'm covered in panic sweat at 6:30 in the morning, hurriedly checking license plates while mentally preparing myself for the worst. Another breath. I can't be a mess right now. I shove my hands into my back pockets, opening up my chest, forcing myself to take a deep breath. Something slides under my nail. More surprising than painful. I pull out my phone with a clawlike grip. There, still awkwardly sticking out of my case, is a business card. *Sydney Oswald.* I turn it over and on the back is Doug Nowak's number. The assistant from the station. Judging by how Nick's been at the site, the whole department is out there. This next day is significant. No one has time for my paranoia. If the car outside my house is nothing, I need to know. If it's something, I can bring it to the police without losing time. Doug implied he wanted to stay on the edges of this case. Maybe running a partial plate is exactly the kind of thing he's looking for? I text him.

It's Liz. Can you run a partial plate for me? I send the letters and numbers.

Standing in front of Mel's house, I note how different it is from the pictures she shared with me at closing. They've fixed the roof. Touched up the blue paint on the outside. They redid the walkway up to the front landing with field stones. I've never been here. We've shared tons of pictures and had hours of video calls. This shouldn't be how I first see Mel's place in person. My need to stay away from this town robbed me of a happier meeting.

I knock on the front door, and it cracks open. The house beyond feels full. I press my ear to the door, trying to discern who's at Mel's this early.

A voice behind me alerts me in the nick of time. "Excuse me!" A woman I've never seen before races past me cradling baskets of laundry. I push the door wide open for her and she hurries through it. I follow after her.

Melissa's house is packed. People crowd the halls and pile in the kitchen. They are all here to support the family. Or to get the real story. No one's crying. The air isn't heavy with grief.

"Such a shame—" a woman whispers in earshot.

I turn to her. "They found Caroline?"

"No. No." Flustered, she takes a step back, making me realize how close I am to her. "Still looking. Here." She hands me a flyer. It's of Caroline, a photo I recognize. From Christmas. It's been cropped, but I can see some of the lights from the tree. She's in a bright red sweater.

Her hair is in two long plaits. There are impersonal stats across the bottom: her age, race, height, weight. I reach out for more and she hands me a stack. Denise, the woman at the station, has been handing out flyers like this for years. I wonder how long I'll be handing them out for Caroline. I look for Mel.

When I reach the living room, I see Mrs. Parker. She is different from the way she was at the site. She's still. Stoic. She sits on the couch while a neighbor talks her ear off. I get bits of their conversation; the woman is offering prayers and help cooking. I do my best to avoid eye contact and look for the kitchen. Before I can retreat to its warm comfort, I collide with a slight woman holding a very full Pyrex casserole dish with a pair of oven mitts. I'm quick to save the dish. Gripping it, my hands feel warm.

"Excuse me—" Before she can finish scolding me, my hands go from warm to burning. We both realize that I've grabbed the pan she was carrying with my bare hands. That pan has just come out of the oven. She takes it from me and deftly places it on the counter. We both look at my palms. They're pink. The heat from the dish fades. Pain sets in. My palms tingle. I grit my teeth as the burn builds.

"Move!" She clears the way for me to the sink. Grabbing my arms, she thrusts my hands under the tap. The pain swells the moment cool water hits my skin. I panic.

"Does it hurt?" Her calm voice invites me to feel the same.

"I don't know." We both watch the water running over my hands. A few people in the kitchen peer over at the two of us. No one races to action. It seems all of them are used to a quick kitchen burn. I never cook.

"How you feeling now?" I'm close enough to her to notice the barrette in her thin blond hair. Baby pink and girly. Not girly as in feminine, but girly as in youthful. The barrette pins her bangs back.

"I'm . . ." My hands feel cold, numb almost. No more pain. "Fine. Thank you."

She lets me go and I realize she has been gripping my wrist right along my scar. It aches from her fingers. I grab some paper towels and dry my hands. When I look up to thank her or to apologize, she's nowhere to be found. The casserole remains. It smells incredible.

Mel and Garrett's home is decorated with carefully crafted decor. The functional hanging rack of pans in the kitchen is nice. Artwork flutters on the door of their fridge. Every piece is lovingly clipped and displayed against the metal. The ubiquitous primary color magnet-letters spell "Baloney" and "Cat," and a precariously placed "F" sits in front of the word "Art." This home is missing its child.

More neighbors mill around in the pantry, putting away food and cleaning. Something like this wouldn't happen in the city. Maybe one or two people, not the entire neighborhood. Neighbors here know one another. They keep up with one another's lives. They care. While they might not be able to join the search, they can make sure Mel's home is ready when Caroline returns. I think back to Mel's text. This must be maddening for her. No one wants her to be alone right now, even if it means suffocating her.

I slide around strangers to find Garrett. He's stationed near the back of the house as the sole end of a strange receiving line. He plasters a painful smile on his face as he gives out shallow hugs and strained greetings. From his stiff movements, I can tell he wants people out of his house and to get back to the site. I notice that Mr. Parker and Nick aren't here. They must be out there already.

When Garrett sees me, he breaks out of the pattern. "Liz!" With his shout, the sea of people parts. He gives me a full hug. "Mel hid in the office." He indicates a far door. "Wait." He points to the flyers in my hands. "She doesn't want to see those. Find me after you talk to her." I give him the flyers.

Careful not to be followed, I make my way to the office. I pause outside the door. The knob feels heavy in my hand. It's like the door doesn't want to open. Still, I pull it and unseal what's inside.

The office is quiet. I can hear the air conditioning hum and there's a clock somewhere, ticking away. Melissa sits in the center of the carpeted floor. She looks like her mother. Motionless. Her stillness is alarming because of its precision. It belies her intent. She's containing herself; she's sitting very still because if she doesn't, she'll explode (or implode) and take everything in arm's reach with her.

Before I enter the room, I announce myself. "Hey."

Mel doesn't respond. She doesn't even move.

People are gathering outside the door. Before anyone can ask me what I'm doing, I slip into the room. As I enter, I pull the door shut behind me. Even the door is reluctant to slide into place. I have to yank it. There. Like that, I'm in Melissa's bubble.

The sound of the door latch clicking jars her a bit. She turns her head toward me. I sit cross-legged on the floor next to her. She kneels in front of a box and holds a stack of multicolored papers in her hands. She handles the papers like they are thin wafers. I'm convinced the slightest movement will disintegrate them, but I know that's not the case. The thing I must be careful not to disturb is Mel. When she doesn't budge, I reach for one of the papers. She shifts away from my touch. In a moment of incredible selfishness, I think this is it. She's going to blame me for losing Caroline. I was supposed to be watching her daughter and now she's gone. Tempted to ask Mel, I stop myself. She hasn't said anything of the sort. I'm doing everything I can to fix this. I shove my worries down, knowing it's my anxiety messing with me.

Mel's phone is a constant beacon of flashes, notifications, and calls. She watches me as each new pulse pulls my focus. She turns her phone over.

Melissa puts the papers in her hands down in a stack on the floor. She grabs another stack from the box in front of her. She looks through each paper and I see what they are. Drawings. Assignments. Art projects. All Caroline's. My heart drops. I watch as she sorts them, making her way to the bottom of the box.

"Can I . . . help?" I ask.

Melissa hesitates. No one has offered to help her. A small part of her opens herself up to the opportunity.

"Yes, but only the piles I tell you, okay?" One by one, we sort through the drawings and assignments. Caroline loved pink.

No. Caroline *loves* pink.

The image I have of Caroline is fading in my head. I think that's why Mel's here. There are pictures and videos, but these are her daughter's creations. They are little pieces of her. Melissa sorts the stacks by year or theme. I can't tell if she is looking for something in the box or if she just wants to touch the work. I sit with her and sort. When the box is empty, Melissa leans forward and runs her fingers along the bottom, feeling her way around the corners. Something builds behind her eyes.

"Her crayons aren't here."

"She had them at the wedding."

"No, the oily ones you got her. They stained her hands. I wouldn't let her use them in her dress. I put them in here."

"Do you want me to look in the living room?"

"No!" Her misplaced frustration stings. "This is where they live and they're gone." I can see the story Melissa is weaving in her head. In her mind, somehow, Caroline came home for her art supplies and then went back out into the trees, like a mischievous child. Like me, she's been searching for the missing thing. The piece that would make everything make sense. I'm looking at license plates, tracking down flyers and a missing girl from high school. Mel is searching through her daughter's art. If she can't find Caroline in the trees, she'll find her here. "They're her favorites. I can't lose them." Mel starts her search again.

I stop her. "I'll find them."

I help her put the artwork back. If Mel needs to imagine that Caroline is with misplaced crayons, then she is. I don't have the heart to pick her vision apart.

THREE

"We aren't supposed to have people in the house—one of the first things they say—but Mel refuses to kick anyone out," Garrett says between puffs on his cigarette. "We only came back to make the flyers. I was up all night finding the right pictures, printing—the minute the neighbors saw our car in the driveway, they flooded in."

"At six o'clock in the morning?"

"Earlier."

Garrett and I stand alongside the house. Judging by the number of cigarette butts, this is his secret spot. It reminds me that smoking is another secret I didn't know about Mel and Garrett.

"Mel doesn't want to think about tomorrow." He cites Nick's grim mile marker. Forty-eight hours. "She wants all this to be nothing, a misunderstanding—I do too. But if it's not . . . tomorrow is all I can think about. I'm getting the media. I'm getting more help. We need to get as many eyes looking for Caroline as possible."

He's right. I spent my morning following up on a flyer from fifteen years ago, when there was one printed today waiting for me. I look at my feet, unsure of what to say. There is more than one kind of cigarette butt on the ground. I know Mel doesn't smoke, but Nick and Mr. Parker do. I guess Garrett has, temporarily, let me into his boys' club.

"Can I ask you something?" I say.

"Don't know if I'll be able to answer but"—he shrugs—"sure."

"Did Mel's dad take you hunting before he would meet Caroline?"

Garrett freezes. Whatever niceties I've earned are about to be rescinded.

From behind a tight jaw, he asks, "Did Mel tell you about that, or did Jacob?"

"Mel did."

"Of course she did." Garrett arranges his thoughts. "Yeah. That happened."

"What did you two do?"

Garrett looks at me. "Jacob took me out into the woods." His gaze shifts past me. It seems like he's watching his memory and deciding how to parse it out to me. "Way out. I was sweating the entire time. And it was early fall, so after a few minutes of that, I was just wet, and freezing." Garrett crosses his arms over his chest, protecting his heart. "He had a gun. A rifle. It was a nice one—one of those guns that can hit a squirrel from a thousand yards away, if you know what you're doing. I had a gun too, but nothing like that. It was some plastic shit from Walmart. The kind you buy for a twelve-year-old on their first hunt. I'm not a hunter. Never have been, never will be. I don't want to give anyone more cause to shoot me, you know?" We share a sad smile. "Out there, we were two armed men, shooting some deer. And that's what we did."

"That all?"

Garrett's jaw clenches and unclenches. I wonder if he has dreams about his teeth falling out. I wonder if they are as vivid as mine.

"He asked me if I'd ever been on a hunt. I told him, 'No, sir'—added the 'sir' for extra protection. He said any man with his baby girl needed to know how to hunt. He needed to know how to provide. And he needed to know how to kill if need be."

Something in the back of my brain records. I can tell every word that comes next is precious.

"Then he helped me shoot my first deer. I hated it. Didn't help that the thing was huge. We had to field dress it." Garrett shivers. "This dude cuts into it like it's nothing. He broke this thing down in minutes. Cut right up the center. Took everything out. Cleaned it. And the entire time he's telling me to watch, to note what he was doing." Garrett has to gather himself for this next bit. "But it didn't feel like he was teaching me. It felt like he was showing off. Like, 'Watch me cut this huge animal down to size.'" For a moment neither of us moves.

Garrett speaks first. "He ever like that with you?"

"Hell no," I whisper.

"Thank God," he exhales.

I don't. I can't. My mind is already starting to churn.

"In high school, did you ever hear about Keisha Woodson?"

"The girl that went missing from that party in the woods?" Garrett's face falls. "Yeah, I heard she got hurt trying to run away with some older guy, something like that?" Garrett shivers. "My mom used to visit her mother, Denise, a lot. Made sure she was staying up on her bills, going to work, all that. We'd bring her food, but she wouldn't take it. Left it to rot outside. She lost her job. Then her house. Refused anyone's help. She stopped talking to her own family. She fell apart."

"Do you know where I could find her?"

"The train station or this bar—Louise's," Garrett says.

"Why the station?"

"Visitors are more likely to take pity on her. She spends every penny on psychics, crappy PIs, and whiskey."

Something he said keeps bothering me. "When Mr. Parker cut the deer, did he . . . um . . ." I have trouble with the image. I show Garrett on my body. "Did he cut up, like, through the sternum to the chin?"

"Yeah. Hacked away at that thing like he hated it." He finishes his cigarette. "He said it made it easier to get to the heart."

FOUR

I spend the rest of the morning and part of the afternoon papering downtown. There's not much ground to cover, but people here like to talk. So far I've gotten heaps of thoughts and prayers. I'm useless out in the trees. Here I'm helping. I'm still part of the search. And if I can find Denise, if she'll talk to me, she might give me more information about Keisha's death. Last night Mel asked me what I thought. I can't get Keisha Woodson and Bonfire Night out of my head.

I never added my story of that night to the narrative because it's incomplete. It's a folded-over memory. I remember the party. I remember it getting broken up by the police. Kids started screaming. I remember running. With some help, I hid.

Then everything goes black.

Over the years I've been able to pull two images out of the darkness: Keisha's terrified face. And teeth. Dark, long sharp teeth. Too big to belong to any animal. If I try to focus, the picture goes hazy in my mind. I can't see any more details. When I woke up, my arm was ripped open and everything was quiet.

Mel's father, Mr. Parker, cuts out the hearts of the deer he hunts. He cuts their chests open. As chilling as it is, I can't jump to conclusions. An investigation proved that what happened to Keisha was an accident. But that's not what her flyer implies. I need more information from Denise.

I head back to the flower shop where I parked my mother's car to get more flyers. The shop is new. I can tell by the brightness of the neon sign and the cleanliness of the glass. What should be a light floral scent is overwhelming. I fight my sneeze and check for Doug's reply to my text. Still nothing.

Please? I add.

I scan the street for where I haven't flyered. There's a restaurant that's just opened. A boutique. A state-run liquor store. And Louise's. I check the time. 4:00. The neon sign flickers in the daylight. They're open.

Louise's is more of a hallway than a bar. There's a jukebox in the corner that still takes quarters. It smells like people still smoke inside. The lighting is dark and moody and red. A tall Black man with a bar rag nods to me when I walk in. Organized in his movements, he cleans glasses and sorts the bottles in the well. This is his tight ship. There are a few locals sitting and chatting or swaying to the music.

"Is Denise here?" I ask.

His deep voice barely carries. "Who's asking?"

"Liz. I owe her a drink."

"Dee-Dee!" The bartender turns to a woman at the end of the bar. She has her back to the wall and is staring out the sole window. She huddles over a short glass of a brown liquor. "Next round is on this girl."

She turns to me and I give her a smile. The look in her eyes lets me know I'm not welcome.

She looks to the bartender. "Terrance, tell that girl I don't want her money."

Terrance turns back to me. "You heard her."

I walk over to Denise. "I just want to talk—"

"You stay right there. I don't need to spend another night in jail."

"Jail?" It looks like Nick had the men to spare. "I am so sorry."

"Uh-huh." She lifts herself off her barstool. "Cops said I'd pissed off the wrong 'saleslady.' Knew it was you. I don't forget a face."

"I didn't mean for that to happen."

She tries to get past me. "Is that right?"

I put Caroline's flyer between us on the bar. "I need your help." I lean in, not wanting the entire bar to hear my conversation. From this distance, her eyes are bleary and sad. She doesn't take her gaze off Caroline's picture.

"You still paying for my drinks?"

"What are you drinking?"

"Hennessy." Denise is not drinking Hennessy, but I'm not mad at her for leveling up.

"Round of Hennessy," I say. Our drinks come fast.

"We're even now." Denise drinks before I can cheers her. She gingerly takes up the flyer of Caroline. "She your daughter?"

"I'm her godmother. She's been missing for a day and a half and—"

"You wanna know if she's gonna end up like Keisha?" She gives me a tired look. "No one ever wants to listen until it's their child." She drinks and turns away from me. "I hope you don't find her like Keisha was. No one should lose their child like that." She gives me back the flyer, done with the conversation.

"Keisha was . . ." Somewhere in the memory that's been kept in shadow for years, I find a half truth. "My friend." It took until my second year of college to understand the tension between Keisha and me. Two high-achieving Black girls, of course we weren't friends. All our lives, we'd been told that there was only space for one. I remember the pressure my mother put on me to claim that spot. I look at Denise and wonder if she pressured her daughter in the same way, or if it was Keisha who drove herself.

"You go to that party in the woods?" she asks.

"No." I roll my wrist away from her, hiding my scar. "Wasn't invited." I see her searching my face. "But I know Keisha was. She was always invited to everything. She, um, she tried to help me with all that. Social stuff. I was just hopelessly awkward, you know?" I smile.

Denise turns back to me and gives me a good once-over. "Still are."

"That's exactly what Keisha would have said." I laugh. For the first time since I've met her, Denise gives me an earnest smile. Just as quickly as it warmed her face, the expression is gone. She drinks again, finishing. I haven't even touched mine.

She waves for another round. "Girl, don't let me lap you."

I settle onto the stool next to her. After two rounds, I have never been more grateful to be a regularly drinking New Yorker.

"What did the police tell you about Keisha's disappearance?"

"She fell. It was an accident. I asked them how she got all the way out there in the woods—there was a party, I know that. But she was farther out, past where any of those kids were. The police said she was with some boy. Said she might have been trying to run away."

"Did you and her ever have any fights?"

Denise lets out a loud laugh. "Ever tried livin' with a teenage girl?"

"Yeah, yeah." I let out a knowing sigh.

"You got kids?"

"No. I haven't, um . . ." I've planned out my life for so long it's strange to not know what's coming next. Not just in my life, but what's coming in the next month, the next day, the next hour. I quickly check my phone. No updates from Doug or Mel.

"Don't have 'em if you don't want 'em." Denise tilts the liquor around the edge of the glass, watching the legs form. "Raising a child takes everything you got and more. You do so much for them, you never think about losing 'em." Denise drinks in one long sip. I can see the tears form in her eyes as she keeps down a cough in her chest. "You know"—she shifts into a wry smile—"when it wasn't my child, I believed what the papers said. I believed what people said. That would never be Keisha." She orders another round automatically. I see the bartender mix her a drink that is more water than whiskey. "She would not be another one of those girls."

That stops my glass on its way to my mouth. "Those girls?"

"The ones who go missing in June? Like Caroline?" Denise studies me.

All I can eke out is "What?"

Denise takes a sip of her fresh drink and shoots the bartender a look. "Some people don't even let their kids out after dark from mid-June till the first week of July." I think of what Keisha said about sneaking out. I thought it was because I was a kid who never broke any rules. I never thought of what rule *she* was breaking. Caroline's friend who couldn't come to the wedding, she said it was because of the girl's parents.

"How long has that been a thing?"

"You from here?"

"I lived up the hill—in Westmont. My mother still does." I scramble for facts. "We never really came downtown."

Denise waits and I see her do something I know all too well. She's controlling her breath, or trying to, in order to sober up. Her mind is reaching for something she can't grasp.

"So, you were a friend to Keisha at that school?"

I nod. "Yes."

"She didn't want to go to high school up there. Said all her friends were down here. When they announced that program to help mix up that school, I was the first to sign her up. Seen too many kids not graduate. Too many kids get stuck." Denise wipes away some sweat that's pooled on her neck. "The first month she was there she'd come home crying, saying how she didn't have any friends. Said she hated me for making her go."

I didn't realize Keisha thought she didn't have any friends. It always seemed to be the opposite. I wait to see if my lie has blown up in my face. When Denise hugs me, I'm so shocked that I barely embrace her back.

"You okay?" I ask.

"One day she finally came home happy. Told me she made a friend. I thought it was a boy 'cause she wouldn't tell me who it was." She holds me tighter. "Glad to finally meet you." Her hug is stable and warm. Just as I feel myself relax into it, she releases me and looks at me. "You saved my girl."

I feel sick to my stomach and it's not just from the whiskey. Denise takes a deep swig of her drink. I stop sipping altogether and wait for my gut to stop spinning. When Denise emerges from her gulp, she examines me again.

"The police came looking for me because of you?"

"Again, I'm so sorry— "

"You're a Black woman who can tell the cops to look into something and"—she gives me one last good look—"they show up." Something opens in her. "You should meet the others."

"Others?"

"We're a mess of mothers." Denise looks so tired. "All kinds of messes. All kinds of mothers."

My fuzzy mind snaps into focus. She's talking about all the mothers with missing daughters.

"How many?"

"Girls who go missing like this? They always taken in the summer. Meet me at the church downtown tomorrow morning. First thing. We'll see who shows."

"That soon?"

"Some of these mothers have been looking for answers for longer than me. If they are still looking, they'll be there."

FIVE

In the parking lot outside of Louise's, I sit in my mother's car and sober up. I check my phone for news from Mel. Nothing. I might be good to drive in a few.

There are more girls.

I remember when Keisha was found. For a few days there were whispers about a crazy killer targeting teens like some slasher film. Tons of kids had "sightings" of a man in the woods. All of them turned out to be made up. The buzz died down. I never heard about the other girls. If Caroline isn't an accident, I need to learn all I can about them.

My phone buzzes.

It's Chris. Drink later?

My face flushes. I leave the text unanswered. I'll deal with him when I can. Currently, it's only the afternoon and I'm on my way to drunk. I shouldn't have had that much with Denise. Seeing the world blur in the daylight makes me feel embarrassed. Drinking is something I do to relax. To have fun. To sleep. That's all.

My phone buzzes again.

Doug has come through for me. Lauren Bristol.

I read the text twice. Lauren is a gossip, but if she's willing to go this far, she has to have more on the line than dishing out secrets over brunch. Doug forwards me her address and I realize I know exactly where she lives.

Lauren is at the edge of the nice part of town. It's my mother's neighborhood, but Lauren is right on the district line. She must have inherited her parents' house. Carefully navigating the turns up the hill, I remember a back way up this mountain.

Like in most places, uptown and downtown aren't only geographic locations in Johnstown. They're also a manifestation of the economic classes and the flood that decimated this place. A tragedy in broad daylight. The floodwater came in the afternoon. Knocked out all communications to and from town. Survivors had to go on foot for help. That first night must have been a nightmare. Relief came once communications resumed. After the town was rebuilt, the wealthy moved to the top of the mountain and the riches trickled down from there. That's why the Inclined Plane was built. Like most things in America, our claim to fame is rooted in tragedy. The higher up you lived, the higher your class. Some nestled themselves along the sides of the mountain. Not quite suburbia, not quite rural. This is where Lauren lives.

Walking home from school, she was the only popular girl who didn't turn in the same direction as all the others. I figured out the district thing when my mother and I moved to our neighborhood. After years of mapping out how to get into the better district, my mother wanted to be smack dab in the middle of a good zip code.

Lauren's house is modest. Nice. She has a yard. In the driveway, there's a navy-blue car. Lauren brought up Keisha at the wedding. She tried to connect the two of us. Lauren is outside working in her garden. A stunning blue rhododendron blooms under her efforts.

That bitch.

She's the "gossip woman" my mother was talking about. Instead of me getting information out of her, she's been trying to pry information out of my mother behind my back. The residual Hennessy is not helping me keep my cool. I should go back to the site. Or hand out more flyers. Lauren waves at me, flashing a shit-eating grin. She's led me on a wild goose chase over her car. She might have messed things up with my one source in the department, Doug. I push my anger down. Screaming at her won't get me anywhere. Getting out of the car, I do my best not to slam the door.

I don't let her get a word in. "Leave my mother out of this. Whatever problem you have with me, you have with *me*."

"Liz? What are you talking about?" She takes a step back, crushing a few blue petals underfoot. "Excuse me?"

"You've been watching my house. Why?"

"Well." She smiles, refusing to meet my anger. "I drive, um . . . I—I drive around at night for some peace and quiet."

"I never told you I saw your car at night."

She stumbles out of the flower bed. She's caught.

"What do you wanna know, Lauren? I'm right here. Ask."

"I have every *right* to talk to who I want and drive where I want." She crosses her arms in front of her. Behind her, a massive American flag slouches from the eave of the house. I don't like thinking about this town and the election. I don't even talk about this town and the election. When my mom started noting the number of American flags going up in the neighborhood, I got scared.

"If you come near my house again, I will—"

"What? Call the cops?" Such an innocent phrase for Lauren. I don't have the patience to answer her. She rests a hand over her heart. "I can't imagine what you must be going through. If I got distracted and lost a child, I don't know what I'd do."

"What do you mean?"

"Chris." The judgment is rolling off her skin with her sweat. "Is he why you couldn't keep an eye on Caroline?" She forces a tight-lipped smile. "Take it from me. Chris is not like . . . that."

I've forgotten how to fight like a girl. I'm used to strongly worded emails and one-upping men in meetings.

"You drove by my house to see if I was with him— Why do you care?" I stop her when she tries to rush past me. "You're married."

"He's Chris and you're *you*!" The words come out of her so violently she drops all of her tools. She doesn't scramble to pick them up. Instead, she looks over her shoulder at the front window like she's checking to see if someone inside can hear us. She looks scared. So scared.

I can't yell at her, she's too terrified, so I firmly ask, "What's wrong with me?" I don't want someone like Lauren to answer that question. I don't need her to. She scoffs and gives me a look that needs no words. It's a shake of the head and blink of her eyes. She shrugs both her shoulders up, rolling her palms open in an oddly parallel movement. It's the same expression you'd give to a child when they ask why the sky is blue, or why the ground gets wet when it rains.

I don't tell people I'm from this town for many reasons. One of them is because of people like Lauren. People who look at me and can only see me in a way that makes themselves feel superior. People like her aren't just in Johnstown. Sometimes I fear I'll find them anywhere I run.

SIX

Before I can drive to the site, or to my mother's, or back to Mel's, my phone rings.

"Liz." It's Melissa. She sounds far away. "She's still . . . we can't . . . I can't find her."

I want to reach through the phone to hold her. "Where are you? I'm on my way."

"She must be so scared and I can't find her." Mel sobs. Her words become unintelligible. Garrett takes the phone from her and explains what's happening. With forty-eight hours closing in we need to think about our next steps. He tells me to rest up. He got Search and Rescue. The dogs are coming. They'll be added to the search tomorrow. I promise I'll be there for the first sweep.

I'm starting to worry for both of them in the trees. A chilling thought crosses my mind. It's the same one I've had all day. *Does Mel's dad cut hearts out of deer the same way Keisha was opened up—the exact same way? Could her death have been made to look like an accident when it wasn't?* Stop. I can't hurl accusations like that without good cause. Doug found a partial plate. I hope an old case file isn't out of the question.

I text Doug: Keisha Woodson. Anything you have. Please?

Like before, no immediate response. I hope Lauren hasn't ruined this for me. I know it's late and I'll have to wait till tomorrow for any follow-up. Until then, I need to pass the time. I need night to come. I need to sleep. I need a drink.

I reply to Chris: I'd love a beer.

★ ★ ★

"If you see the Cannizzaros' place, you've gone too far," I whisper into my phone. From my position at the end of the driveway, it's unclear why I'm whispering at all.

"Like I could miss it. The place is a fortress," Chris replies, distracted by house numbers. "Okay, I see the yellow house with the columns."

I felt strange getting a drink at his place of employment. I asked if he was okay with my backyard. Thankfully, he agreed.

"You just make a sharp left, up the hill," I say.

"Got it."

I hear him coming. I wave. When he makes the last turn, I direct his truck into the driveway like a plane. Oh no. I'm giddy. I don't like this. I quickly knock myself down a peg.

"Hi," I mumble.

"Hey." He flashes me a smile and produces a six-pack. I don't recognize the label.

"What is that?"

"It's from a local brewery—" Another voice cuts in.

"Who is that?" It is my mother, Marie. Mortified, I motion for him to hide the beer. I whirl around to see her standing in the doorway, arms crossed.

"Mom! This is Chris, from high school." She gives Chris a vacant smile. I can tell she has no idea who he is, but she wants to save face.

"Oh, hello, Chris."

She's thinking. My mother prides herself on remembering her patients; she'd never let herself forget a name. So, instead of asking for a reminder, she smiles and thinks. Like she can hide behind the flash of her teeth. I don't know if I inherited my awkwardness from my mother or if it is something all my own.

"Hi, Dr. Rocher. How are you doing?" Chris sounds well versed in speaking to mothers.

"Oh, call me Marie." My mother is suddenly ready to be flirty. I roll my eyes. Her stance on men drastically changed the day I turned twenty-five. It went from *No boys allowed* to *Where are my grandchildren?* overnight. "You two can come in—"

"Mom, Chris and I are gonna sit on the back patio and catch up. Okay?" I am willing her to read the room.

"Let me know if you need anything."

"I will." After a moment, my mother finally leaves. "Sorry."

"Don't be. She's cute."

We walk around to the back. The yard sprawls out from the house. Trees trickle between each of the properties. I pull out two chairs and a table from the set of patio furniture. I motion for Chris to sit, then duck back inside. Once inside, I grab Chris's jacket and flip-flops from the night of the wedding. The wedding that feels like it happened years ago.

Before heading back out, I look at myself in the mirror. My reflection surprises me. The dark circles under my eyes remind me of how my mother used to look after a night of rounds in the hospital. I delicately trace the sockets. There isn't much to do about them now, and it's dark outside, anyway. I try to coax some curls into my hair and head out the back door.

"Here's your stuff."

"Thank you. Here's your beer." He offers me one of the glass bottles.

"I forgot an opener." I turn to go back in. He stops me.

"No worries." He grabs one of the flip-flops I brought out and turns it over. On the underside, there is a bottle opener. He cracks a beer open and hands it back to me, then opens one for himself. We sit.

The moment the beer hits my tongue, I notice it tastes different. With the first sip, I taste the story of the drink. Bitter hops, grapefruit, and something else. There's care; nothing manufactured or pumped or produced. I want to bring it up, but I can't. I'd sound like a fool if I told Chris I could taste the love in the beer.

The way he slouches in the chair next to me lets me know that it's been a long day for him too. Dusk rolls in, casting everything in stunning oranges and reds. I think I can see purple brewing on the horizon.

"How's everything?" Chris asks. We both know that as the hours stretch on, the odds of finding Caroline alive are dwindling.

"It's been two days," I say. "I don't know how to feel." That's true because right now I'm on edge. Painfully aware of everything about Chris, I have something else to focus on and my mind is all too eager to obsess. On the ground, his left foot is a little farther ahead of his right. He's leaning toward me in his chair. He smells . . . Oh God, he smells like I remembered, like wet and heat. Like a boy, in the unbridled, intoxicating way boys are allowed to smell. As a man, he's covered this scent with musk and sandalwood. The same part of me that has been engaging with death craves the opposite. However, I know how to temper my feelings. I let any desires I have simmer in my stomach. One beer becomes two. I tap my phone for light every time it falls asleep. The dark out here still unnerves me, but it helps that I'm not alone.

We talk about everything that happened to the town between high school and our thirties. A few years after I graduated, he "got it together" and went to the local community college. His dad refused to let him inherit the Hearth unless he had a degree. Once he did, he started up the catering part of the business. We revisited places that had long closed or gained new ownership. This strange reacquaintance that should have been happening under different circumstances is going well. Then I remember why I don't drink beer. I feel my stomach expand. I shift in my chair and let out a huge burp.

"I am," I try to backtrack, "I am so sorry."

"That was awesome." Chris laughs. Nervously, I join him. I know he's doing it to make me feel better. "You can take the girl out of the mountains, but you can't take the mountains out of the girl."

The deep darkness of the night washes over us. "I'm still surprised by how dark it gets out here. I've missed the stars." More than lights in the dark, the constellations were my first comfort. Before Mel and I became attached at the hip, I spent my time learning their stories during my frequent visits to the school library. The North Star. The Big Dipper. Ursa Major, the Great Bear. The She-bear and her mirror, Ursa Minor.

In Greek myths, the bears are a mother and her child. When a god loved a mortal, his jealous goddess-wife transformed the tempting young woman into a beast to stop her husband's lust. Then the young woman's son, mistaking his mother for a true beast, hunted and tried to kill her. The goddess transformed the mother and her child into Ursa Major and Ursa Minor, so they could live together in the night sky. I found an Iroquois story about the three hunters who eternally chase the Great Bear through the summer skies. They catch their prey by the end of the season. The animal's blood stains the leaves of the trees red, beckoning the fall. Its bones rest all winter long. By the end of the spring, another bear rises, starting the chase anew. I like a story I found from South Korea the best. A widow with seven sons began dating a widower. To get to his house, she had to cross a stream, so her sons built a bridge for her made of seven stones. Their mother, not knowing who put the stones in place, blessed them, and then those stones became Ursa Minor. There's another version I like less. It says that the mother and her sons ended up living with the widower. However, the widower didn't like her sons, so he pretended to be sick. He said the only cure was a piece of each of the sons' livers. The boys decided to sacrifice themselves and went deep into the forest. Once they were there, a great beast stopped them and gave them its liver cut in seven parts. That great beast became the seven stars of Ursa Minor. Each story has a beast. Some are chased and others are welcomed in.

For years, when I looked up, I imagined my way out. I had no map. The stories gave me something better. An escape. Grounding in the sky. Who finds solidity in the stars?

"If you ever get lost, you can always find your way home," Chris says, breaking me out of the reverie. This is the most we've said to each other since Keisha disappeared. We spoke frequently before that night. When he was a senior and I was a freshman, I managed to test into the same English class as him. I was far ahead, and he'd been held behind. We debated all of our reading, especially *A Tale of Two Cities*. Standing up to him was one of the first times I recall freely speaking my mind.

"Do you remember helping me on Bonfire Night?" I ask. "When the cops came, everyone was running. It'd be easy to forget—"

"I remember." Chris rolls his beer bottle in his hands. "You were nervous at that party."

"It was my first real party."

"You were off by yourself. Looking at the stars. You showed me the Summer Triangle." He turns to me and smiles. "I'm still out there."

"At your dad's place?"

"Kinda. I have a trailer on the land—out near The Rounds. Never thought that would be me. But it's . . . great." He laughs. "You'll think this is funny. I search for that triangle whenever I look up. Took me two years to realize that it's only in that position in the summer."

I join him with a small chuckle. Soon we both fall silent.

He continues, "The cops showed up and started arresting kids. I drove you out on my ATV, back to near my house. I told you to hide in this huge hollow tree." Chris stops rolling the bottle and grips it tight. "I left you there because I wanted to put the ATV back without waking my dad. Had to do the walk in the dark. I was so afraid of him getting mad. He was a clerk for the department for years. Always said it was only a matter of time before they started to break up those parties. I wasn't a kid anymore. Underage drinking was one thing. If you were the one buying the beer, that was something else. He wasn't gonna save my ass. When I got home, he was up, waiting for me. Someone tipped him off. He wouldn't let me go back out. I went to look for you in the morning and you weren't there. I figured you got out. Got home."

I wish I had spent the night in that tree. "I did."

"How?"

Time to plumb the darkness of my memory. "I hid in that tree until Keisha found me—or I saw her—we found each other." I see her face. I see the teeth in my arm. That's it. My brain skips over the rest like it always does. "We got . . . separated. When things were quiet I got out of the tree. Then Mel found me. Mel got me home." Again, not fully a lie, but not the entire truth. I press my scar and it hurts. I can't tell if it does because of my nerves or because I'm brushing over the memory of how I got it.

I can see stars in the city sometimes, but I never stop to look at them. I wonder if Caroline is looking at the same stars. I wonder if Caroline is looking at all. She stays with me like a wound. The throb of missing her had momentarily gone away. It's back. This is foolish. I need to go to bed. Get up early to meet the mothers and rejoin the search in the morning. That is why I stayed. Not to sit here, in my backyard, thinking about a man I haven't seen in years.

"Where's the bathroom?" Chris asks. Happy to be out of my thoughts, I direct him to the guest room on the first floor. I stay outside with the stars.

"What are you doing, Liz?" I whisper to myself. Slowly, I undo the knot Chris made in my stomach. This gradual de-escalation of hope is comforting. Even though he's here, he isn't interested. *Don't pervert his kindness. Remember, he'd never even consider a girl like you.* I repeat these truths to myself, lounging in their rhythm, like a poem learned by rote. By the time he makes it back to the yard, whatever feelings had built between us tonight, I've pulled them apart.

"Your bathroom is fancy," he announces.

"It's my mom's house."

"Still, it's . . . nice." He doesn't take his seat again. Instead, he stands there waiting for me to dismiss him.

"Okay." I'm unsure of what to do. I wonder if my mother cornered him.

"I should go."

"You okay to drive? You need a water or something?"

"No, I'm good." Chris shoves his hands into his pockets, ending the debate. "This was nice."

"Yeah."

"We should do this again," he adds. I give him a noncommittal nod, confused as to if he's offering out of interest or pity. I can never tell. Chris gets into his truck and pulls out of the driveway.

I turn to go back inside, but before I do, I look back up and find the Summer Triangle. Deneb, Vega, and Altair. The same stars I showed Chris and Caroline. In the winter, they'll be replaced by Sirius, Betelgeuse, and Procyon.

Girls who go missing like this? They always taken in the summer. I assumed Denise was talking about the seasons. But what if it's the stars? No, both. The spread of dates Denise gave me contains the solstice. The first day of summer. Tomorrow.

KAYLA

June 2003

"What colors you want?" Kayla asked. Her little sister, Kylie, ran her fingers through the bag of beads like they were jewels. Rainbows shifted through her palms as she picked out the pink and white beads and yellow stars she wanted. Kayla could tell her sister was impressed by how many options there were. Kylie had no idea that beads were cheap, that's why they had so many. She was too young to be aware of class. Kayla understood. But she knew there was nothing she could do to change it at her age. She wasn't going to rob her little sister of simple joys: the satisfying sound of beads in her hair and the sting of hard plastic on her nose when she swung her braids. With a dollop of gel and a comb, Kayla started her sister's hair.

> A man and his shadow live in the trees.
> When they walk in time, both are pleased.
> If one calls your name, or the other tempts you off the path,
> You must ignore both, or face their wrath.

Kayla knew this rhyme was far from anything sweet. It was a warning. It birthed stories of a crazed man in the woods, or was the man inspired by the rhyme? Either way, true or not, that was reason enough to stay out of the trees no matter how many pretty flowers and berries and mushroom caps drew her in. Living on the edge of Johnstown meant she had knowledge of the woods. When it came to her traditional education, her family was changing things for the better.

It meant sometimes they got flyers in little bags weighted with unpopped popcorn. Her mother told her to grab them before anyone saw. Kayla read one once. It was recruiting for the KKK. Or, as her mother said, white folks in search of their own mythology. A dismissive frown covered her mother's fear as she tossed them into the trash. If a group like that was this far north, what did that mean for all their nice white neighbors? That proximity to danger didn't sit well with Kayla's mother. Kayla could tell because of how tight her mother did her pigtails in the mornings. She calmed her nerves in her child's hair. Kayla would undo them at school and the barrettes would crack her knuckles when they released.

Snap!

Myths are as much a part of the slipstream of Black life as joy. Yes, Black folks are masters of joy. Trauma isn't the only thing carried in DNA. Blackness, like any Golden Fleece, is both a birthright and what lies at the end of a quest. What myth lay just beyond Kayla's fingers?

The woods.

Every summer, she faced them for hours as she braided her sister's hair. She didn't need to know the symbolism of making plaits while looking north. She could tell by the feeling in her gut. Woods were to be respected. They had life, in every sense of the word. Freedom could be found in the woods, just as easily as chains. The trees held both healers and hunters.

Summer heat curled little Kylie's hair faster than Kayla could braid it. Kayla wiped her face. When she finished the gesture, she saw something out of the corner of her eye. Like any close sibling, she predicted her sister's movement before she did it. Kayla gripped Kylie's ears and kept her looking straight ahead.

"I saw—?"

"You didn't see shit." Kayla hadn't yet been seduced by swearing and only did so when she absolutely meant it.

The shadow moved again. A sinister presence.

"Don't look at it." Kylie held her sister's face hard. "If you do, he'll get you."

"Who?"

"Why you asking that, big head? Don't give it a name." She sucked her teeth. The head comment was both a nickname and an observation. Kylie had a big head; it took a long time to braid her hair, and she never stopped asking questions. "It's a trick," Kayla said. "If you look, it becomes real. If you don't, it will go away."

Kayla rested Kylie's head against her knee, far away from the shadow, as it continued to flicker.

"That thing wants to take you into the woods and kill you. Eat your heart. You want that?"

The lore had started with Alice. Rumors about her parents. Rumors about the woods. Rumors about her friends. With time, personal details got dismissed. Lost. Only the horrible ones remained.

Kayla reached the bottom of a braid and started to wrap it with a rubber band. "Kylie, if a stranger offered you candy, you take it?"

"No?"

The question in Kylie's answer irked her sister. Still she braided. Her fingertips started to go numb by the end, so she worked from memory.

Kayla reached behind her to grab more beads.

"Kayla?" a voice said. "Kayla!"

Sure enough, her younger sister turned at the sound of her elder sister's name. She looked at the trees. Just as Kayla said, the insubstantial shadow became a man. Before the girls could scream, before they could focus on his face, they ran.

Beads scattered across the yard.

Many things hunt in the woods. Not just men and dogs. Some

things just watch. This particular hunter was a man, but he strained the definition. He liked to remind me about his family. His wife. His child. Every time, I'd meet his eyes with understanding. That life, that tale he wove for me, was the dream. The way he was in the woods was his true nature. So, being a man, he was indeed a Fellow. That's what I'd named him, long before he named me. I am the shadow and he is my flesh. The Fellow. My Fellow.

Just as Kylie reached the door, he pulled Kayla out of the yard and across the tree line. Kayla made noise. She fought. She screamed. She was made braver because she was fighting for her sister. If she was too much trouble, he wouldn't go after little Kylie.

After I was satiated by her heart, and he by his violence, the Fellow asked me, "What happened that night, Jack?"

He didn't need to say when. We both knew who he was talking about. Liz.

I didn't respond.

"She in your head?"

"No," I lied.

"You can have your pets. But if she starts talking, I'll kill her. Strangle her. No heart for you." He was serious. "If it's not me, I'll get my boy to do it. Make sure he gets close to her first."

Kayla's heart taught me I needed a partner worth being brave for. I held on to that hope as I waited for Liz to return to the woods.

New Evidence in Montrose Murder

September 1, 2003

JOHNSTOWN, PA—Evidence supporting child abuse has surfaced in the vicious murder of Kayla Montrose. The teen went missing from her backyard this summer. She was later found with fatal injuries in the woods outside her home. Her younger sister has been re-homed with family at this time while her mother, Pamela Montrose, is investigated.

SEVEN

A familiar dream comes my next night home:

I'm outside.

It's sunny.

I'm running.

I'm always running.

Summer. Hot, not warm. The sun is setting. I'm in my mother's neighborhood. It's also my neighborhood, but I haven't lived here in over a decade.

Jogging past the houses, I clock the ones I know as I go, noting how far I am from my home.

I reach the outlet at the end of the cul-de-sac. No more houses, just woods. It feels like I might continue running right into the trees. A part of me acknowledges I'm not in control. My legs aren't pushing me, I'm being propelled like on a treadmill. The ground and the space in front of me aren't responding to each other like they should. At least, not in a way that makes sense. The faster I run, the slower the houses pass.

My legs stop.

I take my chance to breathe. My chest expands and I greedily take in air.

I look. I look.

I see it.

Right there. Just past the trees, there's a dog.

No. It's huge.

A wolf?

No, not this far south.

A hound?

Maybe, but the fur is too short. And the ears stick straight up.

A warm-weather creature.

It doesn't move like a dog because it doesn't have a master. It weaves between the trees, navigating them in a practiced pattern. The size of the thing is enough to keep me still. Everything in me wants to run again. I want to run home, but I don't want to take that thing with me. So, I stay still as it moves and sniffs and digs.

The sun sets at hyperspeed. A symphony of ambers, reds, and oranges washes over me as a sweet summer chill fills the air. I want to be thankful for the cool night, but the dark is coming and I don't want to be out here with that thing. I take a deep breath. I turn.

I run.

I gain ground and glance back over my shoulder just in time to see the hound emerge from the trees. It's large. Black. Hulking. I will my legs faster. My muscles burn from the effort, but my pace won't obey. No matter how hard I run, the world inches by me.

I don't need to look back again because I can hear the telltale gallop that follows me. Houses crawl past me. The dark spaces between them stretch on forever. By my burning, stubborn effort, I see my house as I round the top of the hill.

I run.

My knees pop in protest. I keep going. Adrenaline wills me forward. The claws of the thing click on the pavement behind me. Each gallop pulses louder than the last. A few more strained steps get me in front of my house. The hound is so close to me that I smell the wild nature matted in its fur.

I scramble across my yard. When I transition from pavement to grass, I slip on the dew. Before I know it, my feet are out from under me.

In my next breath, the hound is on me.

Heat from its body presses me into the grass. I attack it with a tangle of elbows and knees, but I'm flesh and it's fur and bone. I feel myself clench my shoulders to my ears in a primal need to protect my neck. The hound seems to know what I'm doing. It shoves its snout into my collarbone. Its claws and feet force my neck into view.

Teeth emerge from the maw of the thing.

I scream.

EIGHT

Caroline's Third Day Missing

I'm awake when Doug texts me back at four o'clock in the morning.

Meet me at the station.

What happened? I reply.

Urgent is all he follows up with.

Now it's my time to trust him. I try to call him but he declines me. I look back at the text. This early I'll be at the station before most people. Whatever he's found, he doesn't want to text me or say over the phone. My morning is already packed with meeting the mothers and getting to the site as soon as I can. I examine what little I know about Doug. He doesn't like his boss hovering over him. This case upsets him. But no matter how reluctant, he helped me.

I get to the station before sunrise. Doug is outside waiting for me. Quickly he ushers me back. People barely notice me, still arriving and on their first coffees of the day.

"Where are we?" I ask.

"Medical examiner's office. It's in the back of the station. Most places have moved the ME to the hospital. Not here. This place hasn't changed since the seventies." A bitter, burning sanitary smell pervades everything. I stick by Doug's side as he moves through a second set of doors. The whole place feels like a strange hospital. It's clean and well lit, but there is no urgency. No one needs to run because everyone's already dead.

I see a receptionist sitting behind a more welcoming desk than at the police station. Still, there is something off about the whole place that keeps me on edge. We make our way farther back.

After walking through a third set of doors, I figure out what's making me uneasy. It's the smell, or the lack of one. The bitter antiseptic washes everything away. Losing my sense disorients me. I feel like I can't even see the ground in front of me. Even though I know it's there, still, I don't trust it. I nearly stumble keeping up with Doug.

"You okay?" he asks.

"That smell is . . ." I start, but I can't finish my thought.

"You get used to it." He's already at the end of the hall, holding a door open for me. Grateful to leave the strange hallway, I scurry through it.

That was a mistake. The room Doug opened is the home of the smell. I feel like I've been struck in the face. I clamp my hand over my nose and mouth and inhale the scent of my palm. Everything balances out.

"You okay?" Doug asks again. How can he stand to be in here?

"I will be," I say behind my hand. I take in a few more deep breaths of my skin. I've never been this sensitive before. It could be stress. Or dehydration. I know I don't drink enough water. I run through the usual medical suspects in my head, but before I can land on a diagnosis, I notice Doug. He moves forward with a quickness, already in work mode. I see him move to what must be his desk and go through some files. I remove my hand. The smell is still there, but it's become manageable. After a few shallow breaths, I'm okay.

Where Doug's desk sits feels like a regular rectangular office space, but past it the room opens up into a full morgue. Metal tables. Instruments. Backlit charts. Cabinets. Storage. My eyes lock on to a black bag on a metal slab. I freeze. Doug notices.

"Is that a . . ." I can't finish this thought, either.

"Doing a blood draw." He points to a slowly filling bag next to the body. "No heart to pump. It will take a minute."

"You're gonna—" I start.

"Open him up? *No*, no." He uses a gloved hand to offer the chair at his desk. I sit, but I can't take my eyes off the black bag. Morbid curiosity makes me take a large inhale, looking for the smell of death. I get nothing.

"Keisha Woodson?" he says.

"You found something?"

"I pulled her records." Doug places a piece of paper in front of me. Her autopsy report. "There's where her chest was . . ." He notes a single line in the center of the paper. "Cracked wide open. Which wouldn't be surprising for a fall or impact. But this was a perfectly straight cut through the sternum." He points to more markings on her thighs. "She had bruising. Enough for further investigation—this is bullshit. Terrible."

"Who did this report?"

"Oswald."

I add his name to my list of suspects.

"When I started, I noticed he missed things. Often. But this is *criminally* negligent." Doug is upset. Really upset. "Her family doesn't have answers. They never will." He pulls away from me and the chart.

I don't know how to comfort him.

"I . . . I . . . lost my son. Ewan," he says softly. "SIDS. Here one day and gone the next. My wife and I never got any answers."

That's why he doesn't like cases with kids. "We'll figure it out. Get the answers," I say. He won't leave Caroline out there alone. He can't leave her family without answers, just like I can't.

Doug shakes away his emotions. "More than that," he continues. He unrolls a large map of the woods. The forest wraps around town, stretching up into the mountains. Past the city proper, the woods get thick fast. I trace a route I know. Town center to my mother's house. We're at the edge of the suburbs. The forest is basically our backyard. From there, I see that Nick's land doesn't look too far away. The shelves of elevation correct my assumption. Doug rolls the town away, focusing the map on the remote section of the woods the police are searching. Thick with mountains. In a far corner, I notice a small level clearing. Near the clearing is a red X. There are two orange ones on the other side of the map. "Orange is last known location. Red is the drop." He points to the next orange X. "This is Caroline. This is Keisha." Her X is far from Keisha's.

"That's good. Right?"

"If this is a coincidence, but if it's not . . ." He points to the red X. "Is the search going out that far?"

"I don't know." I check the time. "Can I take a picture of this?"

"Go ahead."

I line up my phone and snap a few pictures, getting the whole map. I see the river near the bonfire field. I follow it to Keisha's red X. There I see tons of intricate little lines. They don't look like indicators of elevation.

"What's that?"

"The Rounds," Doug says. "Best map I could find of them. A maze if you don't know your way." I double-check that I have a clear image of the intersecting pathways on my phone.

I glance back at the filling blood bag a few times. Doug's right: It's going slow. Still, seeing the blood move makes me queasy.

He glances up at me. "You gonna faint?"

"No," I say, unsure myself. "What makes you say that?"

"You look pale and your eyes are . . ." He trails off. He stares at my eyes, like, into the workings of them, and gets lost. Not in any kind of lovey-dovey way. He's looking at me with a terrible fascination.

"What?" I try to blink away whatever he's looking at. "What is it?"

"Your pupils look . . ." He trails off again, looking for the words. He blinks a few times himself. "Nothing. Your eyes are dark. That's all."

I know that's not all it is. I've had dark eyes all my life. No one looks at dark eyes the way he just looked at mine. I move away from the blood and Doug and the body and rush toward the sink. Over the sink is a mirror. I really look, stretching my lids apart. As I focus, I see my pupils shrink sharply, making me wonder if they were expanded before. I've always had a hard time differentiating them from the darkness of my iris. I look again. Nothing. Just the brown eyes I've had all my life. I notice my hair. It looks like it's already grown out of its cut, but that's impossible. It must be the product I'm using.

I start to head out and stop. "I might get more names for that map. I'll text you." I have no idea what's waiting for me at the church, but I'm grateful to leave the sterile-scented department. I make my way out of the morgue and back to fresh air.

NINE

What can I say about the Black community in Johnstown? It's as much of a mystery to me as I am to it. My parents divorced before we could make roots here, and my mother always identified with her class before her race. I do know it exists in "the bad part of town." It's not "bad" because of anything inherent. The only crime anyone is guilty of is being poor. Not that there aren't affluent Black people, they just (like myself) keep their distance.

Abandoned houses are a common sight. Streets start and stop, the road is cracked, and potholes gape until they are forced to be repaired. It has been a long time since this part of town has seen any care. The people who live here tend to stay. Generations can trace themselves between the same two or three houses, spanning just a few blocks.

Traveling downtown to meet a group of Black women, I can't help but think of my mother. I always took her isolation as a preference. She isn't always alone, she'll come visit me and her friends in the city. We go to family reunions. She's always calling or chatting with someone somewhere. Never here.

I arrive at the church at the crack of dawn. It's not what I expect. The building barely registers as a place of worship to me. It's too boxy and modern. Looking around, everything in this part of town is relatively new. No stone. Only wood and plastic. This entire neighborhood must have been swept away in the flood. After moving through the parking lot, I press against the crisp metal door of the sanctuary.

Inside, the church is even less churchlike. Its modernity feels out of time. In a few years, this place will disintegrate. Shiny things don't last in this town. There aren't sections to the sanctuary. It's one large multipurpose room. All the chairs are assembled around tables. No cross. The gray low-pile carpet has already turned black in some areas. The long windows have heavy curtains. Most are open, letting in the morning light. I glance up. Popcorn ceiling in a grid. It's missing in some places. Before I can note any more, I hear a voice.

"Morning?" I turn and see an older Black woman in her Sunday best, even though it isn't the holy day. Her wig is plastered to her head with a mixture of summer sweat and gel. Her lavender dress has miraculously escaped the same fate. She fans herself with a matching woven hat.

"Hi." I smile too big, using all my teeth. "I'm here to meet Denise."

The woman eyes me suspiciously. "You the one who wants to listen?" She must be one of the mothers.

"Yes."

She yells over her shoulder. "Toya! Come on out, she's here." She looks at me again. Examining me. "Your eyes are bright."

There it is again. Something strange about my eyes. I rub them with the back of my hand.

"Um. Where's Denise?" I ask.

The woman in purple answers. "Toya would know." She calls again. "Toya, hurry up!"

"I'm comin', Bev," Toya says as she enters from the back. She's in slacks and a loose blouse. Unlike Bev, the heat doesn't seem to slow her down. She fusses with her dense curls in the humidity. I know the feeling, my hair also insists on shrinking up. "Dee-Dee the one who called the meeting. Of course she's late."

"If she shows up here out of sorts—" Bev mumbles to the room.

"She know better," Latoya responds.

"What does that mean?" I ask.

Bev starts to move a table. I jump in to help before anyone can unpack that.

"Thank you." She grabs a seat. "What's your name?"

"I'm Liz."

"I'm Beverly, that's Latoya." Latoya gives me a wave as she deftly constructs a table that should be a two-man job.

"Liz what?" Beverly continues. "What's your family name, sweetie?" She gives me a warm smile. Even with the warmth, her smile makes me nervous. It's false, but the believability of her fake is disarming.

"Rocher."

"Excuse me," she scoffs.

"Rocher. R-o-c-h-e—"

"It's French, Beverly." Latoya sets out more chairs.

Beverly frowns for a moment, then re-ups her smile. "I heard her. I just can't remember the last time I met a French Black." I guess I'm a miracle today. Good thing I'm in a church.

"My mom is Haitian."

Despite her work, Latoya stops. "The doctor?"

"Yeah, that's her."

"Oh, I've heard of her!" Beverly cuts in. "Heard she was nice. I never went to her myself, but I have friends . . ."

"Hell-ooo!" It's Denise. She's in jeans and a T-shirt. She's brushed her hair and washed her face. She put on the airs she needs to be here. No signs of a hangover from yesterday. Of all things, she looks more rested.

"There you are, Dee-Dee." Latoya sets the last chair, making a circle. "You always get here right when all the work is done."

Denise sits. So I do. Latoya stands next to an empty chair. All of us wait. Beverly crosses her ankles, clearly uncomfortable. Latoya folds her arms and checks the time.

Denise speaks up. "The others will be here soon." She looks like a new woman. The hope that was just in her eyes before has extended to her body.

"If they show." Latoya tries to keep the thought to herself, but her voice carries in the wide space.

Moments later, a woman around my mother's age, sharply dressed, enters. Her thick heels sound against the carpet. Her sunglasses stay on. Her glossy ponytail sways as she trots in. She doesn't take any time to make introductions. She hangs her bag on the back of her chair and sits, crossing her legs at the knee.

"Hello, Tanisha," Latoya says.

Tanisha simply raises a hand in greeting. I note the empty chairs—there are at least a dozen still, maybe more. Beverly strains to get a good look at the door.

"I called her, Beverly," Denise says. "Told her someone was here to listen."

"Hasn't mattered to her before," Toya cuts in.

"She'll come." That seems to silence the room for now. Beverly isn't straining her neck anymore, but her eyes are still focused past the circle. Another glance reveals Latoya has situated herself nearest to the stack of extra chairs.

"How many are you expecting?" I ask Denise.

"I contacted everyone I could."

I point to chairs. "This is—"

Latoya answers me. "The right number of chairs? Yes." Denise told me the girls go missing in summer. I didn't realize she meant *every* summer. That gets me to count. By the time I'm done, there are twenty chairs and at least another ten in the stack next to Latoya.

"Can we get started?" Tanisha speaks for the first time. "The girl is clearly not coming."

"I left her a message," Denise insists.

"Doesn't mean she—"

One of the sanctuary doors slams open and a woman who could be my younger sister walks in. She has long blond braids. She wears black shorts and a black tank top. Tattoos curl down one of her legs. She sits far away from any of us. But, even from her distance, I can sense the anger in her.

She looks around at all of us. "This it?" We are outnumbered by empty seats.

Miss Beverly has found someone new to focus on. "Kylie, you couldn't cover yourself before coming in?" She extends her lavender shawl to her. "Have some respect."

Kylie gets up, grabs the shawl, and wraps it over her shoulders. She sits. Silence resounds. I look at this cross section of women and I'm stunned by how different we are and how we are all the same. If Beverly isn't in politics, I'll eat my tongue. She is as put together as any celebrity. Latoya clearly cares for this church and isn't a stranger to a day's labor. Tanisha must have moved here from the Midwest, I can tell by her vowels. They have a softness, not the slight twang people from here have. I used to have that. I worked to get rid of it when I left. And Kylie. She looks to be a few years younger than me. From the ages in this room, and the empty chairs surrounding us. All these women span a lifetime. For all of our differences, there is one striking similarity.

All these women are Black.

All the missing girls are Black.

Beverly starts. "Let's open this with a prayer." Everyone bows their heads. "Dear Lord, we pray for peace today and every day."

Prayers make me uncomfortable. Not the private act, but the public use of them. They feel too intimate to me; it's like wearing your heart on your sleeve. I don't want to see it without warning. I know better than to be rude, but I feel like everyone can sense my unease.

"We pray for grace, strength, and understanding. All is part of your plan."

Denise speaks loudly and firmly, driving the prayer for a moment. "And the safe return of Caroline. Be with her family at this time."

Beverly nods and continues, "Yes, send her home unscathed. In your name. Amen."

"Amen" echoes around. I swallow mine.

"Who are you?" Kylie pushes through the niceties.

"I'm Liz. I went to school with Keisha when she was at Westmont. I'm here to learn what happened." I show them Caroline's flyer. "Caroline has been missing for three days. We are running out of time."

Tanisha clutches her keys in hand, ready to leave the moment this is over. "Alice was the first." Her voice sits right outside her body, reporting the facts. "June twenty-first, 1985." That's way before Keisha. Same year I was born. Same year Mel was born.

"This place was— My husband and I came from Detroit after he got a job at the steel mill. Admin. The industry was drying up. He was here to help shut things down. We were supposed to be safe here. I didn't lock my doors. Told my girl to play outside in the summer. In the city, I'd have been worried, but here . . . what could be out here?"

"Patrice. June twentieth, 1988." Beverly doesn't elaborate. It's clearly still too painful for her to say any more.

Latoya speaks next. "My Morgan went missing June twenty-first, 1994."

"Keisha. June twenty-first, 2002," Denise adds.

We all look at Kylie.

"Kayla's next," she mumbles. "How are you going to help?"

"I'm putting together what I can." I present the best of what I have. "So far, all of your girls went missing not just in summer, but every summer on the solstice, since 1985. It's on a cycle. And they clearly have a demographic."

Beverly raises her voice slightly, making a firm point. "*Our* girls are gone the same day, but not all of them go missing on that day."

"Bev, the girl back in '95 *was* a runaway," Latoya says.

"And this girl now? Caroline? She went missing on the eighteenth, right?" Beverly asks.

"Right," I answer. Just when I thought I had something, it's gone.

Latoya cuts her eyes at Beverly. "Well, we'll have to see if another girl goes missing today." Her sarcasm bites, but her point is made.

Tanisha gets us back on track. "Whoever is doing this is connected to the police department."

"It has to be trafficking," Latoya interjects.

"I don't know about that," Tanisha contradicts.

"How else are they—"

Kylie cuts in, "I got my ass up at dawn for this?"

"Language," Beverly scolds.

"Bullshit. You could have figured that out by sitting on the corner listening to the people down here talk for five minutes. I know you haven't—I saw you lookin' at all these chairs like . . ." Kylie mocks my shocked face. "This has *been* happening, it's gonna keep happening until—" Her frustration gets the better of her. "What's it like living up on the mountain where you don't have to worry about this? Maybe all of us should move uptown, and when they start stealing white kids and eating their hearts, someone will finally give a shit!"

No one scolds Kylie for that. The whole room aches.

"How do you know their hearts are eaten?" I ask.

"Do you know *any* Black folks in this town?" Kylie lands right on a childhood wound and adds salt. Kylie smiles, happy to have gotten to me. "Say that you're out in the woods, after dark, and you hear something, a broken branch, a whistle . . . ?"

"I'd look—"

Kylie corrects me, "No, you didn't."

"What?"

"If something calls your name, if a branch breaks"—she snaps her fingers, the sound echoes—"if you think you saw something. No. You didn't. Don't give it any attention. You let it pass by you in the dark. Or it will eat you alive."

"I heard stories growing up. The man and his shadow. But that's all it is, a story," I say. That was clearly the wrong thing.

"My sister told me not to, but I looked." Kylie's anger leaves her all at once and she sinks into herself. "It called her name."

"The man?" I ask, all ready to ask for a description.

"There was a man. A hunter. But all I could look at was . . ." She goes away behind her eyes. "I thought it was a dog, didn't look like any kind of dog I'd ever seen. Didn't move like a dog."

Before I can ask its size or shape or if it looks like the hound from my dreams or if it has the large dark teeth from my memory, Beverly cuts in.

"Could have been trained—"

"It looked up at me like it knew me. Like it had been watching. I heard it call her name, and I looked," Kylie says.

Tanisha speaks up, "Don't tell me that after all these years, you think your sister was taken by a"—gripping her keys, her frustration manifests in her fingertips—"*thing* in the woods."

"Then what did I see— This is why I don't come. No one ever wants to listen to me."

"I refuse to listen to what you *imagined* as a child," Tanisha replies. "The reality is, this is a sick man who has moved under the radar." Tanisha turns to me. "Denise said you were working with a detective. Are you with the FBI?"

"Um. No. I'm just—"

"A private detective?"

"No."

Tanisha levels a look of annoyance at Denise. "If this is another damn psychic, I'm going to—"

Denise defends me. "She's helping. She's a helper."

I speak for myself. "I'm working with someone from the medical examiner's office."

Kylie laughs loudly. "Seriously? They've never helped before."

She has a point. I remember how Doug was with Oswald versus the man I just saw. Be it justice or a promotion, he wants things to change. Then I'm reminded of what spurred this meeting.

"The police are listening to me. Instead of having to fight for every little step, I—*we* can get so much closer to figuring this out."

"You trust him?" Kylie asks.

Doug has come through for me. Twice. I can't say that I fully trust him yet, but I'm on my way.

"He knows there's something shady going on and wants to find the truth."

Latoya adds, "They *been* doing shady work."

"I tried to cooperate with them," Tanisha says. "The police could have taken evidence, samples, opened cases. Unless there is something staring them right in the face, they won't do shit."

Beverly shoots Tanisha a look. Tanisha half-heartedly crosses herself.

"We're making a map." I pull out my phone. I show them the Xs and explain them. "I'm trying to put everything we have together, to see the big picture."

Kylie gets up and grabs my phone. I let her. She curls herself around the device and makes a few quick strokes. "Here." She hands it back to me and points. "Kayla."

She's made a digital X on the location. I zoom back out. It's between Keisha and Caroline. I now have a row of orange Xs. My chest sinks.

I summon all my bravery. "And where they found her?" She navigates again. Just as quickly, she scrolls out to a location near Keisha's red X.

"Tell me their names?" I ask. "Please." I know I don't have everything they need, but I'm getting closer. After a beat, the names come:

Keisha Woodson.

Kayla Montrose.

Morgan Daniels.

Patrice Carter.

Alice Walker.

Judging by the number of chairs, there are many names missing. "Who else?"

"You never know what it's like to lose a child until you do." Latoya's gaze drifts to the ground as she speaks. "Those who can leave, do. Some fall apart. Some deny it's even happened."

"We all fall apart," Beverly adds.

"Some never come back together," Latoya corrects.

I ask, "What about the community? Everyone—"

"Community doesn't want any part of this." Kylie sits back down. "You have any idea how many church ladies told me my sister was fast, and that's why she disappeared? Or, when she was found the way she was, blamed my mother?"

"How long until they found Kayla?" I ask.

"A week," Kylie says. "Said she was alive out there for a few days before."

"Alice was found the same day," Tanisha says.

"A week for Keisha," Denise adds.

"I'm still looking for Morgan," Latoya says.

We all turn to Beverly.

She doesn't offer anything about her daughter.

Instead, she says, "I don't like to think about why he keeps some of them."

All the missing pieces and unanswered questions turn up the tension in the room. Looking at this small circle, there's what these mothers think, then what the countless other families think, then the Parkers, the police. It's chaos. Purposeful chaos.

"If no one can agree, no one can unite," I say. "Try to get someone to agree to any piece of this: runaway, police negligence, possible trafficking." I look at Kylie. "A monster."

"You think you're the first person to come sniffing around?" she says to me.

"Don't scare her." Latoya waves a hand at her.

Kylie fidgets in her seat. "My mother led the search for my sister in the woods. Dad nearly broke his leg out there. Then she . . ." The room shifts uncomfortably. Kylie doesn't finish her thought.

Tanisha speaks. "It's one sick man."

"A funny man," Beverly echoes.

Kylie gets up. "If you aren't careful, your head will get to you."

Denise's sad voice comes in. "I called all the mothers I knew. Farrah was the last one to do something like this, to try to solve it."

"Where is she?" I ask.

Kylie sighs deeply. "She lost herself. She said she saw a dog. Like I did but . . ." The words fall out of her like a spell, and she is afraid of conjuring what she sees in her mind's eye. "She says she got a bad feeling in those trees over by the old Rosedale Coke plant. Like she was standing on a grave she knew nothing about. Like something was telling her to get out of the place."

A hush falls over us all. We look around, seeing who believes that. I touch my scar. It looks too big to be made by a dog. It doesn't hurt today. Just funny-feeling flesh, but I can already feel the panic mounting in the back of my neck.

"Where is Farrah now?" I ask.

"At her mother's; only person who will take care of her," Latoya says. "She can't be trusted to be on her own." She looks at my list of names. "Brittany Miller was her daughter." I write her name down slowly, taking it in.

"Can I talk to Farrah?"

"Good luck getting her to see you," Kylie scoffs.

Tanisha gets up, ready to go. "She's gonna tell you what we did, just more crazy."

The other women start to leave. Kylie rushes out the doors of the church into the morning light. I glance to Denise and she wordlessly indicates for me to follow Kylie.

By the time I exit the church, Kylie is encased in a veil of smoke. Her vape lights up as she pulls and exhales a plume. She leans against the side of the sanctuary and pulls out her phone.

"You okay?" I ask.

She doesn't even look at me. "What do you want from us? Money?"

I tell Kylie the truth. "I want to help."

She lets out a hollow laugh. "No one wants to help us." Her impenetrable expression is well-practiced and unnerving.

"I'm sorry—"

"Did you do this?"

"No."

"Then don't say sorry. It won't get you anywhere." She frowns as she reads texts. The bubbles populate her screen in a flurry. She's someone who is connected to the world in a way that I'll never be. Her nails click against the screen.

I think about pushing on seeing Farrah, but I see the time. I promised Mel I'd be out there for her.

"Do you think you and Farrah saw the same thing? The same dog?"

"I never like telling them the second part of the story."

"What's that?" Not even I know that.

"If you get taken by this man and his shadow, anyone who looks for you loses it. They go crazy 'cause they're looking for something that can no longer be found. His victims have become what's eaten them."

"The man?"

"No. The shadow." She turns her phone over in her hand, but her focus is clearly on the text chain. "I couldn't sleep at night, just sat up thinking. Looking." That explains how she pulled up the locations on the map so fast. "When they found what was left of Kayla a week later, Momma took a bunch of pills. Didn't work. A few years later, she tried again. Worked that time."

"I'm . . ." My apology dies in my throat.

"Farrah and I *think* we saw a dog. Doesn't matter if it's the same dog, it's . . ." Kylie's in her own memories, searching the wound. "We looked for the truth and it killed my mother. It's killing Farrah. We all saw something out there that we couldn't make sense of. Whatever it was, a dog or a memory, it messed us up."

It's what my therapist told me, sometimes we put things in as placeholders to protect ourselves. I rest my hand on her shoulder. Kylie lets me. Maybe it's her sadness or the residual tension from the mothers, but we share a chill. Beverly's lavender shawl slides under my touch. As it does I see the strangest thing. Something dark slips under my fingertips and curls up into my palm. I pull my hand away. Nothing. A trick of the light.

I look back at Kylie's shoulder and see what fooled me. On her deltoid is a black profile of a canine. Stylized, like a cameo. With two pointed ears.

"What's that?"

"When Mom died, I went to one of the shops here. She hated tattoos. But when I lost her, I was so numb, I wanted to feel something, anything. There was a bunch of flash on the wall and the guy kept trying to get me to pick out a rose or some crap like that. I saw that one, and I knew. He said it's Anubis. The Egyptian god of the dead. Judgment before the end. Caretaker of lost souls. Felt right."

"Why?"

"I know more than enough about death, and I believe in judgment. Whatever took my sister and did this to all these girls? Man or beast, it will see justice before the end."

"Did the dog you saw look like that?"

"I was a kid. I don't know what I saw."

"Kylie—"

"Shh. Shh." She hushes me as she pulls out her phone again. She stares at the text exchange there. "You ever meet someone and just know? Like, you know, 'This man is gonna waste my money and break my heart'? But more than that . . ." She searches for the thought. I know it all too well.

I finish her sentence, "You see how things are gonna end. Not just a feeling but something crystal clear. Like: Three years from now this man will wake up, realize he doesn't love me, but draw it out until Valentine's Day and break up with me before we head to the restaurant. I will eat dinner alone." I glance back and realize that I've managed to grab Kylie's full attention. Proud to have earned it, I hold her gaze.

"Shit."

"I have an overactive imagination."

"That's not imagination. That's a gift." Kylie taps on her phone again, multitasking like a true millennial. "Some part of you knows how things are gonna end long before they do." She puts her phone away. "So, if you have to be the one to end 'em, you know how."

TEN

What the mothers told me and what Kylie said means this has been happening for over thirty years. Ripping families apart. The dates needle at me. The mothers who were there today, their girls went missing on the first day of summer. Today. Caroline doesn't fit. If so, then the person who took her might want to group her in with all these other girls. Or she *is* just like all these other girls and they've changed things up. Or nobody took her and she's out there alone and scared.

I know the rhyme of the man and his shadow, heard it all my life. It's a story, but there are clues in it. The man is obviously a man. The shadow moves in the dark. It can come and go with no one noticing. For someone to keep this up for over thirty years they'd have to be in amazing shape. Or have help. As I arrive at the site, it occurs to me this might not be one person, but two.

Coming back to the field, I find all the decorations from the wedding are gone. The coffee station is now the most established location. The police have brought out power strips. There's a water station. The fire department is still present, but their truck is gone. A few firefighters mill about in their designated corner. Something seems different about them today.

In no time, I spot Mel. She's next to Garrett. Nick is with the other officers in heavy discussion. Mrs. Parker has resumed her usual task of cleaning. Then there's Mr. Parker. He's surrounded by officers. Looking at him now, I notice he looks strong for his age. Lived here all his life, an adept huntsman. But Garrett said Mel's parents love Caroline. Jacob

Parker might not be the man his grin makes him out to be. Then again, looking at how he smiles with both rows of teeth, maybe he's exactly what he presents himself to be. I need to get Mel alone.

Garrett spots me. "Liz!"

In the open field, there is nowhere to hide. I walk over to him and Mel. The moment I get close, Mel pulls me in for a hug.

"Stay with me," she whispers.

Nick approaches us. "I got a good feeling about today." His forced jollity is unnerving. Nothing about today feels hopeful. Everyone at the site is tense.

"You've said that every day," Mel grumbles with a sibling's familiarity.

Nick shrugs. "Today is gonna be it. Trust me," he says with a smile.

I search his face for a clue or a tell. He nods vigorously to himself, a manifestation of his anxiety. We're on day three. Our chances of finding Caroline alive have dropped significantly. I turn back to Melissa. She won't look at me because she's crying. I can tell. I give her arm a slight tug, and she rests her head against me. We watch the officers get to work.

A new car pulls up to the site. It's a regular SUV. Finally, another friend has come to help. I see two women get out and realize they're not Melissa's friends. One has dark hair and a stern face. The other is a short redhead. They aren't in uniform, but they are dressed in a way that feels "on purpose." Their pants look sturdy and their hair is tucked away under hats. The way they move tells me they're here for a job. More officers rotate in the search. The firefighters greet the women. That gets my attention. The firefighters are engaging with them, but not the officers.

Garrett rushes over. "Search and Rescue is here."

"Thank God." Mel sighs.

We all look back at the two women. One leads a leashed sandy pit bull. She makes her way toward the officers. The woman with red hair and her black German shepherd approach us. The similarity between this dog and the one in my dreams spooks me. I wonder if this could be similar to the dog that Kylie and Farrah saw.

"I'm Jessie, that's my partner, Kim, and her dog, Sadie."

Melissa smiles but gives the dog a wide berth. "Thank you so much for coming."

"Of course. We're happy to help." Jessie exudes much more comfort and confidence than the officers do. She fusses with her bangs, tucking them into her cap. Her hair is already secure. It's a tic. Something's frustrating her. "Sorry for the delay in getting out here. The department took their time giving us approval."

"We know. They've been . . . difficult," Melissa says. Jessie glances at me. I keep my mouth shut and my eyes on the dog.

"And who is this?" Melissa asks in a small voice, seemingly equally disconcerted by the large canine.

"Oh, this is Max." The big black German shepherd wags his tail at his name. Seeing this dog with its master drives home the vision Kylie told me she saw. A man and his shadow. There are plenty of intense partnerships, not just man and dog; there's boss and worker, mother and daughter, father and son.

An officer approaches us in a huff. "What are you waiting for?" he shouts at Jessie. Jessie keeps her cool.

"Excuse me?" she replies.

"You got the German shepherd. We want that dog, not the pit bull. We want to find the kid, not maul her."

Jessie's face hardens. "We train these dogs. They don't bite their targets, they signal. And that pit bull, Sadie, will find the girl alive." She refers to the dark dog at her side. "Hopefully, we won't need my dog today. We're out 'cause it's too hot to keep him in the car."

"We need all the dogs we can get," the officer says with a condescending laugh.

Jessie glances from us to him. "Max here is a cadaver dog. This is still a rescue, right?"

The officer hesitates, realizing his mistake. "Yeah—yes. It is." He heads back out.

"Come on, boy, let's get some water." Jessie and Max head toward the water station.

It looks like we'll be going in soon. I break away from Mel to grab some caffeine. At the coffeemaker, I find Nick. He tips the large thermos forward to get the last of it.

He offers me the dark sludge in his cup. "It's mostly grounds. Do you want it?"

"No. Thanks."

"Suit yourself." He adds creamer and two packs of sugar and sips his grounds to get the caffeine. His energy from before has waned. He's running out of steam. I'm reminded of Doug. Both men are desperately working their way up the ranks. Stuck.

"How deep you going in the woods?" I ask. Keisha's and Kayla's marks are at the far edge of the map.

"What do you mean?"

"What do *you* mean? Are y'all going ten, twenty, thirty miles out?"

"Caroline isn't crossing county lines." He drinks his coffee deeply.

"I forgot lost children could intuit man-made borders."

"What I mean is, if she's out there, she's not that far out." I notice he uses "if." Nick knows the search has changed.

"Do you think the dogs will help?"

"Oh yeah." Nick nods vigorously. "You ever been hunting with a dog? They know what's out there long before we do. We had Ace, he was a black Lab. That dog helped me and my dad catch five bucks one year. He was a good dog."

That stops me. "When did you have a dog?"

"It was before . . ." Nick shifts his weight around a bit, then he continues. "He, um, one Christmas, our cousins were visiting. They brought their three-year-old with them. The kid goes tottering right up to Ace like 'doggy, doggy,' you know how kids are."

“Yeah.”

“Well, Ace got spooked and lunged at the kid. Bit him right on the cheek. Nothing too deep, but it was bloody as hell.”

“Oh my God.”

“Mom patched the kid up. Dad took Ace out back and shot him.”

“Wait, he killed the dog?” I need him to repeat that.

“It attacked a kid,” Nick replies.

“Most dogs freak out around kids. They don’t know what to do with them. It made a mistake.”

Nick turns to me. He looks at me like I’m a freak and talks to me like I’m an idiot. “You can’t keep an animal around that you can’t trust. Who’s to say it won’t turn on you?” He throws his cup away and heads back out to the field.

Through the heat, I’m chilled to the bone. What’s underneath the story of Ace digs at me. Mr. Parker disposed of his trusted hunting buddy after years of loyalty because of his black-and-white sense of right and wrong. I look out at the field to see him. Mr. Parker is all smiles and cheer. I can’t stop the story in my head. Mulling it over makes me sick. What else has Mr. Parker sacrificed to his morality?

ELEVEN

"Ready?" Mel extends her hand to me. I never realized how much I associated Mel with the woods. The first time I had venison was at her house. Mrs. Parker made a stew. I remember the bits of deer tasting like grass more than any kind of meat I'd eaten before. Looking at Mel's hand now, there's dirt under her manicure. Raw spots on her palms. She's been out here facing the woods for three days. I wish I had good news to bring her. Instead, I have dead girls, a handful of coincidences, and a feeling that the only way to find Caroline is to figure out what happened to the others. I take Mel's hand. She grips mine back so hard it hurts.

Radio chatter falls to a hush. I watch the dogs dart into the trees, pulled ahead by instinct. This search has always been serious, but this feels distinctly morbid. Everyone around us adjusts. There aren't just humans looking in the trees for Caroline anymore. We all know that searches with dogs can progress for days, but something about this first sweep feels final. Officers head in after the dogs with solemn purpose.

Mel pulls me ahead.

Fifteen years ago she led me out of the woods. I was shell-shocked and she helped me craft a story to tell my mother. One look and Mel knew the piece of flesh that had been ripped out of my arm was bad. Neither of us knew any kind of serious first aid, but she knew she had to keep me talking. We agreed to tell our parents that I tripped and landed on some wood. Then she told me the rhyme of the man and his shadow. Thinking back, I remember that was the first time I heard the story. It was started by Mel and finished by Kylie. But Mel's story was almost sweet in its telling. That there was a curious creature riddled with fear. Controlled by it. Kylie told me the opposite.

Mel and I hear bits of conversation from the others around us. Including her father's loud, booming laugh. What once annoyed me now chills me to the bone. I sent Doug the rest of the names from the mothers I met this morning. With spotty service, I'll never get his reply. I stick close to Mel.

All the while, the trees crowd in around us. There are trails, but soon even those disappear. In the daylight, everything blends into the dense shadowed greenery, making even the sun seem farther away. Mel maintains a good pace, trying to get us away from the bulk of the search. She has always been my safety from the trees. Gradually, the voices muffle. And the only cries for "Caroline" are mine and Mel's.

"Mel?" I ask. "How far out has the search gone?"

"Not far enough. Have you seen anyone?"

"No." I check Doug's map. "You're taking us pretty far out."

"Good." She checks her radio. A quick squawk of chatter confirms that we are still in range. "I bet you the dogs have already led them farther than they've been in days."

"How far is that?" I double-check my phone battery. It's charged.

"They are sticking to Nick's land," she says. "It's like they're looking for something on the land and not where Caroline could have gone. Liz, when they took you to the station, did they ask you anything about me and my family?"

"No. Have they questioned you?"

"Yes." A shiver passes through Mel. "They were pissed we let the neighbors in yesterday. We made sure no one went into Caroline's room. They've been asking about Garrett's and my relationship, my parents' opinions about our wedding."

"What have you told them?"

"The truth. We're happy." Mel rubs the back of her hand over her forehead, wiping away sweat. I pause.

"You okay, Mel?"

She rests her hands on her knees for a moment. "Fine. Which way are we going?" she asks.

I check the map. "North, just north." I try to sound as sure as I can.

Mel runs her hands over the back of her neck. "Okay." We head deeper into the trees.

The rustle of squirrels and other creatures sends jolts down my spine. I swipe the air in front of me every few minutes to clear a low-hanging web or bits of foliage. I have to remind myself that all these creatures are running *from* me. Not toward me. I'm clumsy in the woods, but Mel moves with confidence and comfort.

"Do you remember Bonfire Night?" I ask.

"How could I forget?" Mel huffs as the terrain gets steep. It's vertical enough for us to need to climb at parts. If Caroline is all the way out here, someone had to have taken her.

"Why did you make me go with you?"

"I don't remember it like that." Mel laughs for the first time in days.

"I remember telling you I refused to go to bonfires because they were in the woods and I would be arrested on principle."

"I remember telling *you* that Chris Hartmann would be there and you turned the deepest shade of red I'd ever seen."

I blush at the memory.

"I never knew Black people could blush till I saw you do that." Mel laughs. I join in out of habit, but soon my smile fades. It's not funny anymore.

"Yeah . . ." My mind races back to the conversation and I remember, it wasn't funny then either. I told her so, and she gave me a flustered apology, brushing off her ignorance. She didn't deny my feelings or tell me I was being too sensitive. To me, it was a quiet but definitive moment of our friendship, because she treated me like a person. "Keisha went missing from that party."

Mel doesn't respond, she keeps navigating forward. "Caroline!"

"Keisha's not the only girl who's gone missing and been found in these woods."

"According to Nick, a lot of people get lost out here. It's too easy to get turned around." So Nick knows about people going missing out here. He'd be a good partner, if you needed one. Mel's pace is getting hard to keep up with.

"There are other girls—Black girls—who go missing this time of year and—"

"It's the end of the school year. Kids are outside more, no matter their color—anyone can get lost."

I carefully lay it out for Mel. "One girl, every summer. Some were found a week later with their chests ripped open—"

"Stop it!" Mel's intensity alarms me. "Caroline isn't dead. She's lost."

"I've just been looking into—"

"I—Liz, I asked you what you thought about the search. I didn't ask you to go on a wild goose chase."

"I'm not."

"I don't need conspiracy theories."

"I know." Looking out at the land we're going toward, something hits me. "Do kids still party out there? In that field from Bonfire Night?"

"Oh, no. Dad fenced it off." Mel rests against the side of a tree. She looks up, seeming to map something using the sun in the sky. When was Mel so good at navigating the woods?

"Why would your dad do that?" I ask.

"It's steep here, careful—"

"Your father, Mel." I keep her on task. "Why would he fence off that field?"

"He bought that land years ago, around when Caroline was born." My heart stops. The Parker land isn't just Nick's. Could that be a trigger? His daughter having a Black child? I'll have to wait for Doug to map the others, but if they are all out here, on land he bought, Mr. Parker could hide girls for years.

"Who did he buy the land from?" I ask.

"The state, I think." Mel shrugs. "Whoever had it, lost it."

I navigate down a steep bit of terrain. "What have they asked you about your dad?"

"The strangest things." Mel grabs saplings to steady her descent. "If he ever gave Caroline special attention. If he ever insisted on alone time with her. Messed-up things like that."

"Did he?"

"I don't—maybe? He loves her."

"Yeah, but, anything seem off about it? In your gut?"

Mel turns to look at me. "You're starting to sound like those detectives. What are you trying to say?"

Here we go. "Other girls have gone missing in these woods."

"That's not—I don't doubt it, it's rough out here." Mel stops walking ahead. "I mean . . . Liz, there has to be a reasonable explanation—"

"And I'm trying to tell you!" The jump in my voice startles us both. "One girl—one Black girl a summer. Starting the year we were born." Alice. 1985.

Mel is so still that I can see the effort of her swallow. She tries to put together a few words and fails.

"I wouldn't be telling you this if I didn't think this might get Caroline back." Mel and her family have had their disagreements in the past, but they are still close. Her insistence on letting the neighbors in, her delay in making the flyers. She could be protecting him.

"Liz. Stop."

"The missing girls, the ones found, have their chests ripped the same way your dad hunts—when he field dressed the deer with Garrett? He cut out the heart."

Mel snaps. "Just because your family is messed up doesn't mean that mine is!"

"Whoa! What the—" I bite my tongue. Of course she's defensive. "I'm just telling you what I found. I want to keep you safe."

"Grow up, Liz!" Mel is done. "The detectives are right." She grips the earth and climbs back the way we came. "She couldn't travel this far on her own."

"Aren't you listening to what I'm—"

"I'm telling you what the last few days here have been like. At first, I think, I wanted this to be something big and crazy, but it's not. She got lost."

"Mel—"

"The crayons are back, Liz."

"What?"

"They're back. I misplaced them. That's all. There isn't something bigger going on. Caroline is lost."

I challenge her. "They're just . . . back?"

She reaches into her pocket and shows me a blue one. It has a hole through it, like a puncture wound.

"How?"

"Must have misplaced them. Brought it as a reminder to keep my head on straight." She keeps turning back.

I reach in my pocket for the map. "This is where two of the girls were found."

She ignores me.

"Mel, look!" I push my phone in her face.

Mel grabs my phone. She walks away from me, with the map, pulling us off course.

I stop her. "Did you have a hunting dog growing up?"

Happy to be off the topic of missing girls, Mel latches on to the story of the dog. "Ace? Yeah. He was a good boy."

"Not according to Nick."

"Nick is an idiot. Don't listen to him. Ace was the best." Mel is ready to go to bat for a dog I've never heard her bring up before now. "Ace was loyal and sweet. My dad was—well, he still can be . . ." She chooses her next words carefully. "Dad has a strange . . ." Melissa gets stuck on more words. "He wants the world to make sense, his way, in his time. Even if he's wrong, especially if he's wrong. He'll try to bend the universe to his will."

"By shooting the dog?" I ask.

"Dad might have killed the dog, but he'd never do it like that. He let the dog out, fired a shot to scare him off, and then never let the dog back in."

I look at Melissa with pity in my eyes. I can smell the denial coming off her. If her father was a monster, she'd never see it.

"Mel—" I start, but she doesn't let me finish.

"I saw Ace at the back door three months later. Skin and bones. Living off the land. I wanted to give him some meat or something, but my mom told me not to. She said that if Dad saw him, he'd kill him. I gave him a pat on the head, told him he was a good boy, and shouted at him until he ran back into the woods. I never saw him again." After a moment, she pulls the crayon back out. It looks like a dog got it. Chewed it up.

"There were a lot of people in the house," Mel dismisses.

"Keisha Woodson disappeared like this too."

That gets Mel back to me. She gets right in my face. "Stop it. Stop it. Stop it! Do not compare my child to a drunk girl in the woods. Caroline is not like her! Do not lump *my* girl in with a bunch of runaways and drug addicts." It's almost like Mel has heard the same things the mothers have about their girls. "Caroline is good!"

"Just like I'm 'good'?" My anger makes me flush. With everything I'm learning, it's a miracle my mother and I have lived here unbothered for so long. Maybe it's 'cause we're . . . good. We don't make waves. If you didn't know it, you'd barely even realize that we were here. Nestled in an upper-middle-class cul-de-sac, connected to friends via phone and messengers. Even when I lived here. We've always been hidden. *Good.* I don't like the way that lives in me.

Mel shakes her head. "I didn't—I'm not—I'm heading back."

I don't let her go. "So, me and Caroline are the 'good' ones. What about all the 'bad' ones, Mel?" She doesn't stop. I grab her arm. She wrestles out of my grip.

"You have always thought this place was so backwards—Hicksville—full of rednecks!"

"It is."

"I am here! My family is here! Are you accusing me of being 'one of the good ones' too?"

"I . . . I . . ." I don't know how to counter that twist on my words.

"Ever since you moved away, you think you're too good for this place. That anyone who stays here is stupid—dumb!"

"I never said that."

"You don't need to. Not all of us want to live packed on top of one another, paying thousands of dollars to sleep in a closet, doing jobs we hate, with people we hate, where our neighbors don't care if we live or die—I want my kid to play outside without . . ." That thought stops her rant. Caroline did play outside. She was supposed to be safe. "I don't want to have to drink to live. I saw how much you drank—you always drink. Did you get drunk at the wedding— Of course you did. How is that a question? Is that why you weren't watching her? That why you lost my child? That is why you can't let this go. 'Cause you know and I know this is all your fault!"

I wait for Mel to take it back. To admit she's angry and lashing out. She doesn't. I don't ask her to.

"I'm so sorry, Mel," I say. "I want to help. I'm trying to fix this."

"Help by looking." We both realize she's still holding my phone at the same time. "Are you gonna get this map out again and chase stupid theories?"

"Give me my phone."

"Gonna use this map to accuse my dad of being a murderer again?"

"Give me the phone and we can go back," I concede. She doesn't budge. I try to grab it from her. Before I can, she hurls it into the trees.

I note where I think I heard it thud. I get on my knees and search.

"Liz?"

I keep looking. I need that map.

"Wow." Mel wipes her face. "When you get lost in here again, I don't know if anyone is going to be able to find you this time."

I stop.

I've needed a map, and she hasn't. Even now she's turning back with confidence. I always thought Mel stumbled upon me that night. I never thought she might have found me on purpose.

"Are you threatening me?"

"Forget this. This is crazy." She extends her hand to me. "Come on. Let's double back. Maybe the dogs have something."

I turn away from Mel and dig through the underbrush for the phone. My vision blurs with tears. I don't need to look at Mel to feel her shock. I was the kindly friend who always followed, who needed so little convincing, who was always happy to help. This is so much bigger than our friendship now. It's not just her daughter out here. There are so many others and they all are depending on me.

I hear her footsteps retreat. I dig faster. Her footsteps echo in the trees around me as she leaves. I keep digging. Mud curls under my fingernails. I push layers of underbrush aside and crawl, searching. Out here, this map is all I have.

Purple.

I've never been more grateful for a bright phone case. I grab my phone and swipe. It still works. Opening the map, I see the pathways. A few quick threads will lead me right to the edge of the Parker plot.

"Mel?" I call. No one answers. "Mel!" I yell. I get to my feet. I see the shelf of earth we navigated down. The field from Bonfire Night is somewhere ahead. I start to call again when I remember what Kylie said. Don't call back to anything that calls your name. Nothing has answered me, so far. All I have are my thoughts. I always thought Mel had befriended me out of the kindness of her heart. Now it looks like Mel's friendship might have saved me in more ways than I ever knew.

TWELVE

Why not me?

All my time in this town, that question followed me. Admittedly, sometimes I asked it for purely selfish teenage reasons. Like not getting asked to prom or a kid admitting she only invited me to her birthday party so nobody would think she was racist. She didn't want me there. We weren't friends.

Why not me?

I was a Black girl in this town. I believed what happened to Keisha was an accident. As I search for the site of Bonfire Night, I walk myself through my memory of it again.

Mel convinced me to go. We joined the circle some other kids were in. Keisha was in that circle. She was running it. Keeping everyone laughing. After a while it was clear that, like at that little girl's birthday party, I was being tolerated, not welcomed. I knew this had less to do with me being a Black girl and more to do with my place in the school's social hierarchy. I didn't have one. I moved around from one group to the next. Never popular. Never nerdy. People's ability to categorize me and define me was so important. I want to say it's just high school, but it seems like it's a factor everywhere.

I walked off and sat in the dark. I looked up at the stars. I named them and recounted their stories for myself. They were my way out. What were my stones to build a path? Education and time. I had to get through high school, then I could go to college and get out.

Keisha checked in on me first. She told me not to trust Mel. Then Chris sat next to me.

"What are you looking at?" he asked. Yes, it was nice to be noticed by a white boy. Admitting that to myself now, I hope it will dismantle whatever this town left in me. It doesn't. If healing is what I need, it will take time. If only it was as simple as relieving pain. Pain can be eased or numbed.

"The Summer Triangle," I said. "Chasing the Great Bear." I described the corresponding constellations. Chris listened until we both heard the shouts.

"Cops! Cops! Cops!"

Those words started a blur of events: We ran. I raced away with Chris on an ATV. He hid me in a tree. I waited in the dark. I saw Keisha's face. One look and I knew she was in far more trouble than being pursued by the police. I reached out to her. She reached out to me.

Darkness. Teeth.

Pain in my arm.

I do my best to stay in the memory. Don't let it slip by me again. Keisha reached out for me and was ripped away before she even touched me. Something else got ahold of me.

Keisha disappeared and a piercing dark tooth sank into me. It wouldn't let go. I was too afraid to scream. I pulled, digging it in deeper. I looked out into the darkness that held me. The longer I stared at it, the more something started to take shape.

Something shifts and the memory finally opens:

Upright ears. Large jaw. Claws.

A hound with a maw the size of me.

Its canine tooth hooked into my arm. To free myself, I had to lean toward it to untether my flesh. The beast stank, like brackish water and death. I freed my arm.

The memory folds back over into darkness and silence.

It makes no sense. A hound. Not a face, a voice, a smell, or a clue to who this man is was buried inside my memory? An animal. My lizard brain insists on protecting me still. Like Kylie and Farrah, instead of letting me face my trauma, in my mind, the hound remains.

I look at the map again, rolling my palm up. My scar tightens. I catch the time on my phone before I close it. 7:47 P.M. *What? That has to be wrong.* I look at the sky. It's a subtle shift, but there's no doubt about it, night is coming. I've been out here for hours. Alone. Mel and I didn't bring a pack because we thought we would have ample time to come back. I didn't grab water. Not even coffee. I should be close to passing out, but I feel fine. Not hungry. Not dizzy or tired. That's good. But, even if I turn back now, I'm not getting back to the site until well after dark. I'm close to something, I know it. The path ahead of me curves in a way that it doesn't on the map. No time to hesitate. I take it.

"Caroline!" I hear my voice echo in the woods. If you hear something call your name, no, you didn't. Clearly a legend based on an echo. Hearing it, now I understand. It is terrifying. I come up on another set of paths. This time I can't tell if they're on the map.

"Caroline!" I walk along the path and find myself in a place I've been before. I must be walking in circles, because before I know it, I'm standing at the same crossroads again. I'm in a divide that doesn't seem to be anywhere on the map. This is why they are called The Rounds. I'm lost.

I breathe.

In and out.

In and out.

"Caroline!" I call. I try again. Taking a different path, a different direction. After a few minutes of walking, I find myself in the exact same place.

"Caroline!"

I don't know how many paths I try. Pinks and oranges signal the coming sunset. I start to jog. As the sun sinks below the horizon, I run.

Trees and foliage fly past me. If I'm gonna have to try every path, I'm going to need to burn through them quickly. I scan the trees for something, a trail marker, a break in this endless cycle of forest.

Nothing.

I stop to catch my breath. I gasp it into my lungs. I feel sweat trickle down the back of my neck.

Why not me?

I shake the question away. Now is not the time for this. Now. June 21, 2017. The first day of summer. The day Black parents keep their children inside. A day I never knew about because I was never connected to the community. Latoya's remark comes back to me: *We'll have to see if another girl goes missing today!* My mouth goes dry. There *is* a Black girl lost in the woods today on the solstice.

Me.

Do not panic. Breathe.

In and out.

In and out.

I take a long inhale. In. Then exhale. Out.

Out. A second definitive exhale lets me know that I am not alone.

With all the hope I have, I cry out. "Caroline?" My breathing rumbles in the air, the loudest sound in the quiet of the woods.

In.

And out.

Out. The exhale lingers and lengthens and grows into a tone, almost like a whistle. It stops just as quickly as it starts. I look around me. I don't see anything in between the trees.

"Caroline!" I try again.

This time, the whistle answers loudly and immediately. It's so high-pitched that it could be a scream. I keep looking around me and I can't tell where it's coming from. It seems to be emanating from the trees themselves.

I run.

Feeling the darkness coming, I try to navigate toward the light. In the back of my head I know I'm running west, toward the setting sun, but at least it's a direction I know.

The forest breaks. I take the gap in the trees. When I stop to check the map, the screen of my phone illuminates something in the corner of the small clearing. A shelter. Or something like it. It looks rushed. Made of a blue tarp and rope.

I approach and step in thick mud. It sucks at my shoe. I wrench it loose and lift the edge of the tarp.

The smell hits me first.

Blood.

Then the sight.

The inside of the tarp looks like a wound. Something was slaughtered here. Recently. Whatever did this is still close by. I should get out of here, but I need to know what I've found. A deep red mass. At the edges there's a thin gray layer. It twists around, outlining the heap on the ground. My eyes try to figure it out from the center, then the sides. Moving my gaze around to the nearest point, I see something I recognize. Worms. Massive worms. I lean closer and the smell of shit shoots up my nose, correcting my error: an ashen pile of blood-splattered intestines lies in front of me. Beyond that, a deep red cone draws my eye. Still shiny and swollen with blood, I recognize that it's a liver. I can't name the other organs. Some are dark, they almost look black, others still encased in mucus. Steam rises off the large sections. I don't know if I'll be able to stomach this sight for much longer. Focus. I calculate the size of these organs. They're small enough to be human. A child? To figure out this sick puzzle, I rest my hand over my gut and imagine what lies under my skin. I compare them. The inside of this once-living being is sour and meaty all at once. My stomach flips. I leave the tarp.

Outside, I breathe in fresh air.

In and out.

In and out.

A low hum of a growl stops me. I turn and see a huge black dog on the path. Oh God. I press on my scar to make sure this is real. No. It can't be real. My arm aches. The dog remains. It looks much more solid than a shadow. I try to blink the image in front of me away. The black dog runs toward me. It's smaller. Not the beast from my dreams.

"Max!" That's Jessie. I look again. Max sits right in front of me. Flashlights bounce over me as the search party rushes in.

BRITTANY

June 2012

Brittany Miller was a star. That was clear from her very first dance recital. Other children tottered around the stage and had to be wrangled by the instructors when the music played. Some shrank with stage fright. Most sat and watched the audience as much as the audience watched them. Brittany came alive under the lights.

More than understanding and regurgitating steps, she embodied them. There was adult comprehension in her child's body. Farrah saw this and knew. She was going to get her daughter to greatness.

Farrah had been born and raised in Johnstown. She had a small life. I don't mean this in pejorative terms. Farrah thrived in the box of her existence and never dreamed of anything bigger. It felt too uncomfortable. She saw how Brittany was the opposite. She would be stifled by a small life. Her shine was made to be seen by millions.

There were studios and classes in Johnstown, but if Brittany wanted success, she'd have to get to a city. Farrah threw herself into the task. Brittany had to have all the classes, the cross-training, the hair and costumes. Farrah's husband didn't understand any of this "dance thing" but he knew it mattered to his girl, so he became a dance dad. He learned how to tie tight ponytails and break in toe shoes.

As her parents learned how to support her, Brittany learned something else. As she progressed in her dance skills and became more and more professional, she learned how spaces tolerated certain kinds of Blackness. Her mother's office job, her father's security job, and dance all loved the kind of Blackness that could be categorized, qualified, and controlled. Her mother could make sassy remarks, her father could be strong and stoic, and she could hold rhythm in tights that didn't match her skin color while positioned all the way stage right. The only way for her to get closer to the center was to strive for whiteness, knowing she'd never attain it. What is a little erasure if it ensures excellence? It's just a little bit of yourself. The bit that doesn't fit.

"She'd make a lovely ballerina one day. Just work on her lines." The woman who said this was so thin it was concerning. Her blond hair fell over her eyes, obscuring her expression. She swiped away her bangs like a habit. Though the blonde sat with the other mothers watching the classes change over, Farrah couldn't identify exactly which child belonged to this woman. Honestly, she was too upset to look closely. There was no "one day" for Brittany. She was a ballerina at that moment.

"The teacher says her lines are the best in the class." Farrah smiled to temper her anger.

"Hmm." A wordless judgment from the woman shut down the conversation. Farrah was quick to scoop up her daughter and get her to the next class. Unfortunately, Brittany heard this slight woman and saw her full-toothed, condescending smile. Brittany had long suspected her brilliance, but never owned it. Teachers took notice, choreographers would give her extra turns and more leaps just to watch her do them. While a sullen mother's comment should have easily rolled off her back, like most childhood traumas, it landed in her gut.

The girls in dance showed Brittany how to hide her food. How to measure herself. There was no talk of the consequences of this: the pain at night when she'd grow hungry or how she would get tired. But Brittany was ready to sacrifice anything to this god of dance. Her blood came at the end of the summer and by that winter, her body started to change. The thoughts in her head about what she ate and when and how much became constant. Farrah made sure Brittany had food, good food. She prided herself in the meals she made for her daughter. When Brittany restricted them, Farrah took it personally.

The fight that broke out between Brittany and Farrah was surprising because Brittany won. She did so using her mother's logic: If she was going to win, she had to excel at walking the tightrope of success. If she was going to feel the joy of dancing, she'd have to fit into the role it asked of her. It didn't matter what her genetics were or who her family was. When Farrah heard this coming out of her daughter's mouth, she began to doubt if success and therefore happiness required this actual winnowing away of self.

"Don't let anyone make you small," Farrah said, knowing full well that that was far from a simple desire.

Brittany had imagined how she'd leave the town for years, but she never enacted her plan. She knew summer was the best time. There'd be no one keeping tabs on her in school. Dance had a lull before summer classes. Her preteen brain convinced her to buy a bus ticket and run to the city. Any city.

After months of saving up her allowance and packing her bag, after rehearsal Brittany did a test run to the end of her block just as the streetlights turned on. No farther. She was testing her resolve. Standing in the yellow light, she looked out at the dark path to the bus station and saw her carefully planned future: She'd arrive in New York City the next day, she'd get a room in a hostel, audition for dance companies, and build a life away from her family working as a waitress in a restaurant in Times Square. One day her family would see her on TV and all would be forgiven.

Even as she crafted that lie of a life for herself, she felt her heart ache. If she did this, she'd never get to share her joy with her mother and father. The woman who saw who she was on stage as a toddler and the man who worked hard to make her happy. What was any achievement without their smiling faces in the audience? Brittany turned back. She would have to wait her turn. Get to the city when she was supposed to. Have a name when it was her time. She headed home.

"Brittany Miller." The shadows were out, and they called her name. The Fellow and I ensured she'd never have one.

I often focus on their hearts. I remember Brittany's limbs. She did have good lines. In mourning her, I placed her body in an image of symmetry. I usually never touched them after. The Fellow's son noticed. He didn't say anything. So different from his father, he rarely spoke to me. He looked. Watched.

When the Fellow aged, his son kept our bargain. My New Fellow brought me hearts. I gave him purpose. He liked to watch me consume them. He studied the mechanics of me like he could figure me out. I often wondered if his heart could teach me his curiosity, but I knew better than to take his, even if offered. The Girls' lessons had schooled me about men like him. No matter how I felt, the promise between us was tenuous, at best. He continued to keep his end of the bargain, and I'd keep mine.

Brittany's heart taught me about hunger and how it is used to keep a body in check. If I was to ever be more than a shadow, I needed to eat and eat well.

Brittany Miller Scholarship Fund 2016

[A PHOTOGRAPH OF BRITTANY MILLER: Young ballerina in a pink tutu, matching tights and shoes. Hair in a tight bun. She's mid-pirouette.]

Give the gift of continuing dance education with a charitable donation toward the Brittany Miller Scholarship Fund. Founded by the Miller family in 2013, in remembrance of their daughter, Brittany, the fund hopes to give students opportunities in the community and beyond. Your generosity is critical in ensuring this support. Donations go directly to scholarships, travel costs, and dance supplies. With your help, we can make dance education accessible for all.

UPDATE: Due to unforeseen financial difficulties, this will be the final year of the Miller scholarship. In three short years, the fund has helped 15 local dancers pursue their dreams both here at home and abroad.

THIRTEEN

"What were you doing out there?" The detective sitting across the table from me leans back in his plush gray office chair. He's getting comfortable, and he wants me to do the same. That's what this room is supposed to do. It's filled with familiar trappings: The white table between us and the speckled linoleum flooring are the same as at the high school, the gray paint is the same color as the walls at the DMV. The chairs are like ones from an office. But, the uniformed man in front of me never lets me forget that, while the placard on the door says *Interview Room #2*, this is an interrogation.

He waits for my reply. I finish my third bottle of water since they found me in the woods. They offered me trail mix, but I only want to rehydrate. My eyes land on his face. He looks like a carbon copy of most people in this town. Fleshy and, if you don't know any better, soft. Round features, rounded edges in his haircut. If you get close enough, you can sense power lurking underneath.

"Looking." The end of the word hooks in my throat, making me gag. I swallow. "For Caroline." I make a pathetic attempt at chewing my saliva to keep my jaw busy and my mouth shut. Both of us know what we saw in that tarp. "Why wasn't the—that area part of the search?"

"It was today. Anything particular lead you that far out?" His practiced even keel begs me to add my own emphasis.

"A feeling." That's not a lie.

"Search and Rescue caught a scent, pulled us that direction for over an hour." He shuffles a crisp manila folder between his hands, debating whether he's going to set it down between us. No label on the tab. Another school supply.

"There was . . ." I struggle to keep the image of what was in the tarp out of my head. "Was that—what was that?"

"Those canines track death, Miss Rocher." It's not an answer, just more information.

"Do I smell like death?" is all the rebuttal I can muster. I press the back of my hand into my nose and inhale. A short sniff proves I smell the way I know I smell. Earth and salt and stress.

He looks back at me, eyebrows raised. "Not me you should be asking."

"What was in the . . . the . . . ?"

"You don't know?"

I feel the urge to speculate, but think better of it. I start to think better of all of this. I've been easygoing, easy to work with and easy to trap. They have my fingerprints and my DNA from the wedding.

"Human?" I ask.

"I can't tell you that, but I can tell you that it's of interest."

"Am I? If you think that I have anything to do with this, you're wrong. There are other girls who went missing like Caroline—dig into them."

"What are their names?"

Of all the names I've learned, the person that's been kept from me rings loudest. Kylie and the mothers won't tell me where she is. Maybe he can.

"Farrah Miller's girl," I start.

The detective's hardened visage cracks. "Don't tell me Farrah put you up to this." His voice gets low. "I worked that case—her daughter's case—it was awful. Terrible. But it's closed."

If he wants facts, I can give them to him. "Someone is taking girls. They are abducting Black girls, ripping out their hearts, and dumping them in the woods."

"Stop." He opens the folder. "I thought I'd heard everything, but this is . . . this is sick."

"I know! But it's true." I beg, "Her daughter, Brittany—"

"Your prints are at the scene." He lays photos from the folder in front of me. They're of the intestines in the tarp.

"I was the one that found 'the scene.'"

"Both scenes."

"Like I said, I found them. Of course my prints are there."

He leans back in his chair, taking the photos with him. Too used to searching for clues, my eyes follow them. His head tilts. He noticed that. I'm reminded of what Doug said to me. They are looking for the path of least resistance. And right now, I am standing in the middle of it. Like an idiot.

"Am I being accused of something?" The phrase sounds better on TV than it does coming out of my mouth.

"I'm giving you the chance to do the right thing. We are going to do our due diligence here." He stands. "Are you sure you don't have anything you want to tell me?"

"Yeah. I won't be in here again without a lawyer."

Out in the waiting room, every face I glance at has eyes on me. No question about being watched here. I'm the girl who found a death-tent in the search for a missing child. As much as it makes my insides hurt, I search my memory of the scene for something, anything, that tells me who or what was in that tarp.

I wait for my mother to gather me from the station. I know I have done nothing, but I also know people have been detained and convicted for less.

I do my best not to sprint when Mom comes to pick me up. For the second time in days, she's arrived in her pajamas to grab me from the police station. Just like before, our drive home is silent. I lock my gaze on the world outside my passenger window like one of the bits of nature we pass could pull me out of this car. Out of this reality.

Driving back up the mountain, I realize how flat the town is. In both height and feel. There are no towering skyscrapers here, nothing is more than two or three stories. And the color seems dimmer. I know I found this place dull, but has it always been this hazy? It feels like I'm watching this world through a fog.

We pull into the driveway, and she turns the car off. Like the detective, she waits for me to answer. Unlike him, she doesn't need to ask me any questions.

"Mom, I . . ." As a child, I developed a nasty habit of lying. About anything. Stupid things. It took me years to learn how to get away with it. One night, after I'd barely made a dent in a massive helping of peas, I scraped them off my plate and hid them under the raised lip at the bottom, making a small mashed disc. Then, while cleaning, I swiped it all into a paper towel and carried it to my room. The next day, as I walked to school, I dumped the remains in my neighbor's flower garden. While that was overkill, I'd convinced myself. That was key. Consequences followed. Deer were drawn to the peas. The neighbors weren't able to get rid of them for years. Later, I'd move on to lying about if I'd finished my homework, how I sliced open my arm, if I went to that party in the woods, why my grades were slipping in college, why my fiancé and I broke up.

"You said you were staying here to help Melissa," my mother starts. "Is this helping her?"

"Yes." I feel my face flush.

"It does not look like it." She shakes her head. "At the police station again, Elizabeth, what will people think?"

"I don't care about gossip."

"When your name is in other people's mouths, they twist it up. They make you into something you are not. When people take you outside yourself, that is when trouble comes."

"Trouble is already here!"

She meets my eyes. "Do not raise your voice at me."

"I'm not. I'm . . ." *Breathe*. The dark of the car closes in around me. The need to escalate sits beyond my fingertips. If I'm not careful, I will yell again and she's not who I want to shout at. The skin on my wrist pulls tight as I curl my hand into a fist.

"There's something wrong. I'm trying to help." The words aren't enough. I want to scream that something is wrong and if no one fixes it, everything I've learned, everyone I've spoken to, every story I've heard would all be for nothing.

"Elizabeth"—her concern calms me—"I know it was hard for you to come back here. You do not like coming home." She lets out a decided breath. "But this is unacceptable. Get things in order and make a plan."

"I am." It's a struggle not to scream.

"No. A plan to return to your life." After years of avoiding my mother, finally she is the one who is asking me to leave.

I reach up to turn on the light of the car. "It's too dark." As my fingers slide to find the button, I feel them tremble with frustration.

"Elizabeth?" She wants an answer.

"I will. I will." I repeat the lie, so I believe it. "Mom, did you ever . . ." With all the mothers I've spoken to in the last few days, I've had no time for my own. "Hear anything about the woods?"

"Elizabeth, I am trying to have a serious conversation with you—"

"Anything about girls—Black girls going missing?"

My mother holds her hand up to silence me. "Elizabeth, I have not heard of such things here and I do not need to now." She gets out of the car and I follow her. "I learned the lessons my mother taught me: Do not go seeking the devil and he will not find you."

I didn't sign up for an impromptu sermon. "I'm not looking for the devil."

"You doubt," she replies. "Doubt can open a door in you for anything to walk through." Despite the differences between my parents, they both agree that doubt is the greatest enemy. For the Catholics, it's Doubting Thomas. For my father's Evangelical church, it's the trail of an altar call. Both seek to obliterate this evil spirit. I admit, that is exactly what doubt feels like: a tightening in your chest, a restless mind, a shadow in the corner of your eye.

"This isn't about God." I sigh.

"Everything is, Elizabeth."

I think of the entrails. If I concentrate, I saw intestines, lungs, liver. No heart.

"How big is a child's liver?"

"Elizabeth—"

The organ was dark, shiny, and approximately the size of my two fists put together. "How many fists?"

She gives me a withering look. "No more than five inches."

"Thank you." So if those organs aren't Caroline's, what or whose are they?

In the quiet of my room, all that Mel said finally has time to revisit me. She left me alone in the woods. Something broke then. I want to sleep. No, I want to be numb. I end up counting the hours until dawn. I work with the uncertainty named by my mother. My test isn't one of faith. It's of myself. Not if I should stay or go, but what to do next.

I look at my heavy suitcase in the corner. The bag I strained to lift days ago. I roll out of my bed like a cat. I open it. Beneath my jeans I feel a hard, cool roundness. This is just to sleep. To take the edge off the day. I reveal a pile of tiny glass bottles. Keeping liquor in small containers means I can ration it. Control it. I grab two. Three. The vodka burns down my chest like the bitter medicine that it is. I lie back down and wait. I wait for swimming drowsiness to come. As it does, a stray thought floats to the surface: *What if I only get away with how much I lie because of how much my mother lies to herself?*

FOURTEEN

I can't pinpoint when I started to dream, but before I know it, I'm in it: It's hard to know it's one because the vision itself is dark.

Pure darkness.

My eyes attempt to penetrate the black surrounding me. I can't even see my hand in front of my face. There's ground under my feet, but it's more of a suggestion than anything I can stand on. I test my luck. The thin layer supports me.

I look around. Nothing.

I wait.

And wait.

While I'm still waiting, I explore. I walk. The void stretches out in front of me. I keep going.

I see it.

A strange shimmer in the black.

It looks like a curtain or a web of strings. I reach out for it and make contact. When I pull it, the whole void morphs around my fingers. It puckers and tightens and, for the first time, the space gets smaller. I let go of the curtain, but it doesn't let go of me. It envelops my hand, light as a feather, converting my limb to darkness. Like an itch you can't scratch, I can't shake it away. Cool night continues to climb up my body. I shiver. I try to tear it off, but I'm only successful in tearing at my flesh. It doesn't hurt, the meat of me sloughs off with ease. Pain is replaced with numb.

With no muscle or sinew, the darkness finds a new home in my bones. That's when the cold sets in. I open my mouth to scream and it tries to climb in there too. I don't let it. I bite my lips shut so hard that I taste blood.

Afraid to breathe in, I feel the cold and the dark moving over me. I can't stop it. But, I can't hold my breath forever.

I gasp in air.

The moment I do, I'm back in my dream. The dream from before.

I'm running.

Always running.

Forever running.

Gasping for breath, I've come to rest at the end of the cul-de-sac, standing right in front of the woods. I check my flesh. It's back on my bones.

Snap!

I turn to the woods and I see the hound. But this time, I see a shimmer of darkness behind it. The hound isn't emerging from deeper in the woods, it's stepping out from behind this curtain of night. Before my eyes can focus on the curtain, it's gone, and the hound is in front of me. It looks at me, waiting. We both know how the rest of this goes. I move my weight to my toes and

start

to

run.

FIFTEEN

Caroline's Fourth Day Missing

Eat'n Park was one of three destinations I was allowed to frequent as a kid without question. Church was boring and school always felt strange after hours. Plus, Eat'n Park had freshly baked smiley face cookies. A smorgasbord of Americana: twenty-four-hour breakfast, every kind of sandwich, free refills, stickies (dense grilled cinnamon rolls covered in syrup), and every food I was never allowed to eat at home. Mel and I would go there and sit for hours, nursing lemonades and picking over our breakfast feasts. We'd always finish with cookies. She'd press in the frosting of the eyes before she ate them, watching the color spill out from under her thumb, blinding the cookie to its fate.

Smiley face cookies seem like a good start to an apology. But, after picking up a dozen first thing in the morning, I don't know if I'm the one who should be saying sorry. By the time I reach Mel's front door, the cookies have gone cold and my anger has gone hot. It sits in my throat like a fishbone, poking me with my every movement. She shouldn't have left me in the woods, no matter how upset she was. I shouldn't have pushed my findings on her, no matter how concerned I was. *Am.* Now we both need to come to an understanding. Solving what happened to all those other girls is the only way to save her daughter.

If she's still alive.

If they had found Caroline, Mel would have told me. No matter how pissed she is at me. The detective never confirmed what the entrails in the tarp were. Only that the dogs followed the smell of death. Some of the girls were found a week later. Caroline has been gone for four days. We're running out of time.

I knock on the door of Mel's house. No one answers. I ring the bell. Nothing. I press against the door itself and it creaks open. Oh no. I'm not walking through an open door. I don't care whose. What if Melissa forgets she has a Black best friend and freaks out? It's a silly anxiety. She has a Black husband. Still, I stay on Melissa's doorstep with the cookies.

"Liz?" I hear from behind the crack in the door. It's Nick. "What the hell happened?" He opens the door but doesn't let me in.

"I brought cookies."

Nick doesn't budge. The silence of the house behind him feels settled. This is what this home will be like from now on.

"Where's Mel?" I ask.

"What are you doing here?"

"I need to talk to her."

"No." He leans against the doorframe, turning himself into a wall between me and the inside of the house. He's out of uniform in jeans and a T-shirt tucked into the waist. He has a pack of cigarettes folded into the sleeve of his shirt like some '80s teenage heartthrob. I see that the flag on his hand isn't the only tattoo he has. A blurry bloom of an American traditional chipper ship sits on his arm. Above the ship are stars. Summer stars.

"Summer Triangle?" I point to the constellations on his arm.

He shrugs. "I guess."

"You're the one who put it on your skin." The man who's doing this might know those stars. He'd definitely know the woods. He'd also be both connected to the department but small enough to disappear, like a shadow. "Shouldn't you be at the site?"

Nick shakes his head. "I'm right where I'm needed." He crosses his arms and settles in, just like the detective who interviewed me. This time, the gesture makes me uncomfortable.

"Is she here or at the—"

"She hasn't told you?" He's not as good as the detective at keeping his emotions at bay. No wonder he hasn't advanced in the ranks. "Thought you two were close." The sarcasm in his voice makes my blood boil. She's clearly told him about our fight. "What are you doing, Rocher?"

"What do you mean? I— "

He never lets me get a sentence out. "She said you have some crazy ideas about this search. Said you think we're messing things up on purpose. Said you were comparing Caroline to runaways and troubled kids." Nick rubs the stubble around his mouth. His lips part and I notice that he's someone who has pronounced canine teeth. "We have everything under control."

"Garrett got the dogs. You're not looking everywhere, in every way you can," I challenge him. "Or is getting this solved *your* way and your promotion more important?"

His tone darkens. "Don't put those words in my mouth." There is always a violence to Nick. He keeps it controlled but he unnerves me. "Just because you lost her doesn't mean you get to blame someone else. We're fixing the mess you made. Caroline isn't your daughter, she isn't your blood."

"She's yours. What are you doing to bring her home?"

Nick takes a quick step toward me. I lurch back.

"What are— "

He does it again, and I fumble the cookies. I wind up to slap him, but that's exactly what he wants.

I lower my hand. "Are you fucking high?"

"Go ahead." He grabs my wrist and places it back near his face. "Fight me!"

I jerk away at those words. Ripping my arm out of his hand, I drop the cookies. They scatter over the front steps. I massage my wrist where he grabbed me, the flesh red and tender.

"Why did you— You made me do that— " I get out, but I'm still rattled.

"Alex Edwards." Nick unearths my ex's name. "He was supposed to be your plus-one at the wedding. The two of you had a domestic disturbance call February fourteenth. Both sustained injuries. You had some nasty bruises on your neck. But he was . . ." Nick gives me a knowing look. "Liz, what did you do to him?"

Breath escapes me as his words pull me back to four months ago.

"I'm not giving you another chance to be alone with Mel."

"I am not—"

"Alex said you're unrecognizable when you get angry."

"You talked to him?"

Nick shrugs. "Just wanted to know what you've been up to."

"He . . . he . . ."

The back of my neck aches at the memory of being yanked backward by my hair. Alex always liked my hair long. I never thought he'd use it to tip me off balance and roll me under his weight. When he started to press on my neck, I didn't fight. Everyone thinks they'll scratch, or bite or claw. When faced with death, you are supposed to choose life. *Fight!* His words rattled all the broken pieces of me. He needed me to fix this for him. *Fight me!* He needed my anger to justify his violence. An angry Black woman can be put down without a second thought. A weak Black woman is shameful. When I started to cry he looked annoyed. I don't know what I was more embarrassed about, the fact that I found myself in an abusive relationship or the fact that when faced with death, I didn't fight. I named things to stay conscious, but I could barely make out any shapes in the dark. So I named how I got there:

Blind date.

Whirlwind romance.

Pushed limits.

Fast proposal.

Promotion.

His anger always came out around my job. When we were dating, I thought it was cute that he was jealous of my work schedule. I thought he wanted more time with me. I was wrong. The better my job was, the harder I was to control. I'd be making more money than he was, doing a job that didn't matter, selling wine. Looking at the cracked white plaster ceiling of my apartment, I longed for the stars. No one tells you how long it takes to strangle someone. As I began to fade, my head rolled toward a tall shape in the corner. My floor lamp. A large modern disk with a sharp edge. I felt the cord running under my spine and arm. I wrapped my hand around it and pulled.

Snap!

A dislodged flicker of filament flashed light in my dark apartment before the heavy metal lamp came crashing down on the back of his head. After a moment, he stumbled off of me and searched for his phone to call 911. I didn't need to look at the wound to know it was bad—the amount of blood over both of us told me that. The shame never fully subsided, but another emotion came in.

Pride.

When the cops came to take statements and the EMT patched him up before loading him into an ambulance, everyone asked me what I'd done. Like Nick, they saw me as some monster who lashed out. I didn't mind. A monster could defend itself. Neither of us pressed charges, both too ashamed to show up in court. We avoided each other while he moved out of my place. No one needed to know the truth—I didn't fight. In the burst of light before the lamp fell, my entire apartment was illuminated, except for one distant corner.

In my periphery, there was a settled shadow. It had no need to move. I want to say it had no shape, but it did. Like a well-trained dog, it sat still, like it had always been there. Watching.

My tears speckle the stones of Mel's landing, pulling me out of the memory. My hands race to the sore spot at the nape of my neck, where it's still tender, where it might always be tender. I breathe. Hard. To remind myself that I can.

In and out.

In and out.

I look up and see Nick's weight shift back. He's on the defensive now. He was so ready to fight with words and fists, not tears. He watches me the way Doug does. Like he's trying to remember something about me from a dream or a memory. He also looks at me the way Alex did. Both men have empty blue eyes. My pain annoys them.

I hate that I'm crying in front of him. "It was dark. I didn't want to die."

"Liz." My first name sounds wrong in his mouth. "We're searching at the site and in the lab. If you have anything to do with this, beyond losing Caroline . . . I'll rain hell down on you." After a beat of mutual understanding, he shuts the door in my face.

He's right. Why do I think I can do this? Any of this? How am I going to fight for anyone when I can't even fight for myself? I look at my feet. Cookies cover the porch. I go to gather up the ones that haven't been crushed. On my knees, scraping together crumbs, the sugary chemical smell of them rises. I grab them by the fistful and they crumble between my fingers, mixing with the dirt. This mashing of food and earth should disgust me, but I'm suddenly starving. I bring a handful to my nose, I realize I'm attracted to the earthy smell, not the cookies.

Something red flickers in the corner of my eye. Not a shadow. I turn and see a sole ember smothered in the grass.

Cigarette butts.

There are only three smokers in the family: Nick, Mr. Parker, and Garrett. I stop gathering the cookies and gather the butts instead.

And Mel? Fighting or not, I need to get her away from them. If they did this to her child and others, what might they do to her out there? Nick's threat fresh in my mind, I'm reminded that the cops have my DNA and my prints. But they don't know that I have Doug.

SIXTEEN

A chipper white woman yells from somewhere beyond the threshold, "I have some snacks ready if you're hungry." She totters off back into what I assume is the kitchen or dining room.

I'm in the entryway of Doug's house, not the ME's office. I can't be seen at the station. Doug promised to run home on his lunch break to meet me. Kicking off my shoes, I walk into the hallway. His home is straight out of a time capsule. A quick glance at the ceiling and I see it's that sculptural-looking stucco stuff that was popular in the 1990s. As a kid, my fingers longed to caress those dusty ridges. The wallpaper is something floral and '70s. The hardwood floors shine. I move out of the hallway and find myself in a kitchen. The mid-century is strong in this house. Fashionable mint kitchen appliances hum with heat and use.

The woman in the kitchen isn't making snacks, she is making a feast. It's almost like she knows I'm starving. Her skinny jeans and modern blouse assure me I haven't time traveled. I see a small plate of baby carrots and ranch. I hate ranch. It makes my empty stomach turn. My gaze lands on the shadowed back door. There rest women's sneakers and a pair of men's boots. Both are desperately muddy.

Seeing her fully, I recognize her instantly. "You were at Mel's. Your Pyrex burned me."

"Yes! I'm Kirsten. Doug's wife." Something dings. She does a little footwork as she dances around the kitchen. It's too precise to be a habit. She must have been trained, a ballerina by the looks of her. She is a tiny woman with a large presence. I spot a barrette in her hair. "How are your hands?"

I show her. Her eyes go straight to the scar on my wrist. I do my best not to be awkward about it, but she is staring. Most people ask me if it was some playground injury or a sports thing.

"Shark attack," I say.

She gives me a short laugh before her smile fades. "How is Melissa doing? Must be a nightmare for her. After all that perfection, this is . . . She must really be leaning on you."

"Um." I'm a good liar, but lately it's gotten harder to think of plausible answers. "She's, um . . ."

"Did they find Caroline?" She leans in.

I try to respond, but I honestly don't know. The detectives haven't told me what's in the tarp. But because the dogs found it, I know some part of that bloody mess is human. Mel has stopped responding to my messages. No mention of Caroline or if the search is still going.

"I don't know. She won't talk to me." It's the kind of thing you confess to as a drunk girl in the bathroom in that unspoken camaraderie between women.

"You'll find your way back to each other. I'm sure," she says. Something dings again and she returns to her cooking. I lean against the counter. The linoleum feels worn but cared for. Kirsten takes a sip of what looks like chardonnay. I can smell its buttery notes from where I stand. I have half a mind to ask for a glass. Before I can, the door opens.

"You're here!" It's Doug. Just like his wife, he's a little too excited to see me. He stands in a darkened doorway leading to the garage. The light and warmth from the kitchen seem to be the only thing illuminating this home.

He carries a large box in his hands. "We can head down to the basement. There's more space down there." I follow Doug.

At the edge of the basement steps, my stomach clenches around itself. I stop. It's probably from hunger. I will myself forward.

Doug's basement isn't covered in red string, far from it. It's very clean, organized, and put together. There's the requisite comfy chair, a TV, and a video-game system. They're all piled in one corner. A thin layer of dust reveals their lack of use. The other side of the space has laundry. A dryer rumbles and warms the basement. In the far corner is a bookshelf. I look and see heavy medical textbooks. History of Johnstown. Some books on the flood. A few beach reads.

Unrelenting sunlight pierces the basement window and creates a small spotlight on the worktable between us. Doug puts the box he carried in on the floor and pulls out the map from earlier.

"It's a lot," he warns. I nod. He spreads it out between us. Its vast expanse is filled with red and orange Xs. It mocks me. An X for where each girl was taken and an X for where she was found. If she was found.

Doug starts to take out documents in stacks. "I made copies, but this is everything I have on the girls whose names—"

I cut to the chase. "What was in the tarp?"

"Deer guts." His nose shrivels at the thought of the smell. "But the dog scented. Oswald's breaking it down. Wouldn't be the first time someone tried to cover up a crime scene with animal remains."

"So there are human remains?"

"Not necessarily, could be blood. Human blood. Dogs can tell the difference. Up to us to identify whose."

"That's why they wouldn't tell me." Nick said they were checking the woods and the lab. They must have samples of whatever human they found.

"What?" Doug looks genuinely perplexed.

I catch Doug up on all of it, Mel and I in the woods. Garrett and the deer. My interview with the detective. My run-in with Nick. That I was the one who found the tarp.

"What about the plate you had me run?" he asks.

"Oh. That. A jealous girl. She was watching my house to see if I was hooking up with some guy. Like staking out, late at night."

"You got that plate in the dark?"

"Yeah, as she was speeding away." I laugh.

Doug doesn't find it funny. "Not many people can do that. Chase down a car, catch the plate number, and remember it?"

"I'm observant, always have been." I move us off this topic. "Speaking of, thirty-two years moving under the radar? This is at least two people. Two generations."

"Keeping a secret like this is a one-man job. If our man started young and stayed in shape. Got smarter." Doug thinks. "Also, consistency. The same man who did this, did this and this." He points to locations on the map. "You'd be shocked by the amount of damage one man can do over a lifetime." Doug continues to make his stacks. Transcripts. Crime scene photos. Articles.

My phone chimes.

It's Chris. How are you? Any news?

I quickly turn it off and look back at Doug, only to find him staring at my phone. I can tell he wants to ask, and I can imagine the reason why. He's just taken materials from the department at my request. He's putting his job on the line. I owe it to him to prove he can trust me.

"High school friend. We reconnected at the wedding. He's checking in on me," I say.

"He?" Doug is genuinely curious. There it is again, everyone's obsession with marrying me off.

"Don't worry, Chris Hartmann has enough interest in this town. He isn't after me."

I look back at the map and see the path Chris led me down, where his father's house must be. I find the red X indicating where Keisha's body was found. Looking at where the tarp is, there is a triangle between Keisha, Chris, and that tarp. I don't like them in this proximity to one another.

"Nick said you all were looking in the lab. Any DNA?" I ask.

"Nothing yet."

Finally, I offer what I have. "If something comes up, can you run these? They belong to either Mr. Parker or Nick. Or Garrett. But they weren't in his usual spot beside the house, or the same brand I've seen him with twice now. I'm pretty sure these belong to one of the Parker men." I show him the plastic bag. "Cigarette butts. From outside Mel's house."

Doug stops in his tracks. "I can't test those. Do you know how illegal—"

"No one needs to know how you got them."

He looks at the loose cigarettes. With a heavy sigh, he gets up and digs through one of the drawers and comes back with a plastic bag. He double-seals the butts inside.

"We'll see," he says. He still takes them.

I worry for him. "Be careful. Look at each of these cases. Fumble after fumble." I gesture to all the papers on the table. "It's on purpose. It has to be."

Doug is done stacking. Articles. Autopsy reports. Transcripts. I read them all.

"So many mothers went to the police," I mumble.

"They didn't listen," Doug says. He continues to mark up the map. I move to the stack of photos. I grab the stack closest to me.

"Wait! That's—"

It's too late. It's a crime scene photograph of Brittany Miller. For all the descriptions of the girls, I've never seen what is done to them with my own eyes. She's lying on the forest floor. Open. Like a riddle, her arms positioned at her sides, palms up. Her legs are open. Her body is pulled open. I feel like I should look away, but as much as the image is horrific, it's arresting. Everything looks too red. Her rib cage yawns in perfect symmetry. Though blood congeals in her chest, her heart is missing. This is not how I imagined it. She's not ripped open, she's been meticulously destroyed. Her face is intact. No gnawed-out eyes or gnashed-up cheeks. No animal activity. There never was. I shuffle till I find another photo. Alice Walker. Tanisha's girl. Her undamaged face and limbs let me know she's a child. The rest of her is like the deer. A bloody mess. I can barely tell what is supposed to be there and what is missing. I turn the picture over, but it's in my mind before I can push it away.

"I need some air." I race up the stairs. I need to figure this out before it's too late. Before Caroline gets swept under the rug like all the others.

In the kitchen, I find Kirsten. She's sneaking more wine. Both of us caught, we try to explain our presence away.

"It's so hot out—" she mumbles.

"I just needed some air!" I shout.

She nods.

I notice the glaze in her eyes. She glides across the floor and grabs another glass. She pours another one for herself and one for me.

"Wanna head to the patio?" she says as she walks past me, anticipating my answer. I follow her.

The same MO, different executions. I disagree with Doug. I am looking for a pair of killers. But one girl every summer, what killer behaves like that? I'm not an expert, but I am a woman in my thirties. I've consumed enough true crime to know that killers operate in sprees and have cool-off periods. For someone, let alone *two* people, to be so calculated and controlled feels strange. If one keeps the other in check, if there is an agreement between the two, or a belief. Faith? With the solstice, something about this feels like equal parts worship and rage.

Outside, a muggy afternoon greets us. Kirsten hands me my glass and holds hers out for a toast.

"To what?" I ask.

"To whatever you and my husband are working on down there."

I toast.

I sip my wine slowly, not wanting to be rude, but not wanting to be as drunk as Kirsten. There's something about being out of the basement that's energizing.

"Doug on your nerves yet?"

"No. I think I'm getting used to him."

Kirsten, her voice a whisper, echoes in my ears. "He loves his work.

That means he works too hard. I think that's because he grew up with nothing."

I realize I don't know much about Doug's upbringing.

"Really?" I probe, trying to get more out of her.

"Oh yeah." She sounds happy to oblige. "His family—well, his father drank everything away. Had a good job at the mill until it shut down. Lost his pension when the company went bankrupt. They lost their house and the land they lived on. Doug promised never to let that happen to him. Built everything he has—*we* have. He's self-made. Couldn't afford medical school, so he figured out another way. Put in the work. Got extra training and experience." She beams with pride. "I just wish I could make this house a home for him."

Ewan. I don't think Doug told her that I know.

"I'm sorry. About your son," I offer.

Kirsten smiles. It is filled with the deep sadness of grief.

"Losing a child is . . ." Her gaze disappears into her glass for a second. I move to embrace her, but I see a dark thought cross her face. It's not sadness. It's rage. I can't tell who or what upset her. Before I can say anything else, the thought passes. This mixture of anger and sadness, the shifting emotions remind me of what grief can do to a person, no matter the circumstance or time.

"My husband has a job he takes pride in. He wasn't handed anything. He's struggled just as much as"—Kirsten searches for the right comparison—"well, as anyone else." She hides the shameful notion in her wineglass as she drinks again. When she comes up, she laughs. "Everyone's suffered. What does it matter if one person suffers more than another? We're all in pain." Kirsten rubs her eyes and smiles at me with all her teeth. "It's enough to drive you mad."

SEVENTEEN

"She might not see us," Latoya says. I know Tanisha, Kylie, and Denise have all warned me against talking to Farrah. But after I showed up at the door of the church and refused to leave, Latoya caved.

Kirsten's talk of madness reminded me that all madness has a root. If I can't get to the truth of what I saw in the woods, maybe I can find it in Farrah.

"You listening to me?" Latoya's voice breaks my thoughts. It's getting dark. Night will be here in minutes.

"We have to try." I climb the steps of the house in front of us. Halfway between downtown and uptown, the narrow home is perched on the edge of the mountain. The wood is warped in areas and worn, but has been painted over with care. We're far enough up for this place to have avoided the flood. I wonder how old it is as the last step sags slightly with my weight. I hop up to the porch. Latoya deftly avoids the weak step and joins me at the door.

She raises her hand to the knocker. "If she gets upset? We leave. If she's just talking in circles? We leave. If she doesn't like you? We—"

"Leave. I understand. Anything goes wrong, we leave."

Knock. Knock.

After a long moment, we hear shuffling. "Comin'!" The footsteps approach the door. There's a swipe of the peephole.

"Toya? That you?"

"Yes, Miss Gerri. We're here to visit Farrah."

"We?"

Latoya gives me a look, and I dip my head toward her, centering myself in the view.

I wave. "Thank you for having us on such short notice."

The lock shifts and the door creaks open. A slight, elderly Black woman greets us in a deep green velvet housecoat and slippers. The coat is long-sleeved and heavy. I can't believe she's cold in this heat. She waves us inside.

The house has to be from before the flood. The sculpted wood of the staircase, the dark smooth floors, and the chandelier give away the age of the place. Miss Gerri catches me looking up.

"My grandfather hung that chandelier himself"—she nods in memory—"salvaged it from the flood . . ."

"This house survived the flood?"

"Oh no. Built right after it. Been in my family ever since. We were one of the only—"

"Gerri?" Latoya redirects the conversation. "How's Farrah feeling?"

"You'uns lucky. She has her energy today." Gerri shuffles to a door at the end of the hall. She knocks. "Farrah, your company here. You ready to see 'em?"

A soft voice answers. "They friendly?"

Gerri looks back at us. "It's Toya, you know how she can be." Gerri smiles. "And her friend looks nice. She was polite at the door."

After a moment, Farrah replies, "All right."

Gerri pulls the door open and Latoya and I enter.

Though Farrah's room is in a home, it feels like a facility. A bed, a free-standing armoire, and a nightstand, that's it. The armoire is open. So is the nightstand. There's no place for her to hide things. I never asked how exactly she went mad, but now I suspect she was a danger to herself. I press against my scar. It's hard and numb today.

The room is brightly lit. An overhead light, floor lamp, and table lamp remove all shadows. However, the curtains are shut. A large metal fan oscillates in the corner, moving the stale air around. The room doesn't smell, more that it feels warm and lived in.

Farrah sits on her bed. Her hair is in two French braids, her housedress, a pale yellow with a light pink bow. Her arms rest at her sides, her palms facing up. Her legs are parted, pulling her dress tight at her knees.

"Sit right, girl," Latoya mutters as she taps Farrah's knees back together. Arms open, legs apart. From the picture I saw at Doug's, that's how Brittany was found. Seeing her daughter like that would be enough to break any mother. Looking at her, I realize the story of Farrah is more exciting than the reality. Nothing in the woods made her go "mad." The indifference of the world did that.

Though the curtains are closed, Farrah's gaze is out the window. She's older than me, but she feels like a child in this room. Nothing about her appearance is her doing. She has been lovingly cared for.

"Farrah?" Latoya speaks in the softest tone I've ever heard from her. "How you feeling today?"

"Momma watchin' TV too loud."

"I believe it." Latoya sits next to Farrah. "Farrah, my friend here . . ." Latoya gives me one last glance to check in, to remind me. "She's here to listen to you."

"No one listens 'cept you and Kylie."

"I know, but Elizabeth here wants to." Latoya beckons me over to them. I wade through the grief around Farrah.

Latoya puts Farrah's hand in mine. "Be quick," she whispers to me.

I nod. "Hi, Farrah." I take a breath. "I want you to tell me about—"

"Brittany?" She turns away from the window and looks right at me.

I flinch. "Yeah."

"Brittany is a star. That's why they took her. We can't shine too bright. None of us can. I'm going to take her to classes out in Pittsburgh next summer, get her better training—" Speaking about her daughter brings this light to her eyes. The woman who was in a fugue only moments before is gone. This woman is sharp and alert. I'd follow her anywhere she wants to lead me. Right now I need to guide her down a specific path.

"When you went to go looking for Brittany, what did you see?" I ask.

Farrah hesitates, but her light doesn't dim. "She didn't come home after her rehearsal. I had a shift—I had to work—I thought she was with . . . I wouldn't leave her alone—"

"It's okay. What happened?"

"We had a fight over . . ." Farrah disappears behind her eyes. "I don't even remember. It was so stupid."

"When you went looking in the woods?" I offer.

"I told them what I saw and they wouldn't do anything."

"What did you see?" I grip her hand, pulling her mind back to me.

"You already know." She smiles. "Your eyes are bright. Like mine."

"What do you mean?"

"To find what's in the dark, you have to let it in." Farrah leans in, her eyes searching mine. I feel myself start to tilt back.

"Let her, Liz," Latoya whispers.

I stay and Farrah comes forward until her forehead rests against mine. Eyes still open, she searches mine as close as she can. Hers are like two glossy orbs at the edge of my vision.

"Don't look at the shadow." Her breath slows and so does mine. Soon we breathe together. *In and out.* "People don't look, 'cause looking makes him real." *In and out. In and out.* "But he grows in silence. In fear." *In.* I catch a glimpse of something in her eyes. *Out.* Bent in a fish-eye, the lamps in her room make the night sky in her pupils. Light and shadow. Something moves in the gloss of her iris. Like a dark spot, swimming toward the surface. I'm pulled toward her. I feel one of the many cords wrap around my ankle. I topple the lamp over.

Snap!

It blows, sending a bright flash across the room before plunging the corner into darkness. The side of my eye feels wrong. Cold. Like an eyelash has curled up under my lid. I launch myself away from her. Careful not to hurt my eye, I go to the only reflective surface, the window, to get whatever it is out of my eye. I open the curtains. Night provides a mirror. I look. I can barely see my reflection. Through blurry vision. I don't see anything in my sclera. *I felt it.* I know I felt it. Cool and invasive. There is something in my eye.

Farrah is set off. "Get away from me!" She claws for her covers and wraps herself in them. I close the curtain. She curls up on the bed. Latoya rushes over to her, trying to comfort her. Meanwhile, I'm still backing away. I feel my back press against the wall. "I lost her. I need to go. I need to go find Brittany!" Latoya tries to hold her, but Farrah wriggles away. She makes her way to the door.

Gerri opens it. "What's all this?"

"I need to find Brittany. She's still out in the woods. He's keeping her. He keeps all of them!" Farrah is frantic and driven. I worry she's going to knock Gerri over. But, with the skill of a mother, Gerri reaches up to cradle her daughter's face.

"Calm down, honey. Come on. You need your rest." Smoothly, she leads Farrah back. She curls up and rests her head in her mother's lap, like a child waking from a nightmare. Somewhere between dreaming and reality is where Farrah's stuck.

★ ★ ★

LATOYA AND I both sit on the porch of Farrah's family home. We breathe in the night air. All that Farrah said reverberates around in my head. The madness Kylie spoke of, this is it. Searching without finding anything.

Your eyes are bright. Like mine.

Latoya speaks first. "That help?"

"Farrah is—"

"Traumatized, but not as crazy as people think." Latoya's dark skin glows in the coming moonlight. "My parents weren't ever happy with what the schools taught me. Made me learn about history at home and in the classroom." Something shifts in her. I see the woman who runs the church. "In high school, we had to read speeches by W.E.B. Du Bois, Booker T. Washington—I was scanning something by Marcus

Garvey when I saw Johnstown mentioned in the same sentence as Tulsa and Saint Louis. Couldn't believe my eyes."

"Why?"

"You need to learn your history, child." She sighs. "We all do."

"I know who Garvey is but— "

"Listen," she says. "I don't like talking about politics. But I will say this. All that happened last year, people are walking around shocked, like they didn't know people like that live in this country. Unprecedented times?" Latoya takes a breath, then she tells me about a missing piece of my history. "My great-grandfather was here the summer this place banished us. It was 'cause of some drunk men, too many single men here to work in the factories. And we were taking *their* jobs and living on *their* land. All that same stuff. Everyone in this country says they don't see color, they see hard work, until they start to lose food from their table. If you were one of the good ones you could stay. 'Good' in this case meant time. If you could prove your lineage back seven years, you were one of the good ones. A short time, but the point was made. These bad Black folks? These *new* Black folks? They had to go."

"Did people leave?"

"No details, just . . . clues. Like, two thousand Black folks left in less than a week. They say there was no violence, but that day the announcement was made, ten crosses burned in the hills. This place was listed with Tulsa and Saint Louis. When you put all that together, what do you get?"

I search my education for Tulsa and come up empty. I did learn about the Saint Louis race riots.

"This place has been an open wound since the flood. Probably before." Latoya feels heavy next to me. "Two thousand Black and brown people already disappeared from this town overnight and it's been forgotten."

I'd always been taught the flood, never about this. "Farrah's daughter was a dancer?"

"Best this town had ever seen."

"Kylie and Kayla's family?" I ask.

"Her parents organized for better school funding. They started to get it before she was taken."

"You?"

"Kept that church open with my two bare hands. Kept the community together. We were active too." She smiles. "I tried to get voter registration started before Morgan . . ." Her sadness takes the rest of her words.

Another kind of culling is happening. These aren't random girls. A shadow calling their names isn't a folktale. It was on purpose. These girls were targeted.

Latoya gets up. "This is why I don't look. Searching for my girl, I understand. Digging into the hate that took her . . . no." She walks back toward the street.

"Wait—" She doesn't stop. I run after her down the steps. "Toya!"

"Even if you get a name, and if you find out what's happening, and if you bring that girl home? Farrah is still broken. After all this time, I always thought I wanted to know why, that it might bring me some peace, but if it won't bring Morgan back, I don't want it."

"What about justice?"

"You live in the same country I live in, child?" Her sarcasm bites.

"Please, I'm going to need help—"

"I've given you more than enough." She gets into her car. My heart sinks as I watch her pull away.

EIGHTEEN

I open the door to my mother's house and smell blood. Then mud. I wave my hand in front of my face to waft it away but a metallic tang hangs in the air. I reach for the light. I can't find it. It has been too long since I've been home. Surprisingly, I move pretty well in the dark. I start with a hand out to feel along the wall. Soon find that I don't need it. I deftly avoid the edge of the kitchen counter and move into the dining room without stubbing my toe. Before I can celebrate, I slip on something slick and cold. Trying to catch myself, my body wheels backward and slams into the wall. A framed painting crashes down next to me on the floor. The angle shatters the glass instantly. I grimace from the din of it.

"Elizabeth?" my mother yells, groggy from sleep. I scramble for the light switch. Now, painfully unable to navigate the dark, it seems my familiarity was just as fleeting as it was final.

"I slipped on someth—" Wetness takes my feet out from under me again. I'm slammed flat on my back before I know it. Breath goes out of my lungs. Gasping, I'm treated to an upside-down view of my mother's dining room table. Hanging over the edge, a black unblinking eye, illuminated by moonlight, stares back at me. Brown fur surrounds gray lids and short black eyelashes. The fur builds out in little brushstrokes. The snout has deep dry cracks. A few ticks crawl across the table, fleeing their now-dead host. I see one venture across the eye. The gray lids don't blink the insect away. I stand. When I get to my feet, I see nothing can make this creature whole again.

Before me, on my mother's immaculate dining room table, is a deer. Or what's left of it. The poor thing has been ripped open. Not gutted. Carved. The jagged ribs sag wide and the red insides glisten with blood. I expect to see a stew of intestines. Instead, I see one discernible organ. A heart. The rest of the creature is filled with what looks like bloody ball bearings. A few scatter out onto the ground. I pick one up and roll it in my fingers. It's unpopped popcorn.

Five days ago, the sight of a mutilated mouse sent me racing outside. Caroline's blood on my hands almost caused me to black out. A body in a bag on Doug's table kept me at the edge of the room. The pictures of Brittany's and Alice's mutilated bodies overwhelmed me. Looking at the deer, I'm not afraid. I'm curious. I want to look at the inside of this creature. Cool white bone presses through flesh. I search the pink sinews and red muscles for something I can't name. I get closer, knowing it's there, somewhere. What exactly? I'll know it when I see it.

"Liz?" My mother's voice is close.

I turn to stop her. "Wait!" I'm too late. Her scream is something I've never heard before. I've only ever heard my mother raise her voice to protect someone, me or a patient or a foolish family member. This scream is riddled with genuine fear for herself. I run to her. Doing so, I get another angle of the scene. Nothing else is out of place. The back doors are shut. The windows are closed. Not even the rug is out of place. It's like the deer materialized in our dining room.

I reach for my mother. She's shaking. I grip her tightly and press her head into my shoulder. I shield her with my body. She trembles in a way I've never seen her do before. It rattles me.

This is a warning. The deer from the tarp is staged in my home. Waiting for me. For my mother.

"Are you okay?" I ask.

"I am calling the police."

"No! You can't. They'll think this is me." I try to tell her about the tarp of intestines in the woods and the search for Caroline that I've been banned from. Instead, I grab some dish towels and start to scrub the blood away. It doesn't belong here in my home. My mother grabs the towels from me. I start elsewhere and she stops me again.

"What?" I ask, baffled by her behavior.

"The rod," she finally replies.

"What?"

My mother points to the sliding door. The rod sits to one side. "You forgot to put it back." I feel sick to my stomach. I search for when I last went out through the back door. I can't remember if I replaced the bar the other day or not. I was too concerned with impressing Chris. Idiot.

"Mom, why is it there?"

"I want to be safe," she mumbles and starts to clean. "They have come here before."

"What do you mean?"

She wipes the floor and gathers bloody kernels of popcorn. She wipes them down and shows me. My mind drifts back. The spare keys. I go to the kitchen and open the drawer. There, next to the keys, are bags of popcorn.

"The bags had flyers in them." She takes a shallow breath. "Little recruitment flyers for some group. They showed up on our yard every few weeks after you left for college."

Now I understand why she always visits me and has rarely bothered me about not coming home. It wasn't safe. "And now?" I ask.

My mother won't look at me. She is usually the one searching for me, figuring out what's wrong, and making me face something. I try to meet her eyes. She refuses. While my mother doesn't often choose silence or avoidance, she does when she wants to protect me. I noticed this first when my parents divorced and my father moved out. He left overnight. I remember him in our kitchen for breakfast one day, then never again. We all met in the park next to school a few days later for him to tell me he was okay and to explain that our home was changing. After that day, I made a list of his things:

His clothes.

Shoes.

A few books.

The large-screen TV.

His shoes disappeared first. When I told my mother, she didn't say anything. Every day something of his went missing she did the same thing. Disengaged. Changed the subject. Finally, I figured out she was arranging times for him to come and move out when I wasn't home.

I roll the hard kernels of the bags in my fingers. "Why are you keeping these?"

"Proof. A reminder. About what people say." She starts cleaning. Her frenetic insistence reminds me of Mrs. Parker at the site. Two women, around the same age, hell-bent on making things right. Making things okay. Cleaning up the mess of a man who needed to express his rage. I grab her hands.

"Mom? I'm sorry. Okay?"

"I thank God that it is just this." The waver in her voice is gone. She's cool and clinical. She starts to sort through cleaning supplies under the sink, grabbing the best tools for the job.

"You were here! Someone came in—dragged that thing in."

We've swapped moods. My mother refuses to match my hysterics. In fact, she doesn't even look fazed.

"And, *cherie*? By the grace of God, I am still here."

She snaps on her gloves and looks at the mess. I hear her mutter about setting and staining, but soon her words drift into Creole and I can't keep up. My mother has been dealing with threats, small little threats, unknown to me, for years. The week I come home and start asking questions about the Black girls missing in the woods, this happens.

"Bondye mwen, kisa moun pral di?"

"People will what?" I ask.

She brushes me away, not wanting to have to translate. The message under it is clear. This is the price of living here. In America. My mother will suffer it. She apparently already has. I see Latoya in my mother. Both women of deep faith and women who have had enough. Latoya was done with me unearthing her daughter. My mother is done with me asking her about this. She will suffer this the same way Latoya suffers losing her child. This way, they decide how much they will hurt. Watching my mother work, she shows me there are sides to her that I've never seen at all.

We are good Black people. Good Black folks who don't bring up race. We don't make a fuss; we don't make things uncomfortable; we are calm and cool and collected at all times. Even in the face of death. I think of how I couldn't fight back. I think of how Garrett tolerated the slaughter of the deer.

"We have to get rid of this," I say.

"How?"

Before, I would have asked Mel. I can't involve Doug any further after asking him to risk his job. Also, I just got him on my side, this could be a reason not to trust me. I need to reach out to the last person I have.

I dial and look at the deer. He answers on the second ring.

"Hey," I say. "It's me. I need help." Admitting that releases tension in my chest and back. I bend over and take a deep breath for the first time in minutes. I exhale and my mind finds what I was looking for in the deer's insides.

More.

NINETEEN

"Holy shit," Chris says when he sees the deer.

"Thank you for coming over this late." I usher him through the back door. He was just getting done closing down the bar. He doesn't have time to take off his shoes. Mud and blood are now all over my mother's dining room floor.

"We have to get rid of this," I say. "I know—it looks bad. You need to trust me." I ramble. "Someone is trying to scare me or frame me or both— How do we do this?" I don't give him the chance to say no or to get a question in. Not yet.

"I have something in my truck. We can wrap it up. I'll dump it out by my place."

"You have to burn it or something," I insist.

"I've gotten rid of a deer or two." Chris ducks back out the door.

I look at my mother. "It's gonna be okay." I see her looking at the mud on her floor. She needs to clean. I grab some paper towels and wipe up what Chris has tracked in. At the first swipe, the mud appears to be fresh. I stop. He just closed down the bar. Why would there be mud on his shoes?

The rumple of plastic announces Chris's return. He carries a blue tarp into the dining room and starts to work one side under the deer. I'm frozen like a fool. Chris starts to debate rolling versus lifting the deer up. I don't hear him.

"Where did you get that?" I ask.

"I don't remember . . ." He thinks. "This one just kind of lives in my truck." Chris finally notices my stillness. "What is it?"

Weighing all the options in front of me, I take the most obvious path. "Blue is a common tarp color, right?"

"Yeah. Why?"

The congealed blood against the blue. The tarp I found in the woods. He couldn't run all the way to the woods and back to the bar? But the mud on his shoes—

"Liz?" he asks. "Help me roll this. It's gonna be easier than lifting, don't want to get any more blood on the floor."

Right now, I need to get this out of our house. Before he touches it, I snap a few pics on my phone. Just in case. He tucks the tarp halfway under the deer and I push. The fur slides over the cold hard flesh. I ignore the sensation and get the deer into the tarp. It part rolls, part slides into Chris's waiting arms. He wraps it up fast.

Why not me?

There's that question again. I deny it. I need to stay present. I come around the other side of the table and help him fold in the sides.

"Ready?" he asks. He grabs the end with the head. I have the feet. "Keep it tucked, so nothing leaks out."

When we lift the deer I flash to the crime scene photos. Was this how Brittany and Alice were transported, lugged into a body bag and roughly handled out of the trees?

"Liz?" Chris checks in with me.

I give a quick nod. We start walking the deer out.

He's not bothered by any of this. He's clutching his side of the tarp with one hand and cradling the deer with the other as he moves backward. When he takes the step down out the back door, he takes the animal's weight. It looks like it pains him to do so. He quickly shifts the weight onto his forearms. I see that his hand is wrapped in a bandage.

"What happened?" I nod at his injury.

"I was helping Dad get an opossum out from under his porch yesterday. Perks of living off the grid. Once pests find a structure, they like to stay." Chris flexes his injured hand. "Dad doesn't kill 'em, outta spite. He traps them instead. He's. Um. We don't own the land we live on—not anymore. Been trying to save up and get it back for years, but it feels impossible. Dad gets his licks in any way he can. Like with the possums. If there are pests on the land it's worth less. As long as they don't take up in the house, he lets 'em run free. I helped him set up a trap. It's an old metal thing. Cut me up pretty bad." We make our way across the patio around to the front of the house where his truck is parked. Doug said that something in the remains was human. I've been stuck on Caroline's remains, her blood. It could also be from the killer. From a cut. Chris's looks deep. Probably bled enough for it to sink into the forest floor.

He's here late, in pain, and helping me without a question or complaint. I haven't become a bitter woman in my thirties as much as I've become a smart one. The kindness of strangers rarely applies to me, as a Black woman. And even when it does, I don't trust it. This isn't because of resentment or a lie someone told me. Over time, I've learned to suspect men who are kind without reason. No one operates from the goodness of their hearts.

We reach his truck, and he lowers the back of it to open the cargo bed. It's clean. This deer is gonna ruin that. He places his half of the animal in before coming around to take mine. He shoves the carcass inside and my eyes fall across his back. I know when I'm attracted to someone because I enjoy the shapes they make. The way he organizes his body reminds me of my body in a way that makes me uncomfortable. I look up at the sky, finding an escape in the night.

"You hunt a lot?" I smile to hide how afraid I am.

"Yeah, with my dad. He loves it out there." Chris gets the deer in and sits on the back of his truck. "He broke his foot a while back and it never healed right, but he doesn't let it stop him. Just means I have to go with him every time to make sure he doesn't get stuck somewhere."

I've been so focused on looking for who took Caroline and killed the other girls, I haven't thought about what it would be like to look at him. Now that I'm facing the possibility, I try to form some physical characteristics in my mind. To kill girls like this. To violate them and take them apart. Someone with that darkness in them wouldn't be attractive. He'd have those strange, empty eyes. Looking at Chris's green ones, he looks tired. A little shocked. He has emotions. A blue tarp and muddy shoes are common. It's not him. It can't be. My gut says it's not.

"You ever hear the rhyme about the man and his shadow?" I ask.

"Hell, yeah," Chris scoffs. "Dad and I whistle to each other when we're out there. Never call our names. A whistle will stop a deer in its tracks, give you a clean shot."

When Mel left me in the woods, whatever followed me whistled. If someone were hunting for a deer, that's another basic explanation.

All this is too flimsy. Find something damning, Liz. "You remember Keisha?" I ask.

"I remember she smelled like gummy bears. I don't know why."

I do. "It was the gel she put in her hair."

"What?"

This strange push and pull in me keeps me there, sitting next to him, assessing him and comparing him to the men I'm looking for. He said his father was a clerk; he was tipped off about Bonfire Night. But he doesn't seem like a serial rapist and murderer. Then again, he doesn't have to be, he could be keeping tabs on me for someone else.

I tap the edge of my hairline, hoping I haven't sweated it all away yet. I offer my fingers to Chris. He looks at them for a second. I hold them up to his nose and he understands. He takes my hand. He smells my fingers. My stomach knots again. I've never broken down what I'm attracted to in men. I like to think it's kindness. While sitting here, with a deer carcass behind us, I'm offering an intimate part of myself to a man who I haven't decided is a murderer or not.

"Jesus." I see him go away in his mind, off to high school and Keisha. "That's her. That's crazy."

I pull my hand back. "That's Eco Styler. She always had her edges laid. Why did you stop talking to me? After that party?"

"I was getting my life together. I thought you were mad at me. I was mad at myself. I left you in the middle of the night in the woods. Who does that?"

Mel, I think.

"When I saw you at the wedding, I just wanted to yell I'm sorry. Don't blame you for being pissed with me."

Everyone thinks they know what my anger looks like. They think it's screaming and yelling and fighting. Sometimes anger is a low vibration, the coil before the spring. Sometimes it sinks inside me and paralyzes me.

"We were kids," I say.

"I've missed talking to you," Chris admits. "You don't sound like the people who live here. You aren't interested in the same things they are. You listen. The kids who signed my yearbook, not one of those motherfuckers ever did that. Not even to this day. They come to the bar, but that's it. This town is still made of two kinds of people. People who get ahead and people who have been left behind. Every year, it seems like I know more and more people who are behind. When she—Keisha—disappeared, I thought about it for . . . months. I still think about her."

"So do I."

The person who is doing this must have a lot of hate to kill an innocent child. Or bitterness.

"I should go," Chris says, but he doesn't move. He wants me to tell him to leave.

"Have you ever come across something you can't explain in the woods?" I ask. I feel him try to make a joke and fail.

"A few times. Never look, just keep moving." He stands up. I do too. I go to help him close up the gate, but he indicates he doesn't need me. He lifts the gate and I see something crushed in the joint. It's soft and greasy. And bright pink. I see a few flecks of paper mixed in with the wax of a crayon. Before I can say anything, Chris shuts the bed of the truck.

He heads around to the front and waves. Bye. I barely wave back, my eyes are locked on what I just saw. I know I saw it. That wasn't deer or dirt. That was a pink crayon. Judging by the greasiness, it's one of the needlessly fancy ones I bought Caroline for Christmas. The ones Mel had been looking for.

DIANA

June 1996

People in America love to believe in freedom, even though it isn't free. It never was. Not even for those who emblazon it across their cars, patios, and homes. The history of freedom is much older than plastic flags and banners.

For those who fled north, the color of their skin united them. Some knew only the plantations they'd been born on, others memorized the trails they'd been traded along. A few even claimed to remember the Passage. All who ran did so in search of freedom. They believed they fled their chains. Some brought new ones with them. Shackled to the god of their captors, they praised him with a faith that was once reserved for deities who looked like them and spoke in their mother tongue. Fueled by impossible belief, an unshakable faith was born. Something novel was needed to survive the New World. I should be sensitive.

I miss the 1990s. They were on the verge of something. Everyone knew it. Between the internet and cellphones, something big was coming. None of this mattered to Diana or her parents. They were more concerned about the past. Specifically, a missing piece of it.

Her mother, Renée, especially, was out to prove something: roots. Ever since Diana could remember, her mother had been concerned about where they came from and what Diana was learning in school about the past. Ever a dutiful student, Diana could easily recite lessons she learned about America: Land of the Free, Home of the Brave, Separate but Equal, Winners of an Impossible War. Each segment she learned appeared in her mind like billboards on the side of a highway announcing how far we've come and how far we have to go.

"And where do you see yourself?" Renée asked. Every time, on all these billboards, Diana never saw herself. She also never questioned this. Her lack of existence in this country didn't bother her the way it did her mother. Diana was more focused on a place she couldn't go, but could visit. The past.

The library was one of her favorite places. There Diana discovered a history she saw herself in. Ancient Egypt. Movies cast Egyptians with white protagonists. Diana looked at the drawings herself. Those people were brown and in Africa. Her mother didn't have the heart to complicate Diana's love for this past. She didn't want to point out that most people who were enslaved came from West Africa. North and west were, and still are, very different places. Lumping Africa into a monolith is a side effect of erasure. When your past exists in shadow, you seek your home any way you can. At first, Renée planned to teach Diana about the Iron Age and deities more fitting for her probable origins. But, the more Renée researched, the more she realized, there is no going home for Black Americans, there is only claiming it.

Renée redoubled her efforts to teach her daughter her past. When Diana was in her last year of middle school, Renée founded a small historical society and made Diana her assistant. It was not a job Diana wanted. Oral history was what her mother assigned to her. She had to get the story of a place that lives only in the mouths of people. It was a safe task. In her neighborhood, Diana didn't need her mother to watch her. She had the community to do so. They were all too eager to keep the girl occupied.

"The windy-blows?" The old man on the corner rhymed the name of a much more sinister creature. "'Course they out there. If you hear anything with smarts after dark—whistling, breaking branches, calling your name, don't trust it. Don't even acknowledge it."

One of the ladies who did braids in the summer added, "These old dudes are trying to scare you. Bears are reason enough to stay out of them trees, girl." In collecting these stories, she learned most folks followed these two courses. They either tried to scare her away from the woods with monsters or they'd appeal to her common sense.

A woman from one of the oldest houses in town had a different take. "Don't give it any thought or energy. That's the only way to keep it there." Diana didn't know what "there" the old woman meant: *there* in the woods or *there* as in alive?

Diana was on the verge of something big.

At twelve years old, she was already deep in her opinions. Her opinion of this town was comforting. She planned to finish school, stay here, and have a family. She wanted to indulge in all the comforts small-town life could offer. Diana wasn't someone who felt the need to be coastal.

I've never seen the coast. I don't think I've ever known how to swim.

Neither did Diana, though that wasn't why she wanted to stay away from the coast. She heard it was a place where elites went, and if her snotty classmates were any indicator, she'd much rather stay right where she was. There was no wanderlust in her. Even if she traveled, she would eat only foods she recognized or things she could pronounce. She'd be loud and American, and she'd only ever speak English.

Unlike her opinion of the town, her opinion of the woods was unsettled. The woods were both scary and fun. They were a thing to be respected, but breaking off twigs to build cities for ants was one of her favorite things to do. Years ago, something terrible happened to a little girl in the woods. Some people said her parents abused her and dumped her there. Some people said she got shot by accident and someone covered it up. Some people said she had her heart ripped out by a wolf. Diana dismissed these rumors as stories made up to scare her. A quick jaunt between the trees was too tempting to miss out on because of fear. She set out on a path she knew well, moving quickly.

Hunters like dusk. It's the changeover between creatures of the day and creatures of the night. Diana was wearing the wrong shoes. Her feet, slick with sweat, slipped around in her jelly sandals. She ignorantly assumed she didn't need sunscreen. Her melanin wasn't enough protection. Hidden in the brown hues of her skin, her sunburn had started to make the skin on her shoulders sensitive. She felt the drop in temperature before she noticed the sunset. Her bright yellow top popped against the red undertones of her complexion in a way that was enviable. When she wore it, people couldn't help but stare.

The Fellow easily spotted Diana in her yellow during this shift. And as she made her way along the trail, he tracked her. Halfway down the path, there was a deep bend. That's where she paused, unsure. The hair on the back of her neck rose as she became of someone watching her. Not being well-versed in the eyes of men, she brushed the feeling off and pushed herself toward her own demise. Maybe if she had worn different shoes.

"Diana!"

When she looked at him, she wasn't scared, like the others. Instead, she froze in disbelief. To her, he appeared like a monster in a dream. He was a sudden, awful manifestation of the warnings she knew so well. Diana's mother told her the woods were no place for children to play. To stick to the path. To stay in earshot. The rules of the world didn't extend to the trees. There was something in there with a hunger that nothing could satisfy. A hollow being that preyed on anyone who strayed from the pack.

Sometimes I think of Diana's mother, Renée. She didn't cry like the others. Instead, deep bitter blame rooted in her. She hated her daughter. Renée hated her until she died, years later, from a broken heart. Hating her daughter kept her alive. Hate is active. Hate has drive. But love, like grief, is long and ever-changing. Diana's mother didn't dare love again.

Diana's heart was full of stories. From both the origins she longed for and her home in actuality. She taught me the power of a tale and the purpose in rewriting it.

Ancient Egypt in Education: History's Role in the Childhood Identity of African Americans

BY RENÉE LEAKS

Abstract: In this essay, I consider the role of Ancient Egypt as it relates to childhood identity in African Americans. First, I present the current grade school world history curriculum, specifically when it comes to the representation of Africa, its history, and cultures. Then, I present my findings on self-perception of African American students in those same classes. Focusing on what histories are told and in what manner, I illustrate the complicated relationship African Americans have to Africa in a historical setting. With certain societies held up as exemplary and others omitted or shunned, African American children are often presented with an uneven and incomplete picture of their past. Seeking meaning and identity in African countries or cultures over American culture is a common desire. In conclusion, my findings advocate for a holistic and comprehensive historical approach as diverse as the many groups that came together to create America.

Keywords: Ancient Egypt, early childhood development, African American history, American history.

TWENTY

Caroline's Fifth Day Missing

The next morning, the kitchen smells like bleach. It's so pungent I can't focus. I hardly slept. *Could it have been something else*—I know what I saw. A crayon. What I saw and how Chris is behaving don't align. He feels remorse for leaving me in the woods. This killer would be the exact opposite. If he was trying to hurt me, trap me, why help me? I don't have anything I can use to bring him in. And he's one of the few people I have helping me. I don't know if I can lose any more help in this town. I'll have to be careful. No more being alone with him. I add Chris to my list of suspects. I'll bring him up to Doug and start digging.

In the meantime, I search my memory for something, anything. My eyes ache. My temples and the area above my eyebrows throb like I've been awake for days. I feel the urge to check my eyes. The ordeal of the deer distracted me from the stars I saw in Farrah's eyes. And the thing that crawled into mine. What if it is still there, lurking in my sclera, indicating something wrong with me? I head to the bathroom.

In the mirror, my deep brown irises reflect back at me. I take my phone and turn on the flashlight. I check my eyes. The depths of my irises are dark brown, so dark they're almost black. My pupils shrink and widen. Nothing looks wrong.

My phone rings and I nearly drop it.

"Hello?" I answer.

"I messed up." It's Doug. The pain in his voice is heartbreaking. He sounds like a child.

"What do you mean?"

"I got caught." He sounds smaller than ever. Someone is making him say this. I listen to the other end of the phone. It's open and airy.

"You outside?"

"I'm outside the station, yeah," he says, voice cracking.

"Take a minute, okay? Then go back in there with your head high."

"I can't."

"You can. I know you can," I say, unsure myself, but I'm rallying for him. I need him to be strong for both of us.

"I was running the DNA of one of the officers, Liz. They let me go."

My heart drops. "But the DNA?" I ask, even though I suspect the answer.

"I can't—I can't—" The tremble in Doug's voice is unnerving. "It was this or prison. This or prison." He repeats the phrase like it's what's been said to him. "Maybe still prison."

I let the line go silent. This job is everything to him and it's gone. All because he helped me.

★ ★ ★

KIRSTEN GREETS ME from the driveway. She's already waving at me as I arrive. The smile on her face breaks my heart. She doesn't know what's happened and I can't tell her. I walk up the driveway and she gives me a hug.

"He should be home soon. Doug let me know you were coming by," she says as we go inside, into the kitchen, and she presents me with a perfect turkey sandwich. She pauses before setting it down. This is a move of hers.

I hear the garage door. Moments later, Doug barrels through the kitchen full of uncharacteristic rage. The way Kirsten shuts down tells me this isn't the first time she's seen Doug this angry. She shrinks in front of me and flees to another room of the house. Doug makes a beeline for the basement. I make my way after him down the stairs. Doug is in crisis mode.

"We need to burn it. All of it," he says through clenched teeth.

"We can't. It's all we have."

"It can't be here." He doesn't sound like he did on the phone just now. He's angry. He tears through all the boxes, making two piles. One to burn and one to keep. He decides he can keep the map, any documents he's made, and the few photos that were public record. Everything else: crime scene photos, databases, medical reports, police archives. It all has to go. I try to help him sort.

"Goddamnit, Liz, stop it!" Doug yells. The power of his voice nearly knocks me over. "You don't know what you're doing. You don't know what you're messing with. I knew it! I shouldn't have helped you. I should have let you go right back to the city and leave this place for good."

"And leave Caroline out there?"

"Caroline is gone. Don't you get it?"

"They haven't found her yet."

"Liz, you aren't her parents. You aren't even related to her. You don't need to be deluded like them. Caroline is dead!"

"This is about way more than Caroline now." Doug doesn't know about the deer. "He went after my mom, Doug. He's been going after her, threatening her for *years*. Caroline is more than enough reason, but don't test me. I have family on the line too. Not just my family. This is about Keisha and Morgan and Brittany— My mother! This guy threatened my mother. My—" I want to slap some sense into Doug. I grab the box with the map. He lunges to get it, but I'm too fast.

"Give that back," he demands.

"Why? You don't need it."

"What are you going to do with it, Liz?"

"I'm gonna find who's doing this."

He shakes his head. "Right. That's exactly what— The DNA from both scenes came back. There's a match."

"Oh my God . . ." I almost cry. All of this has been worth it. I look at him, waiting for the answer.

He runs his hands through his hair. "It's not exact, but it's enough to—"

"What do you mean it's not exact? It's DNA! Whose is it?"

"Liz. Please, listen."

I still myself but don't calm down.

"DNA isn't the smoking gun everyone thinks it is," Doug continues. "It's— I'd need another opinion; the department would. I ran the cigarette butts. To do that, I had to use part of your sample from the wedding to rule you out and I got a match."

"Who is it?"

Doug looks me right in the eye. "You."

"What?"

"Blood from the tarp, blood at the scene. They already have your fingerprints. It's yours, Liz."

I twist my wrist to feel my scar's pull. "That can't be." I remember how the wound burned when it healed. "You saw my hands the night of the wedding. I didn't have any cuts. I was just *there*." Mom said the wound itched because of the bacteria. "Someone is setting me up."

"I always thought it was strange that you wanted to help so bad. I never thought that it could be because—"

"I have nothing to do with this! Think about it. It's impossible. H—how?" The question feels empty, but I ask it. "How could I have done this? All this. Gotten back here every summer and . . . and . . . and—someone made sure I found the tarp. Now my DNA *magically* appears—"

"It's not magic, it's evidence."

"Is it you?"

Doug freezes. "After everything I've done to help you, you think—you think I'd lose my job to frame you?"

I don't know. Ever since Mel left me in the woods, I'm doubting everything I've discovered. Accusing Doug is a shot in the dark.

"Do you know what I think?" he continues. "The girls are just girls. And you had too much to drink at a wedding and lost your best friend's kid. This is you trying to cover it up. Mel's life looks pretty damn perfect. Beautiful home. Cute kid. Great husband. You sure you aren't jealous?"

"I refuse to answer that."

"Believe me, Liz. When it comes to you or my job? You are not that special." That cost him something to say. His eyes gloss over. "No wonder you're losing friends left and right. This is everyone's fault except yours."

"You really think that?"

Doug isn't listening to me anymore. He's thinking of the evidence. He, like Nick, is deciding what I am.

"I'll give you a chance to get whatever you need to get in order, but then I gotta tell them what we've been up to."

"I couldn't have done this."

"But here you are." Doug gets that wide-eyed look again. On anyone else, it would be chilling, but on him, it's innocent. He wants to believe.

"You helped me. They'll come for you too. If you turn me in, they'll come for you."

Doug goes for the box of photos and this time he grabs the edge. He tries to wrestle it away, but I'm faster. He's stronger. When I pull away, the box rips right down the middle and everything scatters over the floor. Doug scrambles for the photos. I go for the map. With his long limbs, he tries to snatch the map too, but when he digs his fingers in, it rips.

"No!" I cry out.

He pulls and the map tears. I gather my half and lunge at him. He drops the photos and begins to shred the map.

I scream as I reach for it. My cry morphs into a sound that changes the temperature of the room. It isn't human. Not even remotely. It's a harsh, low, loud snarl that halts the both of us. My hands race to my throat, checking to be sure the noise emanated from there. My neck is warm and scratchy. My hands tremble. I try to imagine the physical logistics of making the sound again, but I have no idea how. I try to think of a reasonable explanation, but I notice Doug. He's backing away from me.

I cough a few times to rid my throat of phlegm. "You liked this when you had something to gain from it, but it never *really* mattered to you." I know that's a lie, but I want to get him fired up. I need him to fight someone else right now. Not me. "It was never your kid missing. It would never be your kid missing, so it was safe."

Doug lowers his gaze. "Get out of my house, Liz." For all the threat in his voice, none of it permeates his body. "Leave, before I throw you out!" he yells.

Compared to the noise I made, his voice sounds so small and thin. I make a quick step toward him and he jumps back. He's afraid of me. I take my time and gather all the shredded pieces of the map. I gather the photos of the girls. His forearms tense when I do. I make sure not to miss a single one. With my pile in one hand, I grab a new box and place it all in there. He looks at me with red eyes. I take the box with me and walk up the basement stairs.

TWENTY-ONE

"Auntie Liz, why don't you come to visit my house?" This was one of Caroline's go-to questions whenever she visited me in New York. For years, she regaled me with stories about her doll collection and her games. She especially wanted me to see her drawings in person and not just the photographs Mel sent me.

"The city is so much fun." I watched her work through my non-answer. She was already figuring out how to ask me again. I was going to have to address her question. "I don't really enjoy going home. And you like coming here." She drew me a map of Central Park on that visit. I hung it on the fridge until Alex took it down. Said it was strange how close I was to someone else's kid. Looking back, I think he was jealous of how much I cared about a child hundreds of miles away. It was a good map. The way she drew the landmarks stayed in my mind. She focused on the lily pads in Bethesda Fountain before the angel. She found the obelisk on the East Side fascinating. Even though it was out of my way, I'd try to pass it on my runs. I haven't run for exercise since Alex almost killed me. Instead, when I wasn't at work, I sat in my apartment with all the lights on. Like Farrah.

Thank God Louise's is open. The dark bar takes me in and I welcome it. I've felt too much today. The vodka from my suitcase will not be enough. Give me the numb. Numb is the only way I'll be able to sleep. Not dream. Get to the next day. If I can get to tomorrow, I can start to fix this mess.

I text Mel for an update. The text bounces back immediately. I check my service and I have full bars. Wherever she is, she must be off the grid. Checking the news, I find no updates. Still no Caroline.

"Liz?" It's Denise. She looks at me with such care that I almost cry when I see her. She can tell what I need. "Let's get you a drink."

In less than an hour, the ache of the day isn't gone, but it's better. Denise sips her Hennessy and keeps me company. She says nothing. She lets me sit in silence, and I can't even begin to thank her.

I barely manage a sigh. "Everyone thinks I'm crazy."

She laughs loud at that. "I know that feeling."

"I'm gonna lose Caroline. They're gonna close the search down, look in the wrong places—"

"I know." Denise drinks deeply.

"They're trying to pin it on me." I finally manage a laugh.

"How are they doing that?"

"Fingerprints. DNA. A deer. Anything to shut me up." I drink.

Denise gives that dark chuckle. "Ain't that some shit? Didn't take any evidence, now they are faking it. Shameful."

"But it's not fake. I'm trying to grab on to these clues, but I'm missing something. If Caroline is alive, where is she? If she's dead, where is she?" I think of the madness Kylie spoke of. This is it. A sick reflection of loss. I try to conjure Caroline and all I get is that sinking feeling that came when I lost her. Her laugh. Her constant questions. The timbre of her voice. All are fading. "I didn't even want to come back here to this stupid town. The only person who ever cared about me—ever—won't look me in the face."

"Ever? I thought you said Keisha was your friend."

"Oh. Yeah." I wave her off, too frustrated to keep up my lie.

"What?" Denise asks.

I could easily explain this away as a slip of the tongue, a momentary misstep, but I know she won't believe me.

"I meant Melissa, the woman whose daughter is missing."

She's not letting it go. "I thought you and Keisha were close."

"We were in the same class—"

"But you didn't know her. Not really."

"She did help me—"

"What else you keeping from me?" The tone of her voice makes me feel like a child again.

"Nothing," I lie.

"Why are they getting all this from you? Fingerprints? DNA?"

"They think I have something to do with Caroline's disappearance."

"Do you?" Her face demands the truth from me. I know better than to spit out an answer. I need to search myself for it first. My mind races back to a few days ago. The train ride feels like a year ago.

"Someone is setting me up."

Denise stares at me, and I recognize the work she's doing. She's assessing me. Weighing me. Judging me and her trust in me.

"Were you at that party?" She doesn't need to clarify. I know what she's asking about. We both do. Her eyes cut right to the heart of me. She's not asking about the wedding. She's asking about Bonfire Night.

"Yes," I breathe. The whole ordeal washes over me again. Me running. Keisha reaching out for me before being ripped away. Teeth sinking into me. I tense my forearms, refusing to rub the scar now. Not in front of Denise.

"And?" she pushes.

"I—I . . . I got away."

Denise looks at me. "What did you do? Lose another girl and what? Live a life that stinks like the coward you are?" She looks at me and sees all the things her daughter never got to be. All the things robbed from her that night.

"Yes." My shame burns my face.

"Why you?"

There it is. The question I've been running from for fifteen years.

"I don't know." I've rehearsed this answer with my therapist. Said it with confident acceptance in her office. This is what I'm supposed to say and the unknown that I'm supposed to accept.

"Don't lie to me. You have to—you have to be special."

"I'm not."

"Stop lying!" Her tone ripples through the bar. People set down their drinks. The song on the jukebox plays, but no one sings along to it anymore. "What do you do? Do you have children? Do you . . . make things. Give things?" She looks at me, into me. She knows. "You have to have something. Be something. What are you?"

"Nothing." The tears are in my eyes before I can stop them. "I don't—can't—I'm not—I'm just . . . Black?" The last word falls out of me like a confession. I don't know who I'm confessing to, or if I'm revealing anything to Denise that she doesn't know. I look at her through my bleary eyes. She's no longer desperate. She's not in pieces anymore. She's back.

"You sure about that?" The question hangs between us, begging for me to take it up. I can't.

Something is coming.

I can't deny it anymore. This feeling has invaded my dreams and my body. So now both are changing. I don't know exactly when it started, but it keeps happening.

Denise is screaming at me. Other patrons pull her away. As they do, I'm not there. Despite how drunk I am, I find the space overwhelming. I drink to make my senses go back to normal. My eyes dim. My sight blurs. My touch numbs.

I don't want whatever my body is preparing itself for.

I don't remember much after Denise yells at me. I don't know how I got home. I grab all the little bottles I have left. I'm still in control. I know that I finish the vodka I brought in my suitcase. I drink until the pain stops. Till this day stops. Till the liquor's soporific warmth carries me to sleep and I welcome it. I climb into bed. Night falls. It's about to get dark. I grab my phone and turn the brightness all the way up. It's my beacon in the black. I don't like the dark. In the dark, I see woods. In the woods, I see Keisha. And Keisha is always followed by teeth.

TWENTY-TWO

This dream is different:

It's night.

I'm in my bridesmaid's dress and barefoot.

I walk through the mud and it doesn't suck at my feet. Something to the right catches my eye; I turn and see a white figure moving in the trees. It's in a dress exactly like mine. The peach-pink tulle of the bridesmaid dress ruffles as it walks. I look closer and see that the figure has no face.

Snap!

That comes from my left.

I turn and see another peach-dressed figure moving in the same direction as me. It struggles through the mud for a few steps before stopping.

Snap!

This one is right behind me.

I slowly peek over my shoulder and see another white, faceless figure. Human in shape, and nothing else. The fingers have no definition; the feet are clubbed, and the face is a smooth white mask. It's wearing the same peach dress as me and the others. I take a few steps back from it and it advances. In my periphery, I notice the others advancing as well. I stop. They stop. I take a step toward it and they all move with me. They aren't chasing me, they're flanking me.

So often we aren't ourselves, but what others make us to be. I need to remember to ask people:

What do you see when you see me?

I turn and move forward again. I keep my eyes on them. They seem content to keep their distance. So I keep walking, pulled on by a need I can't name.

I arrive at the field. The bonfire field. A crystal-clear night sky greets me first. The stars look like they're twinkling, reminding me of what they are. Fire. I want to fall into the darkness between them, but I sense myself being watched. Used to the feeling, I look around, seeking the eyes on me. I find them right in front of me.

A dark figure watches me under the stars.

My peach sisters flank me on the field and approach with me as I get a closer look. I breathe and the breath becomes a whisper. The whisper builds to a whistle.

I feel sound vibrate my bones.

Then build in my lungs.

Before I can stop it. I let out a full-throated howl.

The peach figures turn to face me. I look back at them and see they've gained a feature. Just one.

A mouth. Red and jagged, like a wound. As they approach me, I shrink, unaware of where to go for safety.

The dark figure in the center walks forward. And my peach sisters turn to face it. They flock in front of me.

I can hear their bones crack when the dark figure digs into their chests. I can smell the rending of their flesh. My stomach growls. I feel saliva filling my mouth. It overflows down the sides of my lips. I bring my hand to my face to wipe it away. My teeth feel normal, aside from the salivating.

I cower while my sisters defend me. Their ribs peeled open, blood and shiny intestines spill forward.

Their broken bodies litter the ground around me. The dark figure has won. I brace myself for my death. Instead, it grabs my hands and turns both of them to the sky. Tiny tendrils of shadow dance over the scar on my wrist. Then the figure takes my hand and plunges it into its chest.

My arm disappears into the black, then my shoulder.

I scream.

I'm quickly drawn into the dark wound. Before my head disappears, I see the stars. They've moved during my time in the night. I see a winter sky before I disappear into the darkness.

TWENTY-THREE

Caroline's Sixth Day Missing

A smell wakes me first. It's pungent. Acrid. Sour. I peel my eyes open. I see the vomit next to me.

That doesn't alarm me. The leaves do. I see leaves because I'm not in my bed. Far from it. Pokey twigs and branches greet my hands as I reach out. The faint light bleeding through the trees makes my head ache.

I'm outside.

I roll over. I'm in the woods. Reeling from the realization, I try to get to my feet. I need to get out. *I'm in the woods*. It's night or early morning, I can't tell. I'm in the woods, and I have no idea how I got here. I make my way to sitting and my head throbs. I'm hungover, barefoot, and in my pj's. What time is it? My phone is still clutched in my hand. My knuckles are white from holding it. I release my grip on it. It's dead.

When I stand, I want to retch again. There's nothing in me but bitter bile. My mind scrambles to get my bearings. My thoughts slip on my shock. I've walked into the woods in my sleep. All that running in my dreams was building to something. The thought makes me tremble in fear. My body is beyond my control. No. I am in control. I search for a way home.

Heavy fog settles in the trees. I wonder how far up the mountain I've gone. I'm lost. Fear bubbles up in my stomach and comes out as a short laugh. I walk and the twigs dig into my feet. How did I get this far without waking up?

I remember something about following running water. With no water in sight, I choose to go downhill. If there's water, that's where it'd flow. After a few minutes of walking, it seems to be getting light out. I'm walking out of the night. Good.

It's so quiet, almost silent. Just the occasional crunch of branches and leaves as I tiptoe around tree roots. Then I hear something that makes my skin crawl.

Snap!

Harsh. Decided. An image flashes in my head. A boot on a branch. I freeze. A bird flies somewhere nearby. I move forward, willing myself to calm.

Snap!

I pick up my pace. I'm barefoot and lost. My foot finds itself in mud. Fuck. *Fuck!* Mud means there's water nearby. I take a moment to listen. A subtle flow that should be beyond human sound rings in my ears. I move toward the stream with purpose.

Though I'm disoriented, I'm not winded. I haven't been since coming home. Smells have been wreaking havoc on my nose. Now hearing. I can question this later. Right now, I need to get out of here.

I find the creek.

Snap!

Someone is following me. Whoever they are, they aren't advancing yet. I wash my feet and rinse my face. It hits me. The field from Bonfire Night. From what I remember of the map, it's near a river. It should be close. Looking, I find a worn path. I take it, quickly moving toward the familiar.

The field opens in front of me and relief washes over me. I'm in the woods and I know where I am. There are burned mounds and discarded beer cans. Looks like the high school kids still party out here. I see the fence Mr. Parker put up on the far side to keep them out.

I check over my shoulder. In the trees behind me, I see the figure of a man. His face is obscured by a mask. He lingers at the edge of the tree line, nestled in the fog. Seeing him makes me feel fuzzy, like my body is fleeing from the reality in front of me. I stare at him like a dumb animal trying to make sense of something new. Too seduced by shock to be aware of the danger, I open my mouth to call out to him. I stop when every hair on my body stands up. The small of my back tightens. The nape of my neck goes cold. The man shoulders a rifle.

He isn't following me. He's hunting me.

I take off across the field. Following a memory, I look for the path from Bonfire Night. Chris's home was down one of these paths. I choose one and sprint. I know I might be running toward my demise. But with little else to trust, Chris is my only hope.

Unfamiliar foliage flies past me. I feel like I could outrun a bullet. I see it! The space left by the tree I hid in a lifetime ago. I turn up the path. I pray Chris is home. I can hear footfalls following mine. My feet are bleeding. I'm slipping on mud and blood. I'm going to die. I'm going to die out here, alone.

Up ahead, I smell flowers. Not wildflowers. They smell familiar. I must be imagining a comfort before I end. *Breathe*.

A massive, wild blue rhododendron bush stops me in my tracks. A staple of suburbia in the middle of the woods. There's a flash of silver behind it. Silver and white. I see a trailer between the branches. It must be Chris's. I sprint toward it.

When I get to the door and pull it, it opens. I throw myself inside. A crash lets me know I've woken him up. I press myself against the floor, still afraid of bullets.

Chris stumbles toward me. "Liz?"

I can't catch my breath. "Man—outside—GUN!" is all I can get out.

He grabs a shotgun from his closet and heads out the door. He cocks it, looks to his left and to his right.

"Asshole, this is private property. If you show your face, I will shoot you!" His yell echoes in the morning.

Silence answers him. He waits. He looks. And looks. He closes the door and locks it behind him.

I'm shaking on the tile floor in both fear and relief. As my adrenaline falls, my mind races. The person chasing me had to be the younger one in the pair. Chris said his dad had a broken foot. He definitely couldn't pursue me through the trees like that. It's not him. I was so convinced I was alone. I do have one last person I can trust. Chris.

In the comfort of his home, I start to feel my injuries. My feet burn.

"Are you okay? Are you hurt?" he asks.

I can't answer, I just show him my hands. They are scratched and muddy. He grabs a towel and starts dabbing them. He runs to get hot water and soap. I'm still arriving in the moment. He kneels and cleans my bloody hands and feet. His back curves like the other night when he loaded the deer into his truck. His body is organized to the task at hand. Saving me. I can't remember the last time someone saved me.

I kiss him.

After the initial shock, he kisses me back. Then, before either of us can stop it, we fall into each other.

I don't have healthy sex. This is not that. This is the closest thing to what I think sex should be. I don't try to play things out three steps ahead in my mind. I'm in the moment and in this moment, I want him. When I'm met with an equal passion, I lose myself. It's a strange attraction and repulsion. The blood and mud shouldn't be arousing, but it is. Being this close to him should terrify me, instead, it calls me.

We are all touch and tongue and sweat and fever. There are no tricks or moves or impressing. It's animal satisfaction. My mind doesn't understand it. It doesn't get to understand it. I don't think Chris knows what this is either. Yes, we are familiar with the physics. I know what I'm doing, he knows what he's doing, what we are doing. The difference is us. We're together. There's not a leader or a follower or a giver or a taker, it's all need. Any sort of control has given way to abandon. I'm naked because I need his skin against mine. He is inside me because he needs to feel the depth of me. I'm shocked at how fast I come. It's a natural progression. No, it's a peak, and another one is coming. This. I have dreams about sex like this. I've longed for this overwhelming desire to show myself to another and for them to show themselves to me. He is beautifully open. I don't feel selfish asking him for what I need. He wants to do it, every part of him wants to give me what I want. Before I can think of the time it takes or how I look or smell, he digs himself deeper into my flesh, and I welcome him. I want to see him undone like this. I need it. I need to see that I can make him feel the way I do. So, so painfully present.

How long do we last?

How does it end?

How did it start?

I don't know. I do know I've never fucked like this before.

Now I'm terrified I'll never fuck like this again.

TWENTY-FOUR

I wake up satisfied for the first time in my life. Finally full of something, my mind is quiet. I'm too tired to think. Instead, I tend to my body. I catalogue my new wounds. My hands, feet, shins. All are peripheral to a new energy that lives in me. Glow isn't the word, it's more of an awakening.

Chris doesn't open the curtains, he doesn't want to let the light in on an act that feels more suited to night. He feels for me in the darkness of his bed instead. That's not where I am. I watch him reach for me and then move out into the rest of the trailer. Hunger groans in my belly.

I head out to his kitchen. Looking through the fridge and cabinets, I find some eggs. Pancake mix. Milk. I start cooking. After the smell of breakfast fills the air, I hear footsteps.

"I see you found food," Chris says with a smile. I don't look at him and keep cooking, moving through the motions with a slow familiarity. Needing to touch me, he wraps himself around my back and kisses my neck.

"Morning."

We eat naked and with our hands. We're quiet and content to sit in silence because we don't need words. A peacefulness finally enters my head. That's why I tell Chris the truth the moment he asks me the question.

"Why were you all the way out here?"

"I had a dream. I walked," I confess.

"All the way from your house?"

I wait for the answer to bubble out of me, like before. It can't. I haven't put it together for myself yet. Right now, all I want is to stay in this bliss for a moment longer.

I eat more pancakes. Sticky with syrup, I lick my fingers. The metallic tang of blood cuts through the sweet syrup. The wounds on my hands are painful, but not deep. The taste of my own blood makes my feet ache. Pain is starting to come back.

Chris's phone chirps and he's drawn to it. As he reads what's there he starts to cover his nakedness. He offers me a shirt. Piece by piece, we both clothe ourselves and come back to humanity. Chris plugs in my dead phone and I look around. Chris has a nice trailer. Lived in and definitely not as clean as his truck. The crayon lodged in the back of the bed flashes in my mind. I didn't ask him that night. I need to now. I still don't know what kind of man he is.

"Do you have crayons?"

"No." He shakes his head. "Why?"

"I saw a pink crayon in the back when we were loading up the deer."

"Oh! That." Chris hunches over his phone again. "I was helping my sister move. Box burst. Some of her kids' stuff spilled everywhere." He looks back at me.

I consider his response. I stay silent.

"I don't have kids, if that's what you're asking . . ." He's trying to figure out the leaps my mind is making.

So am I. "Do you know someone who would hunt people—girls—in the woods?"

The question stuns him for a moment. "No. Just animals."

"You ever meet any strange men in the trees?"

Chris drifts back into his memory. "One time, Dad and I came across another father and son. I was young. I didn't recognize them. The dad looked like a dad. But the kid? He was bad news. You could tell there was something off about him. He was beaten, probably. Looked like the type of kid who shot cats, or something."

"How could you tell?"

"His eyes. Even though he was young, they looked empty. He looked cold inside."

I try to picture the face in my mind. I'm met with the many faces of men whose eyes have chilled me throughout my life. All sparked the same feeling, but none of them stuck. No face belongs to the figure from my dreams or the man in the woods.

"Remember the shadows rhyme we talked about?" he asks.

"Yes."

"I looked," he says. "After I left your place, when I was getting rid of the deer. I saw something right on the edge of my vision. And ignored it for a good long while. Then I remembered what you asked me about seeing impossible things and the shadows. I looked. Real quick." Chris's breathing rises from his stomach to his chest. "I saw a woman. Too far away to make out anything specific." He breathes. "There was a little girl with her. A Black girl. She looked rough. And she rushed her away like . . . she was upset with her. I didn't even think of the search because this girl had someone with her."

"Where did you see them?" I pull up the map on my charging phone. I show it to Chris.

"Off these back roads, here, leading to the field." He squints and starts to move the map around, approaching from different angles.

"What?" I don't notice when he grabs my phone to get a better view. Caroline is alive.

"Your map is wrong," he says. He points to The Rounds. "Follow that, you'll end up twirling around in circles."

"The Rounds are crazy." Looks like Doug and I have something else to fight about. Caroline is alive!

"But there's a reason to them," Chris insists.

My brow furrows. "I was told this map was good."

"Simple mistake."

"You saw her at night?" I ask.

"Yes."

That would be the best time to move someone through that area without drawing attention.

Caroline is alive and in the woods.

I am going to get her out.

THE SCALES

CAROLINE

June 2017

I'm going to try and explain my relationship to fear to you. I will fail, but the attempt is important. How do you know what you are if you don't know what you're not? Little strings can come in to complicate things and attempt to gray this binary. When you are afraid, it's clear. Light and shadow are each defined by the absence of the other.

The First Night

Liz finally came back.

She was early.

I needed to get her to stay.

Caroline assured her survival just as much as I did. She wasn't for consumption. She wouldn't be eaten or used as fuel. I needed her alive. This meant I couldn't study her heart, her dreams, or her hopes. I'd get to know her from the outside. I had to leave this place. To do so, I needed to fish for all my missing pieces. Caroline was bait.

I hid the last thrown candle with shadows. When Liz left, I revealed it. The moment Caroline saw it flickering in the dark, she needed to retrieve it. A few steps into the woods and back out. The moment she stepped in, mud invaded her shoes. From the expression on her face, it'd gotten deep between her toes. The squelch of her steps reverberated through the trees like rain.

She moved faster, intent on running in and then right back out. The candle in the bush cast lashes of light into the branches, making long strands of darkness. Caroline approached the candle. She clasped it in her hands. In the prison of her fingers, the light illuminated the blood under her skin. I saw her fixation. Caroline was a girl who sought out shadows.

Snap!

She turned and let her eyes focus on the sound. When Caroline saw me, she didn't scream. She didn't run. Instead, she looked at me. Watching her see me, I saw her fear. Something more elusive lurked under it. What I longed for: unshakable belief.

The Fellow always brought their hearts to me dead. I never saw the Girls. The great muscle in their chests was how I learned who they were. The texture. The taste. The strength.

"Caroline," I said. I never got to do this part. The actual hunting was too dangerous for me. Unlike the Fellow, I had to earn my flesh and fluid. My body had few points of strength and large spaces of weakness.

"Yes?" she answered.

Poor child of technology. No one warned her about the woods and what to do if she heard the distraction of someone calling her name at night. She got the story her mother wove instead. A story of curious shadows, which wasn't entirely wrong.

"Mommy—!" I wrapped myself around her. Careful. This was dangerous for both of us. It does not take much strength to suffocate and it takes even less to tear.

Low branches ripped the edge of her dress and her leg. I put the candle back and pulled Caroline away.

I felt Liz approach. I saw her try to traverse the dark.

She failed.

Liz wasn't ready yet.

The Second Night

"What did you do?" the Fellow yelled. For the first time, I broke our bargain. I poached early, messing up the annual hunt. Caroline's friend Vicky and her upwardly mobile parents would be spared thanks to me. "What the hell did you do, Jack!" This Fellow yelled more than his father did. Young and full of hate. "Jack!" What is an accusation from a man whose voice can't span the depth in his chest? "This one is too valuable."

One drop in this country is all it takes. Being a Black girl is inhabiting a cruel riddle: Your beauty is denied but replicated. Your sexuality is controlled but desired. You take up too much space, but if you are too small, you are ripped apart. Despite the wash of it, that's one thing you can always count on whiteness to do: destroy a threat.

Caroline's white mother gave her credence. She'd get police out here. She'd get searches going. Most important, she'd make Liz stay.

"She stays," I said. I refused to let the girl come to harm. I let her make demands. Her first one?

Crayons.

The Third Night

I watched Caroline sleep. A part of me wanted to eat her heart to learn what was in her head. I didn't. This summer couldn't be like the others. After years of feeding the wants and needs of others, it was time to feed myself.

She was safe with me while the Fellow kept the search, the town, and Liz occupied. The surrounding trees were silent. Shame grows in silence. Once it's brought to light, it shrivels and dies faster than it ever took root. My shame was never so delicate.

When Caroline opened her eyes, I braced myself for her scream. She stared back at me with the fierceness of a little girl. I waited. Letting her decide about me for herself. I wondered if she noticed the food I made them bring her? The water? She didn't. She stared at me instead. Being seen for so long was strange. When she got close to me, I could hear her heart beat. I smelled how well she'd lived.

She looked at me like I was her savior. I've been many things, but never that. Her belief in me differed from his. The Fellow and I had an understanding. A bargain. I fed him and he fed me. Caroline needed me. She inspired me.

The Fourth Night

You learn a lot about a man by telling him "No."

He resented me for complicating our bargain and thwarting the power he held over me: I could not leave these trees and he could not banish me from his mind.

Caroline would not be quiet, she wouldn't eat the food they brought, she wouldn't stop crying. Seeing my Fellow wilt under her commands was enlightening.

If you ever acquire a partner, be sure they love you more than you love them.

The Fellow's partner did. A woman full of fear and rage. She'd always been curious about what he did in the trees and the stories of horror he shared with her. A few whispers were all it took for her to obey. She was a woman who wanted the world to hurt the way she did. I could use that if necessary. Like the Fellow, all she needed was someone to say "yes."

Anger lived in the Fellow in an expected way. Yelling. Clenched fists. Teeth.

Caroline's anger was so quiet it made me tremble.

Like his father, the man craved a legacy. It wasn't enough to kill and remain free. He wanted to ensure that his son had this freedom, and that his son's son had the same. This way, in a world that had increasingly told him "no," his line would remain above it and the inevitable weight of equity would never press them down.

He showed me the palm of his hand. In it was a nub of color. A crayon. Pink.

"Waste," I croaked.

He smiled. That was good. That meant he would move on. However, he pocketed the crayon.

"She's leaving too much behind and those dogs are on our trail." Another smile. "Don't you want to keep her in the dark?"

What did he know of the dark? He'd never faced it himself.

The scent of the dogs sat in the air as they tracked us. The Fellow knew how to throw off a search. The trainers instructed their animals to search for decay. So, when the smell of death was all around, the dogs wouldn't be able to differentiate.

The Fifth Night

"The precinct isn't half-assing things this time. Should have let me pick." There was the accusation. This was my mistake, and he wanted me to admit it. Silence would not force my answer.

The Fellow stood his ground, waiting for my response. He shouldered that stupid rifle and stayed where he stood. The simple tool with its hot lead wouldn't kill me, but it would slow me down. I needed all my strength for what was to come. He couldn't stop what was already in motion. Even in his reluctance, he did my bidding, maneuvering the strings in my plan. That showed me the truth. In his heart, he loved me still.

I wonder what people in town would make of the two of us.

A madman. A murderer.

A prophet. A monster.

That's it. He was the monster. I was his pet.

Pet.

That word worked its way inside me like a chill. It brushed my bones and left me cold. I was not made to be a pet. I was not made to serve a man. I was not made. I was conjured. Before that, I was a creature of the dark. Like him.

"Jack!" he barked. "If you cross me, I'll keep my father's promise. If this has anything to do with Liz, I'll kill her." The threat was real. He suspected what I was doing, but he had no idea of the scope. Everything he'd done, all I'd asked of him and his father over the years, was building to this moment. And to Liz.

No more supplies for Caroline. Soon they wouldn't matter. Her time was coming and so was mine.

That night, Caroline finally spoke to me.

"Are you a *Good Doggy*?" she asked.

This was a new title for me. I hoped to live up to it. After all the Girls had taught me, after years of feeding on them, listening to their secrets, hopes, and dreams, I hoped to finally be Good.

ONE

Nothing good happens in a parking lot. Yet this is where Doug insists we meet. Puppies aren't exchanged between cars. The upkeep of town doesn't extend to this corner of it. Pavement cracks around old faded lines. Chris parks from memory.

"Her hair?" I ask.

"Big brown-and-gold curls," Chris confirms for the third time. "In two . . . poofs." He hesitates around the word *poofs*. It sounds too light and fun to describe a girl some people think is dead. He's just confirmed that Caroline is alive. Someone has been keeping her and hiding her. A painfully nondescript white woman.

"Do you remember anything about her?" I ask.

"It was too dark. She was behind some brush. When I saw Caroline, I froze. She was scared. Terrified." The guilt in his voice is palpable. I recognize the feeling. He saw an impossible thing. Now it's haunting him.

Doug arrives in a dark sedan. I rest my hand on the door handle, but don't get out.

"What is it?" Chris asks.

"I messed things up for him bad. Real bad. Even after he helped me." He hasn't brought the authorities with him. "He protected me."

"From what?"

I think back to the fingerprints, the blood, DNA, all of it. "Myself." I don't have what Doug wants, his box, his files, his work. They are my only collateral. In the end, it's my word against his. "I need his help," I confess. Saying it out loud helps me get my bearings. I get out of the truck.

When my feet hit the ground, though they are covered by Chris's flip-flops, I flinch. The wounds are starting to get sensitive. I make my way toward Doug and his car. He doesn't even try to meet me halfway, almost like he's content to watch me limp. I have to walk all the way across the parking lot before he speaks to me.

"Where's my box?" Doug's all business today.

"I'll give the box back to you after we talk."

Doug looks over my shoulder at Chris in his truck. "You sure you didn't leave it with your boyfriend?"

I do my best not to roll my eyes at him. Bitterness isn't a good look for Doug, but it feels oddly familiar on him. I start to cock my head but my burning feet stop me. "Please, Doug?" I don't like being on this side of begging. "It sucks you got fired, but I'm not sorry about what I asked you to do."

"That's a shit apology. Where's the box?" he presses. "Clearly you don't have it. I'll just send the detectives your address and your boyfriend's plates. I'm sure they'll have fun tracking it down." He turns to get back into his car.

"Caroline is alive." I watch his face.

He blinks over and over again. "How do you know that?"

"Chris saw her with a woman in the woods." I make sure Doug is looking at me. "She's alive, and she needs our help." I'm not letting him back out of this again. Not now. "And one of the guys we're after tried to kill me this morning."

That stops him. "Did you get a look at him?"

"He had a mask on. White. Experienced hunter. Chased me through the woods." I show him my palms, my arms. The scar on my wrist remains. Quickly, I roll it away. I'm not showing him my feet yet.

"You sure you saw someone?"

"I'd bet my life on it."

He nods, but still looks hesitant. His body is stiff and his sweat turns sharp and heavy; he's nervous, or scared. I rub my hand under my nose and the sharp smell of blood makes his scent dissipate.

"Could it have been a dream? A blackout?" He's covering his bases.

"No. This is real."

"Stress?"

I laugh hard at that. "Who cares if I've suddenly become a medium if it means we get Caroline back alive? I'll figure out how to be a witchy aunt after." I'm trying to make him laugh, but Doug's had enough of my sarcasm.

"What were you doing out there?"

"Sleepwalking. Thank God I didn't use your map. Why did you give me a bad map?"

"It's a *great* map!" Doug is really defensive about being called out. "Who told you it's wrong?"

"Someone who knows the place better than you." The moment I say that both Doug's and my anger neutralize. We have the same thought. The killer would know that part of the woods like the back of his hand.

Instantly, I defend Chris. "No. He protected me from the guy this morning. It can't be him. He *saved* me after I sleepwalked out there."

"Do you do that often?" Doug's concern is surprising, especially after our last meeting. He looks at my feet. I glance down and see that blood is visible now on the sides of the flip-flops.

"Never."

He shakes his head. "That's . . ." He rubs his hand through his hair. "Crazy." He goes for the driver's-side door.

I block him. "Look at me, Doug. Does it look like I'm lying?"

Doug does just that. I can only imagine what he sees. My hair is wild. My face and arms are streaked with blood. I have bruises and cuts on my body.

"I owe you an apology," he says.

"Don't apologize. Help me. We need to—"

"We are more screwed than we ever realized." He sighs. This meeting isn't just about getting his box back and scolding me. He's figured something out. It's shaken him. "I was thinking through the DNA test I did. I'm fast, quiet—I wouldn't have been caught unless I was being watched. When the department fired me I lost it and didn't think it through. Someone has been watching me—*us*—every part of this case like a hawk. I didn't even think of it until I thought about the box."

"What?"

"Oswald has been doing everything with these cases for years. You saw me—I run blood tests, get fingerprints—I do grunt work. I thought it was 'cause he didn't think I could do it. Now I realize it's 'cause he didn't *want* me to do it. I thought about what you said about there being two killers? You are absolutely right. And they've been watching you since the night Caroline disappeared." He swipes on his phone and pulls up a familiar face.

Lauren Bristol.

"The car is registered in her name. But she has a husband. I missed it 'cause she didn't take his last name." He shows me a mug shot. The face staring back at me chills me to the bone. He looks like one of the men Chris described to me. Empty eyes. "Tim Oswald. His son. Tim has been in and out of the system his entire life for violent stuff."

I feel bad for Lauren. I ran home after almost fifteen years when I survived a man like that. But for her grief to manifest like this is terrifying.

"I need the box because I'm locked out of the system. I'm pretty sure Oswald determined cause of death for all those girls. If he did, it's the perfect crime."

"So you went ahead and solved this whole thing without me?" I chuckle.

"I told you. I'm about finding the answers." Doug swallows hard. "And that's also where I stop. It's gonna take an army to take out the Oswalds. I need to bring everything to the department and let them take it from there."

"What?" It's all I can say. After everything, Doug still believes. "What if they just bury him, sweep it all under the rug—it's gonna look bad for the department—"

"This is the right thing to do, Liz." He makes for the door again.

I spread myself against the car. "And let them kill Caroline. Have you ever thought about *why* some of the girls aren't found immediately?" I grab Doug, keeping him from leaving. "Isn't it time someone hunted *them* for a change?"

"Yes." He pries my hands off of him. "With the due process of the law."

"Fuck the law. They have actively denied this for decades. No help is coming from them. C'mon, Doug! I'm all in. What do you have to lose?"

"I've lost enough."

"We're both at rock bottom, then."

"You didn't hear me." Doug tries again. "I don't have a job—hell, a career. That was all I had. You're losing sleep? Take a pill. We can't fix this by charging in to certain death. She's alive? Great. Perfect time to bring all this to the department."

"What if you going after him makes him kill her?"

"Do you want justice or revenge?" Doug slides me off the car door and opens it. Surprised by his strength, I struggle to stop him. He shuts the door in my face. I pound on the window with bruised and bloody hands. Doug starts the car.

I scramble for the words. "Wait! Doug, wait!" I shove my fingers through the open window and grip the glass. "Caroline is running out of time. The search party on one end and us on the other? It was enough to make him frame me and get you fired. If we do it again—if we go out there tonight—don't you see this is the only way she comes home alive? We go to the department, they open an investigation. Who knows how many allies he has—she's dead. If we try to get the search changed, drag them out to where he's holding her, if the police look like they are on to him, if they change any behaviors—she's dead. He is exploiting the system; as long as it's running, we can use it to our advantage." I see my words catch him. "We get to Lauren when she's moving Caroline. That's our chance." I remember how I got him on my side in the first place. "If you are right about this, you'll never have to fill a blood bag again. You'll be a legend. A hero." I let go of the window and wait.

Doug turns off the car. "I'm an idiot," he mumbles. He rolls the window all the way down.

"You're in?"

"Yes." Doug nods. "I gotta tell you something. If we let the system continue, the department is gonna keep digging. They already sent a detective to my house. They questioned me." The expression on his face betrays his concern. "They don't do that for something that should be HR—admin work. They're asking people about you. Building a case."

I swallow. "So it looks like I really need your help."

"If they had anything concrete, they would have arrested you by now. They're suspicious. Don't give them any reason to pursue you and they won't."

I comb over the last twenty-four hours. If they've been following me, I've already given them plenty of reason.

"Meet outside my house tonight. We can head into the woods from there, come at them sideways."

"Aside from that, do you have a real plan, Liz?"

"I will by then." I pat the side of Doug's car and head back over to Chris's truck. As I think of a way back to the woods, a plan forms in front of me.

TWO

At the end of my mother's driveway, the silence between Chris and me rings in the air of the car.

"Liz?" His voice draws me back.

I've been here before. A night of passion and connection, now awake, we both are trying to figure out how to say "see you later" like adults. Unsure of what to do next, we go through the motions of a polite goodbye.

"Thanks for driving me home."

"Am I . . ." he starts. "Am I ever going to see you again?" How did a line from a romance novel end up in his mouth? He sounds earnest. I look at him. He seems just as shocked as I am. The disappointment I find in Chris's eyes nearly breaks me. He doesn't want me to leave. The man I'd been thinking about for years is sitting right in front of me, afraid to ask me to stay.

I need to go.

I rush through the correct response. "Chris, I don't— I can't—" I stumble. I still don't have the words. Giving up on speech entirely, I reach for the door.

"I know the woods," he says. "I can help. I know where I saw them. If you are trying to find them again, you're gonna need help—backup." Chris has guessed my plan before I've even said it. He saw Caroline at night. After days of police searches, using dogs, that means she's being moved, using darkness as cover. He unlocks the glove compartment, pushes aside his registration. Beneath it is a folded knife.

"What's that for?" I ask.

"My father told me to keep a weapon on me at all times, 'cause it doesn't take much for people to lose their humanity."

I know that now. I always did, but I have a habit of finding only the best in people.

"Someone is kidnapping girls in this town, then killing them out in the woods. Taking their hearts," I say. It feels freeing to finally tell him the whole truth. I watch him put our previous conversations together.

"Do the police know?"

"They're years behind on this. I can get them caught up or I can get Caroline." I search his face. A steady blank expression is all I get. I know I'm right about time. From the moment I first lost sight of Caroline, from the moment Keisha and I met eyes in the dark, I've been playing catch-up.

"I'm sure the cops know something. They're keeping things close so they don't tip anyone off." As he talks, his words lose their speed and assuredness. Excuses drying up, he knows I'm right. "Liz, you have a good heart. Don't go breaking it over things you can't control."

"What happened to Keisha wasn't an accident." That's what all this boils down to. I'm tired of hearing why Black girls go missing. I know why. I've learned the reasons. The girls are still gone. I don't want to have to tell Chris why he's deflecting or looking for excuses. I want him to intuit it for himself. I need Blackness to exist as it always has and not be conveniently brushed aside for his comfort.

I wait.

Chris doesn't respond.

In his silence, I find what I truly sought in him, in myself. I don't need Chris. I need his belief. I need his desire for me to move him more than thoughts and prayers and a knife. He's wrong. I came here to figure out who or what I could trust. In doing so, I looked for it in everyone except myself. Because trusting myself means admitting the pain I'm in, not just now, but before. Trusting myself means doing things that are hard and dangerous. Trust means I have to face how I've lived and ask myself if it was good for me or for someone else. Here's a start. I don't have a good heart. I have a broken one. Finding Caroline, solving this, is how I start to put it back together. That's why the trees that once terrified me are calling me.

"I need backup."

Chris shifts around in a way that I'm not familiar with. He doesn't want to let me down. It's a fear I'm not used to seeing in someone else. I take a second to memorize this dance in his body, for reference, so if I ever see it again, I'll know. I take the knife and get out of the car.

"Liz!"

I don't turn.

"I'm not letting you go alone. You're looking for her tonight?" Chris confirms. "Where should I meet you?"

"Here. After dark."

"Okay." He nods. "I'll be here." He looks more scared than I do. That's it. There's the help I need.

As Chris pulls away, I look at the knife he gave me. It looks old and well used. I open it. The blade is black. The fine edge surprises me. It's been well cared for. Also, the teeth. It has a serrated edge, like a saw. Little hooks. The edge looks paper thin. A knife this sharp would cut through flesh like butter. With extra teeth, it would make quick work of bone too.

THREE

I'm old enough to remember the importance of a phone call. I remember calling Mel's house, getting her parents, and asking for her. I remember talking about the dumbest things for hours. We'd hear Nick click in and yell him off the line. A warm ear has always reminded me of Mel. Every friend after her has been measured against Mel. Since returning home, I've learned so much about the town I grew up in. And about Mel. I came back to connect with her but we've only gotten further apart. I never questioned our friendship because we were young and grew up together. And because, years ago, when everyone else left me in the woods, Mel saved me.

After all my calls went straight to voicemail, I head to Mel's house. She needs to know that Caroline is alive and that I'm going in after her. When I arrive, I see one police car in the driveway, but that's it. I check up and down the block and watch the front door. The cruiser must be Nick's.

I get out of my car and slowly approach the door. I knock and get nothing. I knock again. Just the echo of a hollow house. There's no way I'm doing this without Mel. In the end, it should be her who brings Caroline home. I give it one more knock. The door gives.

"Liz?" It's Mel. She opens the door fully and looks at me. In our time apart, her eyes have become like Denise's, impossibly bright and hollow at the same time. Her hair is still in the same bun it's been in for days. She grips the edge of the doorframe in her hand. She's not ready to let me in yet.

I need to tell her. "Deer guts. It was deer guts in the tarp. Not Caroline."

"They told me. How did you know?"

"The rest of the deer ended up on my mother's dining room table."

"Is she okay—are *you* okay?"

"I will be," I admit. "Mom handled it like a pro. She was cleaning and . . ." I can't keep my face up in front of Mel. "I'm so scared for her. Someone is setting me up—which is bad enough—but they got to her. *Her.*"

"Because of the questions you've been asking? What you found out about those girls?"

"Yes." I know this doesn't explain everything. I know she's still justified in her anger about me accusing her father. But I hope she sees that this is destroying me too.

"I'm sorry." I can't tell if she's apologizing for leaving me in the woods, or if she is sorry for me discovering what I have. She lets the edge of the door go and lets me in.

The air of the house is heavy with grief. Her house is losing its light. I can tell that things are out of place with items haphazardly put onto shelves or stacked in corners.

Stepping over the threshold reveals the house isn't as empty as it seems. Garrett is in the kitchen with Nick. Garrett is still, eyes fixed on the door. Nick paces with a quiet fury.

"What the hell is she doing here?" Nick asks.

"She wants to talk," Mel says, her voice a breath.

"Get out—" Nick starts, but Garrett stops him.

"Mel?" Garrett asks. "You want Liz here, right?"

Mel nods. "Yes." She sits on a stool in her kitchen. It creaks under her weight. I didn't notice before, but theirs is the opposite of Doug's house. Nothing here is meant to last, it's too white and shiny.

I stand in front of all of them. Though Nick wants me gone, it looks like he isn't leaving.

"Why are you here, Rocher?" he says.

I know Nick will relay anything I say to the department. He'll get the search changed, go after Oswald, and we are screwed if that happens.

"It's important that the search continues as it has once I say what I have to say."

Nick narrows his eyes at me. It's so similar to Mel's expression.

"Nick?" Garrett asks.

"Depends." He shrugs.

Mel turns to him. "Nick, please?"

All eyes on him, temper abated, he agrees. "Fine."

"Caroline is alive. Chris saw her with a woman in the woods." I watch Mel intently. She silently reaches for Garrett. The moment they make contact, it's like he's absorbed all his wife's questions. He launches into them while Mel quietly weeps tears of relief.

"What— How do you— Did you see her?"

I lay out all I know for them. The missing girls, the mothers, Keisha, the woman in the woods with Caroline.

"Thirty-two years?" Nick raises an eyebrow. "No way that would get past the department."

"They're *in* the department, Nick," I say. Could telling Nick completely upend my entire plan to get Caroline out? Yes. But if I don't involve him, he's going to find out anyway. Then he'll have no choice but to tell the department, and Caroline dies. "Oswald and his son, Tim," I say. "And it looks like Lauren too. If any department behavior changes, they'll get tipped off." For the first time since I've known him, Nick falls silent. He has nothing to say to me.

"The cycle, solstice, the hearts," Garrett starts, "it all feels like—"

"A ritual?" I finish. "I can't figure out what or who they're worshipping."

"Do they always find them . . ." Mel runs her hand down her sternum.

"They don't always find them," I say. "And that's not all they do." I don't mean to crush Mel's hope. I need everyone in the room to know what's on the line if we don't get Caroline now. "I want to go out there and try to save her."

"How did you figure all this out?" Nick's not looking at me with annoyance or hate anymore. There might be a bit of admiration, but mostly it's curiosity.

"I listened."

"You need to speak to Detective Turner—"

"They're building a case against me. Right? My DNA is at both scenes." I face Nick now, no longer afraid. "Do you want me to talk to him, or do you want to turn me in?"

The concern that was once on Nick's face is gone. The anger is back. He's getting better at lying.

"They took family off searches this morning," Nick admits. "They think things are going poorly and don't want us there if they find her. Pulled me aside and told me to make sure everyone in the family had their statements together, just in case."

"The rescue mission has been turned into a recovery." Garrett takes a deep breath. Such simple words for a harsh thing.

"I can make sure it stays that way," Nick offers. It looks like it physically pains him, but he says, "Rocher is right. We have to act fast. Using the search as a distraction is . . . brilliant."

"The forest is huge. Where are we starting?" Garrett asks.

"The Rounds. Near Bonfire Night. That's where Chris saw her, and the best place to hide her. Has the search been through there yet?"

"It'll get there late tonight, early tomorrow. Don't wanna be in there in the dark, but they want to find Caroline."

There is more than one way to get out there. "Meet me at my mother's house. At sundown. Be ready to hike."

FOUR

At home, I grab jeans and sneakers, the outfit I was going to wear on my train back to NYC. Seeing what remains in my suitcase, I think back to what this trip was supposed to be. Forty-eight hours. A quick visit home, a best friend's wedding, and a reclamation of self. Figuring out who and what I could trust. I roll my head. The tender spot on my neck has faded. The muscles there are releasing. Too bad they're clenching everywhere else.

I head downstairs. The sun is setting. It's dim in the house, but I don't need to use any lights because I've relearned my home. Ten steps to the landing. Full ninety-degree turn. Then eight more down to the first floor. Directly diagonal, it's six swift steps to a narrow hallway. As I walk twelve steps to the kitchen, I wonder about the history of my home. It's far enough up the mountain to have avoided the flood. I make it just past the kitchen when the overhead lights turn on and blind me.

"Liz?" It's my mother. She hasn't sounded this tired with me since I was a teenager. I guess I'm asking for it since I'm acting like one. She's sitting in the kitchen, waiting for me.

I start my lie. "I'm fine."

"I do not think so."

"I swear."

My mother grimaces. She offers me a seat. I take it.

"I'm just going for a walk to clear my head."

My mother gives me silence again. It's finally happened. We're somewhere we've never been. She can't avoid it. I smile at her, but it doesn't help. That's never been how we communicate. We both press until one relents. For years, it's been my mother pushing me. For the last few days, I know I've taken her to the edge. Now we might be across from each other as equals for the first time in our lives.

"I am making hot chocolate." She rises and retrieves a ball of cocoa.

"It's too warm for that."

"Outside it is. But inside? You look cold."

"Stop. I don't want it."

"More for me."

I stand and watch her work. She grates the cocoa. Warms the evaporated milk. Adds cinnamon and anise. The secret pinch of spices. My nose reveals them to be cloves, cardamom, and dried ginger. The smells are overwhelming. Obvious secret ingredients. I didn't notice them before because I didn't want to. As long as I couldn't name them, the cocoa retained its magic. Now everything about it smells sickly sweet. I start to feel slightly queasy. I want salt.

"Here." She rests the hot chocolate in front of me. I don't even touch the cup.

"That's for you. I said I didn't want it."

"Just a sip."

"It's too hot."

"It will cool." She settles against the counter with her mug. "Tell me, *cherie*. What is going on with you?" She sips her cocoa for comfort.

I watch my mother and see the lack in her. She works hard to cover it. Some of it is deflected onto me. Other parts she swallows so deep in herself, I know I couldn't remove them even if I were a surgeon. There's a secret chamber in her where her doubt runs wild.

"I'm fine. Just tired," I say.

"I had things I thought my mother could not understand when I was your age."

I don't respond.

Marie takes another sip. "For a long time, I longed for my home. I wanted to go back to the heat and the familiar trees and the language I dream in. Then I remembered, I brought all that with me when I came to this country. I had my family. My community. I need not go through anything alone. Neither do you."

"Then why do you insist on being alone, Mom? Why ignore the flyers—why stay here?"

She looks pained. "That will be anywhere I go. What if it follows me? And is worse somewhere else?"

"But you lock yourself up here."

She waves my concerns away. "I can visit you. And now you have finally come to see me." She's trying to dismiss me, but she's made my point.

"And look what happened." I need to handle this. "I grew up here. In this country, in this town, where, no matter how many times I come home, I'm still a visitor. We both are."

My mother's patients used to bring her articles from the internet, certain of their diagnosis. Most doctors deal with this. She always had to answer twice as much. Because her education was different from their own, her expertise wasn't enough. I envy her ability to keep her doubt tucked away. All the other experts in my life are exhausted. I need her experience. I take out my phone. I scan the images and land on the ones I snapped of the deer.

My mother looks at the carcass, disgusted at first. "No, no—"

"You've seen worse, yes?"

"Of course. But when it is surgery, it is clean. Blocked off. I just see the problem, *konprann*?" I do. I take my fingers and zoom in to the chest cavity and nothing else. No strangely cocked head. No limbs. Just white displaced ribs, pink cartilage, and thick musculature that is supposed to come together like music, but has broken apart like a sour chord.

My mother looks. She was right about the liver. What can she tell me about this? At her direction, I do a few swipes and expands.

"They knew what they were doing," she says.

"Like a hunter?"

"Maybe." She points to the floppy arteries that remain. "It is impressive. The cuts here are exact." She focuses on the bone. "But that is a saw. Not a knife or scalpel. It is straight and you can see some dust in the tissue. This deer was not slaughtered, it was deliberately pulled apart."

I look again. I can't believe I've missed it. The leftover tissues were there deliberately. Like in the picture of Brittany Miller, all of it was made to look like something else. Or to copy someone else. Like father, like son? This was taught. Learned. Hence the two styles. I remember how Sydney hovered over Doug. He must have done the same to Tim.

"And the cavity itself, it is cleaned the way I would do it. From the top down. That way, there is less pooling blood. What else do you need, *cherie*?"

"Nothing." My mother looks pitiful. There's nothing she can reveal, or say, or do, to change what is going on inside of me. I see the disappointment on her face, so I clarify. "Silence. I need some quiet."

That's the truth.

I need it now more than ever. Even though I can sense the hurt in my mother, I told that small truth to save her the pain of the lie.

"Do not lose yourself."

I nod. "Yes."

My mother adds, "Are you safe?"

"Yes." I notice the comfort the second lie gives my mother, so I add a smile for extra measure.

"I do not think so. You were not safe in the city."

Shame is a strong thing. It kept me silenced. Now it invites me to open up.

"He hurt me."

My mother doesn't say a word. I watch her try to put together the best thing, and I see her come up short. My mother has missed out on the truth of my life because she can't tolerate it. I've given her the lies because anything except the narrow path of perfection is unacceptable. I had to be good. I *have* to be good. That was the only way for me to survive.

"I was too afraid to leave before he . . ." I look at my mother and see myself. I see a woman hurting and wondering how to build herself back up, and why she has to build herself up in the first place. I see my mother hurting both for herself and for me. I know she wants to fix this. I know she knows she can't.

"I was supposed to start a clinic here. I had everything ready to go and then that girl disappeared from your school. I got scared. The threats came in their little baggies. I shut everything down because I was scared. The anger in this country, it is not like Ayiti. I used to think it was gone. Or neutered. But it is here. It is a matter of who gets to be angry and who gets to seek vengeance or claim justice. The anger here is not the kind that starts revolutions, it is the kind that wages wars. We fight other countries, the news, the politicians, all fight fight fight and bicker bicker bicker. There are lines and systems—rules of engagement. In Ayiti, the government and the people have an uneasy deal. They cross each other often. When I lived there, it made me edgy. The way things are here, people go so far out of their way to smile to your face and stab you in the back. Even with the language: English. You have to put together so many words to be understood. That is not even being heard, just understood." Her eyes go back to the deer. She takes in the gore like a physician. It's a problem to be solved. "When your patient dies and the vultures come, they do not come for your patients who were sickly in the end. They want the ones who could fight. They seek hearts like this. Strong hearts."

I nod. Is this what all the girls are "guilty" of in the eyes of men like Tim and his father?

"Elizabeth? Promise me, whatever this is, you will come home."

"I promise." I do. But I'm putting on such a strong face for her that I can't tell if I'm lying.

FIVE

I arrive at the edge of my driveway and find Doug, Chris, Mel, Garrett, and Nick waiting for me. We outnumber the foes we could be facing by three, but we're going in blind, and at a disadvantage. If Oswald, Tim, and Lauren are doing this, they are united. Looking out at everyone, the cracks in our factions are glaring. Mel and Garrett are here for Caroline, both desperate for her to be returned home. Against the backdrop of the trees, they look delicate. Neither has had a full night's rest in days. It's cruel to ask them to do this. It's worse not to involve them in a plan that could kill their child. I do my best to keep Nick in my sights. He says he knows where the search is going. He says he won't try to thwart our attempt. I don't trust him. But he is right, I need him. If we do encounter the search party, if we need to mask our presence—he's too useful to leave behind. My best shot at this comes from Doug and Chris. Out of all of us, they are the only two who aren't painfully connected to Caroline. If someone can be level-headed in the trees, it's them.

I shove down my fear. This is the only chance we have. Here and now. We're wasting time.

"Ready?" I ask.

No one responds. I notice Garrett eye Chris and Doug with suspicion. I quickly introduce everyone and some tension dissipates. I don't say all of it is gone, because Garrett gives Chris one last lingering look before turning back to me. Now that we have an unsteady alliance, I look out at the woods and think through the next steps.

"What's the plan?" Chris asks.

"We . . ." Doubt climbs into my chest. I don't let it reach my voice. "We head out to where Chris saw Caroline before the search party gets there. Press them from both ends. We're closer from here, and approaching from another angle, we have an advantage." Too bad it's our only one.

"Oswald is at the site tonight. He'll be distracted. At worst, we face Lauren and Tim." Nick pats his gun.

"We're going at night and we're looking for Lauren," I insist. The group seems to side with me more. No one wants to start shooting in the dark. Still, we're not going in unarmed. I have a knife, so do Doug and Garrett. Chris has a rifle. But I know we look more threatening than we are.

We head into the trees.

"You sure of the way?" Nick asks.

"I know it," Chris says as he steps between us, giving me an excuse to walk with him for a while and leave Nick behind. Walking with Chris in the dark, I'm still so aware of him. His breath, the direction he's looking, where his body balances as we head up the steep terrain.

"Damn it!" Doug hisses. I turn back and see him far below us on the path. It seems like he's snagged his pants on some branches. His flashlight waves around in the dark as he frees himself. I realize I've never seen Doug in the woods until now. His movements are clumsy but assured. He's putting on confidence here. Underneath it, he's even more on edge than I am. Or *was*. This place doesn't terrify me anymore. After facing the woods, I know it's not the trees I have to be afraid of.

We get closer, and the paths disperse. We have two choices: walk in one another's footsteps or spread out and trust one another not to alert everything in a mile radius to our presence.

"I'll take front." Nick pushes past all of us before anyone can stop him.

"You know where you're going?" Chris asks.

"Of course." A pissing contest of who has the best directionality starts. Looking at us all, I think the only people in danger of getting lost are Doug and Garrett. I give Mel a quick look and she gets behind me. Nick in the lead, followed by Chris, then Mel and myself, Garrett, and finally Doug. We all crest the mountain and head toward The Rounds.

Nick waves his light around every few moments, clearly something he's been trained to do, or something he's seen on TV. The harsh glow of his flashlight bounces between the leaves and cuts through anything I can make out. I hate that we're blindly following him.

"Why did he want to come? To control everything?" I whisper back to Mel.

"He cares about Caroline," she says back. "And"—she leans in—"he believes you."

"Yeah, right."

"When they started asking questions about you, he told them to back off. That you were helping in your 'own misguided way.'"

The trees start to get denser as we get closer. Chris turns back to me.

"Hey." His familiarity feels intimate. "We're making way too much noise." He takes the side of my palm and runs his finger across the middle with care. "We're going to have to kill the lights and split up."

I look over my shoulder. Mel and Garrett are keeping up. Doug has fallen behind again. I thought bringing him would help with numbers, now I'm stuck taking care of him.

"Stop Nick and stay here with Mel and Garrett," I say. "I'll get Doug."

Chris moves into action. I turn back to Mel and Garrett.

"We're going to have to go dark and split up."

Garrett chimes in first, "Hell no."

"They're gonna hear us coming," I add.

Nick shines a light through a few more trees. "Search party will be coming through here any minute. They should already be here."

I look back and see Doug, a lump of shadow in the darkness. I wave at him to make his way ahead. He does, but it looks like every step pains him. When he finally reaches us, we've agreed on a new course of action without him.

"We need to cut the lights, spread out horizontally, and sweep," I tell him. "Search party will be here soon. We need to stay ahead without tipping them off."

Doug looks at me like I'm a madwoman. "Splitting up. In the dark?"

"That way, if they catch one of us, they don't catch all of us. And they won't see us coming. After a few minutes, we'll adjust." I turn ahead and see that Mel and Garrett have paired off. Nick is doing the math in his head. Clearly Chris is going to choose me. He shines his Maglite at Doug.

"Come on, Nowak. You're with me," Nick groans.

We spread out and one by one our lights go out. I feel Chris grab my hand. He's trying to comfort me.

Snap!

The sound is so clear it echoes around us. I push on. Someone, probably Doug, pushed through a branch. It's fine.

Snap!

There it is again. I do my best to control my breath. I can't lose it out here. Not now. Not after everything I've been through.

Nick motions wildly for us to stop. He crouches. We all do at the same time. Not a moment later, a bar of light sweeps over our heads.

"*Caroline!*" It's the search party.

I press myself against the forest floor. Thankfully, it's not the majority of the party. Or Search and Rescue. I count two officers. They must be the fringes of the fan. They are careful. Thorough. Moving painfully slow. Bits of their conversation reach us.

"West quadrant, clear. Heading back for changeover." The radio squawks in response. Almost instantly, we all hear an echo. From my position on the ground, I see Nick fumble with something on his belt. The officers signal with the radio again. Nick makes a definitive motion to his side, silencing what I've just realized is his radio. The officers freeze.

"You hear that?" one says. They point their lights in our direction.

Why the hell does Nick have a radio? I see Doug and him struggle. I know a silent fight when I see one.

"Anybody out there?" The officers move toward us. I try to press myself farther into the ground. Cold wetness seeps through my clothes. Leaves and rocks press into me. If they find us, this is over. I look for where I can run.

"Hello?"

Snap!

That was decisive. Present. Doug and Nick pause. No one else moves. That wasn't us. The officers pivot their lights in the sound's direction and signal on the radio. After another quick bit of chatter, they go after the noise.

Their footfalls diminish quickly in the trees and their lights fade as they move farther off. Once we are sure they are far enough away, all of us rise. In the quiet, Nick and Doug's fight has grown.

"*Give me that!*" Doug whispers harshly through his teeth. "He has a radio."

"To know our position." Nick tries to wrestle the device from Doug's hands. Doug holds fast. "How else would we steer clear of the search?"

"Why not tell us!" Doug gets the radio away. "Unless he wants us to get caught and turn us in." He puts it on the ground and stomps on it. The sound of crunching plastic twinkles through the forest. I look back where the officers left. They had to have heard that. We need to break up the fight.

"Keep it down," I say.

"What the hell, Nowak!" Nick shoves Doug, but Doug is solid despite his size. Nick swings. Doug easily uses Nick's force against him. A quick shift in his weight and Doug sends Nick's fist hurtling past him. Off-balance, Nick clambers to stay up. On the steep incline, his foot lands strangely. Doug shoves him with his full weight.

Pop!

That wasn't a branch.

Nick bites down his scream. It rattles his whole body. He buries his head in his elbow to muffle his cries.

"Light!" Doug reaches for Mel's flashlight. She gives it to him. Pointing it down, he shines the light on Nick's leg. It's bad. His leg is jammed between two stones, twisted. Enclosed by his pants, his foot points in the wrong direction, and the shin curves at a terrible angle. Blood pools fast.

Doug defends himself. "He was signaling on the radio—"

Unable to speak without screaming, Nick emphatically shakes his head. *No!*

"I know what I saw," Doug insists.

Mel reaches for her brother and then looks at me. "What are we gonna do?"

My mind goes blank. Nick is bleeding. A lot.

"Can you help him?" I ask Doug. Doug tries to look at Nick's leg, but Nick shoves him away. He writhes in pain. He's going to get loud soon. I turn to Doug. He looks lost. Right. He works in a morgue, not a hospital.

Garrett grabs me by the shoulder and turns me around. "Look," he whispers. In the distance, the lights are back. Oh God. I was right, they heard us. I turn back to Nick. His breathing echoes in the trees. We need to leave now if we don't want to get caught.

"Doug, stay with Nick." I see Nick shake his head again. "And Garrett, stay too. Mel, Chris, and I will go on." I see Nick figure out my plan with me. I turn back to Doug. "Give us as much time as you can."

Chris grabs Mel's hand, pulling her away from her brother. I reach out for her when Garrett yanks me back. He catches me before I fall. He gets right in my ear.

"He— Chris was." Garrett doesn't understand why this bit of information is important, but he knows he must tell me. "He was the older guy dating Keisha. I'm sure of it." Mel grabs my hand and I follow her.

We carefully give the officers a wide berth. Crouching along the forest floor, I balance and follow and think. It shouldn't matter that Chris was the older guy dating Keisha, but it won't let me go. That explains why he remembers how she smelled.

The officers' lights pass by us in the dark. Their radios echoing in the trees. They are close. Too close. Chris, Mel, and I separate and hide out of their line of sight.

"Who's out there?"

Light washes between the trees in our direction. We didn't get enough space. I hold my breath and pray. I try to will Nick, Doug, and Garrett to start the distraction even though we don't have enough distance. I'm pressed behind a wide tree. To my left Mel is crouched behind a shelf of rocks. To my right Chris is in some low brush, seconds away from slipping.

I feel someone tap my arm. It's Mel. She points ahead of us. The lights shift shadows as the officers move past. In the distance, I see something more substantial than a shadow move. There's a distinctly human figure ahead of us.

The flashlights catch the shape of a woman.

"*Hey!*" the officers yell.

We all see a woman a long distance away. I barely have time to discern much about her when she runs.

Nick screams.

His pain courses through the air. The lights shift to the guys. Mel, Chris, and I have seen enough. When the officers run to Nick, we run after Lauren. Mel reaches back for my hand and I take hers. We fall into a pace. I hear heavy footfalls behind me. Trusting Mel to continue to pull me forward, I glance back. It's Chris. Mel grips my hand so tight she might break it. I keep up with her. I feel like all my dreams of running have prepared me for this. I do my best to control my breath and find that I can. I haven't run since my breakup. But I'm miraculously in shape now . . . I'm keeping up with Mel. Even Chris is having trouble with her stride. Mel pulls me through more brush and we hit a path. The three of us look. We don't see Lauren.

Mel gasps for breath along with Chris. I keep searching. I crouch close to the ground and look for footprints. Disrupted underbrush. Anything to see where she might have gone.

"Which way to the bonfire field?" I ask Chris.

Without skipping a beat, Chris grabs my hand and leads us north, up the path. With every turn, I troubleshoot. My mind won't let go of what Garrett said to me.

He was the older guy dating Keisha.

Denise mentioned Keisha had a friend, and she thought it was a boy because of her secrecy. Garrett said that was one of the rumors about her disappearance for years. Lauren was too concerned with Chris at the wedding. I thought it was just a misplaced crush, but she followed me at night. I flash back to when I confronted her outside her garden—the same garden she offered my mother cuttings from in exchange for gossip.

Blue rhododendron.

The same rhododendron I saw outside Chris's trailer. The only bit of landscaping. I look at the path around us and my feet are landing in my teenage steps. He knew the map was wrong. He's the only one able to unknot the trails back here. As he grips me I feel the cut I noticed the other night seep through its wrapping. It's deep. My hand is getting slippery with his sweat and blood. He turned his headlights off back then too and navigated in the dark. He's always been able to move in the night like this. The night Keisha disappeared. The night he left me to get help. When he came over for beer, he went into my house. He could have easily removed the bar without me noticing. He had mud on his shoes when he came to help me with the deer. The same tarp. The crayon crushed in the bed of his truck. The guts and blood throwing off the search. Planting or swapping my DNA? How could he do that? Doug said Oswald's reports have been off in the past, and who files those reports but a clerk? Like Chris's father. Oswald could owe him one hell of a favor. Someone has been setting me up and cutting me off from people and driving me toward him from the beginning. Keeping tabs on me. Getting close to me. I thought Lauren was being terrible by saying I wasn't Chris's type because of my race. I never considered I could be messing with their plan.

My stomach pushes up bile.

I yank my hand away and put myself between him and Mel. The break in our momentum sends us in opposite directions.

Motive. *What's his motive, Liz?* That's the one thing missing in all of this. Why would he and his father do this to little girls?

"Liz?" He looks back at me, face sweaty. He's glancing ahead, making sure we keep up. "Come on, we don't want to lose her—we have to hurry!" He reaches for my hand again. I move away. Everything he's said to me over the last few days replays in my mind. I finally land on it. The night with the deer.

"The people who are left behind," I whisper.

He was so awkward when he saw how nice my mother's house was. It's all lining up, and it makes my stomach clench. The person doing this targets any Black family who is advancing or moving forward. Anyone who is getting ahead.

"Where is Caroline?" I ask.

"What?" he says. I hate when I'm right. He is a good liar. And I'm a fool. Another man who used the promise of love to blind me to the darkness in him.

I reach for the growl that's been inhabiting my body, but it doesn't come. I can't do it. I am going to throw up. He takes a step toward me and I reach for the knife he gave me to protect myself and Mel. When I flip it open, I'm confronted with the serrated edge and I realize this isn't a knife, it's a bone saw. Holding it, I see the black blade and hooked edges. The teeth from my memories. This is what made the cut in my arm. The monster chasing me is this blade. The murder weapon. Holding it, my framing is complete.

Now it makes sense. I'll look like a crazy, jealous woman who did something unspeakable to her best friend's child. With someone to blame, anything that comes out is yet another hoop to jump through.

With me being framed for Caroline, any hope of justice for the girls who have gone missing is buried.

"Keisha? You were seeing Keisha the night she disappeared?"

"What are you talking about?"

"Tell me!" I shove Mel behind me and keep the knife between us. I'm crouched. I've never intentionally hurt someone. The thought makes me tremble, but I'll do it.

"Liz?"

"Tell me!"

"Yes—I was young—yes!" he admits. The stumble in his voice lets me know he's well aware of how he looks right now.

"She was younger."

"It wasn't like that."

I can't growl, but I smell something.

Wax. A childhood smell.

Wax and dye.

Crayons.

"Caroline?" I know that's her. I grab Mel and race in her direction.

"Liz!" Chris follows. I pick up my speed and race toward the smell. I feel Mel struggle to keep up. I see a clearing coming up ahead. If we can get there fast enough, we'll have ground and will stand a chance if Chris attacks us. *He has a rifle. Shit.*

I grab Mel at the elbow and throw her forward through the tree line. I burst through after her and turn around immediately. She's gasping for breath. I'm steady. I crouch and wait, firming up the blade in my hands. It's not a gun, but it's all I have.

Between Mel catching her breath and the footfalls chasing us, there's a second of quiet. This is it. I fell for a monster. I invited him in. Through the waves of sickness, I find resolve. Mel gasps in a coughing breath and the sound returns. Footsteps race toward me, cracking twigs in their wake. I brace myself. I squint— No. I need to look this evil in the face.

SIX

"Auntie Liz!" A dirty, bloody Caroline screams my name as she runs through the trees. Seeing her alive brings me to my knees. I catch her and keep my eye on the branches behind her. Chris was right on our tails, where has he gone?

"Where have you been? Who took you? How did you get away?" I ask her.

"Someplace dark." Caroline clings to me. "Him and the mean lady. But Jack let me go. He wanted you to find me."

I scan the trees. "Who?"

"Jack," she repeats.

I've never heard that name in all this. Like I did with Brittany's, I commit it to memory. Not a flicker of movement comes from the woods in front of us.

"Mommy!" Caroline says. I let her go to Mel. The girl takes a step and stops.

"Hey, Care-bear." It's Mel, but her voice sounds all wrong. Mel sounds like she's hurting. I can't imagine the shock of this moment. I prod Caroline forward, but she pushes back into my hand.

I turn around.

"Stay there," Mel says, standing stock-still. She's reaching out for her daughter, but her eyes are screaming at us to stay away. A hand latches over her shoulder. Strong, thin fingers hold Mel still as her center pulses forward.

Again. Again. Again.

Mel's face twists in pain. My mind struggles to comprehend what's happening.

Thunk! The dull sound of a fist on flesh.

Mel's mouth opens in a silent scream of unimaginable pain. Tears stream down her face. The person behind her grunts with effort. Mel tries to turn away or hit back, but everything is happening too fast. I see a flash of metal covered in red. Someone is stabbing Mel! I run to help. Mel stops fighting her attacker and thrashes her arms at me. I stumble back.

"Caroline!" she cries. Her eyes are wide in pain and fear. She wants me to protect her child. Not her. Her expression shifts to surprise when the knife pierces her abdomen. Blood comes deep red and thick. It pours across her shirt. She doesn't even grab her torso at first, she just lurches forward as the knife is yanked out of her. Blood pools across her back.

Kirsten stands behind her.

"Mommy!" Caroline screams and tries to go to her. I race back and clutch her to my side. Caroline starts to cry and shakes against me. I want to comfort her, but how can I? My tears are coming just as fast and as hard as hers.

"Oh! Thank God. You found her!" Kirsten's nice-white-lady voice paired with a bloody knife is a nightmare I didn't know I had.

Mel tries to get up and Kirsten stomps on her back, sending Mel crashing back down to the ground. Her chest hits. Hard. She starts coughing and wheezing. An exercise in futility, I try to will her breath to match mine.

In and out.

In and out.

She can't fully take in air. Blood starts to bubble up her throat in a desperate attempt to breathe. Kirsten hit her lungs.

Kirsten speaks to me like she's hosting me in her kitchen. "Doug told me about your plan to come out here. I knew you'd need help."

Footfalls come in behind me. I turn around just in time to dodge

Doug racing out of the trees. He skids on the ground, trying to grab us. He's found his footing now.

I back up with Caroline and try to keep everything in my eyesight: Doug, Kirsten, and Mel. Mel's wheezing fills the air. She cries out under the pressure of Kirsten's foot. I need to get her and Caroline out of here.

Doug crouches and looks at Mel, then turns to his wife. "You didn't have to do that to her friend."

Kirsten is manic. "It was like you said. I wanted to do it and Jack told me 'yes.' All I had to do was listen. That's all it took."

Doug gives her a suspicious glance and then turns back to us. "Do you have any idea how long I've been looking for you?" Doug should be saying that to Caroline, but he is looking right at me. His searching expression is gone and his eyes are cold. He's sure of his stance. He looks more at home out here than he did in his house or in the morgue. His serenity in the woods and night tells me who he is. It wasn't Chris. It never was. Doug is the man I've been looking for.

"Chris!" I yell. "Help!" He was right behind us, following us. He has to be close.

"He *thinks* he knows this place better than he does, Liz."

"Chris!" I scream. Doug is right. He's lost. No. We are lost on Chris's map, and have found ourselves on Doug's.

"I can't believe the trouble you both caused. Almost had everything tied up. Nice and neat. It was already a miracle of negligence that Oswald hadn't caught my father. I was making sure he, and the department, would never catch me."

A man and his shadow live in the trees.
When they walk in time, both are pleased.
If one calls your name, or the other tempts you off the path,
You must ignore both, or face their wrath.

The truth behind the riddle. A man and his shadow. His partner. First it was Doug and his father. Now it's Doug and his wife, Kirsten.

The shadow. No wonder she's been cooking so much. She's been feeding Caroline. My damning clue for Chris now has a crazy explanation. Kirsten was at Mel's the first day. She must have taken the crayons and then planted them to make both Mel and me crazy with doubt.

"Why?" I ask.

Kirsten echoes her husband. "What makes you think your suffering matters more than anyone else's?" I flash back to our conversation and I remember she was willing to do anything to make their house a home. Doug accused me of being jealous of Mel because he was so familiar with his wife's envy.

"Why these girls?"

Caroline clutches me close.

"Dad showed me what you are. If you knew your place, none of this would have had to happen," Doug says. I don't need him to clarify the "you." Doug prides himself on being a self-made man. I wonder about his logic of "our place."

"What are you doing, Doug?"

"Protecting my home. This town was built by good, hardworking people like me. My family. We *deserve* what we have here. You will not replace us." I thought Doug realized the role he played in a system that kept the girls quiet. He did. He wants to make sure it stays that way. "You were my first hunt." That snaps me out of my thoughts.

"What?"

"Dad taught me not to go after the adults because people make them martyrs. They say their names. It's easier to complicate the blame when a child goes missing."

It takes every ounce of self-control to keep myself still. I need to get Caroline and Mel out of here. He hasn't answered the question he brought up. He's waiting for me.

"Why did you help me?"

"I didn't want to at first, but curiosity got the best of me." He smiles. No. That's not it. He's showing me his teeth.

The gray line.

"I'd never met a Black doctor before. Didn't even know it was possible. Your mother gave me hope. If she could do it, so could I."

The realizations come in waves. The child my mother lost in the ER. She didn't know his age. He got antibiotics too young and they stained that gray line across his teeth. She talked about how he watched her and said he'd be a healer. Doug's dreams were thwarted. He didn't get into medical school. He couldn't afford it. He had to make his own way through. Struggled to be an assistant to a man he could work circles around. My mother had a beautiful home and was trying to open her own clinic. The bags of popcorn and flyers were to keep her scared and small. The deer wasn't just to terrify me, it was a warning for my mother as well. It didn't matter what we achieved or how we did it. We had something and Doug didn't.

It was never supposed to be Keisha; it was always supposed to be me.

Before I can ask, Doug guesses my next question. "When Dad took Keisha he told me never to kill out of jealousy. Only necessity."

"Why did she need to die?"

"I needed to learn a lesson."

Doug and his father played God. They decided who lived in this town, what it needed, and who got to succeed.

"And Caroline?" I ask.

Doug's expression shifts to annoyance. "Another mistake that turned into an opportunity."

If someone this methodical makes "mistakes," it means that there's a major disagreement in whatever relationship exists between these killers. Caroline went missing on the eighteenth, not the solstice. The look he gave Kirsten. Her rage against Mel . . . He didn't want to take Caroline. Kirsten did.

"Kirsten!" If I can get her to disobey him again . . . Maybe . . . "What did the Parkers do? Why did you take Caroline?"

Kirsten considers me, then she hands her husband her knife.

"Liz," Doug responds for her. "You don't get to know everything." He advances on us. "I have a promise to keep."

I speak to Caroline. "Run." I push her away from me. She won't budge. "Run, Caroline!"

"I want my mommy," she whispers. Her little face scrunches in pain. Her mother is bleeding out and I'm telling her to leave.

I wipe away her tears and mine. "I'm gonna help her. You need to run, Care-bear."

"I'll get lost." She shakes.

A voice croaks out. "R-r-r-ruunnnn!" It's Mel. Caroline takes off. In the space between her fleeing, I see Kirsten start to go after her. Mel grabs her ankles. Kirsten falls face-first onto the ground with a satisfying *thud*. I expect to see Doug running after her too. I dig in and get to my feet. Instantly, my shoulders are turned and I'm slammed onto my back. I can't breathe. I feel pressure on my neck. Doug is choking me. I scrunch up my shoulders and gasp.

In.

The exhale won't come because the pressure is back. I know this. I remember this. I almost died like this months ago in a dark apartment far away from home in New York City. Another man I trusted wrapped his hands around my neck because I dared to have what he didn't. I didn't fight then. Now I do. I promised Caroline I would find her. I promised the mothers and Kylie I'd solve this. I promised my mother I would come home. I promised to save Mel.

I need to live.

I thrash as hard as I can. One of Doug's hands slips. A harsh breath *out*, followed by a quick one *in*.

Doug has a knife. If he only wanted to kill me, he'd use that. He's strangling me because he likes this. He wants this. He's using my body, another Black body, for his sick pleasure. The anger I've kept at bay for years starts to possess me. It overrides my fear and gives me clarity. He's gonna wish he stabbed me. Doug has a weak spot in my reach. His eyes. I let go of his arms and go for his face. I try to dig my thumbs in where it's soft. Too late. Kirsten grabs my hands.

"She's strong!" she says.

"Not for long," Doug replies.

It takes a long time to strangle someone. Or it feels that way when you're losing breath. I don't have a floor lamp to smash over his head, to cut his head open so the world knows what he did to me. The shame of keeping quiet has burned in me ever since. I struggle in vain. I let my anger out too late. As it fades, shame, more than fear, starts to fill me. With all I've learned, even with Mel's and Caroline's lives on the line, I'm still weak.

The dark is coming. A permanent one. I fight against dying light.

Snap!

I smell earth. Mud? No. Foul water. Dark and wet. A trace of decay. Brackish. Rotten. I know the flood never reached this high in the mountains. But here it is, the smell from town. The smell that's been following me. Death.

Home.

There's a shadow lurking beyond my gaze. Since the night in the woods in high school, like an old friend, it's been waiting to take my arm again. I fight, but my body isn't working.

Snap!

A branch breaks. The earth under me rumbles. It's the galloping rhythm from my dreams. This is it. Before everything dims, I look beyond Doug and see the night sky. I finally have my stars. Clear and dark. The dome of the world. The lights in Farrah's eyes.

I can't breathe anymore. The rumbling gets closer. I don't know if I should welcome it or fear it. I'm getting too tired to fight. My limbs shudder and fail. Once I relax my muscles, Doug will break my neck and then . . . that's it. I try to stay awake. My lungs struggle to resume their function. My breath is trapped, hiccupping in my chest.

Out of the corner of my eye, I see darkness coming like a wave. The shadow in the woods, the one I've always feared. The dark fold in my memory. The great beast Farrah, Kylie, and I imagined is death itself. The thing that's lived just beyond my reach for so long comes into focus. My muscles give out and blackness crashes over us all.

LUCY

June 1920

Beginnings and endings always have the same feeling. Just different outcomes. Meeting people, you can always tell who is going to change your life. Something in you and in them aligns. Then you're both locked.

Lucy was ten when Grandma Abigail first told her the story of her family. When Lucy never stopped asking questions, it was time to send her to her grandmother's house on Sundays to help and to learn. The story of their family wasn't written down. Instead, it lived in the long tales Grandma Abigail told about people Lucy would never meet in this life.

Passing through the mountains, her family traveled north to settle here in Pennsylvania. Lucy's great-grandmother made her living as a wet nurse. Their family slowly carved out a place for themselves on this mountain and in this town. It all got wiped away in the flood.

"Do you remember the flood?" Lucy asked as she folded. She was helping with the laundry. This was the chore she was best at. Wrangling wide sheets and linens made her feel powerful.

Grandma Abigail sighed. "I wish I could forget it. I was a little older than you are now. We couldn't afford to live in town, so the waters missed us. Put most of it out of my mind, but the smell. I'll never forget the smell."

The sadness in her grandmother's face inspired a new curiosity in Lucy. "And your momma?"

"Momma said the water came the day the rain stopped. There had been storms all week. The dam broke."

"The rain caused it to break?"

"No. That was the rich folks." Grandma Abigail's face scrunched in judgment. "They tried to say it was an Act of God, but ask anyone here. We know the truth." Grandma Abigail described the lake houses built along the dam. Palaces of comfort and relaxation. Somewhere to leave your cares. When it came to worrying over the dam, the wealthy and privileged saw no need. This place wasn't their home. "Between God and the Devil, death visited Johnstown in the middle of the day. Destroyed everything. They found bodies for years afterward, hundreds of miles away. The people who built those cabins caused this, and they didn't take a lick of blame. But it weighed on their spirits. They gave money to put the place back together. Everyone did. The help that came here gave Momma hope." Grandma Abigail gave Lucy more to fold. "After the flood, folks from all over came. Didn't matter what you looked like or where you were from. You rolled your sleeves up and helped. Momma said, for a moment, she saw what this country was supposed to be. You got out as much as you put in. Every man could build his own life and one for his family. Things were like that for a moment and a moment only." Grandma Abigail lost track of the chores. She started folding the same shirts twice. "People with means lifted themselves out of here. And folks got scared—no. They were always scared." Back on task, Grandma Abigail checked Lucy's folding and ushered the girl into the house to help with dinner.

A few more Sundays passed. Lucy moved from asking questions about her family to asking questions about the town.

"How long has it been here?" Lucy asked.

"Since men found it," Grandma Abigail answered.

"How long will it be here?" Lucy asked.

"Until they lose it," Grandma Abigail answered.

"What about the woods?" Lucy asked.

"Been here long before us and will remain long after," Grandma Abigail answered.

"What came first, the man or the shadow?" Lucy asked.

Grandma Abigail stopped in her tracks. "Why you asking about that for?"

"I don't know," Lucy lied. "Just heard some girls talking about it. Saying if you look in the trees—"

"You stay outta those woods or—!" She didn't need to finish the thought. When Lucy and Grandma Abigail lived, there were no men like Doug and his father in the trees. The story was the memory of a warning. *Stay out of the woods*. That was the end of the conversation.

Though Lucy was a child, she knew grown-up anger, even Grandma Abigail's, came from fear. Because Lucy was still young, she thought it wise to see for herself.

Lucy didn't have to look in the forest long for a shadow that did not obey the sun.

What Grandma Abigail's mother didn't tell her about the flood was that its waters cut the people in Johnstown off from the rest of the world. The living ran to get help; the rest were left alone through the night. In the dark, fear reigned. Accounts varied. Some wrote them down. Others took that night to their graves. In the dark, when the earth was a raw wound, when the dead outnumbered the living, when a town cracked open . . .

I woke up.

"Hello?" Lucy said to me. Back then, I didn't fully understand my connection to people. I knew that when they were afraid, I was strong. That's why the flood roused me. All that fear pushed me into painful consciousness. I'd been a thing in the woods, reflecting nightmares for a long time. Yes, the flood made me, but I was always here. Like a story. Or a god.

"Hello?" Lucy said again.

Weak, it took everything I had, but I echoed her. "Hello?"

Shocked to hear her voice double, her eyes widened in fear and curiosity. That made me feel solid. Not like a shadow.

"I'm Lucy," she said.

"Lucy," I repeated. She laughed. Delighted. Her delight exhausted me. It spread me thin. I changed her name in my echo. "Lucy," I said again, using the wind this time. That scared her. When she shook I saw a flash of one of her deep fears.

A dog.

Before I could stop myself, I did what I'd always done. Before I had consciousness and thoughts of my own, when someone saw me, their gaze became a pathway. I walked into them and took the shape they feared most.

She screamed. I felt weight in my claws.

She ran. I chased. With each step, I gained heft. I could move leaves on the forest floor.

I let out a growl. Her fear grew me great big teeth. A massive mouth.

I expanded in size. In her eyes, I was a true beast in the woods. She ran out of the trees. I saw her running for her home. I thought of how there were more people there. All of their fears. I could be endless. The moment I left the trees, I vanished. Disappearing is a pain I don't wish on anything with consciousness. Simply, it is being and suddenly *not* being. When I finally managed to appear again, I was a formless shadow. I had to wait until someone came so I could take the shape of their fears.

They did. And they'd run. Or throw things at me. I got good at using people's fears. I learned how to get enough weight to break sticks and carry my voice on the wind. Once someone saw me and I them, I'd blossom into a nightmare.

Weeks later Lucy returned to the woods. She'd grown brave.

Snap!

And smart. No matter how I entered her vision or her hearing, she turned. She ignored me. A few weeks and this child bested me. It was my time to talk instead of parrot.

"Why?" I asked. Words flowed so freely in my mind. Speaking without fear to power me was torture.

"You gave me bad dreams and I wanna sleep," she said. "Momma said I need to face my fears. Daddy said to ignore 'em. People who come in here and look at you all come running out. So I'm doing the opposite." She crossed her arms.

Defeated. I sat in the corner of her vision and didn't move. That was our relationship for the next few hours until the sun set.

"Why do you need to scare us?" she asked.

"It's what I'm meant to do in the woods."

"What are you outside of them?"

My silence carried my answer. I didn't know. I dreamed of life outside the trees, but I'd never seen it for myself.

When a few stars peeked through the sky, Lucy told me how to use them as a map. Long after she was gone, I would look up at them and imagine all the places they would guide me when I figured out how to leave the forest.

"You were in my dreams, shadow. You don't remember that?"

"No." That was the truth. I hadn't yet figured out how to stay in someone's head. That understanding would come.

Lucy looked at me. I became the hound from her nightmares, but she wasn't afraid anymore. In the little space between her curiosity and her fear, she looked at me long enough that I fell into her eyes. A piece of me crept in under the lid and around her tiny wet orbs. A part of me stayed there, just out of her sight. She left town carrying a part of me. This piece watched the world with her. Deeper than her horrors, I learned her beliefs.

When she died many years later, the piece of me returned. It was full of her stories. Driven away by the shadows she saw in the woods, she left Johnstown. She went west. She had a family. She always slept by the fire, to stay in the light. From my shadow, madness grew in her for years until one day, to escape the dark she saw in the corner of her eye, she lit her house on fire to bring her stars to the earth.

She said this before she left me in the woods that night: "Grandma Abigail said not to give you attention because it goes against God to speak to a demon. Are you a demon?"

"I don't think so."

"Good. 'Cause if you are, Grandma Abigail said, it's only a matter of time until a fool gives you enough attention."

SEVEN

Night.

Stars.

Breath.

I gasp so hard that my ribs burn with the effort. Only when I cough and roll to my side do I realize that I'm free of Doug's grasp. I try to touch my neck. My limbs haven't fully returned yet. My sight is back. I turn my head. I can't believe what I see.

Kirsten is slumped against the bottom of a tree, like she's been flung there. A pile of limbs. I can't tell if any are broken, but she's still breathing, very shallowly. Mel lies in a pool of blood so deep red it looks black. Doug is now on the ground far away from me, looking dazed. He grasps at the air, trying to right himself. Between all of us is a shadow.

The monster from my dreams.

This is no vision or mist. The ground sags under its weight. I just watch and breathe for a moment, letting myself recover.

"J—Ja—ack!" Doug sputters out. The creature rumbles the air with a growl that is clearly the parent of mine. It stands in front of me. Protecting me. I make my way to my knees, still coughing, wheezing, and uncertain if this beast is here to save me.

Looking at it, I see that, unlike the rhyme, it is indeed made of flesh. It reeks. Its fur is short. Worn. One of its erect ears is chewed away. Doug tries to approach "Jack" and its massive jaws snap at him. Doug staggers back. Meanwhile, I get to my feet. Though this beast has saved me, it is still a beast. All the stories about the woods and the monsters in the trees, they're all true.

Jack shifts his weight. This time I stand my ground. Doug pulls the hunting knife back out as he faces off with it.

"I knew you were planning something."

If a beast can, I see the thing thinking, processing. It turns to me. Milky eyes. White teeth. It's an old thing, but it can still hurt me. I'm not afraid. I shouldn't be. He saved me from Doug. It has been in my dreams.

"What do you want?" I ask him.

"You," he says.

I study his shape. He is not a hound. He is not a wolf. Or a dog. He is a massive jackal. A scavenger. Made to feed on carrion flesh.

"What do you want?" I ask again.

"What a god needs."

My mind races to put together what that could mean. Bringing up God leads me to worship. I turn to Doug.

"Have you been . . . feeding the girls' hearts to Jack?" That would explain the ritualistic aspect of the murders. The regularity. Looking at Doug, he fits the definition of the killer in my mind. Hiding a dark nature. Coiled. Ready to strike. I saw the quick work he made of Nick. He wouldn't be happy with one victim a year.

"After everything my father and I did for you, you pick *her*!" Doug yells.

"Picked me for what?" I ask.

If one calls your name, or the other tempts you off the path, you must ignore both, or face their wrath. That rhyme. Wrath easily means death. Destruction. What Doug did to the girls. What could be worse than that?

"To become a god," Jack repeats. Reality feels all glitchy when he talks. The more I look at him, the more it feels like something I shouldn't be doing. My head hurts. Something cold is crawling in behind my eyes.

Your eyes are bright. Like mine. Is this what happened to Farrah? She saw Jack and—looking at him I see the gaps in his form. His flesh slides around in the shadows of him. An internal structure remains. He has ribs. A heart of his own. It squeezes and releases at odd times. He has teeth and claws. He growls at Doug and I feel it. The dreams. My senses. If the monster is real, then this thing bit me. My mom was worried about bacteria in the wound. Now I worry it was something much worse.

"Liz."

I hear Jack's voice rattle deep inside me.

"Whatever he says, don't listen!" Doug says.

Jack's voice groans back in my ear. "You live like me. A shadow. Don't you want more?"

I turn to face the great beast. I see teeth. Then his red mouth opens wide in a roar.

Snap!

I should be cut in half. Instead, I'm in darkness. A wet shadow. I'm inside Jack. The dark place Caroline spoke of. This must be it. Jack's shadows race for my mouth, my nose, like in my dream. I can't stop them. Cold and slick, they climb in through my seeking eyes and run down my throat to my heart. *My eyes!* This is exactly what it felt like when whatever was in Farrah crawled into me. This strange cold burn is also how my scar feels sometimes. These shadows have been gathering and growing in me almost all my life. After Farrah, my senses grew. Drinking dulled my resolve. No wonder I sleepwalked. The shadows wanted to come home.

I hear Jack sigh. He sounds relieved.

"What a world you've brought me." Before I can try to understand, I notice my scar. He's opened it. I can see inside of me. Slick red muscles, blue pulsing veins. In between my tight white tendons I see a piece of gleaming white. Where Jack bit me, one of his teeth nestled and merged with my flesh. It has been there, inside me, for fifteen years. Tendrils of shadow extend into my arm. Those I can feel. They push in. I try to fight them; I'm stopped by my dream. When I tried to rip the shadow out, I only succeeded in tearing myself. Powerless, I feel the cold enter.

My heart races.

It stops.

I press my free hand to my chest. I'm still breathing. Still existing. My sternum goes frosty under my touch. I reach into my shirt to be sure. My flesh feels like clay. I look out into the darkness for an explanation. Nothing.

Pain comes. My dead heart is looking for a way out of my body. I scream. No one and nothing hears me.

Then there is pulsing in my left hand. I look and I see a heart beating. It's heavy. And strong. When it starts to race, I realize that it's mine. Something else is in my chest, powering me now. I look at my heart. It looks normal, aside from the fact that it's out of my chest. I turn it over in my hands.

I try to move around in the dark, but I can't. How am I supposed to move in nothingness? Wait. I've done this. I've been doing this in my dreams. I think of the pain, the blood, and the mud, and it leads me right back to him.

The shadow in my apartment. The hound that has been chasing me. It's been him all along.

"Why didn't you help me?" I ask.

"Why didn't you help Mel?" he counters.

"I tried! I couldn't. I need to—" A sob takes the rest of my words. This creature has watched so many die and never intervened. "I need *help*!" My desperate cry rips my vocal cords.

"With only a piece of me, all I can do is watch," he says. "You need all of me if you want my help." In the dark, his voice feels vast and smooth. "I've learned much from all the hearts. I want to share them all with you."

Before I can stop it, I feel my mind fill with the lives of all he's eaten. My body vibrates with potential and wishes and dreams and promises. I feel Brittany's hunger. Diana's stories. Morgan's beauty. Keisha's change.

And more, so many more. All these girls he consumed. What he took after Doug and his father killed them.

"I want to give you the tools. The power to shape this world how you see fit."

I can barely speak. If my heart were in my chest, it would break. All those dreams and hopes. They've been sitting in him for years.

"You can get revenge now. No need to wait for justice." Jack opens the shadows and I see Doug. Though injured, he searches for me in the dark. He's nowhere near close. "You could snap his neck in your fist."

I see Mel on the ground. She's not moving. I search for the subtle flutter of her breath. I can't focus. This is all wrong. I want everything to be right. To be good. Mel shouldn't be out here. None of this should be happening. My mind starts to go numb with a feeling I haven't experienced in years. Rage. Jack picks up on it and fills my chest with more of himself.

"Wait!" I say.

"Let all your anger give you power. Release it on the world. Don't you want to be a god?"

My heart throbs in one hand and a feather of starlight appears in the other. My arms out at my sides, I realize the shape I'm making, the one Brittany was found in. I hold a heart and a feather. In this ritual of death, I've become the scales.

Anubis.

The god of lost souls.

Jack changes. He makes a shape to suit me: a man with the head of a jackal appears before me. Smiling. Baring his teeth. This is all wrong. Anubis lives in the stars, glossy history books, museums, and, most important, Egypt.

In Anubis, Jack shows me his heart. I know from Lucy he learned the power of belief. From Brittany he learned that flesh could fuel him. From Kayla he learned about finding the right partner. He got his inspiration from Diana's histories. Keisha gave him the nerve.

If he gets out, he doesn't want to roam the world as a canine. He wants to be a god. The dog god. But he struggles to keep the form. He's not Anubis yet. He's still a jackal.

"How?" I ask.

"With you."

Like Doug, he's keeping the whole story from me. I pace through my clues. My abilities have been coming since I came home, so proximity is key. My speed, strength, sight, smell all have grown. When I fought back, he stopped. He can't force me to take on this power, this transformation. In my dreams, being consumed by shadow was inevitable. If he could force me, he would. He's weak. His flesh reeks. He's risking everything to make this work.

"Mel is running out of time," he whispers.

"Help me save her," I beg.

"I can. But if I do, Doug will get away. He'll run. There will never be justice."

The thought alone makes my anger come back. It threatens to overcome me like a wave.

"Tell me how you want to make him hurt and I will say 'yes.' Always."

A chill of recognition stops me from responding. *I wanted to do it and Jack told me "yes." All I had to do was listen.* This is what Kirsten meant. Jack told her to hurt Mel. He said yes. He had her hurt Mel to manipulate me. I need to get away from him and I think I know how. If this darkness is just like my dreams. If pain and mud and blood led me here.

Keisha Woodson.

Her name sits in the center of my mind. I think of her hair gel. The gummy scent. That pulls away from his heavy presence. His need. The open cavern of him.

I understand. The Darkness is not to be feared, for it is full of possibilities. One moment I'm with Jack, the next I'm with Keisha's heart. She is still in her jean shorts and tank top. Her box braids are fresh. On the edge of adulthood, but still a girl. She doesn't speak. My back hunches in memory. But, when she looks at me with respect, something I never saw from her when she lived, I straighten up and walk toward her.

Keisha looks over her shoulder. I follow her gaze and see Brittany. Now whole, I recognize her from her picture. When I reach for her I see all the girls. I recognize some of them from their photos. Then there are the ones I don't know. I weep at the sight of unknown faces. They all look up at me. Silent. Waiting. I feel myself wanting to crumble under their expectation, but I don't. I stand taller.

The Dead know many things. They know the past with an enviable intimacy. They study the present with a focus I'm just beginning to understand.

I ask Keisha my question instead. "Why me?"

"Because you're *good*." She says the word the same way she did years ago. Like the insult it is. "If you were too angry, you'd overpower him. If you were too hateful, the world would overpower you," Keisha continues.

Good.

Special.

Chosen.

I denied my pain. I cut away parts of myself. I made space for someone—some*thing* else. In pursuit of those words, I became the perfect vessel for a monster. I'm Black, but not like *those* Black people. I'm a woman, but not like *other* women. I've fractured myself as goodness demanded of me. I thought the only demon I had to face coming home was doubt. A shadow. What happens when the shadow gets sick of following the man? The answer is: It finds someone it can bend to its image. Jack will be the flesh and I the shadow. Doug and his father need a symbiotic ritual to keep them in check. I wouldn't. I'm good.

"Once you let him in," Keisha continues, "he knows you won't fight. He's seen the world through you. He'll make you think you're saving it while you feed him. Using your flesh as his vessel to acquire more. That is how he becomes a god."

"He leaves the woods and enters the world," I say. I can't even imagine the fear to be had if he succeeds. All the girls look at me. If he gets out, how many others would join them? I can't let this creature that has consumed our hearts get out. Jack says he learned from the hearts of the girls. That is a lie. It's always been. Everything he's done from the beginning has been in service of the emptiness inside him. Once a shadow, always a shadow.

"Do you want his gifts?" Keisha asks. The senses. The dreams. The strength. I think of my life. It's mine and I won't give it up.

"Can he hear us?" I ask.

"He trapped us here, but this place is ours. He stopped listening to us once he had our flesh. Will you give him yours?"

Cautious of Jack's and my connection, I don't respond. Instead, like I've done for years, I hide my feelings. But this time, instead of denying them to myself, I hide them from Jack.

For the first time in a long time, I yearn for my imperfect, incomplete life. I've been so afraid of the story told about me. Now I know I need to tell it myself. For a moment, I rest in being who I am without needing to look through the eyes of anyone else. Seeing all their faces, I know what I must do.

This suffering must stop.

I look at the girls and I wonder about this place that is theirs. Is it Heaven or Hell? I believe it's neither. It is a moment before the eternal. Only a fellow wandering soul can recognize another. Since I found the girls, they aren't lost anymore. Jack trapped them. I can free them. Moving the dark itself, I seek the feeling of belonging and home. Something releases and blinding moonlight fills my eyes. I can't see what's beyond. I sense it. Peace. Warmth. Freedom. They move on, one by one. Keisha squeezes my hand. Then she too passes on. My time here is done. Space with the girls, though brief, is eternal.

I'm alone.

If I deny Jack, he'll kill me and try again. If I accept, I lose myself.

If I can't trust myself, then who?

I know that Jack and Doug are a pair of liars, but I can trust what I've learned about them. Doug wants what I have. Jack wants to get out. He thinks my anger is the key. I can use that.

I let my rage out. Like I thought, it pulls me right back to Jack.

"You let them go?" he growls.

He's hoping to use my pain and doubts against me? All right. I let him in.

"You only need me now," I say. "I accept." The moment I do, Jack flows into me.

"I knew you would."

The dark falls away. I'm standing in the forest. Doug is in front of me, knife drawn, waiting for the attack.

He begs. "Please don't." I call back the shadow that has kept him company all his life. Like the one I took from Farrah, it flows out of him with his tears. I call for the last one in Kirsten and it easily leaves her unconscious form. Now whole, every piece of the creature of the forest and I share one vessel. I have to try *very* hard to keep control.

"Kill him, Liz. For all of us," Jack echoes in me. "For the Girls. For Melissa."

My pain and my rage take over. More than strength, it is unpredictability. Before I can stop the impulse, I'm at Doug's throat. The way he flinches tells me I've moved like a shadow, gone one moment and there the next. I wrap my hand around his neck and lift him high above me.

Unlike him, I'm firm but delicate. I'm doing my best to give him a window to see my weak spot. If he takes too long I'll kill him. I need him to know that. I squeeze and feel the muscles in his neck shudder. I need him to be scared. If he's scared, he'll make the mistake I need him to make. I struggle against Jack's power. He wants me to rip Doug apart. I know if I do, there is no justice coming, only revenge.

"Do it, Liz!" Jack starts to override my resolve. I grip Doug's neck with my other hand. I lift him higher. *Come on, Doug!*

I feel immense pressure in my chest. He's done it. *Finally.* I look down and see Doug's knife sticking out of me, to the right of my heart.

I take a hand off his neck, wrap it around his knee, and squeeze without restraint. My strength alarms me. The pop and following scream let me know I've dislocated it. I drop him. He falls to the ground in pain. I need him injured, so he doesn't get away.

"You stupid girl," Jack says. "You gave him a chance. Look at what happens when you have control. You are too kind. Let me."

Before he can stop me, I grip the knife sticking out of my chest. This will hurt. I close my eyes and start to pull it out. The moment I do, I feel Jack fight me, trying to get my body to keep the blade in and the wound sealed.

"What are you doing!"

I keep pulling. I see blood and rot and shadow racing out of my chest. Good. If I'm so "special" Jack will do anything for me to live, including putting my heart back. When he parts my ribs, I see white with pain. When my chest feels warm again, I know it's back. His tooth lunges out of me, replacing itself with my blood and muscle. After fifteen years, the piece of himself Jack put in me is finally gone.

Jack stands in front of me again. He looks like what he is. A jackal. A scavenger.

He growls. "Idiot! What have you done to yourself!"

I feel where the knife was in my chest. Just as I thought. Jack put me back together, just enough. It still hurts. I'm still bleeding. But I'm alive. He told me all his stories. He showed me his heart. I now know where his "hard-earned" flesh's weakness is: between his well-spaced ribs. I grip Doug's knife. I charge.

From Diana's heart, I know the truth of Anubis, not what Jack would make him. The god of lost souls. It was his duty to guide them home. He would measure your heart against a feather. And if your life was found lacking, it would be eaten. Destroyed.

Before I crash into him, I dodge and roll. I extend the blade and it sticks in Jack's side. He howls in pain. I see the blade has stuck between his ribs. I brace one hand against him and cut. His scream rattles my bones. I hang on to him for dear life as he thrashes. The bone grinds against the blade but, cut by cut, it gives. I stab in again, closer to the center of his chest this time. I remember from the deer, that's where the joints are easier to dig through. I have to put my whole body into it, but it works. He tries to bite down at me. He's too weak. I'm close. I cut through another joint and his chest cracks open.

I fit my hand in. The bone slices right into my fingers. Adrenaline wills me on. I break him open. No blood, only rot pours out. I reach into his chest. His insides pulse with life that shouldn't be. I see his great heart. I wrap my hand around it.

I pull.

JACK

June 2017

Lucy left me longing for the world she fled to. I'd reach out for it at night.

Listening.

Watching.

The tensions in this little town mirrored the whole country's. A constant tally of who has what and who wants it. Who deserved the fruits of their labor and who had to work twice as hard to get half as far. This cycle of fear fed into itself over and over and over. New workers, strangers. A bar fight. Death. Banishment. Flames in the hills. All erased. All repeated. On and on.

When the Fellow found me, he reminded me of Lucy. He saw me and his eyes filled with curiosity. He didn't run away. I searched his mind for fear and saw only darkness that I could inhabit. The man was empty. Bottomless. I became what he needed. I took the shape of the dog Lucy made and never changed. It took a lifetime, but Grandma Abigail was right. A fool had finally come along and given me enough attention. I was fool enough to give him purpose.

I'd watched humans. I knew how they desired regularity. Schedules. I'd keep the Fellow and myself on one. Summer was when I met Lucy. The stars were our escape. They became tenets in our new religion. Like any belief of value, my Fellow passed his desires on to his son, Doug.

The Fellow had been told all his life that he would have a good one. He trained for it. Believed it was owed to him.

He lost it.

He wanted to hurt others long before the steel mill closed. When he saw Tanisha's family coming in to help lay the place to rest, he acted on his pain. He cemented a triangle between him, his son, and myself, with Alice's blood.

I never make anyone do anything they wouldn't have otherwise done. I witness. When they ask me if they should listen to their basest desires, I say "yes." All the Fellow ever needed was a "yes."

He offered me hearts because I was his. I had a mouth because he needed me to eat. To chew. After that, he didn't care what I did with the muscle. He wasn't checking the woods for my waste. His attention gave me strength and solidity. His worship gave me flesh. With the hearts he gifted me, I crafted what I could: Ribs. Fur. Some muscle. I learned more from the Girls' hearts and shifted my form. I lifted my ears. Shortened my fur. I knew what I wanted to be when I left these trees. I could be only a jackal in the forest. In the world, I would be a god.

The longer the Fellow worshipped me, the more he took my shadow inside. But, no matter how many times I tried to leave while inside him, I got pushed out. I'd take up more space in him and try again. Failure. Again. I tried until I cracked his ribs and inflamed his organs. How would his body last in the world?

I used the hunt we created to seek a new vessel. The hearts he brought me were strong. And the Girls' bodies were still growing. If I could get into one before she was an adult, I could grow with her. Slowly ensuring there was enough space for me.

Why not his son? Doug?

If his father was any indication, I'd burn through the boy in an afternoon. A man like him with my power would be too destructive. This world would put him down. But someone unlike him? One who was used to keeping everything locked up tight?

Doug is the only reason I found Liz. His insistence on and obsession with her and her mother made me watch her. I did, and I saw.

Liz had the perfect heart.

Its tempo was flawless. The muscle was taut. And its capacity rivaled the cosmos. With this marvel in her chest, I could use Liz if I let her grow. If I kept her safe. Special.

Doug called Keisha a mistake, but she was just as planned as the others. The Fellow and Doug needed their same old ritual. I needed to start one of my own with Liz. Deeper than looking at her or climbing behind her eye, I bound the strongest piece of myself to her. A tooth. We grew together.

When the Fellow died, I took his body. It still couldn't get me out of the woods, but it gave me weight. I could break branches and echo calls. But it smelled too strong and was too delicate for me to hunt on my own . . . yet.

The more I learned about Liz, the more I delighted in her return. She had eyes full of starlight and so much space in her. We'd do so much more than walk out of the woods. Every night, I looked up and longed for Liz.

I remember being lost. I remember the stars. I remember searching for substance in them when I was lonely.

Both Liz and I did that.

I think that is why Liz and I were inevitable.

Liz was strong like I knew she'd be. Like a true lover, she knew exactly what to do. She used her strength, her blade, and her teeth. She went for my side first. That wasn't the fatal blow. That came when her fingers gripped my chest. They cracked open my ribs. Her nails rent my flesh. I was only the shadow of a dog god's body.

When death comes for Death, it does so in the present tense. Each moment is every moment. Some use this last second to revisit their lives, or just the parts of it that matter.

What will I do?

In this second, I don't know.

By the next one, I will.

Before it's over, I feel her hand around my heart. A moment of incredible intimacy. I know I'll never be held like this again.

The second I see my heart leave my hard-earned body, I'm done.

I'm surprised by my relief.

My emptiness feels vast.

The weight of my matter? I'll find out. But now

Now

Now?

After a life of shadows, finally, in death, I am seen.

On June 28, 2017, Detective Turner (DT) interviewed Caroline Washington (CW) in the presence of her father, Garrett Washington (GW) at [redacted].

DT: It is presently, 0900 hours on June 28, 2017. Currently at [redacted]. This is in regards to case number 6345-034. Thank you both so much for agreeing to speak so soon after the incident.

CW: Are they . . . are they . . . Dad?

GW: She wants to be sure you've locked up . . . um. The people who took her.

DT: Both are currently in custody and no danger to you, I promise.

GW: Good. Go ahead. You can answer the detective's questions.

CW: . . .

GW: Caroline?

CW: . . .

DT: Caroline, do you want to tell me what you're drawing?

CW: Is it okay if I tell him, Dad?

GW: Of course.

CW: Can I have more paper?

DT: Here you go.

CW: I'm trying to remember something from my dreams.

DT: Do you dream about what happened when you were in the woods?

CW: Sometimes.

DT: Can you tell me about it?

CW: You won't believe me. Or you'll treat me like a little kid. I know what I saw.

DT: What did you see?

CW: Someone took me from the wedding, but he didn't hurt me.

DT: Do you know who that was?

CW: That was Jack. He was bad too, they all were, but he didn't hurt me. He wanted to.

DT: How do you know that?

CW: He told me. But he wanted to hurt Auntie Liz more.

DT: Did he say why?

CW: He thought she could help him get out.

DT: Of where?

CW: The woods. That's where he was trapped.

DT: How did you stay alive out there?

CW: Kirsten, the mean lady, she brought me food. And crayons. Doug didn't want Jack to get Auntie Liz.

DT: Was he protecting her?

CW: No. He didn't want her and Jack to see each other. He said something very bad would happen.

DT: He was there? *(showing her a picture of the suspect)* Is this him?

CW: Yes.

DT: Did he touch you—hurt you?

CW: He wanted to. Jack stopped him. Jack protected me.

DT: Can you describe this Jack person to me?

CW: He's a shadow.

DT: Can you explain that?

CW: *(holds her hand out and makes a shadow on the wall)*

DT: A shadow?

CW: Yes.

DT: Are you sure?

CW: Yes. He didn't want to be a shadow anymore.

DT: What did he want to be?

CW: . . . like us and like him. Something real, but with all of his unreal things.

DT: When it comes to the night in question, how did you get away?

CW: Jack let me go so Auntie Liz could find me.

DT: Then what happened?

CW: I found her and Mom. Mom . . . Mommy . . .

DT: You don't have to answer anything you don't want to.

CW: . . . Jack told me lots of stories.

DT: About?

CW: This town. His life. The hearts he's eaten. Those were the only stories he had to tell. *(Caroline draws, dotting her paper.)*

DT: What's the truth?

CW: For a long time, Doug and his dad killed girls like me. Black girls.

DT: Do you remember any of the names Jack told you?

CW: Alice. Alice Walker. Keisha Woodson. Brittany Miller. Kayla Montrose. Diana Leaks. Morgan—can you write them down?

DT: Yeah—yes. *(Detective notates.)* Go ahead.

CW: Morgan Daniels. Eboni Lewis. Patrice Carter. Tricia Harris. Aisha Smith. Sandra Hill. Calli Jordan. Nia Davis. Yolanda Brown. Lexi Jackson. Rachel Adams. Imani Jones. Jada Mitchell. Alexandra Thomas. Brianna Hall. Gabrielle Allen. Shanice Bell. Makayla Watson. Chantelle Bryant. Zina Wilson. Taylor Hayes. Tiffany Johnson. Krystal Simms. Cassie Clark. Whitney James. Jayla Kelly.

GW: Good job, sweetie.

DT: Th—thank you. For your time.

END OF VIDEO RECORDING

EIGHT

Caroline's disappearance didn't bring the media, but Mel's death did. A sweet white mother murdered trying to save her daughter from a serial killer. Everyone came for Mel.

Standing up at the pulpit at her funeral, I can't help but remember, "Mel asked me to speak at her wedding." My chest hurts when I breathe too deeply. Jack healed the worst of it, but cartilage, skin, and bone will take time. "She was joking. Trying to get me to relax and laugh. Melissa Park— Washington, was more like a sister to me than a friend. We fought like sisters. We were there for each other like sisters. She was one of the few people I could trust."

My words echo in the church, another thing this town has a lot of. Only Mel's immediate family is allowed. Standing in front of them, I should be terrified, but I'm in too much pain. My body hurts. So does my soul. Getting Caroline out cost us Mel. Life doesn't add and subtract evenly. It isn't balanced on scales. I will spend the rest of my life replaying that night, looking for what I could have done differently. The past is so easy to see. I wish I could have that clarity for the future. Whenever I try to unpack my guilt over what happened to Mel, I'm overwhelmed. After everything, I think I only know how to live in the "overwhelming" now.

When the service is over, I go back to Mel's house. The only reason I'm allowed is because of Caroline. Since the woods, she refuses to leave my side for more than a few minutes at a time.

I pull into the driveway and see black stars. Summer stars have been spray-painted across the front of Mel and Garrett's blue house. I see Nick doing his best to usher his parents past them. Garrett carries Caroline inside. Once they are all in, Nick and Garrett come back out. I turn off the car and join them.

"Kids," is all Nick can say. I know better. This is Doug's doing. Not him personally, but the people who have started to listen to him.

"There's paint in the garage," Garrett says as he walks toward it. I follow him. He sorts through various home improvement supplies and abandoned projects looking for paint. I watch him.

"How are you?"

"Here." He stops. "That's all Mel wanted for the wedding. It was why it was all so last-minute. She wanted to celebrate what we had right then. That whole day and every day after she kept telling me to be *here* with her. Not ahead or behind. All I could think about was tomorrow. Now . . ."

All we have is the present. In grief I exist moment to moment. It doesn't mean grief doesn't visit my dreams or wrap around my body in the middle of the day. It does. I keep going because I know that's what Mel would want. For us to be here. Now.

He finds the paint.

I look at the constellations on the house. Instead of conjuring tales or myths to escape, I tell myself the truth:

I gave as much of my statement as I could to the police. There was only so much I could say before they would throw out everything. I'm glad they didn't ask me too many details about the massive bruise on my arm and severe cuts to my chest. I don't think they would have understood that's where my heart left my body and where a shadow put it back. I still don't think I fully understand everything that happened.

Garrett and I return with the paint. Nick's opened a beer. He offers Garrett and me one. Garrett takes his. I don't.

"No," I say. "Thank you." I've been numb for enough of my life. Since Jack left me, I'm living my life without being watched. Having a quiet moment alone feels like an act of revolution.

Doug has been talking, of course. I was right to sense ambition in him. He's ready for the cameras. He baits them every day from prison awaiting trial. Kidnapping. Attempted murder. Assault. Rape of a child in the first degree. Murder of a child in the first degree. The charges and counts rise every day as more families come forward. The same for Kirsten.

The stars are from Doug. He is peddling his ritual of hate to anyone who will listen. Some are. Painted summer constellations are popping up all over town and beyond. Though he was betrayed by him, Doug still worships Jack. This is how he ensures the jackal gets what he wanted. People are taking little pieces of his beliefs into the world. There is no shadow to please, no killing to be done, and no offerings to be made. But people are telling stories, starting legends, and inspiring fear. Doug only knows how to live as Jack's shadow.

"Auntie Liz?" It's Caroline. She pokes her head out the door, looking to me and me alone for permission to be outside.

"Come on," I say. She sits on the lawn with her sketch pad and crayons. She looks at the stars on the house.

"What were the other ones? The winter ones?" she asks.

I'm happy to tell her. "Let's start with Orion."

Nick sits on the front porch. He looks naked, having to navigate with his crutches and without his gun in its holster. He left the force. He's not talking about it yet. I don't know if he ever will.

I grab some paper and join Caroline. I draw . . . nothing. Lines. Color. Anything to keep my hands busy.

Caroline pauses in her sketch of the night sky. Nick finishes his beer. I consider my next color. We've all come to a pause, listening for predators.

"Auntie Liz?" Caroline whispers to me. "How do you map with the stars?" I recognize the question. It's from her time with Jack. Both Jack and I used them to plot our ways out of this town when, in actuality, neither of us could ever really leave it behind.

"Start with the North Star. That's how you build your compass," I say.

Caroline nods and keeps drawing. We sit together until my picture of random lines and shapes and colors comes together, a messy representation of my mind. There are angry streaks of red. Mournful mounds of blue. Chaotic neon.

Garrett brings a ladder. I exchange my crayon for a paintbrush. Under the watchful eye of Caroline, Garrett, Nick, and I start to paint.

Latoya was right. Seeing the girls struggle to get the bare minimum doesn't feel like I thought it would. Justice is a tricky thing. I've inhabited the scales of it. Those whose cases went cold are now seeing movement again. The ones who were dismissed as runaways are now being properly investigated. Court dates are coming. Witnesses are being scheduled. Little by little, everything is starting to get sealed up. The scars remain. The one on my arm doesn't hurt anymore. No numbness. No fire. Just skin. I've seen Black women become heroes and villains. To live and live well? That's what I want.

I haven't seen Chris since that night in the woods. He texts me questions sometimes. **What happened? Are you okay? Are you still here?** I can't answer him. I don't know how long I'm going to stay home, or if I'll ever go back to the city. If this is the intercostal of America, the ribs, it's also the fastest way to its heart. If we tear ourselves apart, God help us.

Three coats of paint and the stars are covered up by sky blue. I start to help clean up when Caroline stops me.

"Here," she says. She hands me her drawing. I look at it. In the time we've painted, she's filled every inch of the paper. There are white and yellow orbs representing the winter constellations. The true feat is the night sky itself. The blacks, blues, and purples she's used to make the sky cast the dark in many fine textures. It makes my eyes search for shapes in it. The crayon strokes look like little tendrils emanating from a source. I find it. There, in the lower right-hand corner, if I squint just right, I see the profile of a canine with two upright ears.

I search Caroline's eyes. They aren't light or dark, but red with tears. I know I gathered all the pieces Jack left in people. I wonder about Caroline. I search her eyes from time to time to see if he left a bit of himself in her too. If a shred of him is in this child, I'll take the monster in again. In a heartbeat.

"Auntie Liz?"

I give Caroline a smile the way I like to smile. The way I did before Jack. One-sided and close-lipped.

"Thank you, Care-bear."

She runs back inside.

The boys have finished putting up the paint. I'm alone outside in the setting sun. I look at the drawing again. I find what I've been looking for all along: the truth.

I don't know if Jack is really dead. I don't know if something like him can die. I'll never forget what it was to become the beast. The truth I have told no one is, what Jack did to me worked. All that anger he craved? It didn't go away when he did. A lifetime ago, Denise first laid eyes on me outside the train station, and she told me nothing good came from being hateful and hollow, but my anger could be useful. So many have used my anger to silence me, to hurt me, to manipulate me, to try to kill me. I know it's because they are terrified of what I could accomplish if I used my anger for myself. Everyone in this town—this country—is so afraid of the other, whoever the "other" is today. If there's one thing fear can do, it's make a beast out of a shadow. It turns us all into monsters.

The enemy of the shadow isn't light. It's sight.

The sun sets. It's dark. Quiet. Out of habit, I name things.

A drop of blue paint.

My mother's car.

A pink crayon.

I bend to pick it up. Something flickers at the edge of my vision. I still myself and get a glimpse of what's on the other side of my grief. It's not an emotion or place. It's action. I will pick myself up. I will fight.

Another moment and the shadow enters my sight.

I turn.

I face it.

AUTHOR'S NOTE

One of my favorite things about going home is the train ride. The nearly eight-hour journey, replete with incredible views and long stretches of quiet, is perfect for reflecting and writing. The only interruptions are occasional announcements for small-town stations and landmarks like the Horseshoe Curve and the Rockville Bridge. I can't go home without traversing history. While this book has always been a work of fiction, writing it has required a personal journey through my hometown's past.

In fiction, the events are made up but the emotions are real. As I delved into this story, I started to demand touches of reality around its location. No matter how many towns I imagined and mapped, they all ended up looking a little too familiar. With each draft I rebuilt my hometown: Johnstown, Pennsylvania. After we'd moved every three years of my life until middle school, Johnstown was where my mother and I set down roots. Ever since arriving I've had an uneasy relationship with the town. So, like Liz, to get to the other side of this novel I had to face what homecoming meant to me.

I still remember the first weekend my mother and I visited. Sitting in the back of a job recruiter's car while they toured my mother around downtown, I stared out the window and noted clues: water lines on buildings, brass bars, strange concrete locks in the riverbed, the presence of a vehicular inclined plane. All across town I encountered scars of a tragedy. By the time I studied the unit of history in school, I was ready to put all the pieces together.

The Johnstown Flood of 1889 occurred on a Friday afternoon at the end of May. About fourteen miles upstream of the town was the South Fork Dam. It changed ownership over the years, which meant its upkeep varied greatly. As it aged it frequently sprang leaks and there were concerns over its integrity, but no action was taken. After days of heavy rain, on the morning of May 31, 1889, the South Fork Dam was on the brink of failure. Workers tried to relieve the structure, but it was too late. The dam was there one moment and gone the next. In a little over an hour, the South Fork Dam emptied, sending 20 million tons of water hurtling toward the town below. Laden with debris from its path down the mountain, a wave of floodwater thirty-five to forty feet high hit Johnstown at forty miles per hour.

Harrowing firsthand accounts describe indiscriminate destruction. Some houses were completely swept away, while others suffered minimal damage. Some families were spared while others were decimated in seconds. Entire trains were swept off tracks. Four square miles of downtown Johnstown were destroyed. The debris piled up against Stone Bridge, which spanned the Conemaugh River, and caught fire. It burned for three days straight. The previous days of rain and the flood itself knocked out the telegraph wires. With night falling, survivors had to wait until news of the tragedy trickled out to be rescued.

Once notified, help came swiftly. In my research, I found donations from groups all across the country and internationally. Not just monetary help—people offered their labor and expertise in supporting and rebuilding the town. The American Red Cross, led by Clara Barton, arrived on June 5. This was the organization's first major peacetime effort. When the waters receded, the death toll came in. More than 2,209 souls perished. Bodies were found for years after, some hundreds of miles away.

Once the town started to heal, one question came to the forefront: Why did the dam fail? Of all the hands the South Fork Dam passed through, its most recent owner was the South Fork Fishing and Hunting Club—an affluent retreat for Pittsburgh's elite; a who's who of

America's ruling class. Among its members were Andrew Carnegie, Andrew Mellon, and Henry Clay Frick. These men made their fortunes in the same industries Johnstown and many other towns in the rust belt were known for: iron, coal, and steel. The club was a getaway from the worries of work and the city. Thus, when the dam was modified or cared for, it was done so to suit their interests before anyone else's. For example, one alteration included lowering the dam to allow for carriage travel, thereby reducing its ability to discharge stormwater. After the flood, litigation followed. But after years of lawsuits and investigations, the flood was determined to be an Act of God. Though these men donated to the relief effort, they took none of the blame. This is where being a local changed my view of history.

According to articles and textbooks, the fault for the flood was vague and hazy. The blame was passed from person to person and organization to organization with aplomb. Finally, in 2013, the truth came out. The South Fork Fishing and Hunting Club misrepresented their modifications of the dam. Their changes jeopardized the structure's integrity and directly led to its collapse in 1889. If you asked anyone in Johnstown, they could have told you that truth years ago without batting an eye: This happened because of the negligence of the wealthy.

Sometimes excavating history means confirming a truth people have collectively known for years. Other times, it means digging up a past that has been left in a shameful shadow.

Growing up in Johnstown, I collected clues around a different historical event. These hints were more evasive than brass bars. Johnstown is very segregated, in both race and class. Traveling from downtown to uptown and beyond, there are distinct differences at every latitude. I lived in the haven of small-town America; kids could walk to school unchaperoned and people seldom locked their doors. None of these assurances could explain or soothe my near-constant anxiety. I was one of three Black kids in my entire school, in both middle and high school. I accepted this as a fact of living where I did. Who'd ever heard of Black folks in the middle of nowhere? But when I picked at that rhetorical question and tried to pull it apart, I got pushback. There was something there. For a town that valued hard work, rebuilding, and rebirth, there was no reason for it to be so divided. Of all things, with the industries in town, it should have been blended across all areas. In pursuing the source of my anxiety, another historical event in Johnstown's history found its way into my novel. Here I must thank Cody McDevitt and his work in *Banished from Johnstown* for helping me solve another mystery about the place I call home.

In the summer of 1923, much of the United States greatly feared the possibility of a race riot. In Johnstown, only two years after the Tulsa massacre, a drunken brawl in the predominantly Black neighborhood of Rosedale resulted in the deaths of Robert Young, a Black man, and white police officers Otto Nukem, Otto Fink, Joseph Louis Abrahams, and John James. To save the town from full social upheaval, Mayor Joseph Cauffiel handed down a decree: "I want every Negro who has lived here less than seven years to pack up his belongings and get out." He banned Black and Mexican laborers from coming to the city. He banned gatherings of Black citizens for any reason except worship. To find the outcome and glean the fallout, we must collect the clues. The decree was never enforced. But two thousand Black and brown people left Johnstown the following week. Cauffiel was quickly admonished and lost his office. However, on the evening of the edict, ten crosses burned in the hills of Johnstown.

To me, this banishment and the Johnstown Flood are inextricably linked. They carry hard truths hidden in their details: The carelessness of the wealthy destroyed a rising working-class town, and white fear and anxiety drove off a substantial part of the town's Black population. I was never under the impression that everything in my hometown was without conflict. I know what it means to live in America. There are other towns with histories like Johnstown's. But because it's *my* town, I must face it. Out in the woods, if you see or hear something that makes your hair stand on end—no, you didn't. But learning, naming, and confronting what makes us afraid and uncomfortable, no matter how ugly, is key to understanding and ensuring it never happens again. Sometimes anger comes with truths like this. I don't think that's a bad thing. Anger fueled some of the writing of this book. My discomfort drove me to weave together all the clues I needed to craft my complex idea of "home." Often, anger is only there to mask fear. Once fear passes, all that's left to do is take a look at the truth. Sometimes it's the only thing that can inspire change and allow the space needed to heal.

ACKNOWLEDGMENTS

From an early age, my parents instilled in me a love of the library. My childhood is filled with memories of checking out stacks of books and falling in love with each and every one of them. Both my mother and my father fostered my love of language throughout my life: They read me stories until I memorized them. They gave me cash to tear up the book fair. They gave me space and time to read every summer. They never banned books from me. If I could comprehend the world, then I could learn about life on the pages. For that trust, I'm forever thankful for Anne-Marie Sterlin and Derick Adams.

In its infancy, this book was lovingly witnessed and critiqued by my writer's group, Re: Group. Thank you, Charlotte Lang-Bush, Jordan Tierney, Jack MacCarthy, and Kacey Stamats. You all gave me the care and confidence I needed to complete this novel.

I will never be able to thank Sonia Hartl and Annette Christie enough. They changed my life. They sent me an edit letter that taught me how to revise by teaching me to listen to my writer's gut. For years I was too afraid to dream my dream of being a writer. Sonia and Annette helped me make that dream a reality. Thank you to my Pitch Wars class for being there for me every step of the way. Special shout-out to CJ Dotson, Angela Montoya, Diba Bijari, and Zahra Zelle for reading drafts of this book and for your continued support. Thank you, Brenda Drake, and thanks to all the volunteers who helped run Pitch Wars.

Thank you to NYU's Department of Dramatic Writing. Thanks to the faculty and the class of 2022. Thank you, Komal Surani, Anuhea

Brown, and Gareth Mattey, for listening to all my crazy plot pitches during revisions. Thank you to Robin Epstein for giving me grace, space, and guidance while I did these edits.

Kerry D'Agostino is a gift of an agent, who met me where I was and saw where I wanted to be as a writer. Thank you to the entire team at Curtis Brown: Holly Frederick, Madeline R. Tavis, Sarah Perillo, and Mahalaleel Muhammed-Clinton, among others. I'm such a lucky, lucky writer.

Thank you a thousand times to Jenny Chen. I still remember the vibration of excitement we had in our first Zoom call. My gut said, "She wants this just as much as you do." Jenny read *Jackal* and saw how to make it even more brave and stunning. She and her assistant, Mae Martinez, guided me through this incredible revision. By the end, the book smelled even more like me than the initial draft did. I love it. I'm obsessed with it. I'm so proud of the work we did and that I get to call this book my debut.

The entire team at Bantam has been a dream. Thank you, Allison Schuster, Allyson Lord, Jordan Forney, Yewon Son, Quinne Rogers, Loren Noveck . . . and everyone else who has helped bring this story to life.

Thank you to my incredible gremlin, Thisbe, aka the goodest dog in existence.

It took a village of people to make *Jackal*. I'm forever grateful for all who got this book here and who will carry it into the future.

ABOUT THE AUTHOR

ERIN E. ADAMS is a first-generation Haitian American writer and theater artist. She received her BA with honors in literary arts from Brown University, her MFA in acting from The Old Globe and University of San Diego Shiley Graduate Theatre Program, and her MFA in dramatic writing from NYU Tisch School of the Arts. An award-winning playwright and actor, Adams has called New York City home for the last decade. *Jackal* is her first novel.

erineadams.com
Twitter: @IAmEEAdams
Instagram: @IamEEAdams